Philip Warren is a pleasant, thoughtful young American in search of a future. He has taken a year off his lucrative law practice to wander the eternal cities of Rome and Paris, detouring down to the mysterious relics of ancient Egypt, encountering a kaleidoscope of weird, sad, comical, beautiful, bizarre and sinister characters, most of whom exert their varying influences on Philip to take up their causes or embrace their philosophies.

With his urbane and lucid wit and his uncanny ability to make the reader 'feel' the reality of his vision, Gore Vidal has produced a genuine masterpiece of modern fiction.

'*The Judgement of Paris* is the best and most ambitious of Vidal's novels, the richest in texture and the most carefully executed. In it, with the help of classical myth and a cosmopolitan setting, he has found his way to a dramatic statement of his theme'
– *New York Times Book Review*

'He has a fine comic talent derived partly from Christopher Isherwood, Ronald Firbank and the early Aldous Huxley, but something fresh and gay of his own as well'
– *Manchester Evening News*

'A novel full of vitality and creative energy'
– *Scotsman*

D1140237

Also by Gore Vidal in Panther Books

Myra Breckinridge
The City and the Pillar
Julian
Two Sisters
Washington D.C.
Messiah
Williwaw

Gore Vidal

The Judgement of Paris

Panther

Granada Publishing Limited
Published in 1974 by Panther Books Ltd
Frogmore, St Albans, Herts AL2 2NF

First published in Great Britain by
William Heinemann Ltd 1953
Made and printed in Great Britain by
Cox & Wyman Ltd, London, Reading and Fakenham
Set in Intertype Times

NOTE: The brief quotations from Hesiod, Homer, Pindar, Sophocles, Anaxandrides, Plutarch and Cicero which appear in the course of Chapter Twelve are F. M. Cornford translations while the Plato excerpt is from the Jowett translation. The anonymous medieval text which prefaces Part Three is from Helen Waddell's *Wandering Scholars*. Also, before I am accused of plagiarism, I think I should here confess that the exchange between Lord Glenellen and Mr. Norman which occurs in Chapter Twelve is a deliberate paraphrase of the quarrel between Brutus and Cassius near Philippi: Act Four, Scene Three of Shakespeare's *Julius Caesar*. And finally, my last borrowing, I should like to thank Mr. Antony Tudor for his kindness in allowing me to appropriate the title of one of his excellent ballets for this work.

G.V.

Part One

'But what are kings, when regiment is gone,
But perfect shadows in a sunshine day.'
            Marlowe: *Edward the Second*

CHAPTER ONE

She wore her trauma like a plume. When she was seven an elderly man attempted to have his way with her in a telephone booth at Grand Central Station (her mother had been buying a ticket to Peekskill). Although in no way defied, the shock was great and, to this day, she was so terrified of the telephone that she was forced always to compose innumerable messages on pale blue paper for the instruction and pleasure of those acquaintances whom she might otherwise, in a less perilous era, have telephoned.

That was all there was to it, he thought sadly, studying this one paragraph typed neatly at the top of a sheet of fine white paper: there would be no more; he was confident of that. She was lost to the world, trauma and all, and the contents of those messages on blue paper would never be known. She had emerged in his mind one day, clear and precise, a lady of the highest, most Meridithean comedy, with just a trace of something more racy, vulgar even, to give her a proper contemporary relevance, but he had lost her for good after that first paragraph, watched with helpless resignation as she sank back into a limbo of unarranged words, convincing him that he would never be a man of letters: not, of course, that he had ever thought too seriously of becoming one ... rather, it had seemed a pleasant way to spend a life, composing sentences day after day with a tight smile on his lips and a view of mountains, or the sea, from a study window.

His failure was complete, however, and he knew with a sad certainty that his lady of the blue notes (not a bad title, he thought, wondering if there might not be a double meaning in it: something to do with music) would remain unrevealed for ever, this paragraph her *alpha* and *omega*. But that is that for now, he thought, and he gave up literature as he had given up painting and music the year before, having composed one art song to a three-line Emily Dickinson poem, and painted one non-objective painting in the style of Mondrian. 'I am not an artist,' he murmured to himself with some satisfaction, putting the paper back into his suitcase and ending for ever a never too urgent dream of creativity.

The problem of what to do with his life still existed, of course; but time undoubtedly would arrange all that, he decided, removing the Hotel Excelsior, Napoli, tag which had only this morning been stuck on his new suitcase by a hotel porter whom he had never seen until that moment and who expected, but never received, a large tip for his superfluous service, thus further darkening the none too bright reputation of Americans in post-war Italy. There had been a scene as he got into the taxi but he carried it off well and at the station, as an act of contrition, he gave the cab driver a thick pile of torn and dirty lire.

He hated scenes, he decided, looking out the train window at the green countryside, rippling uncertainly beyond the solid fact of glass, shimmering in the heat of a white spring sun. But Italians need them, he thought wisely, it kept them from succumbing to a hopeless lassitude, especially now that June had come.

Philip Warren sighed happily. He was here at last: Italy, Europe, a year of leisure, a time for decision, a prelude to the distinguished fugue his life was sure to be, once he got really to it, once the delightful prelude had been played to its conclusion among the foreign cities.

He glanced out the window again, looking instinctively for modern ruins which he hoped would not be there: the way one reluctantly examines the remains of a dead dog on a country road; fortunately, there were no ruins in sight, except the ancient, the respectable ones, bits of an aqueduct arched over the plains of Latium, brown-brick against the Apennines ... The Apennines, he said the name aloud, with reverence, and as the conductor came to take his ticket, he quoted Macaulay to himself, those heroic stanzas which had made his nose tingle with excitement when he had first read them, years ago, under an apple tree in his grandfather's orchard.

'Roma?' inquired the conductor, a slovenly man with a body which no uniform would ever fit, including the one he wore. Already, after one day in Italy, Philip had discovered what the last dictator had not: uniforms are not adapted to the Italian figure.

'Roma,' said Philip with a smile and a gesture, indicating that he could speak a great deal more Italian if he chose . . . he had even rolled the 'r', giving, though he was not aware of it, a somewhat Scottish burr to that wonderfully evocative name.

The conductor did a number of things to the ticket, chatting all the time. Philip continued to smile intelligently until the conductor, recommending him to God, left the second-class compartment and he was again alone, the only passenger in the compartment: the only passenger in the whole car, for that matter, since very few people travelled from Naples to Rome in the middle of the day in the middle of the week.

It's going much too well, he thought, arranging his grey-flannelled legs on the seat opposite him, conscious that his shirt and collar were still fresh and that his hands were clean, untravelled. On the boat he had dreaded the confusion of arriving in Europe for the first time, without a reservation, no place to go, victimized by the natives, pushed this way and that by furious crowds and, finally, torn apart by an enraged mob, as a blood sacrifice to the dollar, totem of the new Rome of which he was a citizen. Fortunately, except for a debacle or two with the local currency, he had been well taken care of; he had felt like a royalty when the man from the Excelsior picked him up right after Customs and drove him in lonely splendour through the streets of Naples. He had hardly been able to resist an impulse to nod solemnly at the crowds of olive-skinned people in the narrow streets, waving his hand at them in that curious circular manner affected by the British royal family, inherited, no doubt, from the more recondite Druidic ceremonies of their blue-tinted ancestors.

Then a night at the Excelsior, all marble and smelling of new paint: it had been shattered by various bombardments during the war since it was right on the bay, the celebrated blue semi-circle of water which contained within its symmetrical arms many of the world's ships. Everywhere, or rather at the railway station and at the Excelsior, the only places he had seen in Naples, he had been received with a courtesy which had in-

11

volved of course, a continual disbursement of lire on his part ... but then he knew that good will cannot be had for nothing in this commercial world, and he was willing to pay a little for the flashing smiles of the Neapolitans.

Outside, the countryside was becoming suburban and, as he watched, his heart beating more quickly, the buildings of Rome appeared all about him, rushed past him as the train pulled into the station and he was there, finally there.

Since he had only two suitcases, he carried them himself through the crowd of porters who fought to get them away from him. Finally, having got through to the outside, flushed and breathing heavily, he climbed into a cab. A porter shut the door for him; then he extended his open palm, smiling villainously. Philip having no stone to give him, gave him nothing; his mother's integrity was questioned as his cab pulled away from the station.

'This is your room,' said the clerk, showing him a room as scrubbed and neat as the young clerk himself, a fresh-faced Swiss. A big balconied window looked out on to a quiet street of tall trees against the baroque façades of seventeenth-century houses, all embassies now, remarked the clerk, opening the window and letting in the sunlit air. Then, after a quick briefing on the meaning and the uses of the various bells, Philip was left alone in this handsome room with its feather bed and numerous pillows, its old-fashioned bathtub hidden, along with a bidet, behind curtains. Very happy, he unpacked.

Now then: what does he look like? What sort of man or boy or youth is Philip Warren? Well, it is much too early to draw any conclusions about his character since he is hardly yet revealed. On the other hand, there is a great deal to be said about his appearance. His face, certainly, must be described before he ventures out into the Roman afternoon and as he has not yet looked into a mirror (the usual device for describing one's protagonist) I must say that, first, he is young and that, second, he is handsome. Now of course he is not remarkably young, unless twenty-eight is considered very young, which perhaps, nowadays, it is as our population grows older and older and the period of incubation in the schools and colleges is prolonged to an inordinate degree ... but then the world is as it is and Philip Warren is twenty-eight and fairly handsome, slim, unem-

12

barrassed by over-developed muscles, flat-bellied (could one ever have a protagonist who was young and stout?) and though not tall, not short (all things to all men obviously); he is, then, of middle height, his face more square than oval, his cheekbones prominent. His nose is unheroic, small and stubby, making him look even younger than he is. His eyes are a dark blue, not very interesting but, as one writer once said of another writer's eyes, interested. His skin is still boyish and taut and except for a deep line between fair brows he has no outward marks of age or experience or character in his face.

His body, for those who are interested in such things, was well-formed and greatly admired by the not inconsiderable company which had, at one time or another (and on some occasions at the same time) enjoyed it. On the inside of his left thigh, near the groin, a small pretty butterfly had been tattooed, a memento of the war when he had been a junior Naval Officer on leave in Honolulu. His speaking voice was manly but marred by the faintest lisp, a defect which he hated although, unknown to him, it was his greatest charm for, instead of sounding sissy as he imagined, it made him seem very boyish and charming: a puzzled youthful man in need of a woman's protection. As a result his success with women was quite remarkable not only because of this boyishness but also because he genuinely liked them in an age and nation where, generally speaking, they were less admired than usual.

'Do you play bridge?'

'Why yes,' said Philip, turning, as a stout bald man moved apologetically into the room from the hall.

'I'm so glad. I do hope you'll excuse my dropping in like this but your door was open and I live right down the hall and we do have so few people in Rome who even *play* bridge, much less *want* to play it. You do want to play?'

'Yes, not now, though. Some other time perhaps.'

'Of course, of course ... I was thinking of the future, not the present. You play it decently, I hope?'

'Rather,' said Philip, meaning 'rather decently' but, in the excitement of the moment, he found himself parodying the other's British accent.

'I'm so glad. Are you from home?'

'No,' said Philip, already alerted. 'I'm from America.' He blushed as he said this unaccustomed phrase, as though he had

13

begun suddenly to unfurl and snap, all red and white and blue in a chauvinistic breeze.

'Yes? Well, one never knows any more. The world is becoming one at last, is it not? Pleasant thought, or is it? Ah well, soon it will be a *fait accompli* and no concern of ours. My name, if I may introduce myself, is Clyde Norman.' Information of this sort was formally exchanged and Mr. Norman gave him a card, a very proper sort of card which declared that Mr. Norman was a director of the Fabian Trade Mission, otherwise undefined. 'I've lived in Rome almost all my life, you know. Stayed here all through the war. Very risky. Quite a story in all that, I suppose. If one likes stories, eh? But now I'm sure you have many things to do . . .'

They agreed, then, that it might be a good idea to have a drink together, to celebrate Philip's arrival.

Mr. Norman was splendidly knowing, decided Philip, as they strolled from the hotel to the Via Veneto: the fashionable street of Rome. He was able to say something amusing about almost everything mentioned or, at least, he spoke as though what he said might be amusing if one fully understood the various references.

Dingy youths stood on street corners, peddling black market cigarettes, candy bars and currency. The streets otherwise were discouragingly familiar. The buildings were either severe and formal or baroque and formal, their stucco façades a weathered grey-gold, the colour of Rome. The day was so very fine, however, that this momentary disappointment was succeeded by a sudden elation, a blitheness which he had seldom experienced since childhood. He controlled a sudden impulse to slip away from Clyde Norman, to run as fast as he could until he had reached the Forum, where he would sit among the broken marble and recall Horace and Keats and think how good it was to live, or to die, for both seemed equally desirable, the dark and the light, one meaningless without the other, twins and opposites. But he dared not mention this to Mr. Norman who was, he gathered, more concerned with details than with abstractions.

'In thirty years, one picks up quite a bit, you know. One comes to know the city behind the city, if you get what I mean.'

'I certainly do.'

'England is like a foreign country to me now. I hardly know how to act when I'm there, and the climate ... do you know English weather?'

'By reputation.'

'Damp, very damp. And from September to May everyone has a cold ... ah, here we are, the Via Veneto.'

They paused for a moment, surveying this celebrated thoroughfare. Mr. Norman was somewhat proprietary while Philip found it not strange at all. The street reminded him of a minor avenue in Washington D.C., except that it curved up a slight hill to a massive brick arch and fissured wall behind which could be glimpsed the rich green of gardens, the gardens of the Villa Borghese according to his companion, who indicated various other sights of interest: the Excelsior Hotel, an outdoor café called Doney's where, presently, they sat in iron chairs at iron tables, the pavement between them and the main part of the café.

'This is the centre,' said Mr. Norman. 'So many cities have no centre. London, for instance, has none, or rather too many: the Strand, Parliament and the Abbey, Piccadilly Circus, Buckingham Palace, the various squares ... all very stuffy and impersonal ... no place where one can go and see *all* one's friends, from every class. No cafés like this one where, sooner or later, everyone in Rome one wants to see will come. I have always thought London must have been like this in the days of the coffee-houses.' He ordered apéritifs with unfamiliar names. Then they sat back to watch. Philip felt as though he were sitting in a theatre just as the lights had begun to dim, that expectant moment before the discordancies of an orchestra trying its instruments becomes an overture. Mr. Norman, with a smile, figuratively tapped his music stand with an imaginary baton and the curtain rose as one of the late dictator's mistresses, a plump little woman in black, walked slowly between the crowded tables of chattering people, accompanied by a plump little chow on a leash, a chow whose sad face was a doggish facsimile of her own.

'I always thought mistresses were beautiful,' said Philip, who had thought nothing of the kind but, having been trapped in a role: naïve, youthful, American, had the good manners not to confuse the other by assuming a character closer to his own.

'They say she used to be,' said Mr. Norman, watching her as she nodded to numerous acquaintances who nodded back and then, when she was out of earshot, discussed her eagerly, her health, morals and current fortune.

'But then . . .' said Mr. Norman, solemnly, pausing as though expecting an epigram on the nature of courtesans to spring sharp and original to his thin bluish lips; but since none came he took a sip of his apéritif instead. He was, Philip decided, one of those charming men whose way of speaking is so ceremonious and shrewd that they seem to be scoring one linguistic hit after another on the all too vulnerable target of human character while, actually, they do little more than repeat the clever sayings of other men . . . which takes a good memory, decided Philip tolerantly, not to mention a sense of timing and, finally, a style which was set if not by Dr. Johnson by Horace Walpole in the great days of aristocracy, when the perfect pearl of the Renaissance was misshapen by a rigid manner and the baroque was born of that tension between nature and artifice. Philip wondered if he would have an opportunity to tell Mr. Norman that the word baroque came from the Spanish word *barocco* which meant a misshapen pearl . . . no, not now; later, perhaps, if they spoke of architecture (Philip was good at guiding conversations into home waters where, with infinite skill, he could scuttle the barks of others with some torpedo of esoterica, some bit of knowledge, properly timed; it was, he knew, the surest way to total unpopularity in a pretentious age). But for now he would be agreeable, the moment for defining baroque not having presented itself; and the other, unsuspecting, unaware of his young companion's pirate nature, continued to explain Rome to him.

'There are of course many different sets in Rome. The Church group, the government (which isn't much these days), and the old nobility which is very fine and very distant, set apart. One hardly ever sees them. They live the way they've always lived in those *palazzi* and they are quite scornful, I suspect, of the rest of the world, of people whose ancestry does not go back to the Republic, as they maintain their own does, to the Republic and even farther in some cases, to the gods.'

'But then doesn't everyone go back that far?'

'Yes, but the descent is not recorded.'

'Caesar traced his family back to Venus, didn't he?'

16

'Fully documented, too. Which proves I think that all genealogy is myth,' said Mr. Norman smiling, displaying two rows of British teeth in a state of only partial repair. 'But tell me why you are here, Mr. Warren, if I may ask.'

'You certainly may,' said Philip cordially; then he paused awkwardly, destroying the illusion of cordiality with this ill-timed hesitation; discreetly Mr. Norman began to murmur, to back away from the personal until Philip, the reason for his hesitation still not clear to him, said at last: 'To travel. I have a year, you see.'

'A year? Is that all? I mean a year for what?'

'A year to travel in, to make up my mind.'

'About your future?'

'Yes, about the future.'

'I wonder if one can ever do precisely that.'

'You mean come to a decision about life in a given period?'

'Yes, to make a positive, irrevocable decision. I shouldn't think it could be done, or should be done.'

'I would like to try, even so,' said Philip vaguely, distracted by the sight of a well-known American actor who strode quickly by, scowling like Cato and carrying under one arm a new and shiny book with its provocative title in bold black letters on red: *Decadence*. The actor disappeared into the door of the Excelsior Hotel.

'Accept the moment: there is nothing else.'

'Perhaps not. Still, I am nearly thirty and . . .'

'You look so young! I thought you were a college boy.'

'Thank you . . . and I feel I must really decide what to do with the rest of my life.'

'Even though, terrible thought, it might be, considering the state of the world (and pardoning the impertinence of my gloom), very short?'

'Or, considering my natural cowardice and cunning, longer than the average.'

'Ah, now you exaggerate. I only suggested that your life might be shortened to convince you of the very real folly of making long-range plans: they are just *not* the thing nowadays.'

Philip appeared to ponder this pronouncement while the waiter brought them more apéritifs, pronouncing their name 'Cinzano' as he slopped the glasses before them on the table.

The day, Philip decided, was perfect in every way: effete

17

fluffy clouds burdened the west, preceding the golden globe of the afternoon sun as it sank rapidly through the blue to the seven hills of the city, to the sea and to the new world beyond that. The day was warm, without wind but not hot, not the way he had been warned it would be in the spring. Conscious of weather and bemused, he said yes and he said no as his pleasant companion advised him to accept what was since there would be, for all he knew, no more and, as he had already planned to do precisely that, to live as he pleased for a year, he found that he could agree with the older man and, by agreeing, could establish a tentative friendship.

'What precisely do you plan to do with this year of yours ... this climacteric in your life?'

Philip smiled. 'I haven't the slightest idea. Sit at this café, perhaps. Or go and walk in those gardens over there. Or journey up the Nile to its source, dissolving imitation pearls in cups of gin, or would they dissolve in gin, do you think?'

'I don't know much about imitation pearls; gin is another matter. But, seriously, you have no plan?'

'None.'

'Wise! Very wise ... and then you're so fortunate.'

'In what way?'

'To be young.'

'One doesn't realize it at the time. I'm not conscious of any serious blessing. Perhaps I will be one day.'

'You will. How extraordinary though that you should feel that way. Are you really so detached? Or, like so many of the politic young men nowadays, have you merely learned the proper responses?'

'You're much too quick,' said Philip, taken aback, not prepared for the other's shrewdness for, of course, it was true: he had learned to say many things which got him easily and with no exertion the respect of his elders, statements which he knew well in advance would amuse or shock or please and which had little or no relation to what he actually thought. It was a schoolboy's trick and he felt a sudden shame to be playing again the brightest boy with the headmaster, as though he were still fourteen and ruthless, without a heart.

Mr. Norman had the grace not to pursue his advantage; instead he remarked: 'And then you are fortunate because you have money.'

Philip laughed. 'I have none,' he said.

'But you are able to travel well ... That's what I mean by having money. You are not caught in a web of chicanery, trying to make your few pounds support you by doing all the squalid black market things.'

'In that sense I suppose I'm fortunate ... I have the correct nationality.'

'Indeed you have.' Mr. Norman drank his Cinzano moodily and Philip watched the street become more crowded as the golden light darkened and the evening star shone silver over the gardens. He was aware, after this discussion of currency, that he would be called upon to pay for the apéritifs and this thought did not sadden him for he was, after all, a young man with an income, a small one but sufficient for the traveller's purpose and he knew that he would entertain many strangers before he was done, and though none of them might prove to be angels in disguise they had, he knew, a right to his hospitality since he had come among them to learn what he could.

'Rome,' he said, changing the subject, 'is not as hot as I thought it would be this time of year, in June.'

> ' "Faire is my love that feedes among the Lillies,
>   The Lillies growing in that pleasant garden,
>   Where Cupids mount that wellbeloved hill is,
>   And where that little god himselfe is warden," '

intoned Mr. Norman unexpectedly, his voice becoming resonant, like that of an actor stepping on to a stage in a familiar role. An Italian couple at the next table turned and looked at him as he quoted Bartholomew Griffin. When he had finished, he asked Philip if he had ever considered the arts, or an art (in other words, literature), as a possible career.

'No. I once thought I might write. I suppose everyone who has been shown certain books thinks he might become a man of letters ... it seems so easy to do a novel: a little talent and a number of impressions and the models, the great models, are always there to follow if imagination falters, but, in spite of all that, I could get no further than a first paragraph which I wrote coming over on the boat ...'

'You hardly gave yourself time to unleash the lightnings, as it were.'

'I'm afraid that to unleash that one small spark exhausted my talent. After a paragraph I decided it was too much. . . .'

'What was? the paragraph? Fancy!'

'No, the whole business. I could see to the end of it too clearly.'

'You know your own mind. I suspect that that's a burden to you for it is the confusion, the passionate confusion which produces art and, more important to you and me, produces the high experience of a life.'

'My system is superficial,' said Philip. Now we shall break into song, he thought to himself grimly, as the Cinzano began to have its effect and both grew wise and comfortable and confiding, drawn together by alcohol and the approach of evening with its promise of artificial light, dinner and strangers on the prowl. He was about to define everything rather than something . . . he had a gift for the general: the particular always tripped him up since he could not handle facts with any interest . . . he was not, however, allowed to continue for Mr. Norman had got suddenly to his feet and was shaking the hand of a stooped middle-age man with a fire-red face in which, shadowed by a bird's-beak nose, two watery blue eyes danced about, unable to focus on anything (although Philip was aware that he himself had been immediately comprehended by the newcomer in one quick intense glance).

'Sit with us, Ayre,' said Mr. Norman. 'I want you to meet a young friend of mine, a new friend, only just arrived from America. His name is Philip Warren.'

'How do you do?' said the older man in a curiously accented British voice, most of the stresses falling in unexpected places, a Welsh voice as Philip later learned. 'I can sit just a moment. I'm expecting Guido. I said I'd meet him here. He's late. Why is he always late? Why?'

'That's just his way.'

'There is of course a possibility that *I* am late. I never know.'

'I'm sure he'll be along presently,' said Mr. Norman with quiet authority and then he turned to Philip and said in a voice from which every trace of pride had been resolutely banished to accord harmoniously with a Stoic attitude: 'This, Mr. Warren, is Lord Glenellen.' Since they were now all seated, Philip could only incline his head respectfully at the peer who was now insulting the waiter in faultless Italian, or what sounded to Philip (and to the waiter) like faultless Italian. Mr. Norman watched his countryman with some satisfaction, smiling at the more colourful epithets and frowning furiously when the waiter attempted a mild insult or two on his own.

'About the coffee,' said Glenellen finally, as the waiter walked away, 'coffee I had yesterday. It made me ill.'

'What will you have now?'

'Not a thing. I think perhaps I'll go to the Excelsior for some decent coffee.'

'And not wait for Guido?'

'He could wait for me, you know. There *are* worse fates.'

'Of course, Ayre, of course.'

'You're an American, aren't you?' The blue eyes, milky as though filmed by cataracts, fixed on him disconcertingly, avoiding his eyes, though, concentrating instead on the line of his chin, the curve of his mouth.

'Yes, from New York, the state. . . .'

'Ah, I know. I know. Don't tell me. There's a state named that as well as a city. I was there, you see. Long, long ago, when Harlem was the thing to do. I adored Harlem. Is it still there?'

'Very much so.'

'Do you go there much?'

'No, almost never.'

'Well, times change. Where do people go?'

'Nowhere in particular. There seems to be little difference now between one part of the city and another. The East side is no different from Greenwich Village.'

'Ah, the Village! I had forgotten all about it. Has it changed much? Is it still amusing?'

'I expect so. I don't live in the city, though. I live up the Hudson River, at a town called Hudson.'

'All great civilizations,' announced Mr. Norman, checking in, 'have flourished on the banks of rivers. There has never been a civilization of any importance on a lake, for instance.'

'Is that so?' Philip was polite.

'Do you plan to stay here long?' asked Glenellen.

'I have no plans.'

'A gentleman of leisure,' said Mr. Norman, with a father's smile.

'Fortunate boy ... to have no plans. Now I, on the other

hand, am burdened with plans. I have every day and every hour of every week outlined for months ahead. Dinner with this person and tea with that one. A week-end at Ischia; a week in Vienna. I think sometimes I am over-organized because, in spite of all my activity, I have no time for work.'

'Work?'

'Oh my goodness, yes.'

'He composes,' said Mr. Norman, giving a brother's smile this time at the lean figure beside him. 'He composes music,' he added, 'chamber music.'

'When I have time,' said Glenellen uneasily. 'Tell me: where are you staying?'

'He's at my hotel,' said Mr. Norman. 'Isn't that a co-incidence? I barged right in on him this afternoon and asked him if he played bridge. He does. Aren't you pleased?'

'I am pleased that he is here, Clyde,' said the other courteously. 'Besides, you know perfectly well that I seldom play cards.'

'Ah, your barren life, Ayre. I had forgotten.'

'I have my compensations.'

'Yes, yes, indeed yes. Innumerable.'

'And unmentionable!' They both laughed loudly and Philip looked from one to the other, puzzled as one always is by the private references of acquaintances newly met, the eclectic jokes which suggest vast unexplored areas of vice and virtue unrevealed to the outsider.

'But to consider you: you intend to follow your instinct, obey your whims, travelling here and there without a plan?'

'Exactly. I shall look at buildings I have heard about, absorb as much scenery as I can ... I'm just a tourist, you know, not even a student like the rest. Then, when I've had as much as I can take, I will go home and do something.'

'Do something? Do what?' Glenellen leaned forwards as though suddenly eager to know the truth, to attend at a revelation.

But Philip was not equal to the moment, nor for that matter was he in the mood to be examined, to speak of himself when, for once, there was so much outside himself that he wanted to see and to know: he resented the attentions of these two odd Englishmen who, for all he knew, were mocking him.

'Whatever I can,' he said with a heavy attempt at lightness.

'Take a job . . . I'm a lawyer, you know. I graduated from Law School last June, from the one at Harvard.'

'A lawyer?' Glenellen pronounced the word as though not quite sure what it meant. 'How peculiar. No, I don't mean peculiar: I mean to say it seems so strange to find a personable young American who is not trying to be a painter or some such romantic thing among the ruins of our old Europe. I suppose, Clyde, that we see only the romantic ones, the ones who have got away for a time.'

'I think it most impressive, his being a lawyer. Original even.'

'But, my dear Clyde, does one *want* to be impressed by young men? Isn't it far more agreeable to be *pleased* by them, charmed by their freshness and impracticality?'

'*I* am charmed,' said Mr. Norman, patting Philip's knee as the sun unexpectedly set: the light going from gold to grey, the air from warm to cool.

'Will you go into politics?' asked Glenellen.

'I may, yes. I've thought about it. My family is in politics, back home.'

'You find it interesting?'

'Oh yes . . . but for a career, I don't know.'

'And what are your politics?'

'Darkly reactionary, I suppose. In practice, however, I should, if ever in office, devote my time to staying there.'

'No convictions . . . wonderful youth!' exclaimed Mr. Norman, drinking the rest of his Cinzano. 'How different you are from the young men of my day. How much more sensible. Tell me, would you like an ice or something? a little cake? This place is noted for its pastries.'

'I don't think so . . . thanks.'

Glenellen looked at him thoughtfully. 'I would like very much to have a chat with you one day about European politics. I have certain attitudes which may interest you, certain schemes which . . . but more I cannot say, for now. Though let me add that when I was your age, I, like you, was interested primarily in the progress of my own life, my time given to music and, of course, to my many hobbies. . . .'

'Your hobbies?'

'A joke of Lord Glenellen's, Mr. Warren,' said Clyde Norman quickly, too quickly, thought Philip, and he wondered what was not being said for his benefit.

'A joke, Mr. Warren, yes, a joke . . . and here is the wicked Guido. Late! You're late! Hear me?'

The wicked Guido heard and he smiled a smile like polished bone. He was a slender well-proportioned Italian boy with a head like a Michelangelo and a body, as much as could be seen through his suit (a great deal), as fine as a Donatello; he was nearly as vain of it as the long-grieved Narcissus had been of his own water-captured face.

'This is Guido,' said Mr. Norman urbanely as he and Philip rose and shook hands, while the high clear voice of the seated peer inveighed against the boy's character, accused him in English and Italian of monstrous crimes, denunciations which were received by the youth with a lovely smile and a serene disregard of what was being said.

'I was on my way stopped,' he said, finally, when the querulous voice had for an instant paused; his English was good if original. 'I find my brother has taken the only white good shirt of mine and so I went to my brother to receive the shirt once more for me. I want to look nice,' he added simply, expressing his philosophy in five words.

'Shirts, suits, shoes, watches. . . .' Glenellen sighed and turned to Philip. 'Those are the only things that really matter to these people.'

'I like the motor-cars, too,' giggled Guido. 'I like to drive very fast in *Alfa Romeo*. Oh good car, good car. I take cars apart. I know about things inside. Were you a soldier?' he asked all in one breath, noticing Philip as though for the first time.

'A sailor, for several years.'

'In the war? In Italy?'

'In the war . . . in the Pacific.'

'I knew many soldiers here. You might know some of them maybe. Nice men . . . very kind. I was fourteen years old so they gave me presents. A camera was given to me by one captain but it was stolen from me by one thief I know and he sells it.'

'Come, Guido,' said Glenellen, rising. 'You can tell your stories to Mr. Warren another time.' He turned to Philip. 'I would like to see you again one day soon, if I may.' They shook hands. 'Do you know the Baths of Nero?'

'I'm afraid not. I've only just arrived.'

'That's so. Of course you wouldn't have had a chance . . .

24

Well, should you have a moment to spare, do drop by tomorrow afternoon around four. I always arrive at four and leave at five, like clockwork. .... Marvellous for the figure, I've found. Not that you need to think of that quite yet, but we could talk. I have a plan which might interest you. Now I'm off. Many thanks, my dear Clyde, for introducing this young man to me.'

Farewells were made and Glenellen hurried away, followed at a more leisurely pace by Guido, immaculate in his good white shirt.

'Splendid fellow,' said Mr. Norman as they watched the older man and the youth turn the corner beyond the Excelsior Hotel. 'Difficult of course ... one of the last of those eccentric peers my country used to produce with such abandon in the old days. The supply seemed inexhaustible but now of course, with currency restrictions and so on, Ayre is the last, the very last of a great line ... and under a cloud, too.'

'A cloud? But why?'

'Oh, for so many reasons. His life has been too colourful for one thing, too many hobbies. Then there was the scandal about his wife. I suppose you were too young to remember that.'

'What happened to her?'

'I'm afraid he set fire to her at a party in the British Embassy at Berlin. There was the most terrible fuss made ... relations were strained at the time and this was added fuel to the blaze, as it were. They got him out of Germany as quickly as possible. The Ambassador was furious and the party, needless to say, was ruined.'

'And his wife?'

'Lady Glenellen was burned to a crisp. Fortunately they were able to get the Glenellen diamonds back ... she had been wearing a good many of them at dinner, a number of quite important pieces too. The settings were badly melted, I believe, but Ayre had them remounted later in the Etruscan fashion, a stroke of genius as it later developed, for he started an Etruscan vogue which lasted a number of years.'

'Was he never prosecuted?'

'For making Etruscan art the vogue? Heavens no! He received a decoration from the Pope.'

'I meant prosecuted for burning up his wife.'

'Ah well,' Mr. Norman gestured vaguely, 'she was an unpopular woman, a great hypochondriac and a bit of a religious maniac, too. Then, of course, there was some question as to whether the fire was his fault or hers.'

'Who *was* responsible?'

'Who can say? All I know is that, as the ladies were getting up from dinner to go into the drawing-room, he picked up the candelabra and hurled it at her, shouting: "Be Joan of Arc, *if you dare!*" It was the addition of the "if you dare" which saved him from more stern consequences since the phrase implied, you see, a certain choice in the matter. That she elected of her own free will to *be* Joan of Arc demonstrated a deliberate choice on her part and, as a result, he could hardly be held responsible for an act in which she so obviously concurred, perhaps even precipitated, since it was well known that she had always expected some sort of martyrdom ... ever since the day she married Glenellen, fully aware of the extent and the nature of his hobbies. Her life was one long expiation for the original sin, as Catholics say, of having been born.'

'You must tell me about his hobbies one day.'

'I should be glad to, but, best of all, observe him yourself. He will tell you all; show you everything ... he has no discretion, alas. You should go, by the way, to the Baths of Nero tomorrow.'

'Are they interesting?'

'I have always thought so. It depends upon one's taste, of course.' Mr. Norman looked at him furtively and Philip experienced a sudden weariness as he recognized the ancient pattern, traditional and obvious, displayed for his pleasure by Mr. Norman ... a pattern somewhat frayed beneath the light of street lamps, revealed perfunctorily, with little hope and less ceremony. He gave it back to Mr. Norman: gently, firmly, he folded it up and placed it on the table before him; then, wiping the dust from his hands, he guided the conversation to an end.

Mr. Norman sighed. 'I shall see you at the Baths then. I often go there for the health's sake ... to lose weight. I get stout in the summer and slim in the winter, unlike the rest of the world.'

'Does Lord Glenellen live in Rome or England?'

'In Rome. He isn't allowed to enter England.'

'Why not?'

'They disapprove of him ... at least the Home Office does.

Being officials, they have no humour. They don't recognize his very real value.'

'Why do they disapprove?'

'The hobbies again. But now it's getting very late. Where do you plan to have dinner?'

'I hadn't thought.'

'Then try the hotel. The food is very good there. I should like to dine with you but I have a function I must attend ... dull sort of affair, part of my job, I fear.' When the waiter came there was a struggle for the check which Philip won, as both knew from the beginning he would.

'Awfully good of you, really, but now of course you must allow me to take you to dinner one night this week. I know a charming place I'm sure you'll like. Do you have a car? No? Well, there's another place just as good near the hotel. Until tomorrow then ... the Baths of Nero.'

'Where are they?'

'Near-by ... the hotel will direct you.'

They parted and Philip made his way alone through the darkening streets to the hotel, elated and curious, aware not only of himself but of the city, too; for an instant, he was no longer separate but a part of it: an airy and fantastic bridge across the gulf challenged him and, deliberately, he moved across it, above the dark division, to the other side where strangers were.

CHAPTER TWO

His first dinner in Rome was as good as Mr. Norman had predicted it would be. He had dined alone with a volume of Byron's *Don Juan* before him on the table and, as he ate antipasto and minestrone and chicken and drank chianti (the sort of Italian dinner that was served in America but seldom in Italy except at the better hotels, for tourists), he read of Don Juan's shipwreck and he wondered, as he often had before, whether or not the poem was intended as a parody, especially the hilarious account of the famished mariners who ate one another, beginning with Don Juan's tutor Pedrillo; as Philip munched chicken he read of the disposition of the tutor's remains:

> 'Part was divided, part thrown in the sea,
> And such things as the entrails and the brains
> Regaled two sharks, who followed o'er the billow—
> The sailors ate the rest of poor Pedrillo.'

Excellent, he thought, murmuring the last couplet to himself; it helped him understand Byron's remarkable vogue as a popular poet: almost everyone is interested in extreme situations like murder, rape, cannibalism ... the Victorians not excepted. Idly he wondered how Jane Austen might have handled incest in a novel. When he got back home he would ask one of his literary friends at Harvard; then, smiling to himself, he heard very clearly the voice of the most perverse one, the brightest, saying: 'But, my dear boy, what on earth do you think she *did* write about?' He wondered if he himself might one day learn the conversational trick of appearing never to be taken aback when confronted by the most appalling of paradoxes. It was a trick, he knew; one he'd not yet learned.

Feeling somewhat stuffed, he left the dining-room, receiving the respectful bows of the maître d'hôtel with a bemused expression which he hoped would be thought dignified but gracious. In the lobby the pink-cheeked desk clerk gave him a dolorous cocker-spaniel look and wished him a good evening.

A good evening? It was more than that: a splendid evening! warm and star-scattered. There was no moon, but he was too happy to object to this one omission as he strode down the Via Veneto in the direction of the *piazza* where he had been assured the Colosseum might be found. He hummed the only aria he knew from *Tosca* as he followed the curving Street of the Tritons towards the *galleria*. On the way he passed restaurants and *trattorias* all open, bright with undiffused light and loud with the noises of people eating and laughing and singing sad songs. Then he turned into the *galleria*, a massive arcade, not unlike a gothic cathedral except, instead of a groined ceiling, it had dirty glass panels high over head. Shops and bars like profane chapels edged the nave. Young boys and girls stood about soliciting buyers, older youths sold drugs and lire and lovers

28

with a sharp good humour, very different from the manner of such salesmen in other cities. Nothing was sordid here. The pimps, though shabby, were not at all sinister, and the boys and girls were cheerful, obviously more pleased than not to be making money in such an easy way. The young Swiss at the hotel had already instructed Philip in the current prices for girls, for virgins, for women and, with a blush or two, he had even quoted (from hearsay only, of course) the price for boys, and the one for men – there was a distinction, Philip had been amused to discover, but when he had pressed the young Swiss to define that difference he had only blushed all the more deeply and said that really he didn't know, he'd only heard tell, as everyone had.

But tonight Philip was not, for once, interested in finding a companion. He was on a mission of the spirit: to behold certain of the more profound Roman symbols by starlight; so, spiritually mighty, he was able to pass without a glance the prettiest of the Roman girls, the most voluptuous of the Roman maidens who watched him go with sorrow for they obviously thought him attractive; unlike so many women of the North they took a very real pleasure in love-making and the fact that when it was over they expected prompt and complete payment for the act by no means meant that they had done what they had done without enthusiasm, contingent, of course, upon the behaviour, the age and the character of the man involved. Money they knew was the same everywhere and in that knowledge they were indeed similar to Northern women, but they also knew that men were by no means all the same and here they differed from their cool sisters who lived so far to the north of the inland sea.

For a moment he paused in silence before the dark and rather unimpressive palace where, on a balcony, the fallen dictator had made so many appearances, burdening the newsreels of Philip's boyhood with a rock-jawed, insensitive face tilted with boundless assurance to a classic disaster. Few people frequented the square at night as though in deference to that battered ghost which still seemed, Philip felt, to brood over the palace, arm raised for ever in a facsimile Roman salute; dwarfed, however, in death as in life by the fantastic marble monument across the square, the pillared white temple of the first modern Italian king, Victor Emmanuel, now a resident with the dictator in that

29

limbo which some clever god has no doubt devised with the express purpose of maintaining the one-time great men of our world in a state of eternal discomfort, of perpetual desire and thwarted will. Philip, meditating comfortably on the folly of human enterprise, crossed the square, dodging the occasional cars which darted about, lights blazing and horns shrieking. He paused and asked a policeman where the Colosseum might be. Having had this one sentence already prepared for several weeks, he was confident that the other would be able to understand. The young policemen, with a gravely stupid frown, shook his head wonderingly and Philip said: '*Grazie*' and turned down the street which seemed most likely to lead him to his goal.

It was the right street. He sensed that instinctively and he toyed with the idea of pretending to himself that he had been here before, that some atavistic memory was leading him on to the centre of the ancient city, over paths which in another life he had walked many times: a general returned from Parthia followed by his legions. He chuckled at the thought ... more likely a prisoner from the island of Britain, a fair-skinned oaf with shaggy beard who'd probably get a better price at the slave market than an African, but not so good a one as an Asiatic.

Suddenly the modern buildings ceased and on either side he saw dark canyons a dozen feet lower than the street, and he could see dimly by starlight the ruins of the Forum, pale familiar shapes of broken buildings, shattered columns and arches, an occasional dark massive section of some government building still intact, reminiscent in style of nearly every railway station in every American city. He walked slowly, quite alone. There were no other pedestrians and he wondered if perhaps the Romans had some feeling against frequenting ruins at night, the fear of ghosts, of all the bloody happenings which had taken place among those broken rocks, the centre once of a world of fine law and some order, an age of silver untarnished by that Christian blight which had coincided, somewhat suspiciously he'd always thought, with the dark ages.

The avenue widened and there before him, illuminated by several floodlights, was the Colosseum, far higher than he'd ever imagined it to be, solemn in its age. He paused, awaiting revelation. None came, however ... he was aware only that his legs were rather tired from walking and that his left shoe was pressing too tightly against his little toe. There it was thought, all of it, precisely as he'd imagined it would be from the various photographs he had studied years ago in school, in the days when he had read with excitement the stories of Livy and the *Lives of Plutarch* and the splendid, wise letters of Cicero. Now by the floodlights which managed to diminish rather than enhance this relic, he was able to regain in a rush that youthful fascination with the past which, like a sudden tide in the blood, returned: a love of the old not merely because the old was in itself romantic nor because the worst of the dull sad moments had long ago been winnowed out by chroniclers too busy describing great deeds to note that the human condition (how he loved this echoing phrase: the human condition!) was constant in its confusion, in its vulnerability to pain. . . . No, he loved the past for another reason: continuity, that was it. He'd always known instinctively that when he died the poignant progress of one Philip Warren would end for good. He had known this from the day he'd first been told about death: when he was four years old and his grandfather had died in the room next to his. War had only confirmed him in this knowledge. Men whom he knew, and often had liked and admired, became after an air-raid so many torn limp carcasses in canvas bags at the bottom of the sea. Their personal belongings sent home to a faraway family (equipment gone through carefully beforehand, however, to make sure that no unusual letters, lewd photographs or contraceptive devices would be sent on to shock the grieved family). Nothing remained of these warriors but fast-blurring images in the minds of friends whose primary interest is never the devout recollection of the good dead but survival. Somewhere Thomas Hardy had written a poem on this theme, he recalled. But Philip, because he understood and respected change, valued the past, his own and the world's became, as he pondered, all the more impatient with detail, more curious about the whole design of which only tantalizing fragments had been revealed by scholars, men not unlike himself, in temperament at least, all haunted by the fact of change which they attempted, in the only way they knew, to define, by fixing the near-true moment in the careful prose of history.

' "Oh call back yesterday bid time return," ' Philip whispered as he descended a deep flight of steps and approached the crypt-like building, eroded by weather and scarred by all the visiting

Northern warriors. With a sense of one about to make a discovery, he entered a dark archway, pausing midway through the building, suddenly alert, as he realized there were people all about him in the dark. He could see no one but he heard breathing, an occasional whispered word; finally the lighting of a match revealed a pair of lovers while, behind them, stepping hastily into the shadows, thieves and murderers foregathered to contemplate acts of violence. Yet, though conscious of danger he was unafraid, protected by his own conception of this battered place: no one is murdered in a dream, he knew, and like a dreamer he walked out into the open and observed with nostalgia and delight the tiers of seats which circled an arena whose floor had been torn up by archaeologists to reveal the complicated passageways beneath. This was Rome.

'Do you think the ruins of Madison Square Garden will ever be as impressive?'

He jumped. The voice, a woman's, laughed pleasantly; he turned and saw that she was behind him, seated on a fallen column.

'Perhaps,' he said evenly, moving towards her. 'Have you been here long?'

'On this column? No, not very, a few minutes. . . .'

'How could you tell I was an American?'

'Only an American would come here at night and walk out into the arena. An Italian would have hid beneath the arches, doing business.'

'Are we the only romantics?'

'It would seem so.'

Was she young or old, he wondered, pretty or beautiful or plain? He could not tell. She was no child: her manner was too mature, too confident for a young girl. He would have to get her out of here, he decided; manoeuvre her into the light and then . . . well, he could not predict what might happen since, currently, he was dedicated to the idea of a classic detachment and he was wary of any involvement which might threaten this high, cool mood. His life had been, for the last few years, unpleasantly confused with the rapid arrivals and departures of women who had all discovered, some sooner than others, that his boyish manner concealed a resolute love of independence and, against those who came to this discovery late, he had learned to fight with growing skill a series of delaying actions which would have done credit to that Fabius Cunctator who had so often and so brilliantly harried the great Hannibal near this very spot. Philip's master stroke had been, of course, his sudden departure from America which ended, as far as he was concerned, several difficult alliances. So, remembering the immediate past and aware of his own weakness, he was cautious as he stepped beside the shadowy figure on its pedestal and caught the odour of her perfume.

When he had finished a speech on the romance of far places, there was a pause. He watched her still figure, wondering if she was preparing a response of equal gravity or whether she had just stopped listening to him. He strained to hear her breathing, and he did: deep breaths, slow, unexcited breathing: that was too bad, he thought, wanting suddenly to prove his power. Then he remembered that he, too, was invisible and she had no idea what he was like. She was as curious as he, however.

'You're a student, aren't you?' she asked.

'In what sense?' he parried, remembering this stylized phrase so often used in intellectual debate when one warrior of the word, needing time to compose a new strategy, invites the other to lose his way in definition.

She laughed again, mockingly. 'Now I know you must be a student. Scholarly young men always want to know in what sense any question is intended.'

He laughed, too. 'I was stalling,' he said, wondering whether he should tell her a lie or not. If she were old or plain he would not for a moment have hesitated to make himself sound as romantic as the occasion and the setting insisted that he be. If she were desirable he would of course be romantic about *her* and stick only to the facts, favourably arranged. Which should he do? What should he be? He paused, knowing that his decision would be irrevocable, that, if she were to be one day a lover, it would never do to begin by telling her that he was one of the heroes of the Air Force, now doomed to travel feverishly about until the cancer which had already begun to spread to his nerve centres (explaining that tiresome lisp) finally, and in great agony, brought him Icarus-like to earth. No, he would play it safe, he decided; and moving closer to her, he said: 'I graduated from Law School a month ago.'

'How young you must be,' she said, and his heart sank: he was positive now that she must be sixty with a strong resemblance to his mother. He backed away, wondering if it was too late to speak of his fatal disease.

'No, not so young,' he said.

'Then you are one of the veterans who went back to school.'

'Yes.' He waited for an opening.

'What was it like, going back? Didn't you feel too wise to be taught?'

'I always felt too wise to be taught,' he said, stumbling into an epigram, 'but not, I hope, too wise to learn.'

'Oh, I hope not.' And again he caught the mocking note in her voice. Well, I earned it that time, he thought, grimly. 'You're a lawyer now?'

'Yes . . . believe it or not.'

'It doesn't seem so incredible . . . there have been other lawyers.'

'I know, but I never thought I should be one.'

'Why not? what would you have rather been?'

'I don't know . . . probably nothing at all. I would have made a very fine dilettante in the eighteenth century . . . the sort that had theories on everything and wrote long careful letters to friends.'

'You were born too late for that. Everyone must struggle now.'

'A pity, isn't it?'

'I don't think so.' She was now going to become serious, he could see, and the advantage would all be his. He had been on the defensive as long as she questioned or mocked him; but now she was vulnerable and he felt very much better. She said: 'I suppose it's fashionable now to avoid responsibility, to speak lightly of Armageddon as though it were really of no concern.'

'What can one do, though?' he asked. 'I've always admired those flippant souls who go about their business, ignoring the horror . . .'

'I don't.'

'What can one man do, or fifty men, or even a million .. if you could imagine a million men, or fifty of them for that matter, being united on any policy. What can they do? How can they alter the direction of life?'

'You sound so fatalistic. . . .'

'Not really,' said Philip, wishing to get the conversation back

34

to earth again, to himself and to the story he had planned to tell her of the sanatorium where he'd spent the last year, and of this final fling before the end (had he not been warned that if he came down to sea level before the five years of his cure were up he would die?).

But she was resolute. So resolute that he no longer really cared what she looked like: he disliked women of strong character and he had been fortunate in his life, having known comparatively few and none well.

She persisted. 'Well, let's say, then, for the moment, that I agree with you, which I don't, I accept your theory that individuals have no direct effect upon grand affairs; yet I see no reason why a man shouldn't act. In other words, even though one knows his gestures have no ultimate meaning, no real effect, it doesn't mean that a man's action is worthless for it has, after all, some value to himself and to the others who are, in one way or another, immediately touched by it. By acting he expresses himself, the act itself is an assertion, an expression of his will . . . I sometimes think that the whole excitement of politics is just that: to state one's position (more or less honestly) and then to pursue a single end until it is obtained.'

'Even if the end is only political office?'

'The end should be more noble, I suppose, but the holding of high office is all a part of what I mean . . . making an important design of one's life.'

'I would rather be passive, interpreting the world for my own private pleasure, than bustle around upsetting people, the way the biggest operators do.' He wondered why, of all the possible roles in his repertoire, he had elected to play this curiously weak one with her. He believed, of course, everything that he was telling her, but on the other hand he believed so many other things, many of them quite contradictory. Well, he would have to be consistent, he decided rather sadly, marshalling a number of references for the coming attack; but the attack didn't come. She shifted ground; she became personal.

'Have *you* any interest in politics?'

'Only a spectator's.'

'But you're a lawyer.'

'What has that to do with it?'

'You know perfectly well what that has to do with it . . . the law is the first step in most political careers.'

'So?'

'You'd probably do well in politics. Have you money? Aside from what you earn?'

'I have enough. I've never earned anything yet ... except my Navy pay.'

'Are you married?'

'No, and I'm not likely to be.' This was better. He was about to inquire into her status but she gave him no opportunity.

'Then obviously you have everything ... and how you could enjoy yourself if you wanted to!'

'Talking to dull people all day? Smiling at my cretinous constituents and promising them all the things they have never had? It doesn't sound like fun to me.'

'But can't you imagine yourself the head of state? making important decisions? striking an admired pose for your ... cretinous public?'

'Too easily ... I fight against the temptation.'

'Then you *are* tempted?'

'Of course but the fact that I'm reasonable now doesn't mean I should act reasonably if placed in a different situation.'

'Then you *could* imagine yourself involved in politics?'

'I can imagine myself involved in anything ... the one virtue of having served in a war is that one quickly learns nothing is unlikely. I can do anything.'

'But would you like it?'

'I would have a real contempt for the whole business.'

'But would you like it?'

'Probably.' He qualified, partly from conviction, out of a desire to be as nearly accurate as words would allow, and partly to see what she would say next, to determine, if he could, the reason for her curious urgency.

'Ah. ...' She had got her way and for a moment she did not speak. Both stared across the betrenched arena towards the tiers of seats on the other side: stars shone large and white in the black sky; beneath the dark arches of the building, struck matches, for brief instants, glowed like fireflies on a summer lawn. The air was still; there was no wind and, though he tried, he could not hear the sounds of the modern city which he knew must be all about them, outside this much-scarred oval of antique marble. An occasional voice, muffled and secret, came to him from the archways but, excepting those near-by voices, the

36

rest was silence. What would she say? She asked him where he was from and, when he told her, she laughed and asked him his name. He told her this, too, and she said: 'I know your family.'

'Oh no! I'll never escape, I see.'

'Why escape? You have so much to do ... Philip, and there isn't much time.'

His name sounded odd to him, spoken like this in the warm Roman dark by a stranger, by a woman who apparently knew all about him though he knew nothing of her.

'What do you mean, not much time? Are you speaking prophetically?'

'Oh no ... just relatively, I suppose. I was thinking how short lives are at best, and since you are thirty ...'

'Not quite.'

'Not quite ... and presuming you live to be seventy, your life at this moment is half gone.'

'Nearly half.'

She laughed and repeated: 'Nearly half.'

'Then, of course, you could so easily be killed in a new war. But somehow I feel you will survive it.'

'So do I. How did you guess, though, that I'd planned to avoid it?'

'I'm intuitive, I suppose.'

'You must be. Yes, I've very elaborate plans for keeping out of the trouble. First, I shall have all my teeth taken out. ...' He paused; then: 'Where did you know my family?'

'In Hudson. In the county. My husband knows your father very well.'

'And your husband, what's his name?'

'Rex Durham ... my name is, as you probably know, and a poor joke it is after all these years, Regina.'

He said nothing for a moment; he was surprised and amused and, against his will, more than a little impressed. All his life he had heard of Rex Durham and he still remembered, years ago, when Durham had married Regina: Rex and Regina. For fifteen years he had heard stories about them ... their parties, their deeds (both amatory and political); Durham was the boss of the Party which was the boss of their state and the state, often as not, was the boss of the country. Philip's father had always been proud that he knew Rex well enough to call him by his first name, while his mother had always thought Regina lovely, in a hard sort of way.

'No wonder,' said Philip at last, 'you're so interested in politics.'

'No wonder,' she echoed. 'Tell me, though, have we ever met before? I must be honest and say I remember almost no one I meet, unless I've been briefed in advance.'

'No, we've never met. But I was thirteen when you were married ... I remember that very clearly. My parents were at the Albany reception.'

'I remember, too. I mean, I remember your mother and father that day. I was twenty then,' she added self-consciously.

'I know.'

'Time passes,' she said. 'Shall we go?' She stood up, facing him in the dark. She was taller than he had suspected, not much shorter than himself, and her body was indeed slim. Her face he had imagined from the many photographs he'd seen of it: dark hair drawn severely back, thin mouth, arched nose, and black eyes with thick brows. He knew all the details, knew they made handsome photographs; he was curious, though, to learn how those familiar features looked in life.

Beyond the Colosseum, they both stopped as though by mutual consent beneath the first lamp-post and examined one another with, he thought uneasily, that shameless eagerness which in the past had meant only one thing ... and that one thing, he'd already decided, was out of the question for a number of reasons, all good.

As he looked at her he wondered if, perhaps, electric light was not in its way as false as photography. For this light was stark and dramatic and it made her face deathly white. It made the features bold as it cast its dark shadows in all the hollows, emphasizing her large deep-set eyes. She wore no hat and her hair seemed pale and rather dull, not grey nor yet blonde but somewhere in between; not dark like the newspaper photographs, nor as severe. She seemed very young to him or, rather, ageless; a woman with handsome features and a tranquil expression.

'I thought you would look older,' she said, smiling.

'I thought you would, too,' he said, without thinking.

She laughed at this; yet, suddenly self-conscious, she stepped out of the light. 'You're not very gallant,' she said.

'I'm sorry. I didn't think ... one of those unfortunate sentences that doesn't mean what it says.'

'Don't make too many of them or we'll never get you elected.'

'Am I running for office?'

'Of course. Let's go back to the hotel ... you must meet Rex, you know.'

'Now? this very minute?'

'Why not? Are you afraid?'

'No, just uncertain. I never know what to say to politicians.'

'He isn't like a politician. Besides, you'll have to learn how to talk to everyone easily. There's a trick to it ... watch me some time in a group, or Rex, or any old-timer for that matter.'

'You'll really teach me all those things?' He was careful to disguise his amusement.

'Of course.'

'Why?'

'For reasons of state,' she said evenly, as though the sentence had been long prepared in her mind awaiting the proper moment to be spoken, to disguise, he was quite sure, her true intentions whatever they might be.

'I haven't consented yet,' he said lightly as they approached the mammoth white confection which contained the martial spirit of that dull king who fathered the no less dull and now, thought Philip, fortunately defunct royal house of Savoy. A bat suddenly swooped across their path, circled in front of them and doubled back to the vast ruins of the Forum behind them.

'But you will,' she said seriously. 'You'll see, I think, that you must. For many, many reasons that I will give you one day, if you like.'

'I should like to hear them.'

'I should like to tell them to you. I wonder why you seem so much younger than you really are.'

'Because I lisp, I suppose. It's my cross ... before my voice changed I was considered the sissy of all time. After it changed I was considered very sweet and everyone wanted to protect me.'

'The way I do?'

'I don't know. By the way, how am I to succeed in politics if I can't talk straight?'

'Stop finding difficulties.'

'Tell me, do you know Lord Glenellen?'

'No, I don't think so. Why?'

'I only wondered.'

It was almost midnight when they arrived at the Excelsior. The lobby was nearly empty as they turned to the right of the desk and walked down some stairs to a still crowded bar. As they walked between the red damask walls, he caught a glimpse of her in the mirror and saw her, he realized, for the first time. Among the glass and the red and the well-dressed people, she moved with purpose, pale and strange, foreign not only to this room, to these people, but in a sense to all that was familiar. He wondered with some amusement how she managed to please her husband's political friends, for she was abrupt in a way sure to be resented. But then, too, it occurred to him that she might after all be a good actress and that the figure he saw crossing the room was an actress hurrying from her dressing-room to the wings, mumbling lines to herself, oblivious of the supers who stepped aside, making way for the star.

Philip stepped forward like Ganymede prepared to meet Jove and, with a smile, he shook the hand of Rex Durham who had risen to greet them. The introductions were quickly and skilfully made and before the first Scotch and water had been brought Rex had been told all that he would ever need to know of the past life and deeds of Philip, who said nothing while his protectress (or temptress, he was not sure which) instructed her lord.

Rex Durham was a tall man, heavily built, with a great head, large grey eyes, which, Philip noticed, could look either commanding or stupid . . . nothing else. The brow was massive and deeply lined and his hair was a thick chrome-silver, while the square strong face was ruddy and healthy, for he was just fifty, powerful, admired, and married to a remarkable woman, a combination of good things which, Philip reflected, might combine to destroy a lesser man. But Rex was in no sense a lesser man. He was a major one. He was, at this moment in his history, leader of the Party and in rank a member of the Congress. He believed, like all good bosses, that it was wiser to remain out of important office, away from the direct influence of the frivolous ballot box which could occasionally (though, he saw to it, not often) upset the most reasonable of combinations for the most irrelevant of reasons. He represented, Philip recalled, his own district on the melancholy-green banks of the Hudson River, a rural old-fashioned region, not much changed in essence since Washington Irving made it strange with his fancy, his dream of Dutch legends.

'Been waiting for you for half an hour, Regina,' said Rex clearing his throat oratorically, trumpeting.

'I lost my way,' she said. 'Then, when I finally got there, I met this young man and we talked for a long time. He walked me back.' Rex looked at Philip with large grey eyes, empty, not seeing. 'He's one of your constituents,' she added, 'that's why I've been so nice to him. He's Judge Warren's son.'

'Judge Warren! Old friend of mine, young man. I'm very fond of your father, very fond indeed. Do remember me to him when you write him next. We've been through a lot of campaigns together, the Judge and I. Wonderful old devil.'

Rex's manner had changed and his eyes glittered as he reminisced. 'But isn't that remarkable, Regina,' he said, turning to his wife with an ingenuous air, 'your finding a boy from our own backyard right in the middle of the Colosseum. . . .'

'In the middle of the night, too,' she added. 'I thought you would be pleased.'

'Certainly am. So you're Judge Warren's son. . . . You were in the war, weren't you?'

The catechism was then read through with a degree of simulated interest and vigour on both sides; Philip impressed by the older man's legend, while the older man, used from habit to flattering young men who were in some way politically connected with him, or might be, or should be, conducted the questioning with ease. It was soon done and they drank Scotch thoughtfully as the room suddenly filled with noisy young Americans, cheerful and handsome and a little drunk. The boys had crew-cuts and wore seersucker suits. Their innocent faces were tanned from long drives through the golden countryside with their girl companions, short-haired and full-skirted. They filled the bar, four couples, collegiate and simple. Not one pair of horn-rimmed spectacles in the lot, thought Philip, lulled by the giggles and jokes of the newcomers, curing any possible sickness for home he might have had.

'They're really enjoying themselves,' commented Regina with

an inexplicable neutrality; he was disappointed that she did not share his pleasure.

'Glad to see it,' said Rex. 'World is in such a state, they may not have much longer to play around in. I'm all for a good time. What about you, Philip?'

Philip agreed that he, too, was in favour of a good time and Regina sighed; then Rex talked politics. He mentioned great names, many great names. He did not drop them to impress, the way an ordinary man might have done. No, he fired them in volleys. He was discreet for all his bluffness, and Philip knew the other was trying deliberately to appear frank while saying nothing that a reasonably dedicated reader of *Time* magazine might not have known. But the effect was all that could be desired and Philip listened with pleasure to a description of the Pope's views on the world's state.

'Grave, very grave.'

Then he reported to Regina on his day and they spoke over Philip's head as though he was not there or was a child.

'Saw Jim this afternoon, after I left you.'

'And he said . . .'

'Wouldn't be able to play ball with us . . . going to handle the whole thing through State . . . regardless.'

'But didn't you tell him . . .'

'How could I? As long as they have confidence in him, I'm helpless.'

'But not quite.'

'No, not quite . . . the President . . .'

Their conversation at this moment became so very grand that Philip wondered if he should not tiptoe out of the room which had, with only a magic word or two, become, somewhat incongruously, a residence of majestic intrigue, despite the boisterous young people at the next table who were debating whether or not they should drive to Ostia that night and go swimming. He listened, aware that he was, if only for this moment, close to the whirring centre of the world, of the vast delicate machine which would determine the future for all of them or at least execute the inscrutable design which, with or without the machine's connivance, included one crisis after another, good and bad (for some good and for others bad) as it had always done, without benevolence or malice, master of the machine of which Rex Durham was a part, perhaps even at this moment the key, though Philip did not know this ... nor, for that matter, did anyone, he thought ... wallowing lazily in huge abstractions, conscious that of all those now in the room he was the most detached and, paradoxically, the most engaged with the question if not the answer; the question which, with one illusion or another, the boys and girls, the man and his wife, managed to obscure until at the last they would be confronted with it, with the end of it all, and Philip sighed, end of both question and answer alike.

Rex Durham predicted a major war within thirty-six months.

'Let's not talk about that,' said Regina uneasily.

'We must, though. It would never do to be unprepared again.'

And here we go again, thought Philip: all his life there had either been talk of a war just ended or one about to begin or, and in a way best of all, a war in progress. Somehow the fact was never so terrible as the anticipation, as the gloomy predictions which his family in particular had indulged in all his life, confident as they were that they would some day be swept away by a common catastrophe, a major war or, failing that, a popular uprising. They belonged to that small class in America which regards itself as aristocratic, a wealthy class, nicely educated and as old in a tradition as the people of a new country can be ... which is old enough, thought Philip, trying to recall the origins of the Durham family, deciding at last as he recalled some half-forgotten bit of gossip that Rex must have belonged to one of the new families, a self-made man or the son of one. But soon it would make no difference if his own father's prediction were to come true or not: the old man believed their days were numbered and that the old freedom their class had enjoyed was, with each year, being surrendered bit by bit as the taxes increased and the business of the government became larger and more oppressive, more concerned with the details of its citizens' lives in an effort, partly benevolent and mostly political, to sustain a majority of the voters in the grey and uniform security of a nursery where the eccentric and the private would not be permitted; and their own society, for the most part as stolid and as nearly virtuous as any reformer could wish, would vanish and their lawn-circled houses would serve to house girls' schools and asylums for the insane (the latter drawn more and more, Philip was certain, from the wise and the sensitive and the formerly free).

Yet Rex Durham, concerned only with the pleasure of power, would be, he realized, quite unsympathetic to this view. He would say that times have changed and that times must, if one is sensible, be moved with. He publicly deplored Socialism and the government's taxation programme but, in private, he would admit that his Party in power would not behave differently for after all armies must be maintained and unhappily governmental charity can never be withdrawn.

But Rex had got to his feet. Rex was going to bed. Rex was tired.

'It's been a pleasure, young man. I hope we'll see a lot of you now that we're all here in Rome together.'

'How long do you plan to stay, sir?'

'Ten days more. Then to the Vienna Conference, and then home.'

Tall elms, only somewhat blighted, black twisted locust trees, glittering copper beeches, green lawns and silver river: home . . . it was the same place for all of them. Philip bade the Durhams good night or, as it turned out, only Mr. Durham for Regina said that she was not yet sleepy and that she would like to sit up a few minutes longer.

'Regular night owl,' commented Rex, as Philip knew he would (he'd got into a terrible habit of guessing what others would say before they actually spoke and he was rather alarmed at how often his guesses proved to be accurate).

Then he was alone in the bar with Regina for the young people had, with a good deal of noise, departed just before Rex, their destination as far as Philip could determine still undecided.

'It's late,' said Philip.

'Yes,' said Regina, 'very late.'

Contemplating the lateness, they looked at one another across the table, aware of the silence in the room, empty except for a sleepy waiter on a high stool behind the bar.

'Do you like it?' she asked.

'Yes, very much,' he said, not sure what she meant, willing to match her ambiguousness with his own.

'I do, too, very much. You'll spend a year in Europe, then? A year travelling?'

'So I've planned.'

'Afterwards you'll come home?'

'I may come home, yes.'

'But you may not.'

'It's possible. The year has only begun.'

'Only begun,' she repeated thoughtfully, then: 'You will be coerced, you know, by all of us.'

'Am I as valuable as all that?'

'Of course . . . don't you think you are?'

'Naturally, but I wasn't aware that the world valued me as much as I do.'

'But it does.'

'A great responsibility.'

'Of course. You *are* responsible . . . that is the meaning of the whole business.'

'What business?'

'Being alive . . . responsibility, action, to live usefully.'

'For others?'

'Why not? Wherever the greater glory lies.'

'One wants glory?'

'Oh, more than anything else! To live grandly, to shape the world!'

He laughed. 'It's too rich a diet for me. In any case, I've already given you my opinion of politics.'

'Shallow, smart opinions . . . You didn't mean what you said.'

'But I did. Besides, I'm a shallow person. That's why I've come to Europe, to improve my mind, to grow deep.'

'You're making fun of me.'

He smiled. 'No, not at all. Only I don't think it's worth the trouble. . . . You're wasting so much interest on me. Let's talk of something else . . . of Mr. Durham.'

'My husband? What of him?'

'An unusual man.'

'I think so. A political genius, if politicians can be said to have genius. I respect him.'

'Will he be president?'

She looked at him without expression; as though she had not heard or had not understood. She answered elliptically: 'Is he the sort, do you think?'

'I don't know. I mean, after all, he's your husband.'

'Yes, he is. Would you like that office?'

'I don't think so.'

'It could happen.'

'Nonsense.'

'You don't know, you don't know,' she repeated, shaking her head. The bar-tender who had been asleep fell off his stool. He got to his feet, blinking.

'Tell me something else,' said Regina.

'What do you want to know?'

'Tell me . . .' she paused; then changed the question, 'Tell me a story,' she said.

'Any sort?'

'Yes, please.'

'Once upon a time there was a mother who had five children. She was very proud of them in her way, but her way was very severe for she was ambitious. She made up her mind that she would make them the most successful children in the world and so every day she beat them until she had taught them how to fly. In time they got so they could fly very well indeed. They could glide and soar and do arabesques five thousand miles up; naturally people thought very highly of them.'

'Then what happened?'

'Oh, they flew away from home and joined a circus and became very rich.'

'And their mother?'

'They never saw her again. They didn't love her at all.'

'Do you like that story?'

'Not very much, but it's true I'm afraid.'

'I don't like it either.'

'It's getting late.'

'Is it late?' She looked at a small diamond watch.

'Is there time?' he asked.

She nodded.

CHAPTER THREE

The ultimate moment. The splendid act. The joining of body and spirit in one breathing centre about which the earth and stars revolve, counter to all the established laws of the empiricists who know only detail, and that partly, while lovers know truth wholly. Or, to put it less grandly, it is great fun indeed for the light-hearted . . . solemn and emotionally edifying for the rest, the ones who are aware of the tradition involved in the long duet, and who approach it reverently, even fearfully if the Puritan spirit has by chance spoiled them as it has spoiled so many, even now in these relatively enlightened days when most of the fear has gone out of the act.

Union. An end of loneliness, exaltation, a moment compared to which all other moments are tedious and unbearable. What more can one say? Well, rather too much, I fear. Since Pindar, it has been said all in a rush (and presumably before that in Babylon, China, Egypt and the gnomic land of Crete), and so nowadays one must confine oneself to the peripheral rather than to the central aspects of the business, the splendid game in which we are all, to the best of our capacities, engaged.

Now, part of the pleasure one gets from reading novels is the inevitable moment when the hero beds the heroine or, in certain advanced and decadent works, the hero beds another hero in an infernal glow of impropriety. The mechanical side of the operation is of intense interest to everyone. Partly, of course, because so few of us get entirely what we want when it comes to this sort of thing, and, too, there is something remarkably exciting about the sex lives of fictional characters. For one thing, there is so much clear and precise talk both before and after the act. So much talk that one feels far more clearly engaged than one does in life where the whole thing is often terribly confused and clumsy and one hardly knows where one is, if anywhere. Then, too, there is a formidable amount of *voyeurism* in us all and literature, even better than pornographic pictures, provides us at its best with an excitation occasionally more poignant than the real thing.

I have, of course, over-stated the case, and Philip presents something of a problem at this point. Like most young Americans of his age and class, he has a tendency towards promiscuity, towards 'emotional brashness', as an eminent English critic once remarked, rather sternly, of contemporary novels and their faithless, aimless protagonists. Philip is not, of course, aimless but his approach to sexual matters lacks the solemnity which those of us who care deeply for man's highest emotion demand of that most intimate union between man and woman. Taking all of this into account, it would, I know, be wisest to avoid the subject altogether and begin this new chapter as though nothing untoward had happened that evening in the Excelsior Hotel. One could indicate, perhaps, that the relationship between Regina and Philip had somehow magically deepened or, better yet, a fistful of asterisks tossed over the page might solve everything; and one would be praised for reticence since there are always a great many American ladies (of both sexes) who tell one that there are enough unpleasant things in the world without writing about them in books ... lovemaking, significantly enough, being considered very nearly the most unpleasant activity of all. But, nevertheless, I feel obligated to myself, if not to the reader, to reveal as candidly as I think proper what happened between Philip and Mrs. Durham on the fourth floor at the Excelsior in a room separated from Mr. Durham's by a sitting-room and a locked door.

First, despite the essential beauty of the act, the union was not well made. There were a number of small frictions, tiny annoyances, which almost always occur between two people who are not yet properly attuned to one another and who are also over-excited by the novelty and the danger of what they are doing.

Philip had only half his mind on what he was doing. The other half was listening, somewhat frantically, for the sound of Mr. Durham rattling the locked door and demanding entrance. Philip had placed his clothes on a chair in such a fashion that he could get into them with a speed which always did credit to his military training (shirt inside jacket, drawers inside trousers). Regina did her best, however, to put him at his ease, remarking that Mr. Durham seldom demanded his marital rights, his energies, as far as she knew, being devoted to the greater business of controlling presidents.

48

Now, to be frank, one hardly knows how far to go in describing precisely what happened. There is the brutal school, which uses any number of squalid words to get to the point. Then there are the incredibly popular lady novelists, who titter and leer, describing the hero's great, rough (yet sensitive) hands and the back of his bronzed neck (for some unaccountable reason, the back of the neck has become, in the male at least, an erotic symbol of singular fascination). Then there are the sort to whom the business is very beautiful and very fine, the centre of the book, tender and warm and serious, very serious. Much is described, as much is left to the imagination. One is moved and, should the novelist be a good one, the scene can have a remarkable immediacy. Yet, in this particular case at least, we must attempt another method. For Philip is not brutal nor is the back of his neck bronzed nor is he in love with Regina. He finds her attractive and desirable and it seems to him like a very pleasant way to spend his first night in Rome. In other words, to go back to that same English critic, he is 'emotionally brash', though it is to be hoped that in the year of self-discovery he has so wisely elected to embark upon he will come into a proper relationship with another human being, thus giving a certain emotional richness to the deed which, in Regina's cool arms, he lacks.

Cool arms. Now we come to it. At seventeen minutes after two o'clock they entered the bedroom. Regina turned on the light, took her rings and bracelets off and accepted his embrace. By two-thirty, more or less, they were both undressed and investigating one another with some pleasure. Regina's body was very fine. She was not too heavy. Her waist was slim and taut. Her hips were somewhat large but handsomely curved. Her breasts were not in the least unusual; they did not sag while, on the other hand, they did not point skywards like mounds of ice-cream, the way the glands of young women in magazine advertisements are supposed to point. Her skin was rather brownish and quite smooth.

Philip has been described already in some detail. It should be noted here, however, that he had very little hair on his body, a characteristic which seemed to appeal enormously to Regina, who caressed his chest and belly with some intensity. Genitally, he did not in the least resemble those lewd markings on the walls of public conveniences. He was properly and sturdily endowed, normally shaped and without any peculiarities. He was capable of a spirited performance, guided by an intuition of the other's rhythm which often bordered on the miraculous. Tonight, however, due to nerves, his performance was violent and boyish rather than sensible and manly. Conscious of this tension, Regina helpfully murmured an occasional direction, but the stars were not right and the climax, which lasted seventeen minutes, counting preliminaries, of course, was not epoch-making in either of their lives. On the other hand, it afforded both some relief and the previous atmosphere of tension was succeeded by a state akin to euphoria.

The final details are not particularly relevant. Needless to say, Philip was anxious to leave, afraid of that locked door opposite the bed through which at any moment he expected to hear the rumbling of the husband's querulous voice. Regina turned on the light and they looked at each other with considerable interest, even critically now that desire was for a time allayed. Happily they found that even under these somewhat exacting circumstances they were still charmed by one another and it was immediately apparent to them both that they would, with some pleasure, repeat the act whenever in the future an opportunity should present itself.

Regina gave a number of dates and times when she felt opportunities would arise. They decided that, all in all, late afternoon was the best time to meet and his hotel the best place in which to reaffirm their passion. After a few more remarks (all whispered) they parted and Philip returned through darkened streets to his hotel where an ancient Swiss with pale orange hair unlocked the front door and led him through the shadowy lobby to the lift, which unfortunately was out of order; blithely, however, he climbed three flights of stairs to his room and then, tired but happy, he went to bed and slept without dreaming until noon the next day.

He was awakened by a gentle but insistent rapping at the door. 'Come in,' he said, sitting up, still half asleep.

'I can't,' said a faraway British voice. 'The door is locked.'

'Wait a minute.' Philip grabbed an enormous bath towel and wrapped it about himself like a cloak; then he opened the door and admitted Clyde Norman.

'Ah, you were bathing,' said Mr. Norman, rather pleased.

'You Americans bathe every day, I'm told. Go ahead. Don't let me interrupt you.'

'Oh, that's all right,' said Philip vaguely, 'come on in.' Now that he was awake he did want to take a bath but modesty prevented him: there was no bathroom, only the curtained alcove which contained the bathtub and the bidet, this last an object of considerable fascination to Philip who thought it wicked.

'Don't you find it terribly unhealthy, bathing I mean? Doesn't it open up the pores dreadfully? I have a weak chest and so I take no chances. I never bathe.'

'I'm afraid I've never thought about it,' said Philip, getting back into bed. Clyde Norman went to the window and pulled back the curtains, admitted a flood of yellow light. In the street Philip could hear a newsboy shouting.

'You don't mind, do you? It's quite warm out.'

'No, not at all. I've only just got up. I was very tired, you know ... the train and all that.'

'I should think so. Your first morning in Rome! How wonderful for you!'

Mr. Norman sat down in the room's only arm-chair, crushing Philip's trousers beneath him. 'I come,' he said, making himself comfortable, 'from Lord Glenellen, who would like you to play bridge with us tonight at his place. There will be only four people, counting yourself, should you come. Ayre, myself, you and Ayre's secretary, a pleasant Welsh boy named Evan Morgan who can't sing a note.'

'Sing?' Philip was beginning to wake up at last.

'The Welsh all sing,' said Mr. Norman easily, 'like your Negroes.'

'Do they?'

'Of course they do. All except Evan, who doesn't sing one note properly, though Ayre likes to listen to him. Ayre claims he's the only real interpreter of the Bardic songs ... a minor peculiarity of his Lordship's and, to my mind, the only really insupportable one. The poor child is often called on to render a song or two after dinner and once every season there is a recital ... all very sad, but then one must allow for human nature.'

'I suppose so. Yes, I should like to play bridge. What time?'

'After dinner, at ten. I'm afraid we won't be invited to dinner

51

. . . Ayre hates to serve food though he's one of the richest men in England . . . or, I should say, *out* of England.'

'He seems unpleasant,' said Philip sharply.

'Yes, doesn't he?' Mr. Norman was bland. 'It's very strange how unsympathetic people seem when described by a good friend. But of course in life all the unpleasant characteristics are blended in such a way that, to the friend at least, the result is most agreeable. To an outsider, Ayre must seem a monster. His reputation is not only frightful, it's frightening. Yet I find him one of the dearest people in the world.'

Mr. Norman paused sentimentally and Philip looked away uncomfortably, afraid he would find a tear on the other's sallow cheek.

Fortunately Mr. Norman changed the subject. 'What did you do last night?'

'I went to the Colosseum.'

'But there was no moon.'

'I know. I wanted to see it, anyway.'

'And did you? Could you?'

'Oh yes. It's lit up on the outside at least. Inside it was dark.'

'Rather dangerous, too. You should be careful.'

'I met an American couple while I was there.'

'Of course. I should have known that the Colosseum at night would attract all sorts of Americans, as well as murderers and thieves and pimps. Who were they?'

'The couple? A Mr. and Mrs. Durham.'

'Not the politician?'

'The same. Friends of my family.'

'How very interesting! I've already met them, or rather I've seen them at the Embassy. There was a garden party given for them last week. It rained. Do you know them well?'

'No. I'd never met either of them before.'

'How strange they'd be sightseeing in the middle of the night. He seemed such a hard, shrewd man . . . so very American.'

'But she is different.'

'Yes, she seems to be. Rather like an Englishwoman, if that's any description.'

'I see what you mean. Anyway, we all went back to the Excelsior for a drink.' Philip had a natural inclination to cover his tracks, an instinct which was at the same time usually undone

52

by a need to discuss at length everything which had happened to him or might yet happen to him. He was sufficiently wise, however, to include Mr. Durham in the starlight meeting, to allay any possible suspicion on the part of Mr. Norman who, fortunately, had none at all along these lines but perhaps a suspicion along others or, at least, a hope, faint but persistent.

'Then you must know them quite well by now.'

'Not even Americans work that fast.'

'But you'll see them again.'

'Very likely, yes.'

'I see.' Mr. Norman shut his eyes ... it was a trick he had when he was about to make an announcement, or to change the subject. Philip, wanting now to have his coffee and a bath, wished he would make his pronouncement quickly and go. Mr. Norman was capable of a mild surprise or two, however, for instead of some vague observation he asked a question. 'You care much for politics?'

Philip moaned softly.

'I've heard nothing but politics for the past twenty-four hours. No, I'm not interested in them at all. I have decided that I'm going to be a water colourist,' he said inventively, surprising even himself with this choice of profession.

'How nice. Whom will you study with?'

'A Russian who lives in Paris. You probably don't know him.'

'I see. Well, isn't that nice?'

'It's what I've always wanted,' said Philip softly, gathering the towel about his neck and pointing his bare feet like a ballet dancer. Mr. Norman watched the toes, an unpleasantly rapt expression on his ordinarily serene face. Philip wondered absently if perhaps Mr. Norman liked boots.

'Do you approve of the Communist Party?' asked Mr. Norman at last, with an effort removing his somewhat febrile attention from Philip's toes to his face, unshaven for two days now and covered with a golden stubble.

'No,' said Philip.

'Do you approve of monarchy?'

'Why?'

'I should like to know. If I seem to pry, do tell me and I won't ask you any more questions.'

'Yes, I like kings very much. In a decorative sense.'

'I see, I had to know.'

Mr. Norman laughed apologetically. 'Fortunately, you said what I thought you would. You see, we've already looked into your history . . . rather thoroughly, if I say so myself.'

'We? Who's we? And why are you interested in what I think?' Philip was not agreeably surprised by this admission, this unexpected development.

'I can't answer either question yet,' said Clyde Norman smoothly, enjoying the mystery.

'I'm not sure I like this at all,' said Philip, sitting up and swinging his legs over the side of the bed, the towel falling about his body in toga-like folds.

'Don't be alarmed. It's just that both Ayre and I were quite impressed with you yesterday and we may ask you to help us in something.'

'In what?'

'I'm afraid I can't say. Ayre may tell you tonight. In fact, I can say almost certainly that he will tell you tonight, ask you to become one of us.'

'Oh no . . . none of that,' said Philip a little harshly, causing a blush to come to Mr. Norman's usually pleasant face.

'I am speaking of a political movement,' said Mr. Norman evenly, retaining some but not all of his usual dignity.

'I know,' said Philip, confused and embarrassed. 'I meant . . .'

'I'm sure you will be interested in it. The fact that you know Rex Durham makes you all the more necessary to us . . . if you will but help us.' He paused impressively, once again master of the dialogue.

'I'd like to hear all about it,' said Philip contritely, eagerly, willing to do anything to erase the memory of his ungraciousness.

'Good,' said the conspirator, getting to his feet. 'I shall call for you at eight. We will dine in a pleasant *trattoria* I know and then on to our bridge game.' He chuckled and, with the noise of Philip's good offices and protestations of friendship in his long hairy ears, he departed, well-pleased.

Philip bathed. Then he had coffee sent up and he drank it thoughtfully. Finally, dressed, with a minor anthology of major poetry under one arm, he set out for the Forum to commune with that splendid age to which he had always been mystically drawn, as though to a point of origin always known but until now too obscured by distance to be more to him than a dream of home, a ghost or a shadow of a time of splendour. And so he came to the great pit which contained the squares and streets, the monuments and office buildings of that age and, after buying the inevitable ticket, he passed under a triumphal arch and walked solemnly down the grass-grown, moss-decked Sacer Via towards the hill where Capitoline Jove once sat in his temple and where today the tower of a building of state, the work of Michelangelo, dominates this golden marble wreck of a world which still contained for Philip, despite the shattered walls and broken arches, a certain grandeur divorced from reality perhaps but, in effect, in essence, no less valid for that reason ... a world which he wished to absorb directly, the way he had, years ago, the stories of Livy and the poems of Horace (translated ecstatically with the aid of a trot).

It was both more and less than he had expected. He had not anticipated such vastness: the ruins of the various basilica and public baths startled him with their unaesthetic massiveness. They seemed too ponderous, too calculated to overawe. He wondered what a savage must have thought, coming from the foggy green forests of Germany to this stern behemoth of a city, this centre of the world. He stood looking up at a dome still intact, the work of the penultimate and gentlest dynasty, and he tried to think of it the way it had been ... he failed completely, as he always did. He had no visual imagination, only an emotional one; he could simulate attitudes and re-create forgotten moods but he could not with any success people the past with figures that seemed to him visually convincing. The Forum was altogether too much like Times Square on a Saturday night when he stared at it very hard, trying to imagine it as it was, Cicero and Nerva, Catullus and Julius but he got only a double exposure of the jostling, noisy, sinister New York crowd against these delicate columns which contained only sky and summer air ... tall umber walls emerging from green unexcavated hills and cliffs where coins and urns and marble heads lay buried in subterranean rooms, smothered in the fine brown earth of violent and unremembered days.

Tourists wandered in and out of the Temple of the Vestal Virgins, remarking upon their reflections in an oblong pool of stagnant water greener than the Tiber, like a pea soup which has sat too long and gathered on its surface an iridescent, rainbow scum. Thinking of the Vestal Virgins, Philip crossed the atrium of their house, past a series of statues which looked for all the world like a conclave of club ladies, serious and benign; at the first bench, an austere one of marble, he sat down between a pair of Corinthian-capped columns which supported a solid fragment of pediment on which a frieze had once been chiselled, a design now lost except for a man's shoulder and arm, preceded by the tail and buttocks of a prancing stallion.

He looked about him. The day was cool and the sky was clear and yet, in spite of this total realization of an old wish, he was neither excited nor content. He felt lethargic, the way he had always imagined a man who has come suddenly into a long desired place in the world must feel: this is it; the rest will be repetition. He shut his eyes and the sun was warm on his eyelids. He breathed deeply, wanting to absorb all this, to be all this. But he was himself, he knew, opening his eyes suddenly very wide and staring straight into the sun, going blind for a moment, lost in a green-gold world of Catherine wheels.

And then, as several American ladies, well-dressed and confidently equipped with Baedekers, studied reverently the remains of the Ministry of Colonies, under the impression it had once housed the god Dionysius and his erotic mysteries, Philip read:

> 'Oh rose thou art sick!
> The invisible worm
> That flies in the night,
> In the howling storm,

> 'Has found out thy bed
> Of crimson joy,
> And his dark secret love
> Does thy life destroy.'

This suited his mood, he decided gloomily, reading it again.

'Do you really think that's what they did?'

'Of course, Claire. I have read all about them.'

'Just think, it happened right here, right where we're standing!'

Philip glared at them, imagined satyrs sweeping them up in hot goatish embraces and bearing them off to catacombs, their hats, handbags and Baedekers scattered among the ruins as final

56

witness to their shameless impiety. But they moved on, un-molested, and he repeated: ' "Oh rose thou art sick!" '

Feeling a little ill himself, though not much like a rose, be-wormed or not, he wandered off towards Capitoline Hill and its memory of Caesar's death and of Jove and of *his* slow death at the hands of that Eastern mother and her mortal son.

There was a telephone message from Regina when he got back to his hotel. He called her, and after some trouble with a non-English and possibly non-Italian-speaking operator, he got through to her at her hotel. She sounded very far away.

'What did you do today?' she asked as they made awkward conversation, behaving like strangers who have contacted one another reluctantly and at the insistence of a mutual friend. He told her where he had gone and what he had seen.

'Real sightseeing,' he added, obscurely ashamed at not having been more like the other Americans here, the worldly ones who spent their days in the cafés talking and their evenings prac-tising hobbies with the cheerful and ever amenable Romans who, for money, were available for any activity, the more ec-lectic the better.

'Are you free this evening?' she asked.

'No, I'm afraid that ...' He told her where he was going, pleased that he could at least claim a certain social success for himself in this strange city where he had had letters to no one, except that unofficial one, a large draft on youth and charm which, in proper proportion and for a time at least, can buy the vitiated heart of the world.

'Perhaps another time then?'

'Tomorrow at five?'

'The day after at five?'

'I should like that.'

'So would I.'

'Shall we meet here?'

'If you like. I have so many things to tell you.'

'So many things,' he repeated. And then, since neither could think of anything else to say, made shy by the intimacy of their short acquaintance, they said good-bye to one another and the two tiny mechanical clicks emphasized the distance between them.

Philip went down to the bar of the hotel at seven o'clock, only to find Mr. Norman was not yet there. Two cherubic American ladies were drinking orangeade in one corner of the rather bleak clean little room with its tile floor and odour of antiseptic: a 'sincerely Swiss' room had been Mr. Norman's comment on it and, perversely, he liked it and made it, after Doney's of course, his club.

One of the ladies said to the other: 'Would you like a straw, dear?'

'No. No thanks.'

'Oh . . . I *like* a straw.'

The fact that this exchange struck Philip as very funny indeed reveals a great deal about his character and his attitude towards humanity, an attitude which could not be called compassionate yet, on the other hand, was not malicious or contemptuous; it was detached, ironic, and rather confused for he had a spontaneous tendency to accept people at their own valuation while, later, upon reflection, to believe nothing they had said and to question whatever he might have observed them do. This duality was the proof of his youth and essential goodwill. He had not yet come into the full manhood of his race where confusion is contained by tedious conduct and by an indifference to paradox, by that lack of curiosity which best characterizes the American man at his opulent, mature peak when the world seems familiar if not good and his strength, not yet melted away by age, is in every way adequate to life in the jungle.

Mr. Norman wore a handsome dark blue suit with unusually narrow lapels which made him seem quite foreign, while the striped shirt with plain white detachable collar only added to his quaintness in Philip's eyes. He apologized for being late, allowed Philip to pay for a quick round of Cinzanos. Then they went to Mr. Norman's *trattoria,* a small dirty place with a great many electric-light bulbs and an accordion-playing tenor who sang 'Catalina' with a ghastly tenderness which cloyed Philip but pleased Mr. Norman, who asked for a number of other songs all having to do with the fate of Italian maidens who love unwisely in Amalfi, Sorrento and Venice.

A very fine *pasta con burro* was followed by an *entrée* which Mr. Norman claimed was the specialty of the house: lumps of pink meat containing unexpected bits of bone served in a tepid white cream sauce.

'What is it?' asked Philip as he felt a filling loosen, his teeth coming down hard on a bit of bone.

'Goat,' said Mr. Norman with a happy smile. 'It *is* good, isn't it?'

The Palazzo Mettellio was a large building covered with buff-tinted stucco and roofed with tile; the façade, as presented to the square of the Mettellii, was as shabby and inexpressive as the fountain in the centre of the square which was attributed to one of Michelangelo's students, the one who failed the course, according to Mr. Norman, as they paused to stare at the dirty water which trickled from a number of unusual outlets placed frivolously in various parts of the several marble ladies who were oddly involved with bowls of fruit and a dolphin.

The interior, however, was very much more impressive, thought Philip, as they were led by an Italian youth across the long entrance hall whose ceiling was encrusted with gold decorations and paintings of heaven where various members of the Mettellii were prominently displayed, chatting with the higher ranking personnel of the heavenly host.

'There is no electricity in the Palazzo,' said Mr. Norman as the boy led them through the great hall which, though handsomely tapestried, was not furnished. At the end of the hall they paused while their guide lit a new candle. 'Ayre has never liked electricity.'

'Why not?' asked Philip as they followed the boy up a wide marble staircase which curved into darkness, a place of unexpected draughts of air which made the one candle flicker crazily. 'I don't know. I never asked him,' said Mr. Norman. 'I don't think he minds it in other people's houses. I'm glad you mentioned it, though. I shall remember to ask him.'

They followed the will-o'-the-wisp flame down a long corridor to a massive door of carved oak which the boy, bowing theatrically, pushed open to reveal a small brilliantly lighted chamber with walls of carved wood and heavy brocade curtains. A carved table and four chairs were in the centre of the room beneath a small crystal chandelier which glittered with many candles. A fire roared in the pink marble fireplace and before it, in leather arm-chairs, sat Glenellen and a plump young man with blue eyes and dark curly hair. Both rose as the newcomers entered.

'Behold the young American!' exclaimed Glenellen, moving forward in a stately glide and taking Philip by the hand; then, still ignoring Mr. Norman, he led him to the fireplace where he was introduced to Evan Morgan: '... my secretary. An invaluable assistant. Invaluable,' he repeated, looking at the young man solemnly. 'When the truth is known one day, as it must be, he will be made a Chevalier of the Order of St. Jerome of Padua. Mark my words and recall them at the proper time,' he added, deepening the mystery by putting his forefinger to the side of his nose and winking.

'Did the meeting go well today?' asked Mr. Norman, by way of reminding the other of his so far unremarked presence.

'I don't know what you mean,' said Glenellen blankly; then he smiled, revealing his terrible teeth. 'Ah, Clyde. You came after all. I was just saying to Evan here, I wonder if Clyde will come tonight and play a rubber or two of bridge with his old friends, and here you are. Do sit down by the fire. And you too, young man. I like a fire this time of year; these old palaces get so awfully damp. Fire dries them out. Dries me out, too, though I doubt whether that's such a good idea. Eh, Evan? Well, let's have a drink. Evan, ring for Guido, would you? And tell him to bring ice. Dreadful boy, you met him the other day, I think.' Philip nodded. 'If he doesn't learn to concentrate, I'm afraid I shall have to lock him up again.'

'Lock him up?' asked Philip.

'Oh yes, often ... with chains. He likes that best, he tells me.'

Guido appeared with a tray of glasses, bottles and a silver bowl of ice. Philip studied him carefully but the boy's face revealed nothing at all. No scars attested to Ayre's grim reference and when he had set the tray down on a console he left the room. Evan mixed the drinks. Glenellen was disappointed to hear that Philip preferred Scotch to absinthe.

'I suppose I have the best absinthe in Europe,' he said proudly, 'guaranteed to make a weak head dissolve. But then nothing that is good is for the weak, is it, Clyde?'

'An interesting idea, Ayre,' said the other non-committally, turning to Evan. 'Did you have a good day?'

'I think so,' said the young man, glancing uneasily at Glenellen. But that peer was daydreaming, staring into the blue-gold flames of the fire as though anticipating the birth of the Phoenix or recalling his wife's death, thought Philip, suddenly remembering Mr. Norman's story of the Embassy dinner.

'Did you hear from the Vatican?'

'Yes, the Monsignor came.'

'The Polish?'

'No, the Austrian, the old one.'

'And he felt . . .'

'That we would get considerable help at the proper time.'

'From whom?'

'The Cardinal.'

'Which one?'

'The fat one . . . you know, the River Po.'

'Ah yes. But no news from above?'

'None. *He* must remain aloof.'

'I suppose so, but perhaps at the proper time . . .'

'The proper time, and all will be forthcoming, or so the Monsignor indicated.'

Evan turned to Philip and asked: 'Mr. Norman tells me that you're a friend of Mr. Durham?'

'I know him slightly.'

'He'll be in Rome another month, I hear.'

'A few weeks, I think. I'm seeing them day after to-morrow.'

'Ayre,' said the young man, nudging his employer who had so identified himself with the flames that his face had turned a sympathetic scarlet and his gaze was as abstracted and as flickering as the fire itself. He responded to the nudge, however; his eyes focused on Evan.

'Yes, my boy?'

'The Durhams. He knows the Durhams.'

'And *who* are the Durhams?'

'You know perfectly well, Ayre,' said Mr. Norman. 'He is the President's right hand.'

'Which President?' His eye might be focused but his mind was not, thought Philip, wondering if this was the work of the absinthe which he had drunk.

'The American one,' said Mr. Norman patiently. 'Mr. Durham is here on a mission to the Italian Government. The President is relying on him. Our young friend has Mr. Durham's ear . . . isn't that enough?'

'Why didn't you tell me this before, Clyde?' said Glenellen, suddenly brisk and business-like. 'I could have made preparations. If I had only known I could have told the Monsignor when he was here today. Why, why didn't you tell me?'

'I did tell you, Ayre. Yesterday we discussed the entire thing and you suggested Mr. Warren be brought here tonight ... to play bridge.'

'Bridge?' said Glenellen hopefully, clutching at the one reference which seemed most concrete. 'I haven't had a good game of bridge in four years, since the German occupation.'

'Ayre was here during the war,' explained Mr. Norman quickly.

'He was opposed to the Nazis ...' began Evan.

'*Parvenus!*' interrupted Glenellen, throwing his glass into the fire. It shattered among the flames.

'But he had some friends from the old days, from the old German court. They protected him,' finished Evans.

'You have influence with this Durham?' asked Glenellen suddenly, his foggy blue eyes on Philip's.

'No, none at all.'

'He is being modest,' said Mr. Norman. 'His family is politically very close to Mr. Durham.'

'How do you know that?' asked Philip, surprised.

'Oh, I know a lot of things about you.'

'Clyde, this isn't the young man you told me about yesterday, is it?'

'The same,' said Mr. Norman wearily, appealing to Evan who was now at the other end of the room fixing drinks.

'I sometimes think, Clyde, that you try deliberately to confuse me. Young man, how do you stand politically?'

'Nowhere at all,' said Philip.

'But you disapprove of chaos?'

'I suppose so.'

'You recognize the importance of human affairs?'

'Yes and no,' said Philip, not understanding what this meant.

'Have you an adventurous nature?'

'Oh yes, yes,' said Philip. Why else would he be here? He added to himself, intrigued though still confused.

'Do you play good bridge?'

'Fairly ... I don't know. It depends.'

'In that case. Clyde had better be your partner. I usually play with Evan anyway. He understands my bidding. The only other good player in Rome.'

They rose and went to the card table and for two hours they played while hot wax from the chandelier overhead dripped on the table, got in their hair, and Glenellen cursed but made no attempt to move the table somewhere else. Finally, when the game was over and the eccentric playing of Glenellen and Evan had triumphed over the more conservative game of their opponents, Ayre rose from the table and turned to Mr. Norman. 'It was good of you, Clyde, to bring this young man here tonight. We must remember, however, that discretion is of the greatest importance and that it is altogether too soon to admit him to our order. Watch him, Clyde. Study him. Question him and if he seems trustworthy and valiant bring him to me next week.'

'But the Durhams, Ayre . . . they won't be here for ever.'

'The Durhams can keep,' said Glenellen sharply. He turned to Philip with a smile. 'You must not mind being tested, my boy. We all are, every day, in one way or another, if not by man by God. I am sure you will not be found wanting.'

'But will he *want* to serve us?' asked Evan reasonably. This question was ignored, however; Clyde Norman sighed. 'Very well, Ayre. It's your organization. Where shall we meet next week? And when?'

'Thursday will be the best day,' said Glenellen. He frowned. 'Not here, though. This place is being watched twenty-four hours a day. The Baths.'

'The Baths?'

'Yes, Clyde. The Baths of Negro, at five o'clock.'

'But, Ayre, I don't think . . . I mean.' He gestured futilely in Philip's direction. But Glenellen was already ringing the bell for Guido to show them out.

The meeting with Regina went off very well indeed. She arrived on time, simply dressed, discreetly made up, and Philip, when he met her in the lobby, thought her most desirable, more attractive even than she had been the night of their first meeting. They decided to take a walk in the near-by gardens of the Villa Borghese for both were a little shy at first and he wondered whether or not to invite her up to his room: he was not yet free of the American fear of desk clerks which has rendered the great game so depressing in his own country.

The day was fine, cool and at this hour golden, elegiac in

mood, with rococo clouds arranged above the rolling meadows and dark woods of ilex trees which comprised the gardens, contained in part, along the Via Veneto, by a fragment of the wall of Rome and by a most heroic arch where, on either side, families lived like cave dwellers in the thick masonry. They paused by a silver pond beneath the dark green ilex trees. Priests strolled up and down; lovers sat together on the benches, silent and passive, watching with selfconscious eyes the children of others as they played, sailing little boats on the water, playing tag between the trees.

'What can they mean?' he asked at last. He told of his evening with Glenellen. He had wanted to amuse and interest her without becoming too personal and, since their supply of mutual reference was seriously limited, it was best, he decided, to stick to anecdote until they had known one another long enough to have a whole language in common, a world of easy familiar reference in which they could meet without resorting to the neutral or to the irrelevant.

'I'm not sure,' she said with a frown. 'It's a mystery. They all sound quite mad.'

'I thought that, too, but amusing.'

'I wonder if it's wise ... your seeing them, I mean?'

'Oh, I think so ... What harm could it do?'

'Well, one never can tell. The present government here isn't having an easy time of it, you know. Some think there may even be a revolution this year.'

'But after all, I'm just a visitor. I'm not interested in any of their politics ... I'm not even interested in our own.' He smiled at her to see if she would take up the challenge as she had at such length the first night. But today she was in a different mood; she turned away and walked to a bench near-by. They sat down. A soldier with one leg and a face creased from the wars and bristled like the back of a black boar came up to them and successfully begged a lira from Philip.

'Do be careful, though,' she said, looking at him; her blue eyes serene ... no matter what her mood, they never changed expression.

'I'll see them once again. ... I promised Mr. Norman I would ... and that will be the end.' He chuckled. 'Well, at least I haven't got in with the usual group.' Philip was suddenly conscious that his head was aching terribly. He shut his eyes and pressed his hand against the lids; inside his head the universe was definitely and brilliantly exploding outwards infinitely, and he with it. He opened his eyes and blinked.

'What on earth is the matter?' Regina was staring at him, alarmed. 'Are you sick?'

'I don't know,' he said weakly. The light hurt his eyes and he half shut them. 'I have a headache. That's all. Came on me all of a sudden.'

'Do you have them often?'

'No, never . . . not like this.'

'We'd better go back then.'

'No, not yet. Let's sit here. It'll go away. I've probably eaten something which disagreed with me. I . . . Oh!' He groaned, recalling the dinner the night before. 'Goat!' he exclaimed, and he told her of the dinner. Then, when the pain was less acute, they got up and, slowly, as though he were an invalid only just arisen from bed, they walked down avenues of ilex, of evergreens, to the Via Veneto and to his hotel where at his insistence she went up to the room. He ordered tea and aspirin and then, after this had arrived, sick though he was and in spite of her cautioning, they made love, the warm gold of the afternoon imprisoning the room with bars of light.

This time, it should be noted, all went well in spite of the fact the phone rang at the most important moment and continued to ring irritably for some time, as though the caller suspected he was being ignored deliberately. Then, when they were through, both knew (though neither was indelicate enough to mention it) that, in spite of his headache, it had gone very much better than the first time. Philip especially enjoyed it and he felt relaxed and easy when, finally, exhausted, they lay side by side on the bed and he smoked and she drank tea and the conversation reverted once again to Glenellen.

'I'll find out about him, if you like,' she said.

'I wish you would. And by the way, why should he be so interested in your husband?'

'I don't know. But the fact that he is means that he's up to something politically. If you want to do anything in this country you have to go to the Americans.'

'And your husband is the American to go to?'

'So they think.'

'I see.' He blew a series of elliptical smoke rings. They

65

watched the pale rings distend and vanish in the golden mote-scattered light of the room. When the last one had vanished, she sat up in bed and propped a pillow behind her head. He looked at her with interest and pleasure, relieved in a way that the novelty was gone (usually it went in the first five minutes) and that he could regard her without that distorting of perspective which in his initial lust inevitably performed on any immediate object, beloved or not. So now what he saw he liked dispassionately and he could, he knew, in time and if all went well, love or at least grow accustomed to her in such a way that he might think himself in love: that grand nineteenth-century passion which had never, at this moment in his life at least, touched him with its burnished wing ... although, if questioned, he would no doubt insist with some severity that he had loved and suffered in his day, adding as all philanderers do that the promiscuity of his more recent years had in no way atrophied his power to love one person wholly, should that person, by some miracle, materialize in his arms after the usual dalliance with a responsive stranger. Thus did he believe love would come, quickly, suddenly, utterly transforming some stranger into a creature as desirable and as unique as those goddesses who, in ancient days, would for love of a mortal become temporary exiles from the heroic beds of heaven.

But the transformation was not destined to be made that day. Regina, sensing no doubt what he was thinking, suddenly pulled the sheet about her and said: 'Rex thought you very charming.'

'I'm glad. I prefer you, though.'

'But he can do more for you.'

'Oh no, not that.'

'But for someone who professes to hate politics you must admit you're involved rather deeply all on your own.'

'You mean the Glenellen business? That's just idle curiosity. He makes me laugh.'

'Do I make you laugh?'

'No. No you don't, not at all. Should you?'

'I'm not sure.' She sighed. 'I must go now. Rex is waiting.'

'When shall I see you?'

'Any time you like. Tomorrow?'

'Tomorrow. The same time?'

'I'll be here. How do you feel now?'

'Rather odd.'

'I wonder if you should see a doctor?'

'No. I'll be all right. I'll sleep it off.'

But the next day he was worse. The night had been terrible. He now had a fever as well as a headache and he tossed about unable to sleep until, shortly after dawn, he took a shot of brandy and at last slept fitfully, tormented by nightmares, by all the childhood monsters of the fever world. When he tried to sit up he grew dizzy, his head throbbed and his eyes ached, dazzled by the morning light. Confident that he was going to die, he rang for some tea and some brandy to hasten the end. He wondered if they would bury him in the Protestant cemetery, near his favourite poets Keats and Shelley. He could imagine the fuss his mother would make: his body would be shipped back at great expense and deposited with the other Warrens on the banks of the Hudson where he had, he recalled lugubriously, played as a child. The thought of his own premature death, complicated by the very real discomfort he was in, so moved him that he was tempted to cry, not noisily but softly, in a manly way. The arrival of the waiter, however, immediately lessened the pain, brought him again into a proper relationship with the living as they exchanged greetings. Then Philip drank the tea and the brandy and felt somewhat better. He was contemplating whether or not to get up and take a bath, to try and draw the fever out of his aching joints, when Mr. Norman entered the room, a friendly smile on his face.

'Do excuse me for barging in like this but I'm to tell you of a little change in our plans. Ayre has been called to Milan on business and so the meeting will be postponed for a week. I hope that's all right with you.'

'Anything is all right with me,' said Philip gently, beginning to die now that he had an audience.

'What *is* the matter with you?' Mr. Norman was alarmed. 'You look perfectly frightful.'

'I am sick,' Philip whispered and shut his eyes, feeling rather better for having drunk the brandy.

'Ah, you've caught it,' said Mr. Norman with some satisfaction, proud of his adopted city's treachery.

'Caught what?'

'We call it Roman fever, and everyone gets it. It lasts about a week. Possibly it's from the water, or perhaps it's just because the city is so low . . . used to be malarial, you know. There was a time when no one could stay here during the summer.'

'But what do I do?'

'I'll get you a doctor. Nice chap I know, a German. He'll fix you up in no time. Meanwhile, of course, you'll have to stay in bed and miss this splendid weather.'

'I don't care. I don't care about anything.'

'By the way, I telephoned you yesterday afternoon but there was no answer.'

'I wasn't here. I was walking in the park.'

'Now that's odd because the manager said you were in your room.' Mr. Norman chuckled maliciously.

'I take long walks up and down the corridor,' said Philip, wishing Mr. Norman would go away. His wish came true for Mr. Norman, after this final indication that he knew precisely what the other was up to, departed with the promise to send him the doctor immediately.

Illness becomes the young, in moderation, of course. It makes them pause in the midst of their physical euphoria and contemplate their own mortality. For young men like Philip the body is unobtrusive, something to be fed and washed like a motor-car and, from time to time, relieved in different ways. It gives no trouble and, served properly, can be the best of all possible toys. Philip's was no exception. He was vaguely fond of his body. He admired it dispassionately, without vanity though not without some complacency when he compared it to others and found it not only decorative but useful, always equal to the admittedly not very rigorous tasks he set for it. But now after twenty-eight years of loving care, something had gone wrong. He had had, of course, all the childhood illnesses but none of them had been severe, while his maturity had been marked by the most resolute health. Yet now, in an instant, he had been laid low and at first he wished he was dead; then, suddenly aware of what it would be like to die, he wished he were well and thousands of miles away from this city which had so gratuitously returned his passionate admiration with a well-aimed blow in the most unexpected quarter.

He convalesced slowly and, after the third day when the fever broke, agreeably. He read. He sat on his balcony in the cool sunshine and surveyed the life of the street with a detached eye, aware that he was set apart from the others, the busy men and women out of doors, who did not know, as he did, that man is vulnerable and the flesh, after a certain age, corrupt and festering, preparing for its final dissolution. The morbidity of such conjectures appealed to him hugely and once the pain left he found that he almost missed the knowledge of the body it gave him, the sense of the secret actions and counter-actions of the flesh which caused him to live and to be, which would cease all too soon when the mechanism, unbalanced at last, would degenerate into dust to be rearranged in time into other apparently less sentient forms ... though of this he could not be sure and, until he was, he decided, death would find him furiously protesting, if not terrified.

Regina came to see him every day. They talked of many things and she spoke often of politics, of his natural gift for them (though how she knew he had such a gift was never apparent to him). She tempted him in every way she could to go home when she did and to prepare for a great career: the Presidency would be his in twenty years, she indicated, though fortunately not in words, for this revelation would have embarrassed him and shaken his faith in her practicality. Presidents, they both knew, ruling out divine appointment or intervention, are the result of various compromises of the moment, compromises between extremes which cannot be predicted in advance from one year to the next ... expediency governs the lives of nations as it does, though fortunately to a less marked degree, the lives of individuals. Yet he was touched that she had such faith in him. Her calm assurance, however, was bewildering: she spoke of the winning of future elections as a fact. Four years in the Assembly, then ten years in the Congress, then the Governorship and, at last, the Presidency. It all seemed easy when she spoke of it, so definite. She told him how the elections could be won, which person could do what for him and, knowing her power, he could not, at least when it came to detail, doubt what she said. In his weakened state he found himself more receptive to this gaudy dream of domination than ordinarily he would have been. And she, seeing that her companion was making some progress, pressed on until at last he was almost ready to agree to go back in two months' time and begin the ascent: wondering always what it was that she wanted from him, what he must give her in exchange. He did not like to ask and so he held back from the final declaration she so much wanted to hear.

One morning he awakened to find that he was well again. He stretched and unsuccessfully tried to recall what the pain had been like; but he could not remember ... even the memory of the fever was gone.

Mr. Norman, who had kept careful watch over him during his illness (had even encountered Regina briefly in his room), arrived shortly after breakfast.

'You look very well, very well indeed.'

'I'm going to go out today.'

'By all means. Get more air ... won't do you a bit of harm. Summer is here and the day is fine. I've been up since seven.'

'It'll be nice to get out of this room.'

'Has Mrs. Durham called you yet?'

'No, I'm seeing her tonight.'

'A lovely woman,' said Mr. Norman, looking in the mirror and combing his thin hair straight back. 'She's quite a nurse, too, isn't she?'

'She's been very kind,' said Philip, pulling the blanket about him and getting up. He felt strong and confident, ready for almost anything. Which was fortunate, for Mr. Norman had, as usual, a plan to which Philip, with a number of unexpressed doubts, finally agreed: at four o'clock that afternoon he arrived, alone, at the Baths of Nero.

The Baths were in a small side street. A large, soiled plaster head of Nero hung above the door through which he passed into a dingy reception-room. A man who spoke no English indicated the price, which Philip paid, wondering, as always, whether or not he was being cheated. He was then led down a spiral staircase to a large well-lit room full of cubicles with wooden numbered doors. Men dressed in sheets or towels padded up and down the corridor; when he entered several stopped their patrolling and stared at him.

Now, it should be remarked at this point that Philip is neither naïve nor innocent. He has had a varied and interesting life

70

which has included a thorough indoctrination in almost every human activity. His own tastes were set when, at thirteen, he seduced a high school senior, a much admired girl of eighteen and the object of his older brother's less virile attention. The excitement of this conquest had gone to his head and so, for fifteen years now, he had untiringly repeated that first experience with various partners, in his enthusiasm and pleasure increasing rather than lessening as he grew older. Over the years, however, he had been offered any number of opportunities to explore other ways in the company of excited strangers. When he was fifteen an older woman, a respectable family friend, had tried to get him to beat her with the silken cord of her dead husband's dressing-gown. He had refused her sternly. A year later, at prep. school, he was invited to indulge in certain erotic ceremonies conducted by the school's leading athlete, a strong passionate boy who died in the fire of a bomber the year the war ended. In spite of his adulation for this young hero, Philip's natural modesty combined with a precocious love of his own pleasure, caused him, with great politeness, to refuse the invitation. Later, in uniform, seldom a day went by without some form of adventure presenting itself. Elderly men bought him drinks and invited him up to their rooms for a night-cap. He refused them all, even though on occasion he would accept a drink or two at a bar. The men's rooms of various railway and bus terminals of the country were brilliant with generous invitations which he always declined pleasantly as he continued his own quiet and orderly progress. He was never outraged, unlike the neurotic whose balance is precarious at best. In fact, everything interested him in the abstract and several times when friends of his had tried to sell him on this or that variation he had admitted that it all sounded very interesting and that perhaps at some other time he might give it a try. But that other time never came and meanwhile Philip covered the field like a quarter-back with good interference.

From time to time, however, he has become involved in situations which had he been less of a traveller, less curious, he might never have known about, much less become involved in ... proving, perhaps, that he has an inclination towards forbidden vice; a very slight one, however ... certainly not enough of one to render enjoyable this visit to the Baths of Nero where, after tying a small white apron about his loins, he timidly opened the door of his cubicle and stepped out into the hall.

Slowly, barefoot, not liking the thought of the dirty coarse matting under his feet, he walked down the hall towards a small sitting-room where a number of middle-aged gentlemen were smoking and chatting and drinking apéritifs provided by the management. They paused in their conversation and looked at him very carefully. Several were noticeably aroused and one sighed audibly as Philip, blushing furiously, walked past them to the thick glass door of the steam room. He caught the words: 'Inglese, Americano.' He wished he had not come. He had known perfectly well what it would be like: the world of the Turkish bath was no secret to him nor, for that matter, was the character of Mr. Norman. Idle curiosity had brought him here and now, he decided grimly, he would have to go through with it.

Hanging his apron on a peg beside the other aprons, he stepped into the hot room.

It was a large room with stained-glass clerestory windows which gave it a faintly ecclesiastical air. On three sides of the room a broad white marble shelf had been built and here, in Roman fashion, a number of figures reclined or sat. Off to the right was another door of glass, the door to the steam room. A fountain decorated the centre of the hot room and cold water trickled from the fountain's mouth into a basin where the clients dipped their hands from time to time, cooled their faces. The most unusual feature of the room, however, was a number of unusually handsome Italian boys, with deep chests and velvet skins, who wandered about the room with preoccupied expression, stopping here and there to say a few words to this or that person. They were, Philip could see, the quarry, the central attraction of the Baths.

The men on the marble benches were for the most part middle-aged though there were some very young ones, Philip noticed, as well as several incredibly old ones not yet free of the cruel and insane master . . . though very nearly free of the flesh itself. They talked in all languages, laughing and joking like club men. There was a significant pause when Philip entered and, as he walked across the room to a vacant place on the bench, he was aware that he was being judged, point by point, like a prize bull. Simulating indifference, however, he swung himself on to the bench and modestly crossed his legs. The conversation resumed, although there were many glances in his direction and one young man, a lean American with a crew-cut, came over and asked him if he would like to go back to his room with him. Philip shook his head politely and smiled. 'I'm meeting somebody,' he said. Sadly the young man went away and Philip rubbed himself until he began to sweat, trying not to notice the various odd duets about the room.

He didn't have long to wait for, in a great burst of sound, talk and laughter, the peer, red and leathery as a salamander, entered from the steam room, a towel arranged about his head in the fashion of the Pharaohs, He was accompanied by Evan, who looked handsome with his clothes off, and Mr. Norman who did not.

'Ah, there you are, my boy. Hardly recognized you, Hardly recognized you, indeed,' hummed Glenellen, inspecting him quickly, professionally. 'May we join you on the slab?' They arranged themselves like corpses around him; Glenellen sighed voluptuously. 'The heat, the heat,' he murmured, 'ah, the darling heat.'

'We come here every day,' said Evan, who looked as though he would rather have been anywhere else: he was sweating profusely, unlike the two older men who seemed to absorb the heat greedily.

'Good for the soul,' said Mr. Norman, hesitantly patting Philip's calf; Philip moved out of range.

'I should think you'd all get very thin,' he said, for want of anything else to say. He had never felt more out of place and already he had begun to plan his escape.

'Source of life,' intoned Glenellen, sitting up and looking at the youths who stood in decorative attitudes around the fountain, showing their wares to the would-be purchasers, talking in low voices among themselves. 'Give me young lips that taste of fruit,' said Glenellen, smiling, revealing carious teeth. 'What say you, young man?'

'Oh, by all means,' said Philip distractedly.

'Aren't they lovely? Like young gods. Commercial young gods, but still divine.'

'Very nice,' said Philip, not wishing to give offence or to be thought gauche.

73

'Which would you pick?'

'I don't really know,' said Philip beginning to blush, aware that Mr. Norman was watching him with great amusement.

'You can have any one you want,' said Glenellen with a royal gesture. 'I will treat you to one.'

'I . . . I'm afraid I'm not in the mood today.'

'Nonsense. A healthy boy like you is always in the mood. Come now, don't be shy. Take your pick . . . my party, you know.'

'Are they very expensive?' Philip stalled.

'Five hundred lire, that's all . . . *prixe fixe*. Here, at least; on the street you have to pay more. Well . . . what about that dusky Venetian blond? Wonderful type . . . how Titian would have loved that face . . . and Michelangelo to sculpt that torso. I almost want him for myself . . . but after you. I will be generous. You are my guest today.'

Philip did not know whether to reveal himself as a womanizer and a tourist, or to dodge the whole thing gracefully by going off with the boy for a polite length of time. Mr. Norman, a mound of white dimpled flesh, saved him by remarking: 'Before we play, Ayre, I suggest we do our business. Besides, you must remember that our young friend has been very sick these last few days. He may not be in the mood for the game.'

'He looks all right to me,' said Ayre suspiciously, 'but you're right, we must set to work.' He sat cross-legged on the marble. The heat, Philip decided, was good for him. Glenellen was far more alert than usual, even rational. 'Evan, go take one of the boys and cool off. You always look as though you were going to turn into a weeping willow when you come here.'

Evan, obviously pleased, scrambled off the bench and walked over to the fountain, where he engaged a small sinewy Sicilian in conversation. They came to terms immediately and, with a wave to the others, Evan followed the young man out of the room.

'He always likes those small muscle-bound boys,' said Ayre peevishly. 'He has no taste. No love of beauty. Poorly educated, that's the trouble, like all the Welsh. Where were we, Clyde?'

'Business. Mr. Warren.'

'Ah, yes. Mr. Warren, we need you.' His voice was urgent. He looked about furtively to make sure that no strangers were listening. 'We've examined your record carefully, both of us, Clyde and myself, and we've decided that you can be of great use to us in our movement. Before I go into detail, however, I must impress upon you the need for secrecy. If you feel that you cannot for any reason respect my confidence, I wish you would say so now and I will not continue ... my lips will be sealed.'

'Well,' began Philip uncertainly, torn between curiosity and a fear of involvement.

'I accept that, then, as your pledge,' said Glenellen, rearranging his red, loose body upon the marble. 'We know that politically you are in sympathy with us. Your comments on politics have been duly noted and interpreted. In short, Mr. Warren, we recognize you as a fellow royalist and we wish for a short period to utilize your talents in our movement to restore the House of Savoy to its rightful place in our adopted land.'

It was out at last. Philip, who had long ago decided that Glenellen was the head of an international opium combine, gave a sigh of relief; pleased to know what it was all about, a little disappointed that the more glamorous alternative had not materialized.

'What do you think, Philip?' asked the suet-white lump on his other side, a flaccid, breathing shape which contained a soul as passionate as any other's.

'I don't know. I mean, I haven't any idea what you want me to do.' Philip was immediately furious with himself for having taken the wrong line, for not having immediately opposed any suggestion that he join the cabal. He realized, however, that it was now too late, at this moment anyway, to back out; he had indicated interest and he was partly committed.

'Two things,' said Glenellen promptly. 'We need a courier to go to Amalfi next week. Most of our people are already known to the police and are being watched. We must send someone they cannot suspect and someone they don't dare touch. The fact that you are an American and new to Rome is all in your favour. You have never been seen with me. This place is safe, by the way. My own house, of course, is watched but, if you remember, there was no moon the night you came and there are no lamps in my *piazza*. The second thing is the more difficult and the more important: we want you to try to enlist Mr. Durham on our side. We feel that if he could present the true

75

facts of the case to your President he would intervene and restore the monarchy. The Republic is a fiasco. Everyone knows it. Any day now, the Communists will take over and that will be the end of Italy. We have great resources behind us ... great men are helping us ... but we must proceed cautiously and not force an issue too soon. Above all, we must get the American government on our side. Naturally, we have any number of people at work in Washington but it has not been easy to interest your government. Since you are on the best of terms with Mrs. Durham, you could, if you chose, exert considerable influence in that quarter, adding immeasurably thereby to the total effort in which we are all engaged.' He paused, the foggy blue eyes beneath the Egyptian head-dress alert, the usual vagueness replaced by an unfamiliar concentration which impressed Philip, against his better judgment.

'I'm afraid,' he said at last, 'that there isn't much I can do about the Durhams. They both know what they think and I'm sure they wouldn't take any advice from me on foreign affairs ... after all, that's his speciality, you know. And, to be practical, even if I could influence him, that still doesn't mean it would be any help to you. The President and Congress don't respond to that sort of influence when it comes to a national policy ... at least, I don't think they do,' he added, suddenly appalled by the unexpected pedantry of his reply; it was not as if he knew what he was talking about. He persevered, however, covering up this involuntary expression of doubt by several more dogmatic remarks on American foreign policy.

'But that doesn't mean,' said Mr. Norman smoothly, 'that one can't try. Every little bit helps, you know. Mr. Durham can supply us with information either directly or indirectly; we can discover what his government is thinking, learn how to change, if possible, that thinking. Oh, there are many ways to accomplish our ends, many ways, and there are many of us at work on different levels. You could try, at the very least ... if you wanted to.'

'Perhaps,' said Philip doubtfully, already intrigued.

'Will you deliver the papers for us?' asked Glenellen.

'What are they?'

'Very important documents. I can tell you no more. In any case, they must never fall into the government's hands. If there is any danger you must destroy them.'

'Where are they being sent?'

'You will take them?'

'Depends on where you want me to go. I'm travelling for pleasure and I have only a year and many things to see. I don't want to waste any time.'

'Waste any time! Young man, do you realize that at this very minute Umberto, our martyred king . . .'

'Amalfi,' said Mr. Norman quickly. 'I'm sure you will like it . . . one of the loveliest old cities in Italy, and the bathing is excellent.'

In a reckless mood, Philip accepted the commission. Both Mr. Norman and Lord Glenellen profusely complimented him on his wisdom and thanked him for his wise partisanship to their high cause. Mention was made of several decorations which would be given him when a grateful king once more adorned the Quirinal Palace. Although Philip questioned them further about the movement, he received no new information. They would not tell him whether Umberto himself was involved or what stand the Vatican was taking. They suggested darkly that they had powerful friends who would, at the right moment, declare themselves king's men. As for his own role, instructions on how to proceed would be given him in a few days, said Mr. Norman. It was understood, though, that he would not have to leave Rome before another week, in which time it was hoped he would have made some headway with Mr. Durham. Philip agreed, dubiously, to much of this: he could already imagine himself in front of a firing squad composed of Republican soldiers.

At that moment, however, his bitter vision was cut short by the return of Evan, breathless but otherwise cheerful. The Sicilian youth also returned a moment later, unruffled and businesslike. He joined his *confrères* at the fountain and they conversed seriously, like a group of brokers on the exchange. It was obvious, even to Philip, that they were discussing the price of their commodity.

'Good?' asked Mr. Norman.

Evan nodded, catching his breath at last. 'Awfully.'

'Better than Guido?'

'Well, Guido is Guido. I mean, there could hardly be another.'

'No, I suppose not.'

'We have forgotten our friend!' cried Glenellen, sitting up. 'We've done nothing for him. Shown him no hospitality. Evan, go get that blond one over there, the Venetian beauty. I'm sure he will provide Mr. Warren with a fine welcome to the Baths of Nero.'

'But . . .' Philip got no further for Glenellen then proceeded to celebrate in extravagant phrases the virtues of the baths and how, on more than one occasion, their existence had saved civilization. Even today, he implied, the serious work of Rome would be tragically affected if the lawyers and businessmen could not make an occasional visit to the baths on their way home to their wives and children. According to Glenellen, every Roman would be hopelessly frustrated and neurotic without this marvellously organized release.

Evan returned without the blond. 'He won't come,' he said, upsetting Glenellen's entire system.

'Won't come? And why not?'

'He says that our friend here is too young and too good-looking, that he only likes older men. He asked me to introduce him to you instead.' They all laughed: Philip with relief and Glenellen with almost childish pleasure. Then the boy was brought over and presented to Glenellen who quickly, and in Italian, made the necessary arrangements. Philip who only a moment before had congratulated himself on his narrow escape was not yet safe, for Glenellen, with all the insistence of his monomania, summoned a powerfully built adolescent, with a body like the David and the face of a stupid angel, to be Philip's companion.

'A gift!' exclaimed the peer warmly.

It was too late for Philip to retreat. He submitted without a word, aware that Mr. Norman was especially enjoying his discomfort. Led by Glenellen, they left the room for their various cubicles and those transports of commercial bliss which have ever engaged the highest talents of the finest poets, but will not for once concern us here.

After making a date to see Philip in two days' time, Glenellen disappeared with his Titian. Mr. Norman, too, had engaged the services of a temporary friend, while the satiated Evan ordered wine.

When the others were gone, Philip turned rather hopelessly to the youth and told him, first in English and then in French, that he would get his money all right but that due to some fundamental perversity in his own nature he would rather forgo the pleasures of the couch. The youth knew neither French nor English. He smiled charmingly and said: '*Si?*' Then he followed Philip to his room.

It would be startling to report that the stalwart Philip succumbed to pagan vice, that the habits of his maturity were in an instant undone by this classic figure which, against his will, he found himself admiring. But we must remain true to the fact of Philip's character and report, truthfully, that nothing much happened. When they got into the cubicle the boy removed his apron and hung it on a peg. Then he looked down at himself and smiled with an ingenuous vanity, as though to say: 'Isn't this handsome?' Philip smiled back. They stood facing one another for a moment. Then, a little bewildered that nothing had happened, the boy sat down on the edge of the bed, Philip, feeling silly standing over him in such a small room, sat down too, several inches away from the smooth olive-skinned flank. The boy then asked for a cigarette. They had a cigarette. The boy felt Philip's arm muscle and nodded admiringly; then he flexed his own arms and Philip gingerly touched one bicep with his forefinger. Another silence. The boy changed his position on the bed several times and Philip sat bolt upright beside him with a frozen smile on his lips. Finally the boy frowned and, indicating himself, suggested by signs that perhaps he was not Philip's type. Philip quickly put the lie to this by demonstrating with gestures that the young man's body was all that could be desired, but that (and here he made certain universal signs in the air) it was not a woman's body. This revelation quite astonished the other. He talked a great deal, stating, as far as Philip could tell, that all Americans, English and Germans liked Italian boys and even Italian boys, though they didn't make too great a thing of it, liked Italian boys.

He then demonstrated graphically that he was all a woman could desire and that women were all that he desired even though he came every day to the baths not only for money but for the companionship of his friends, the other youths about the fountain. ... How could Philip understand all this? Never mind. He did. One of the first things one learns in travelling is that people understand one another if they want to, no matter how great the language barrier. And so, on a friendly note, their

79

brief encounter ended. The boy put his apron back on, borrowed another cigarette, shook hands and left the room with, Philip knew, a hell of a funny story to tell the boys in the hot room.

'It is the most absurd thing I've ever heard.'

'I suppose so ... but then to me anything which has to do with politics is absurd.'

'Well, you certainly won't go.'

'I'm not so sure,' he said perversely, waving to a waiter who responded as all waiters do by distractedly going off in the opposite direction. They were seated in the open at Doney's, their backs to the street, facing the pavement and the afternoon display of new alliances and costumes, all rosy in the light of the setting sun.

'But Philip, you may get into trouble. Just remember the Communists may take over Italy any day now. There isn't a chance in the world of the monarchy being restored and even if there were that madman Glenellen wouldn't be involved in it.'

'So you do know who he is.'

She grimaced. 'I found out after you mentioned him the other day. Do be careful. He's really bad business, and mad as a hatter.'

'But I want to see Amalfi.'

She sighed. 'That's another thing, of course.'

'Is it really lovely?'

'Oh yes. I went there with Rex once, years ago, when we were first married.'

'How will the swimming be?'

'Wonderful, this time of year; but stay on in Rome. We'll be here two more weeks before Rex has to go to Vienna.'

Finally a treaty was made after many speeches, border disputes, hostages surrendered and compliments exchanged; their affair was, at the end, no longer the same, weakened by policy but, like a fracture that has healed, strongest at the point where the break occurred. When two people are fond of one another the first quarrel, the first sign of wills in opposition, comes as a shock, destroying the vain illusion that two can be one: a knowledge that is saddening but, happily, soon obscured if the new alliance is intelligently fashioned, defined by sensible treaty. The covenant, then, to which they both agreed was that he go to Amalfi, that he not mix in politics, that he await with mounting impatience her arrival some ten days later in a small English car called a Hillman, very fast with a convertible top and room for only two people in it.

CHAPTER FOUR

'I don't know why, but I can hardly believe that this is the room where Ibsen wrote *Ghosts*.'

'Probably because this is *not* the room. It's over there, across the hall.'

'But the manager said distinctly that it was the first room to the left.'

'Well, dear, this is the first room to the right.'

'So it is, Bella. I'm sorry. I was hasty.'

'And there seems to be someone in it.'

'Why, so there is. I wonder who?'

'Not so loud, dear, he's asleep.'

'Do you think it's an American?'

'Good heavens, how can I tell? I mean, he's asleep.'

'Now *you* are talking loud.'

'Come along, May. Let's look in the *right* room now.'

'It's really terribly thrilling! I love Ibsen, don't you?'

'Oh yes, yes.'

'What was *Ghosts* about, by the way? I don't seem to remember.'

'Tuberculosis.'

Philip waited until he heard them withdraw; then he rolled over and opened his eyes, unpleasantly aware that as usual in the heat he sweated more sleeping than awake. Slowly he got to his feet and, like an old man enjoying his discomfort, he crossed the room and shut the door, wondering why he had accepted this ridiculous mission. Considering bleakly the nature of the House of Savoy, he put on a bathing suit and a dressing-gown; then he left the room.

The hotel was a rambling, odd sort of structure on top of a steep cliff at the town's edge. In the centre of a Moorish-style patio with delicate carved arches of yellowed plaster, ancient tiles, cracked and smooth from age, were arranged in oriental patterns about a lily pond, shadowed by a single orange tree. He crossed the patio, went down a dark cobbled passageway, as steep as a castle's entrance; then he stepped out into the street.

He stood a moment blinking in the hot sun. Below him was the town of Amalfi, surrounded by steep cliffs and green hills, cut by a narrow ravine through which a slender foaming river ran, curving down through terraced stone houses to the luminous blue sea which sparkled a hundred feet below him, vivid in the noon light.

He crossed the street (the hotel was at the hill's top and there were no other houses near-by), and descended the steps which had long ago been cut in the rock of the cliff.

He had had a brief recurrence of the fever coming down the day before on the train and now, today, he felt tired and irritable, obscurely despondent, without direction, conscious of no real centre to his life. The thought of his secret mission depressed him further and he wondered if it might not solve everything if he drowned himself in that warm blue sea beside which he now sat in his bathing suit, one foot in the water and his face turned blankly to the scorching sun, like a tired love-offering to the occupant of the far-ranging golden car.

Then, bored with sunlight, he looked about him at the sharp brown rocks which edged the peninsula at this point; there were no beaches here ... only cliffs and rocks while, at the town's centre, the ravine and the river were contained by wharves, the focus of Amalfi which, like some great pink amphitheatre, was fanned out over the green and umber hills on top of which dead castles, relics of the crusades, of the busy bold Normans, rose in solemn silhouette against the sky.

It was all very lovely, he decided sourly, giving up the idea of suicide for the moment.

'Est-ce que vous parlez francais ou anglais?'
'Oui, je parle tous les deux.'
'Are you American?'

'Yes.'

'How nice, Bella. We were right . . . at least, I was.'

He recognized the voices: The two ladies who had awakened him in search of Ibsen's *Ghosts* appeared. They stood now before him in white dresses and wide hats, cameras over their shoulders and, in their hands, great handbags containing, he was sure, pills and lotions, guide-books and expensive cameos. They were American, plump, no longer young, resolutely cheery. . . . Their mannerisms and costumes were so alike that they seemed to be identical twins, although he was sure that, examined carefully, there must be any number of differences easily remarkable to their friends.

Everyone was introduced. Bella and May Washington were sisters, teachers of English and Social Science, respectively, in the Bigelow Clapp High School of Dubuque, Iowa. Both were unmarried, they hastened to say . . . and both were virginal, he decided, sublimated to a degree that was scarcely human.

'Isn't it nice?' said Bella, sitting on the rock to his left.

'So lovely and warm,' said May, perching on a rock to his right. He pivoted about to face them, the sun on his back now.

'We saw Pompeii, did you?'

'Not yet. I passed near it on the bus from Naples this morning.'

'Then you only got here today.'

'A few hours ago.'

'We've been here a week.'

'We must really apologize for breaking in on you like that but May had been reading about Amalfi in the guide-book when lo! and behold she discovered that Ibsen had stayed at our hotel and that he had written *Ghosts* there so we hastened to discover which had been his room and the manager very kindly told us. By mistake we got into your room. May's mistake.'

'Yes. Silly of me, wasn't it? I never seem able to follow directions. It was so interesting, though, seeing the room. I asked the manager all about Mr. Ibsen, and he said that he remembered seeing him years ago when he was a little boy, when the manager was a little boy.'

'Tell Mr. Warren what he said about him.'

'He said that he had whiskers and that he refused to eat *pasta* . . . isn't that interesting?'

83

'It certainly is,' agreed Philip.

'Will you be here long?'

'About two weeks,' said Philip, imagining those two weeks: A sun-scorched time of dazzling sea, of restless nights until Regina came, when his loneliness would quite possibly increase. *'Dies irae,'* he murmured to himself as he was told what to see in Amalfi, which churches were lovely and which were tacky, which stores were expensive and which were reasonable and full, yes full! of fine cameos, old and rare. Would he like to see one? Yes? He was shown a large yellow cameo of Minerva, or was it the goddess of liberty? No, more likely Minerva. 'I mean, after all in those days the Goddess of Liberty was rather *de trop,* as the French say. Not at all proper to reproduce in a monarchy like Italy,' which reminded him again of his mission and, thinking of it, he shuddered suddenly in the hot sun, afraid of what might happen.

'And then he was killed by the Count's servants and eaten by wolves.'

What on earth was she talking about? he wondered, aware that he'd missed an entire anecdote.

'How terrible!' he exclaimed. Then, to show interest: 'Where did the wolves come from?'

'The forest, naturally. The castle was surrounded by a forest in those days and there were wolves everywhere. Certainly proves the legend, though, doesn't it?'

'I should say so.' Philip was now ready to go swimming but they had other plans for him: they wanted to take his picture. So he posed for them against a rock, looking out to sea like a tired Hermes prepared for flight.

'Thanks so much. That's our hobby, you know, taking pictures. We have seventeen scrapbooks now.'

'That's a lot.'

'It certainly is. Of course we travel a great deal. This is our fourth trip to Europe . . . the first since the war.'

'Bella likes Italy. I like France.' Their views were presented to him and he passed judgment as tactfully as possible and then, before they could draw him out, he rose and excused himself and with some style dived into the warm seas, narrowly missing a sharp rock which might have split his head, providing the sisters Washington with an unusual snapshot.

He left the hotel through a back door, wondering whether or not he should have worn a cape. In his coat pocket, fastened with a safety pin, was the document which he was to deliver to the 'organization'. But before he could meet the 'organization' he would first have to present himself at midnight at a certain antique shop where the proprietor, according to Glenellen's verbal instructions, would receive him warmly if he remembered to say *'O lente, lente curite noctis equi'*. He had been drilled in this one sentence by Clyde Norman, and as he walked down the narrow street he murmured it over and over to himself.

The street fascinated him: steep and only a few feet wide, a cobbled path between the windowless façades of buildings, broken here and there by deep-set bolted doors. The only light came from the fragment of moon overhead and from the lights of the town at the foot of the street. Feeling disembodied and faintly unreal, he walked liked a ghost through the warm wine-odoured darkness, the stale heat of the day lingering in the quiet air; he wondered what would happen if, irrationally, he began to shout and batter at one of those metal-studded doors.

His mood changed when he stepped into the circle of dim electric light which illuminated the level part of the town, the stage of the amphitheatre. Men and youths stood about on the wharves in groups talking, their shadows long upon the sea. In the open cafés men and women were singing loudly and, Philip thought, rather well, on pitch and melodiously. He was aware of curious glances as he walked in front of the main café ... foreigners, tourists rather, were still a curiosity in this country so recently conquered by the foreign armies, and he knew that his appearance and, in even greater detail, his clothes were being discussed as he strolled the way conquerors have strolled for a thousand years through the cities of this much shattered land.

In front of a pool hall he asked a policeman where the antique shop he wanted was and the policeman, and affable man, was able to tell him, in English. After thanking the man, he strolled up the main street of the town.

The farther he walked away from the sea the narrower the streets became, while the long dark shapes of the mountains on either side grew more oppressive by moonlight as they converged and the town in irregular ranks continued on up the hillside, almost to the castle-crowned summits. Near the fast and narrow river, contained by masonry and spanned by medieval bridges, was his goal, the shop of Signor Alberto Guiscardo. A sign in Gothic script announced Signor Guiscardo's name and business. Philip pulled the bell; there was a loud jangling.

After a long wait the door was opened by a young boy who spoke rapid Italian until, seeing that Philip did not understand him, he stopped abruptly and made a motion for Philip to come into the house.

The first room was the shop, large and musty, crowded with furniture and mirrors and paintings all jumbled together like a looted museum. The next room they entered was a comfortable modern drawing-room, small, well-lighted and airless. The windows were all shut and Philip wondered if he would be able to stand the heat and the odour of incense which burdened the torpid air. He was invited to sit down; then the boy disappeared. Philip had just picked up a book which someone had left open on a coffee table when the tinkling noise of a Mozart quartette filled the room. He put the book down nervously and looked about for some sign of life; there was none. The gramophone was in another room. He was about to pick up the book again when *it* appeared. Philip started with dismay. Then, controlling himself, he got to his feet. *It* was a fat middle-aged Italian in a Sulka dressing-gown (mulberry with gold figurings) who wore over his face a rubber mask like the ones sold in American drug-stores. This particular mask depicted, in the most life-like manner, the rosy features of a plump somewhat vacuous hog.

'How-do-you-do. How-do-you-do. Please don't get up. Sherry? Yes? I always drink sherry, too ... late as it is. I've nothing stronger, in any case.' A glass of sherry was produced from the sideboard. Philip took it, still staring at the pig's face of his host.

'Now let us chat,' said Signor Guiscardo, settling comfortably into an arm-chair. 'You wonder at how well I speak English? So do I. I have never had a single lesson. I've never been out of Italy, in spite of my numerous ... I repeat, numerous ... friendships with Americans and English people. You are American?'

'Yes ... just visiting.'

'Have you been to Capri?'

'No.'

'Do you plan to go there soon?'

'No. I shall probably go back to Rome when I leave here.'

'You must under no circumstances miss Capri,' said the Pig solemnly, taking the sherry through a slit under the snout.

'If it's so very interesting, perhaps I will go there.'

'Do, by all means.'

There was a long pause as they sipped sherry and Philip sweated in the heat and looked longingly at the sealed windows. It did no good, however, for his host obviously had no intention of opening them. Finally, when the silence got too oppressive for him to bear, Philip said the magic words Ayre had drilled him in before leaving Rome. '*O lente, lente curite noctis equi.*'

No sooner had he pronounced the incantation than the Pig stood up abruptly, spilling sherry all over its mulberry dressing-gown. Hand to its head, as though the piggish jowls might burst, it rushed from the room leaving Philip bewildered and a little frightened. He was nearly ready to make a run for it himself when his host reappeared. This time the dressing-gown was of stiff brocade, dark green with a *mille-fleurs* design. On his face he wore a new mask, that of a goat, a pale astonished-looking goat with haggard features and unhealthy red little eyes.

'I think this is more becoming,' said the Goat quietly, returning to his chair and folding his hands in his lap.

Philip half expected to see cloven hooves instead of hands. 'So do I,' said Philip, refusing to betray the very real alarm he felt.

'So much more in keeping with the tone of our discussion.'

'I couldn't agree more.'

'What were we discussing?'

'I had made a Latin reference. I had quoted a line of Ovid.'

'Of course. In the excitement it had slipped my mind. Do you like the classics?'

'Very much. Especially Horace.'

'Superb, superb poet. But I must say Catullus is more me.'

'I'm not surprised.'

'You're not despised?'

'No. I said that I am not surprised.'

'Oh.' There was a pause. The Goat looked at him thoughtfully; then it said: 'How is milord Glenellen?'

'Very well. He sends you his regards.'

'Send him mine . . . when you see him.'

'I shall.' Philip was suddenly relieved that the conversation had, for the first time, taken an anticipated turn. 'Shall I give you the papers now?'

The Goat threw up its hands as though in terror. 'Under no circumstances, my dear young man, are you to give me anything. Ever! Do you understand?'

'But I thought . . .'

'I don't care what you thought. You are not to give me anything. Do you realize that I am watched every minute? I can take no chances. There are a number of people who await with eagerness my downfall. I wish to disappoint them.'

'Well, of course, if you . . .' The Goat had rushed to the window and was looking out into the darkened street, presenting, Philip thought, a dreadful vision to any passer-by, civilian or spy.

'I can advise, however,' said the Goat suavely, satisfied that at the moment the street was empty, the enemy in hiding. 'Not only can I advise, I will, with your permission, suggest.' He looked inquiringly at Philip who nodded gravely. 'In five days the moon will be full. You will proceed to the ruined church of St. Elmo on the slope above the St. Elmo bridge . . . you can't miss it . . . and there (you must arrive at midnight precisely, not earlier not later) the committee will await you in front of what was formerly the high altar. Deliver your papers to them.'

'Are you sure you don't want them?'

'As sure as I am that the House of Savoy will return to its proper place among us,' said the Goat with an intense piety, in keeping with its sacerdotal features.

'In that case, I had better go. I hadn't planned to stay in Amalfi quite so long.'

'You're not going to leave without delivering the papers?' The Goat was anxious.

'No, I am going to leave you . . . I mean, I don't want to impose myself on you longer tonight. You have been very kind.'

'Not at all. I'm only sorry I couldn't have been of more help to you. But I'm sure that you appreciate my position in all of this.'

'Of course. You must be careful.'

'Not for myself, either,' said the Goat with dignity, like a martyr discussing an *auto-da-fé*, 'but for Italy and for our king.'

The silence that followed this pronouncement was so long, so reverent, that Philip was tempted to steal quietly away. The Goat, however, was not finished. 'Are you by any chance interested in antiques?' he asked in a different voice.

'No,' said Philip cruelly, 'not at all.'

The Goat appeared to be depressed. 'That's a pity. I have some exciting bits and pieces, you know.'

'You see, I have no place to put them,' explained Philip, wishing now to be more gracious, regretting his own harshness.

'I know how it is. In case you know of anyone who might care for some rather unusual items, do send him to me.'

'I certainly will.'

'I am sure you will enjoy yourself in Amalfi,' said the Goat. 'We have everything a gentleman needs.'

'I haven't been well,' said Philip. 'I plan to rest here, to get some sun.'

'We have quite a number of fair-haired people in this section ... where do they come from? Ah, who knows? From those great barbarian armies which once ranged up and down this ancient realm, taking their pleasure where they chose, clothed in the rough skins of beasts like so many golden forest gods. Then, later, the Normans came, from whom I am descended on both sides, the blood of Plantagenets like some heady tide in my veins, pulled this way and that by the waxing and the waning of the silver moon; and from the Normans a new vitality infused the old stock, and the kingdom of the Two Sicilies flourished for many years until it came under foreign dominion and corrupt houses reigned; at last, under a mongrel Bonaparte, God willed that it cease to be and Italy accepted Savoy, as I do, although only temporarily ... until that glad day when my own nation is free again and I, my dear sir, am restored to my rightful place as the first prince of Europe, as the rightful king of Naples.' The Goat stopped, one arm stretched out before him, upraised as though awaiting the anointing and the orb.

'May that day be soon,' said Philip quietly, now very alarmed.

'It will come,' said the Goat, arising and peering once again out the sealed window at the dark street. 'It will come. In the meantime, I will devote my days to the restoration of Savoy, knowing that once they have returned the task of Plantagenet will be more easy, that our day must surely come.'

Philip rose. 'Now I must really go, sir,' he said, adding the 'sir' as he'd always been told one must with royalty. The Goat-King got to its feet, too.

'We've enjoyed your visit. You must come back to see us soon, by daylight, on a mission of less state.'

'I will, if I may.'

'And should you perhaps want an interesting object or two, or know of a friend who does, why, bear my little shop in mind.'

'I will, sir, I will indeed.'

'I shall show you out myself.' He led Philip down the dark hall of the dimly lit shop. Here they paused for a moment and the Goat rummaged through an antique Renaissance chest. At last he found what he wanted. 'It is from Pompeii,' he said. 'Keep it as a little memento of our agreeable meeting.'

'Thank you very much. I will,' said Philip, pocketing the small object which was quite heavy for its size and obviously made of metal. Then he was led to the door, which was opened after a good deal of unbolting and unchaining, like a fortress Philip thought; he turned to say good night to his host who had, in the meantime, somehow managed, between the shop and the front door, one final metamorphosis: this time the altogether too realistic face of a grey wolf stared at Philip, its red eyes glowing luminous in the dark.

'We must meet again. Until that day, however, do not forget your rendezvous: the church of St. Elmo the first night of the full moon.'

'It has been a great pleasure,' said Philip, backing out into the street with an agility which would have done credit to Little Red Riding Hood.

Two days later, at lunch with Bella and May Washington, he felt in his back pocket for a handkerchief (the day was hot, the meal was a heavy one and all three were uncomfortably damp). The handkerchief was not there but the present from the king of the Two Sicilies was ... he'd forgotten all about it, had not worn these trousers since that night. While the two ladies were devouring chunks of hot fried veal, he examined the object. Then he tried unsuccessfully to hide it under his napkin but he was not quick enough for the beady eyes of Bella Washington, like an eager raven's, had caught the glitter of metal and she swooped figuratively upon it (the width of the table and the plates of hot veal kept her from literally seizing it). 'What is that, Mr. Warren?'

'A present someone gave me the other night. Nothing of importance,' he said unhappily.

'Oh, do let us see it.' And there was nothing for him to do but hand them the small bronze phallus, executed in perfect detail by some long-dead Roman, an amulet to inspire fertility or perhaps just an object of no significance, fashioned for the sheer fun of it, a bauble for a lady to wear about her neck (there was a hole at the base through which a chain could go).

'What on earth is it?' asked Bella. 'Is it very old?'

'Very. Roman . . . or so I was told.'

'Let me see.' May took it and after a quick glance she blushed, betraying a knowledge of mysteries denied the virgin. She looked at Philip accusingly, as though he had done this on purpose to reveal her secret, to taunt her with memories, no doubt still vivid, of past events never to be repeated in this bleak world. She gave it back to Bella who asked what it was.

'An amulet, dear,' said her sister, recovering her composure.

'Isn't it meant to be anything at all? It looks like something.'

'A tree,' said Philip helpfully. Bella glared at him, still suspecting treachery, her expression suddenly so intimate that it made him uneasy, conscious of his own generic relationship to this symbol which the puzzled Bella returned to him with the remark that she thought it very nice.

'Do you know the church of St. Elmo?' asked Philip quickly, changing the subject, guiltily avoiding May's eyes.

'Oh yes,' said Bella. 'We loved it. So ruined.'

'One of the more interesting examples of Romanesque,' said May, her manner still constrained. 'We recommend it very highly. Or have you already seen it?'

'No, not yet. Someone told me it was quite interesting. An antique dealer, a man named Guiscardo. Have you met him yet?'

Bella nodded. 'We liked him,' she said. 'He sold us some marvellous cameos, like the one you saw your first day here. I thought it was a real bargain.'

'Did he seem in any way unusual?'

'Oh heavens, no . . .'

'Of course, he did,' said May. 'His English – why, I've never heard an Italian speak such correct English. He was a most fluent conversationalist and his grasp of the idiom was firm. His remarks, too, were cogent and well-expressed on nearly every topic we discussed.'

'On every topic,' said Bella benignly.

'You are correct, Bella, as always. On every topic. And he kissed our hands when we left.'

'Both hands?' asked Philip, willing to play the grammar game as long as possible; he was an avowed anti-semanticist.

'Her right hand and my right hand,' said May Washington coolly, making it very clear that only good manners had prevented her from declaring open war on him and, through him, on all men for his earlier revelation of that ancient shape of all betrayal.

The sisters Washington charged off to a near-by castle after lunch and Philip, left to himself, wandered disconsolately about the hotel bowing gravely to the other guests, a dozen or so Europeans from the prosperous north of the continent, red-faced and long-haired, demoralized by the heat, Going out on to the terrace which overlooked the town and the glittering, tiresomely, monotonously vivid sea, he decided that this was not at all what he had expected Europe to be like. He had imagined himself moving comfortably and decorously through an unusual landscape containing various examples of celebrated architecture in whose historic shadows he would sit with lovely young girls who spoke English with charming accents and drink Pernod and Dubonnet with him while he discussed literature and politics with intellectuals who had gathered about him for his pleasure and instruction.

But, of course, it hadn't been like that at all. He had been naïve, he decided, sitting on a bench in a shady corner of the terrace, to think that the world would arrange itself so neatly for him. Actually he was aware already of a lengthening present curving from one mystery to yet another, composed of unexpected happenings that were affected always (subjectively at least) by the irrelevant demands of the irritable flesh. Yet one day he would know. He was confident of that.

Then Regina, all in green, joined him on the terrace. 'Here I am,' she said.

'At exactly the right moment, too,' said Philip, standing up, but not taking her hand or kissing her. 'I was just this moment thinking of the flesh.'

'How flattering! A woman my age always enjoys being thought of as flesh, a decorative cushion for the lust of men. I knew that it was wise of me to come before I was expected.'

He pulled up a chair for her and they both sat down. She was extraordinarily handsome, he thought . . . her face darkened by the sun and her hair beginning to bleach.

'Has anything happened?' asked Philip, wondering how long it would take to reconstruct their affair . . . since the days that had separated them had provided each with a different memory of what had been at other meetings; memories which had been further distorted by separate ponderings: what one forgot the other treasured until at last they met on a hotel terrace overlooking Amalfi, and they were strangers.

Sex without love in this late-romantic age is considered to be one of the more disagreeable aspects of man's nature, to be ranked somewhere between murder and grand larceny. Those men and women who over-indulge their senses in this regard are, at best, considered weak and, at worst, villainous, quite capable of the other two misdemeanours.

Yet nature, finally, is the master and even the most bigoted must admit that moral attitudes change from generation to generation, as dramatically as women's clothes. Both murder and grand larceny, if conducted on a large enough scale, are universally applauded, blessed by all our institutions; while even the laws governing sexual behaviour vary from time to time, though never to the same extent as murder does, since obviously no man or woman is so constituted as to be able to show through personal example and on a sufficiently impressive scale what nature is capable of in the way of variety. Then, too, our sexual lives are hopelessly dominated. according to the mental therapists, by early mishaps and bad examples; it is no wonder then that we have as many different ways of love-making as we have people in the world ... and this in an age which desperately needs at least one rock on which to set a dogma, one single constant, one standard for all.

It has been suggested that most of the suffering mankind has undergone so far has originated with the same impulse which, simultaneously and paradoxically, has given us civilization: the insistent need to proselyte. The vegetarian must convince all mankind that vegetables are the way not only to health but to grace, while in the sphere of religion and politics should any of the zealots be given a church or a state or a mob or a foundation with some cash to use as they please, it will go hard indeed for those unorganized civilians who like meat, representative government, state control, capitalism, hot baths and extra-marital sexual relationships conducted with dignity in hotel rooms downtown. The zealots must reform their neighbours, even if they find it necessary to kill them first. It is the only sort of tidiness their minds are capable of and with a truly heroic sense of symmetry they go about their ancient mission, holding committee meetings, instituting pogroms and inquisitions.

Does Philip believe these things? Should this digression be attributed to him or to his author? Both, I think. All in all, since he is mine, he had better come around to my way of thinking ... you see? Even in this small instance, power has gone to my own level head; I insist upon agreement. But now since the point I began with seems to have enlarged into a denunciation of the proselytizers, I must return to the original suggestion that there is a popular mistrust of those who have sex without love, or without the sanction of the various institutions, secular and religious, which guard mankind against pleasure.

Philip does not love Regina ... in the sense that love means to venerate, to prefer to the exclusion of all else. And Regina? Does she love Philip? Who knows? Perhaps she does but since, in this instance at least, we choose to give only Philip's side, her attitude must remain, as the attitudes of strangers always remain, enigmatic. I can only report that a few minutes after their conversation began on the terrace it ended in his bedroom, a room with a view of the bright sea and the blinding sky.

She had come away from Rome sooner than planned for Rex had suddenly been sent on a tour of factories in Western Austria and she had used this trip of his as an excuse to get away, to come to the seaside for a little bathing, to escape the heat of Rome which reminded her, she said, of that famous hymn by St. Francis written during a terrible medieval summer and bedecked with sun-images still vivid centuries later.

They spent the long days together; on the rocks, bathing in the warm salt water, boating, exploring caverns and listening to legends as old as the gods and as remote. At night, avoiding Bella and May Washington who watched with eyes too interested to be disapproving, they strolled about the town visiting the waterfront cafés, drinking with the sailors and whores until, tired at last, they returned to the hotel and made love with an intensity which diminished as the moon grew great until, by the time the moon was full, Philip found his passion succeeded by a solicitousness which was more good manners than tenderness. Yet they needed one another and both knew that although there would soon be a change, this was not the time. He tried not to consider the future, unlike one of his idols, Stendhal, who always imagined the end of every love affair even before it began.

The afternoon of the day he was to go to the church of St. Elmo to fulfil his mission, he and Regina rented a rowboat from a red-haired sailor and they rowed from the town to a grotto which could only be approached from the sea. They moored the boat to a large rock at the grotto's mouth; then they took off their clothes and swam nude in the cool dark blue of the cavern, away from the glare of the June day.

The water was warm and the air cool. For a time they paddled in and out among the stalactites which supported, church fashion, a central nave from which dark forbidding-looking passageways extended into a watery darkness, sacred to old forgotten deities, terrible and proud. Finally, bored with swimming, they climbed up on a rock off to one side of the central nave and lay side by side together in the dim blue light and stared at the groined odd ceilings and Philip wondered if there were bats here, hanging like furry fruit from stone branches, asleep, fearful of even this pale light. Regina took off her bathing cap and let her long dark hair fall free upon the stone.

'It's lovely, isn't it?' she said at last, her words echoing through the nave, repeated endlessly from wall to wall like the talk of gossips. They both laughed; they talked in whispers, not wishing to be overheard by the guardians of the grotto.

'If one could only prolong such moments,' said Philip, wishing he had said something more spontaneous, less trite. But insincerity seemed more and more to be his way in love affairs as he tried always to please the other, to say what the other expected him to say, his own true feelings sacrificed in the process: perhaps because I do not feel at all, he thought gloomily, turning on his side to face Regina, aesthetically pleased by the sight of their bodies side by side, prototypical of their sex, the first man and the first woman . . . or the last. He wondered what it would be like to have no consciousness, to be just that, a half with no other function than to become, easily and blissfully, a whole.

'But we can,' she said, still on her back, her eyes shut and her dark hair gathered under her head like a cushion. 'You can come on to Paris with us next month. We could see each other every day . . .'

'What about Rex?'

'What about him? He has his own philandering to do.'

'I thought you said he wasn't interested in such things.'

'No . . . or at least I should have said he isn't interested in me any more. He likes young silly creatures and I'm just as pleased with the arrangement. I have no false pride about my role in his life. You see, we're very happily married. We have the same interests. We enjoy politics. He'd be quite helpless without me, professionally at least.'

'Does he know about me?' Philip, like all young men, was eager to know everything everyone thought of him, the more uncomplimentary the better. He liked to think of himself as a ruthless buccaneer who strode across the world shattering sensibilities and conventions with the fury of his progress but he knew, of course, at the same time, that most people thought him rather a lamb . . . a conception based on his small nose and his babyish lisp.

'Of course not.' Regina laughed. 'Why should he? We never discuss our infidelities. As a matter of fact, he thinks you're a promising young man.'

'Promising what?' Philip was disappointed.

'A great career.'

'In politics?'

'What else? Is there any other?'

'Of course, but since I probably won't pursue any of them either, I can't imperiously throw an easel or a violin at you. I can only deny what you say with the uneasy authority of a theoretician.'

'Well, desert theory long enough to think of what you might be able to do in actual fact, if you chose. What you might become.'

'But I don't choose; *they* choose . . . the others, the voters.'

'If you choose now I can promise they will select you at the proper time.'

'A machine?'

'*Deus ex machina.* Whatever you want to call it.'

'Give me time,' he said, suddenly serious.

'How long a time?' She sat up and looked at him. Her body upon the dark rock was smooth and fine as the white marble statue of that girl-saint who lies sprawled on the floor of the catacombs near Rome, martyred beneath the cross and the fish.

'Give me my year. Then I'll know.'

'You promise?'

'I promise. I must have the year first, no matter what I do.' Then, feeling the tug of sex, he took her and they made love on the hard rough surface as lovers before them had done since the days when the gods in human form wandered about the earth seducing mortals and rewarding them with curious gifts, with crowns and genius, with constellations in their image spangled across the black fields of the night or if the mortals refused to yield to these passionate gods, they were struck down, destroyed, transformed to winter shadows or to summer flowers, their beloved forms becoming green laurel on the slopes of hills or wild-flowers in the fields where the thunder sounded.

'Must you go?'

'I said I would. I promised Glenellen.'

'But you promised me you wouldn't.'

'I didn't really promise. I said I would try to get out of it. But it was too late. Besides, what harm can come of it? They are all perfectly harmless lunatics.'

'I'm sure they are but you don't want to get into any trouble with the police.'

'Why not? You can get me out.'

'That's no reason to do anything foolish. Suppose they shoot you.'

'Oh, for God's sake! and suppose I get run over by a taxicab? There's more danger of that happening, you know.'

'Do as you please,' she said. And he did.

He left her at eleven o'clock that night. They had dined with Bella and May Washington whose curiosity had finally got the best of them ... May especially (the one who had suffered) was eager to ferret out if possible the nature and the enormity of their sin. Regina handled her beautifully, however, and, when dinner was over and Philip excused himself, the sisters Washington were fawning on Mrs. Durham, eager to win her favour.

In the middle of the sky the white moon rode among black and silver clouds, blown north by a south wind ... hot and gusty ... the dry desert wind of Africa tempered with the sea's salt but not much cooled from the long journey. The townspeople seemed more exuberant tonight than usual, as though celebrating unconsciously some old festival of the moon's fullness.

Philip paused a moment before the largest waterfront café. Inside men and women were singing and dancing. One tigerish, black frizzy-haired woman (descendant of some Moorish or Carthaginian sailor) was doing a wild dance for the men, her skirt pulled up to her fat thighs, her legs moving like fleshy pistons in time to the music.

Philip, as unobtrusively as possible, slipped into the café and watched until, amid laughter and curses and cheering, the dancer stopped and the usual sentimental laments were wrung stickily from the fiddle and the accordion. Everyone was hot, sweating, flimsily dressed and happy, all that he'd ever imagined the joyful peasant to be. Yet he knew that if he looked closely he would see what the outsider never saw: fear, antagonisms, envy ... all the usual human characteristics accentuated by this summer land, the violence checked by pleasure in the evening, by piety and labour during the bedazzled day.

A young Scandinavian, thin and horse-faced, so blond that his face seemed eyebrowless, lashless beneath its straw-like hair, appeared and asked in English if Philip were an American.

'I thought so. I can always tell. Have a drink.'

'No, I can only stay a moment.'

'It is very gay here tonight.'

Philip nodded, looking past the other at the revellers who were now singing opera, loudly and without shame.

'Do you like Europe?' persisted the Scandinavian in his prim heavily accented voice, his pale eyes magnified by black-rimmed spectacles.

'No,' said Philip, inspired, 'I don't.'

'But why not?'

'Because it is dead, finished ... and the roads are bad. The trains are not on time. The various conveniences, such as they are, are not sanitary and the women are lewd, immoral and, I'm told, diseased. But I want to thank you for asking me that question ... I now know what I want to do, where I want to go. I'm going to return immediately to Waco, Texas, where I belong. Good night.' And feeling much better, Philip left the café and turned into the street which led to the Bridge of St. Elmo.

Even these ordinarily dark streets were well-lighted for the doors that were usually sealed against the night were open and townspeople sat on their own doorsteps or lounged about the cobbled streets beneath the full moon which hung, rich and golden, swollen with summer, among its clouds, like a lantern in the dark.

On the other side of the bridge. however, all was quiet. A few houses were set back against the hill on terraces above the town, accessible only by foot. Set apart from these houses was the ruin of the church of St. Elmo, surrounded by olive trees and ilex, by giant cypresses, all black and mourning in the moon's light.

But before he could get to the church he first had to climb many steps, each, it seemed to him, more steep than the one before and he was thankful for the south wind when he finally arrived, breathing heavily, at the top of the steps where he paused a moment to rest. Amalfi was below him, its yellow light gleaming in a pattern as inscrutable as that of the white stars which shone everywhere, one behind another, in the midnight sky. Far out to sea, a ship with blinking lights was making its way to Africa and, as he stared at the ship on the dark horizon, a star fell in the west, a delicate sudden arc of light.

He turned and walked slowly down a narrow flagstone path

to the grove of trees where the church, black and silver in the light of the full moon, stood like a ship wrecked on a sandbar, roofless, its windows like idiot's eyes and its towers gone. He stood for a moment looking up at the cracked stone towers; insects whirred dryly in the trees and, far, far away, he heard the faint tinkle of music, the echo of laughter in the town below.

Conscious of his danger, dreading ghosts more than police or communists, he entered the church and stood in the roofless nave surveying the shattered arch beneath which the high altar, now a mound of rubble, had once been. As he moved down the nave the noise of the cicadas abruptly ceased. He stopped then, waiting for the ordinary sounds of the night to resume, but they did not; the silence persisted. He looked up at the moon, now bone-white, no longer golden, sailing through the black and silver clouds which separated solid earth from empty sky like an antique shawl from Spain thrown over that one-half world beneath the moon.

He waited, trembling, before the mound where the altar had been. Minutes, hours, years, eras passed and still he waited, frozen by moonlight into a pallid facsimile of his living self. He saw the church as it was: stained glass, wine red and cerulean blue, filled the empty windows and translated clear sunlight into rainbows, while figures in vivid costumes moved about in ritual attitude and celebrated the ancient Mass. Then windows shattered and the roof fell; the towers crashed down the hillside and, as he stood there, even the walls which still stood buttressed all around him fell at last and he was alone in the dust, the burnt stumps of cypress and ilex and olive around him, and the sea where the town was.

He moved. The cicadas resumed their monotonous whirring and the moon was hidden by clouds. He looked at his watch and saw by its luminous dial that he had been there ten minutes, that it was now fifteen minutes past twelve and no one was there, neither conspirator nor policeman had shared with him the ghosts and the constant shadows.

'Hello!' he said in a loud voice, which frightened him; but no one answered. Resolutely he explored the church, pushing his way past the fallen masonry into chapels where wild grapes grew . . . he went everywhere except down into the dark hole behind the high altar where, he knew, the illustrious dead had

100

once been buried in ice-cold crypts, the earth of their bodies now holding, indiscriminately, nests of scorpions and the roots of flowers . . . in decay, as in life, the fine balance between good and evil kept, continuity maintained. Then, satisfied that no one was in the church, he left.

As he stepped across the stone threshold he noticed something gleaming on the lintel. He picked it up, but since the moon was hidden he could not identify it in the dark . . . it felt like an empty balloon or a bag. He put it in his pocket, and went down the steps to the world again, his vision lost already . . . the material world, as the Cathari once maintained to their regret, being the work of Satan, while the spirit was God.

Regina listened with amusement to his story of the empty church and his moment of vision.

'Then your time wasn't entirely wasted . . . you at least had a revelation.'

'But of what?' Philip was irritable, conscious obscurely that he had been made a fool of in a way he did not understand.

'It would seem obvious from your description. I've always suspected, though, that revelations are valuable only in themselves, not for what, if anything in particular, they reveal. It would seem that you saw the life of one building from its beginning, centuries ago, to its end, when not only the ruin will be destroyed but Amalfi as well. Nothing remarkable about that Since nothing endures it's quite logical to conclude that Amalfi is not eternal, that one day the sea will make a bay of what is now a town. . . . Since the exact date of this phenomenon was withheld, you do not qualify as a prophet.'

'It all seems quite pointless, including your analysis,' said Philip, tired and angry. 'I'd like to get my hands on that antique dealer.'

'Forget about it, darling. Why bother? Now we can go back to Rome. You've had your moment as a courier, a conspirator . . .'

Philip, remembering something, reached in his pocket and pulled out the rubber bag which, upon examination, proved to be a mask of a grey wolf's head, quite realistic, with red eyes which reflected light the way the tail-lights of motor-cars do.

'This must have been Guiscardo's,' said Philip.

'Do you think he was there all the time?'

'Perhaps. I wonder why he didn't speak to me, though ... if he was.'

'He wanted to see what would happen.'

'Yet what did happen?'

'You will never know now.'

'I suppose not. Shall I return the mask to him?'

'No, keep it as a souvenir.'

'Of what?'

'Of your monarchist days.'

He snorted and shoved the mask into a waste-basket. They were in his room, seated in front of a tall window which overlooked the sea.

'Shall we go back to Rome?' asked Regina at last.

'I suppose so. I would like to see more of this country first.'

'We can drive slowly.'

'We might even go to Capri,' suggested Philip.

She nodded. 'It's lovely there this time of year. Crowded, though.'

'I don't mind.'

'You will see nothing but Americans.'

'I've a feeling the best way to go to get to know them is to see them in Europe.'

'You're very right ... but do you want to know them?'

'No, but for a budding politician I thought it the right thing to say.' They laughed at one another. Then he took his jacket off. As he did, he noticed the safety pin which fastened Glenellen's documents to his inside pocket. He undid the pin and held the plain white envelope under the lamp.

'Do you think I should open it?'

'Of course. How will you ever know what's inside?'

'But I shouldn't really.'

'Why not? Your mission is over. You'll have to destroy it anyway. Open it. I can't wait.'

He tore the envelope open and took out a single sheet of paper on which had been written one word in letters which he recognized to be Greek, a language he had not studied in school.

'What on earth does it mean?' he asked, bewildered.

'Let me see.' Regina took the paper for a moment; then she handed it back to him, smiling.

'Well, what does it mean? Can you really read Greek?'

'Oh yes . . . there's no end to my talents,' she smiled.

What does it say? . . .'

'I can only tell you what the word means. You'll have to interpret it.'

'Why?'

'Because it's a message, for you I think.'

'But that's ridiculous, I was supposed to deliver it to the royalists here.'

'Then perhaps it wasn't intended for you. In any case, *you* must decide. The word is *Asebia*.'

'And it means?'

'Failure to worship the gods . . . a capital crime in ancient Greece. It was the principal charge brought against Socrates.'

'I am very confused,' said Philip.

'A confusing age,' said Regina with a sigh. 'How lucky none of us knows what will happen.'

The vulgarity of Mrs. Helotius was one of the few really perfect, unruined things in Europe; it was a legend and, unlike most highly publicized phenomena, never a disappointment to the eager tourist who (properly sponsored) had got himself into any one of those five villas which decorated the spas of fashionable Europe like rough diamonds, bases for her considerable operations. There was about her a completeness lacking in more human, more frail beings who, though dedicated like herself to the achievement of a major social position, might, from time to time, make an exception here and there, squeeze in a cousin or old friend at a luncheon for some Cabinet Minister or a reception for one of those exiled kings who, at this period in the world's stormy history, were gloomily making the rounds: Venice, Lausanne, Rome, Paris, Cairo, Capri . . . all the pleasanter places where they would be in demand, where dinners would be given for them by the vigorous hostesses, thus delaying the moment when the gold bars, the tiaras, necklaces (even the crowns!) would have to be converted into currency to support their state, the ultimate reckoning delayed by, among others, the tender if ruthless hospitality of Mrs. Helotius who never let up, who never missed a trick.

She might have really got away with it if she had been better born (officially she had never been born at all for that area of the world where she had first appeared fifty-two years ago had changed nationality so many times that all records had long since disappeared), or had married less richly. But, as she freely admitted to her intimates (those creatures to whom she accorded precedence either because of birth or well-rewarded talent), she had started from scratch, as had Helotius, a Greek who had made more money than any honest man should out of figs in Asia Minor. Later, when he became British, he married Mrs. Helotius whose family name had never been revealed to her intimates though all of them called her by her first name, Zoe ... she liked of course to be addressed as Countess since once, having been carried away by a stunning dinner party she'd given for a Cardinal who was to have been the next Pope, she had presented a great deal of hard cash to the solemn institution, the Roman Church, for which, in due course, she had been created a Countess and given a decoration. This had all happened some years ago; the Cardinal and she had since drifted apart for, as it turned out, someone else got to be Pope and her time was now more and more taken up by the royal waifs who gravitated to her like flames to a crafty moth; so the loss of the Church had been the grain of the Blood.

Helotius was dead. He'd been thirty-seven years older than Zoe at the time of their marriage and, presumably, during the twenty years they'd spent together he had grown no younger. He died leaving her the figs and a lust for position which, until that moment, had gnawed secretly at her vitals ever since, as a child, she had scrubbed the floors of her underprivileged home in that part of the world which, even then, was in the throes of being torn from one nation by another. Money was really not important to her; clothes and servants and houses had, in themselves, no charm for her. She always said that a bit of horsemeat and a cold boiled potato was the best meal in the world and little did her fine friends know that she meant what she said. But Position was something else and fortunately she now had the money to achieve it. Her career began two months after Helotius died. She had gone to the finest couturier in Paris and she ordered the couturier to make her a wardrobe which would knock everybody's eyes out. He did.

There were those, of course, who laughed and thought her in bad taste but everyone else followed her activities in *Vogue* and *The Tatler* with feverish interest, aware that money was being spent and that something must be done about it.

She was vulgar, of course. But then she was rich, and the villas were being bought at the rate of one a year. At the end of five years she was a Countess and her implacable design was now fully displayed across the ravaged old world of Europe as everyone came to her lunches, her dinners, her ballet parties and her fêtes. The birthday of the British king was always the occasion of her greatest effort: it usually took place at night on the Eiffel Tower which was acquired for the occasion; unkind people said that her observation of this particular day was because George VI was the last hold-out. She had never been presented at his Court. The time she had invaded the Royal Yacht Squadron at Cowes with a bouquet of roses, thistles, shamrocks and leeks was not considered cricket, although she did get one glimpse of terrified majesty before she was led away.

But even her enemies were now forced to admit that she had won through and that, very likely, her vulgarity had been more of an asset than not. Had she been more sensitive she could never have endured the contempt of the established figures of this world; the fact that she had ignored their hostility in the end gave her a certain moral dominion over them. If she was really so sure of herself, they reasoned, perhaps there was something to her after all and, certainly, she entertained richly. So, finally, almost everyone came round; the ones who did not were considered stuffy and not in fashion.

Yet despite these triumphs she was, in her own estimation at least, a long way from her goal; and in this she was fortunate. A lawyer gets to the Supreme Court and that is that. A politician gets to the Senate or to the Presidency and that is that: there is no place left to go. But for Mrs. Helotius the world was an enormous jungle full of lions to be bagged and no one, not even a woman as well-equipped and devoted as herself, could hope to assemble more than a fraction of them under her roof. To add to her frustration new lions appeared every season, and how was she to know if they were to reign for a number of seasons and become legitimate or be devoured in the first few months of their maturity? (She did not bother with the cubs except as background.)

All in all, however, she did not make many mistakes. She never read contemporary books but she was able to skim reviews and study the authors' biographies on the dust jackets and determine with remarkable accuracy whether the gentle-man in question was 'there' or nearly there, or gone. She did not handle lionesses unless they were either royal or very noble. In science she was guided by *Time* Magazine and the various selections of the Nobel Prize Committee. In politics and re-ligion she was infallible and, as for society, she had every Regis-ter, every Peerage and Almanac available while her secretary-companion, Lady Julia Keen, an impoverished daughter of a bankrupt Earl, was in complete charge of a portable filing case where everyone was neatly indexed according to age, general appearance, income, connections ... all recorded with com-ments of the number of times they had been entertained at the five villas and the number of times they had entertained her at *their* villas. She was, as one ill-natured editor who had failed to be invited a second time to her house remarked, the Havelock Ellis of the social world. As for her stratagems; well, you know as well as I do how she wrote Bernard Shaw whom she'd never met that H. G. Wells, whom she'd never met either, would be at her house on a certain day; then she wrote Mr. Wells that Mr. Shaw would be at her house eager to make his acquaintance. And that is how the two great men met one another, and Mrs. Helotius, for the first time ... or so they say.

Now she was in residence at Capri, and Regina and Philip, just up from Amalfi, were lunching on the terrace of her house in the company of twenty brilliant creatures, the best to be had on Capri at that moment: a British Field-Marshal, a Spanish Marquis, four American novelists (they were everywhere that season), a number of politicians, and a dozen men and women whose names are known to everyone who reads about the doings of the international set.

The house and the terrace, the day and the island were, Philip thought, marvellous. He'd never seen such vivid colours: burn-ing green and blinding blue, flashes of flame-red and flame-yellow flowers among the green, stirred gently by the south wind, and by the more drunken guests who wandered off the flagstone terrace to look down the steep rock cliff at the sea below, the town off to the left, white and powder-pink.

The house itself was not large: a dozen bedrooms, half as many baths, and the usual offices. Nothing more. Of the five villas it was the smallest but, because of its setting, Mrs. Hel-otius always spoke of it as her 'jewel'.

'You will so enjoy meeting the Field-Marshal, Mrs. Durham ... and there are a number of people from your Embassy whom you must know. They will know *you*, certainly, and be so thrilled to meet you if they haven't already. Do come to lunch, both of you.' She had said this last with a sharp rather puzzled glance at Philip. 'The Field-Marshal is so sweet.'

And so they came to the lunch and the Field-Marshal looked exactly like his famous self, not sweet at all, and Regina knew a number of the Americans and all the Italians. It was a good way to spend his first day on Capri, thought Philip, who was thoroughly impressed by now, much more so than he'd been that morning in the main square of the town when Zoe Helotius, dressed in a Swiss dirndl and wearing dark harlequin-shaped glasses, swooped down on Regina, a hairy-legged Italian Duke in tow.

She was more elegant now, however, She wore one of her couturier's creations, a gossamer grey affair with emeralds the size of egg yolks at her raddled throat. Her hair was a dark red, streakily dyed to give it the illusion of authenticity which succeeded very well, in the sense at least that all the women present were profoundly aware of the expense such hairdressing entailed. She was a short lean woman, unusually shaped, with no waist at all. Her features were tiny, except for the chin which was slightly undershot. She was always carefully painted and her face was lifted once a year until now it was almost totally expressionless, as though fixed for all time by some Medusa, in a mood mid-way between surprise and doubt. Her voice was harsh, very English, seldom betraying her obscure foreign birth.

They had dined at a buffet. Then, drinking champagne, the guests moved about a dainty gazebo which, banked by flowers, overlooked the sea below.

'Shall you be here long, Mrs. Durham?' inquired Mrs. Helotius, gazing over Regina's shoulder at the Field-Marshal who was grimly tearing one of her finest yellow roses apart.

'I'm going back to Rome tomorrow. Then on to Paris.'

'With your husband?'

'Oh yes. He has a job to do, you know.'

'Indeed I do. All Europe knows. All Europe awaits his report with bated breath,' she said dramatically, averting her eyes from the Field-Marshal who was now heading purposefully towards a bush of white roses with much the same expression he'd undoubtedly worn on his face the day he had ordered one of his divisions into the worst engagement of the last European war.

'I am sure his report isn't that earth-shaking,' smiled Regina.

'Nonsense. He has the President's ear,' said Mrs. Helotius intensely, betraying her near-Oriental origin by an exotic over-emphasis which was very un-British and certainly not American.

'You must let me give a party for you next month in Paris,' she said at last, gracefully accepting the fact that she would learn nothing of Durham's mission from his wife, no minor state secret that she could whisper to some interested statesman to make this visit to her seem worth while in a political as well as in a social sense.

'We should like that very much.'

'You come too, Mr. . . .'

'Warren,' said Philip, who was wondering just how Regina was going to explain him.

'. . . met him just yesterday in Naples. His father is one of my husband's very good friends . . . a judge . . .'

'Ah, the law,' intoned Mrs. Helotius, surveying the gazebo, wondering who was drunk and who was not. Lady Julia marked a minus after each name in the filing cabinet to denote one instance of drunkenness or bad behaviour. Three minuses excluded all but the most eminent from the hospitality of the villas and the Eiffel Tower.

'Well, what do you think of her?' asked Regina as Mrs. Helotius hurried away to defend her rosebush from the Marshal.

'Much better than I'd imagined.'

'She is wonderful.'

'Quite up to expectations. I'm glad we came.'

'To Capri? Or here?'

'Both . . . aren't you?'

'I think so. I must go back to Rome soon.'

'When?'

'Tomorrow, I think.' For a week now they had been together growing dark in the sun and easy in one another's arms. Neither had referred to her plans or to his or to whether those plans would, after this week, coincide or not. It had been his idea to visit Capri. They had connecting rooms at the hotel and, as she had predicted, everyone she knew was on the island. There were no secrets here, which did not disturb Philip much. He had nothing to lose and, all in all, he was more proud than not to be Regina's lover. Her attitude was, as usual, unknown to him, disguised by that serenity which he'd come to value far more than intensity or passion, preferring this Regina to the one he had known in Rome, the one who had tried to appeal for some reason of her own to his ambition.

'Will you stay on here?' she asked, not looking at him, smiling pleasantly as a young American presented himself to her.

'A little while. I'll be in Rome before you go,' said Philip quickly; then he said how-do-you-do to the young man whom Regina introduced to him as Robert Holton, of the State Department.

The three chatted amiably. Holton was one of those smooth, well-educated youths Philip particularly disliked, not objecting to their smoothness or the fact they had gone to Harvard as he himself had, but rather to the way they mixed opportunism, charm and earnestness in such a fashion as to render (to him at least) their every remark suspect. Young men dupe older and wiser men but never their own contemporaries with whom they must compete for the good places of this world. And Holton, carefully dressed, beginning to go bald, cautious, no doubt sensed the other's hostility for presently he went away.

'He used to be in Wall Street,' said Regina, as though anxious not to talk of themselves now that, in a moment, a plan had been made for the next meeting, a promise exacted, 'but he got into the State Department this year. I used to see him at Mrs. Stevanson's in New York. You know her, don't you? Blue hair ... that one. He had an affair with a charming Italian girl whose name I can never remember. He treated her badly ... or she treated *him* badly. I've forgotten which. Oh, here comes the great Field-Marshal ...'

And, smelling of all the roses he had that afternoon destroyed, the warrior talked for twenty minutes until Lady Julia Keen, under orders from their hostess, led him away.

'It seemed that Mrs. Helotius was staying at Antibes many years ago at the house of some very grand friends, when some less grand friends at Cannes invited her to lunch soon after she arrived. She wired them she couldn't possibly get over ... that she was exhausted from the trip. She then received a card from them saying how sorry they were that she couldn't make it for lunch since the P. of W. would be there. Lunch was nearly over, when Zoe arrived, dusty and dishevelled, her Daimler boiling in the hot sun. "Where is he?" she said to the startled host. "Where is who?" "Who? Why, the Prince of Wales, of course." "Oh, the Prince isn't here. Just us, and the Provost of Worcester." '

Robert Holton was full of stories about Mrs. Helotius and Philip enjoyed them. Since Holton was staying at his hotel they saw a great deal of one another after Regina's departure and Philip's first unfavourable impression had been soon succeeded by an amused neutrality. He did not like young men. He'd never had a close friend among his contemporaries and he thought it unlikely that he would begin to care for one of them now. He enjoyed the company of older men if they were civilized (his standards were precise) and he liked pretty women. Young men, however, always brought out the worst in him, made him irritable and competitive. He had often thought that he might, at one time at least, have had a fling at pederasty if it had not been for his dislike of those aggressive masculine traits which inevitably kept him at a distance from his contemporaries; although, and this paradox was, he knew, quite logical, his few friends at Harvard and in the Navy had either been gaudily effeminate and amusing, or else masculine but understanding, interested in him for reasons which were, whether declared or not, distasteful yet flattering. He had known an intimacy with such men that he realized he would never know with ordinary men whose line was straight, less comprehending.

At first Holton seemed to him to be like these others he had known in school, but after several days in one another's company, he struck up at last against that familiar density, the sudden wall which he recognized as being similar to that which guarded the area of his own central interest from invasion; and Philip was relieved even though he realized that their alikeness would prevent any sort of relationship, that it might in time, he knew too well from experience, cause hostility, even violence, like two young bulls in a field together.

But after all the problem, as he considered it one afternoon on the rocks where they swam, was academic. They were companions for a week or so and nothing more. Only because he liked insoluble problems did he examine as dispassionately as possible his attitude towards Robert Holton and towards all men of a certain age and quality who, no matter how pleasing their character, how admirable their many virtues, constituted a threat to his own integrity, to that love and pride of self which was both the charm and the vice of his own youth, as it was of theirs.

Holton, however, was very nearly as neutral as he himself and they were able to spend the days together blandly, eating and drinking and bathing in the sea. At night there were various parties, expeditions to bordellos where everything was handled blithely and gracefully, with all the Italian pleasure in the natural communicating itself to these two Puritan boys who realized, each in his own way, that such pleasure, all pleasure, was evil and that only pain was good; consequently neither could exact more than a temporary physical satisfaction from any act, while both would far more likely (though this would not be easy to prove) have been exalted spiritually to ecstatic heights by some calculated frustration and its attendant anguish. But the young and the unengaged in these fiery last days of the Christian era of which I write were not allowed the excuse of faith or the rare delight of conscious martyrdom ... rather, they were allowed to play any game they wanted, to invent the rules as they went along, to do exactly what they pleased as their culture, more brilliant, more fine than ever, approached its diffuse end and they themselves, liberated as they were from the arbitrary ways of the old church, from its superstition and dogma and bloody intolerance, had not yet managed, at this point in time at least, to exorcize the mean devil of guilt, the sense of sin which their faith had, with such care and patience, nurtured for two thousand years. Now, though the churches themselves had died of their own victory long before the last of the wars of religion began, the fear of pleasure and the hate of loving persisted, a withering frost at the heart of summer, and all the martyrs, clinging upside down like bats from the rafters of heaven, no doubt felt that their work had survived the vicissitudes of knowledge much better than even they might reasonably have suspected. Perhaps, though one must not look too far into the irrelevancies of the future, their great monument, that core of gleaming ice in each man's heart, might yet become

111

once more the focal-point of a new, more fatuous orthodoxy in which the dream of the martyrs would at last be fulfilled in the vast design of some dogma from which there could be no deviation since the mind, as the later Christian scientists have discovered, can now be controlled: drugs will extract a truth or a fact from any man and, no matter how strong he may be, he will recant on schedule with apparent calm, while virtue becomes the monopoly of the state and the hero vanishes – the happy citizens, identical in quality, going about their assigned tasks, eating, thinking, dreaming all alike, the ice within so much heavier than the mountains around them or the continents beneath their feet, a weight which anchors them securely and for all time to the dull earth.

Does Philip know this? All men know it or rather feel it, in different ways. Were he examined he would say perhaps that he disliked the cold, but whether he would choose the fire is doubtful; yet neutrality bores him and, unconsciously, he does await the thawing of that spirit which was frozen by a long accretion of laws of conduct, empiric and mystical ... to be unfrozen, if at all, by some act of loving outside the jungle that the flesh is, that the mind is, too; the beloved shrine of the saints shattered at last by some central force, the glacier exploding into a million particles of ice, brilliant in the light of the fire outside, as the flow resumes, like a wide river in the spring or like those myriad galaxies of burning stars which, they tell us, are eternally flowing outwards from some dark cold centre to the void where nothing was before.

'I had a talk with Julia Keen the other day,' said Holton thoughtfully, 'and she told me some wonderful stories. But best of all, when she'd finished, she leaned forward her face close to mine, and whispered: "You know the most important thing in the world?" I shook my head, expecting to hear something quite unusual. "Tipping! It does wonders." '

Philip chuckled. 'I shouldn't be at all surprised if she weren't right. I suppose women like her need service more than anything else.'

'Mrs. Helotius is less well organized, as far as I can tell. She can get people together, but I don't think she has ever stopped to consider why she has brought them together. I'm sure all that activity of hers hides a terrible vagueness.'

'Does she really make those funny remarks people say?'

'I only heard her make one. She was at a dinner and Serena Bondi, the bitch of all time, turned to her and said: "Zoe, have you heard that extraordinary story about your friend General X? They say he's homosexual." And Zoe, with her best I'm-going-to-understand-this-or-else manner, said: "Poor thing, but they tell me it's not dangerous now. They've found a cure. A cousin of the King of Spain nearly died of it until finally they gave him this new drug and the bleeding stopped immediately." '

Holton told story after story and Philip listened, drifting off from time to time, his eye following the curving flight of gulls above the sea and his mind now pleasantly unfocused, untroubled in the bright sunshine. When Holton suggested they have a drink he refused gently, softly, for he was like the soft day, bemused and passive. And so Holton, with an amiable word or two, left him and climbed the hill to the nearest bar.

Philip closed his eyes and dozed in the sun.

CHAPTER FIVE

He arrived in Rome on a hot, grey day, windless and enervating. The Via Veneto was crowded with tourists who seemed very nearly depressed as he himself; the chatter at Doney's was more subdued than usual and, from time to time, anxious glances were turned skywards as though a storm or the Second Coming was imminent. Far away, beyond the Alban Hills thunder rolled. He told Clyde Norman that he wished it would rain.

Mr. Norman had been sitting alone at a table gloomily chewing a meringue glacé, the whites of his eyes a liverish gold. He had greeted Philip cordially but without enthusiasm. He, too, wished it would rain.

'I haven't been well,' he observed briefly as Philip sat down.

113

'What's the matter?' Philip tried not to sound as unsympathetic as he felt. The Amalfi adventure still rankled.

'Liver. And, for some reason, when I'm having a liver attack I eat all the wrong things. A demon drives me to larger and larger meringues, more and more curries and heavy veal ... until at last I'm forced to go to the hospital for a few days, or even weeks, and live on bread and water. The body! How I loathe it.'

'I'm sure that mess you're eating will do the trick.'

'Send me to the hospital? Very likely. But I can't stop. I just can't stop. By the way, have you tried the nougat here? It's splendid, but be sure to take the little bits of paper off – otherwise it has rather a nasty taste. Will you have something to eat?'

'I don't think so. A drink, perhaps.' A drink was ordered. A thin, middle-aged lady nodded to Mr. Norman, who bowed deeply into his meringue as she passed, her expensive high heels clattering on the pavement.

'That,' said Mr. Norman with some show of interest, 'was Daisy Fleech.'

'And who is Daisy Fleech?' Philip regarded each digression as a personal affront, since obviously Mr. Norman must have known about the Amalfi fiasco ... if he had not been responsible for it, which was not unlikely, considering the general confusion in which the conspirators moved.

'She was one of Mussolini's mistresses.'

'Is every woman in Rome an ex-mistress of Mussolini?'

'Of course not,' said Mr. Norman, a little sharply in his turn, fixing his golden orbs upon Philip. 'I thought everyone knew who Daisy Fleech was.'

'I'm afraid ...'

'She was a portrait-painter of some renown. She specialized in politicians and, being of a romantic nature, she had affairs with as many of her subjects as possible. It was her expressed ideal to have a child by every major head of state in Europe ... or rather, the head of each major state, which would, theoretically, give her a fine family of comfortable proportions: five or six children, no more. Unfortunately, nature, as you can see, neglected to make her very attractive; yet in spite of that handicap her success in her chosen field was quite high. She failed with Lenin, one hears, but most of the others capitulated and, of them all, Mussolini was the one who made the most profound impression on her, for, just below the elbow, she has two little scars where he bit her arm through to the bone. She is quite proud of them and will show them to you any time you like. She has even had a rather curious bracelet made of gold and amethysts so arranged that they set off the scars.'

'Did she have any children?'

'No, alas. It seems that she was like our great queen ... "of barren stock". But she had an interesting time.'

'I went to Amalfi.'

'I wondered. I didn't want to ask.'

'Why not?'

'Well, Ayre is the one you must report to. I'm only a small cog in the organization. Did you enjoy Amalfi?'

'I liked the bathing ...'

'Excellent water ... so warm. I shouldn't mind going down there myself, but the sun is the worst thing in the world for a liver complaint.'

'Everything else went wrong, though.'

'Wrong? In what sense?'

'In every sense. I wasn't able to deliver the message.'

'Oh.' Mr. Norman sighed and looked distractedly about, as though for succour.

'And Guiscardo was no help at all.'

'I don't know him.'

'You know who he is.'

'Who who is?'

'Guiscardo.'

'Oh ... I do wish you'd talk to Ayre about all this. I'm sure he'll make much more sense than I will.'

'I can hardly believe that,' said Philip, growing angry. 'Of all the people involved in this idiocy, he is the one who had consistently made no sense at all ...'

'Hobbies,' murmured Mr. Norman depreciatingly.

'What are they, by the way?' asked Philip, deflected for a moment from his calculated denunciation.

'Oh, one thing and another ...'

'Such as?'

'Can't you tell?'

'The young men?'

Mr. Norman blushed. 'That too, of course. No, I meant the vagueness you referred to.'

'What about it?'

'Narcotics, my boy ... he takes heroin at the moment. But don't ever think he isn't making sense. He is. The difficulty is that when he's under the influence his tempo is somewhat different from that of a ... civilian, and consequently he tends to skip certain details in a conversation which, were they supplied, would make him very easily understood, even admired, for he has an excellent mind, you know.'

Philip decided to postpone his scene. Obviously there would be no point in dissipating his wrath on Mr. Norman, who was not, so far as he knew, directly involved in the Guiscardo business.

'I suppose I'd better report to him, then.'

'I think it would be a good idea.'

'I shall also tell him that the House of Savoy can be restored without my assistance.'

'Oh ... I'm sorry.' Mr. Norman looked as concerned as it is possible for anyone to look with a mouth full of meringue. He swallowed noisily and repeated: 'I am sorry. I had so looked forward to our working together.'

'My connection with the movement wasn't intended to continue after Amalfi, anyway.'

'What about Mrs. Durham, though?'

'Mrs. Durham?'

'Yes. I thought you were going to approach her about our cause. I thought that was why she went to Amalfi.'

'How did you know she was there?'

'One hears things.'

'She came to Amalfi, and we did talk once or twice about your party and she was all against it.'

'I was afraid of that. You weren't able to change her mind at all?'

'Not at all. As a matter of fact, I never tried. We only talked about it.'

'Oh dear. This *is* discouraging. Well, I suppose everything will work out properly in the end. By the way, how did you like Zoe Helotius?'

'How did you know I met her?'

'Someone saw you at a party she gave on Capri.'

'You know everything.'

'If only I did! But how did you like her?'

'She was pleasant enough, I suppose. I only talked to her once ... briefly.'

'Fabulous woman. I remember such a funny story they used to tell about her. It seems she was staying with some rather distinguished people at Antibes ...'

Philip listened for the third time to this story, idly comparing its delivery to earlier accounts, awarding finally the prize for recitation to Mr. Norman. When they had done laughing, an appointment was made for Philip to wait upon the Lord Glenellen at his palace on the following day, to report the failure of his mission in the south. Refusing nougat and another Helotius story, Philip left Doney's and, walking quickly, he got to his hotel before the rain in quick warm drops fell on the dusty streets, while thunder clapped above the gardens of the Villa Borghese.

Raindrops were in her hair and on her face. She had worn no hat. 'Why wear a hat when the rain will ruin it?'

'I'll dry you off.'

He took a towel and partly dried her hair and face, liking the familiar scent of rain on woman's hair, recalling once how he had made love on the banks of the Hudson during a summer storm and how, when the moment came, lightning had struck a near-by tree, revealing an unsuspected truth in its sudden white glare.

'I'm glad you're back,' she said, when he had finished and they lay side by side on the bed.

'I got tired of Capri.'

'I thought you would.'

'I don't like that sort of thing.'

'What sort of thing?'

'People who are interested only in people ... or is that what I mean?'

'I don't know, my darling. You must know what you mean, though.'

'Yes, I suppose I do. It's not that I object to malice and gossip. I'm capable of both myself, I know, but it isn't my principal interest.'

117

'What is?'

He grunted. 'Here we go again.' He arranged the pillow behind his head. 'Myself,' he said at last, 'but it sounds so awful to admit.'

'No one else?'

He paused. Then he repeated, not looking at her: 'No one else.'

'Sad,' she said, with no inflection.

'Should there be someone else?'

'That's not what I mean, Philip,' she said. 'I'm not really very romantic either. I've had affairs. I have a husband. I've liked some men, adored others. But I will admit to you now that I have never loved anyone either, nor have I ever once put someone else's interest before my own.' She laughed softly. 'We're a fine pair of lovers, aren't we?'

Illogically, this hurt him. He did not care a great deal about her, of course, but for either to admit this truth to the other when their bodies had so recently been joined was a form of brutality which he had never before encountered. Seeing his momentary dismay, she kissed his hand.

'But I adore you,' she said lightly. 'Don't look at me as though I'd done you a frightful injury.'

He recovered. 'I was just startled to hear you say something so frank.'

'You don't think I'm ordinarily frank?'

'No ... it's just that I've never known a woman to say anything like that, so soon after making love.'

'Perhaps I merely said what you were thinking.'

'No. That would have been childish. But then I'm not so sure anyone ever really sacrifices his comfort for another person ... which is, I suppose, the ultimate test and definition of love.'

'Oh, many people do.'

'What do you want from me, then?'

Regina sat up and faced him.

'A great deal.'

'But not love.'

'Not what we usually call love, no. I don't want self-sacrifice, no grand adolescent gestures or frenzies. What I want is something else again.'

'I don't know what you mean.'

'You will.'

'When?'

'Soon, I think. Part of it has to do with our discussion that first night.'

'But how could all that help you or, should I say, gratify you?'

'That is my business.' She spoke more sharply than she had intended, and for an instant Philip had a glimpse of another Regina, one like her name, cold, unfeeling, indifferent to everything but power and its impersonal logic; but the vision was brief. She was herself again. She apologized for the sharpness with which she had spoken, but, as she resumed her early role, he sensed with some uneasiness that the Regina he had seen so briefly might be, after all, the real one; and so, in that one instant of doubt, the affair ended. What might come after would perhaps seem unchanged and though they could still make love, talk intimately, affectionately, he was withdrawn, no longer committed or sympathetic, a stranger with all the privileges but none of the demands of the lover. Regina, if she was aware of this withdrawal, did not show it. She talked of other matters.

'Did you see much of Zoe before you left Capri?'

'A quick and poignant meeting in the square,' he said, selecting a number of artificial phrases to disguise his confusion, to give him time to recover. 'She was guiding the Field-Marshal about the town with a look of terrible triumph. I believe she thought I had written a book, for when I said hello to her she told the warrior that he should read it. Unfortunately the book, whatever it was, must not have sold very well because, before I could identify myself, they were gone.'

'So like her.'

'Why does everyone say "so like her"?'

'Philip.' He looked at her then.

'What's the matter?' She seemed puzzled, even defensive.

'Nothing's the matter,' he said weakly. 'Nothing at all. I'm just rather put out by the whole damned trip.'

'I thought you enjoyed it.'

'I did, parts of it.' But he could not add the sentence she wanted to hear. He went off in another direction. 'It got on my nerves, that's all.'

'Have you seen Glenellen?'

'I go tomorrow for dinner.'

'What will you tell him?'

'What happened, what I think of the whole thing.'

'Do be careful.' Then she got up and dressed. Philip put on a dressing-gown and sat down in an arm-chair by the open window. Monotonously the rain fell.

'Where's your husband?' asked Philip suddenly.

'Rex?' She paused, his hairbrush in one hand. 'He's gone to Florence for a few days. I have to meet him there.' She brushed her dark hair back, her eyes watching not her own reflection in the mirror but his.

'How does he feel about your . . . trip?'

'We never discuss those things.'

'Have there been so many?'

She turned round, smiling, and faced him. 'Now, Philip, for some reason you want to quarrel with me. Heaven knows why . . . but I'm not going to quarrel with *you*. If I've done something you don't like, then tell me what it is. But please don't be disagreeable.'

Since there is never any way to handle reasonableness when one is in a bad temper, Philip was forced, rather foolishly, to apologize, to say a number of things he didn't mean while Regina, the calm mistress of the situation, continued to arrange her hair.

'The rain is almost over,' he said at last, examining the broken lines the drizzle made, as it slanted palely against the dark wet trees across the street.

'Would you like to drive with me to Florence next week?'

'I thought you said Rex was there.'

'That's right. I'm joining him. We're going on to Paris the first of next week.'

'I don't think it's such a good idea, my seeing him. Do you?'

'Why not? He likes you.'

'But . . . well, after all . . .'

'Don't be silly. Besides, it's no concern of his what I do when I take a trip. I thought I'd explained all that to you. In any case, should he have been suspicious, he wouldn't be if he saw us together. Obviously I would not travel to Florence with my lover.'

'I don't understand.'

'Oh . . .' She came over to him where he sat and looked down at him for a moment, smiling; then she said: 'It's my plot, don't

120

you see? Our going to Florence is part of it, the most important part. Do humour me. It's for you, after all.'

'For me?'

'And for me too, in a way. But that's my problem.'

'I'm not sure if I'll be able to get away,' he said, having always found it easier to conceive than to sustain an attitude . . . the thought of hurting anyone's feelings distressed him, more from cowardice, he knew, than from any regard for the sensibility of others, even though he was able, when he chose, to identify himself with their problems. In fact, he had a tendency not only to see the other person's side in a discussion but, often as not, perversely, to see more good in it than in his own. And, on occasion, he had ended by warmly agreeing with an antagonist, even though, a second later, outside the other's aura, he would revert to his former position, having earned (unjustly, he always thought) a reputation for being a *faux bon homme*. But for once he was not sure how to approach the situation since, very simply, he did not understand Regina. There was an elusiveness which he could not define, a continuous suggestion of mysteries which she never chose to reveal and which, though he had tried, he could not comprehend. It made their discussions remarkably one-sided, and now, since that moment early in the afternoon when he had glimpsed the hidden image, impersonal as cold marble, he was more at a loss than ever . . . not sure of anything, he parried with her, discussed the trip to Florence in all its aspects, ignoring of course any mention of the real reason which he could not guess and which she obviously was in no mood to reveal.

'I still think there's something awfully indelicate about my driving to Florence with you when your husband is there on political business. Perhaps he doesn't care, but others will. And since he does represent the United States, it would be rather tactless of us to give the gossips something to talk about.' The piety of these remarks, the sudden reverent mention of their homeland rather sickened him, but he was too busy making a point to worry about his own fraudulency.

She took his remarks seriously, thereby reducing considerably her moral dominion over him. For several minutes they batted the shuttlecock of patriotism back and forth, each hitting it higher and higher until, as so often happens, it quite disappeared in the star-spangled red, white and blue heaven.

And Regina, having demonstrated a surprising lack of humour, repeated a few of her old arguments almost word for word, pleading with him, exhorting him for a reason never given, to come to Florence, not only to be her lover but to ingratiate himself with her husband for the sake of a political career which he had already, in one way or another, declined.

When the rain had stopped she left. He had given her no definite answer and he had been, he realized sadly, childish and hostile; this depressed him as all weakness in himself did, for, as a rule, he was at ease with everyone, especially lovers. But Regina was different ... how different he could not tell, and because she puzzled him he felt, quite correctly, that he was at a disadvantage and he was undecided as to what course to follow: whether to break with her at once and for good or to go to Florence and examine the mystery close to.

He stood in the tall window looking down in the street. He saw Regina get into a taxicab and drive away. The boys who bought and sold black market money were reappearing in the street, busy as ever, while overhead the grey broke and the sun shone.

'You will find Ayre somewhat changed,' said Mr. Norman, as they crossed the dusty parquet of the great hall and Philip noticed for the first time the threadbare ensigns of ancient battles which hung from the walls at regular intervals, between portraits which, cracked and flaking, stared darkly at him; the Mettellii in solemn conclave expressed their contempt for the dust and the new age.

'I always find him changed,' said Philip. 'Each time I see him he's a different person.'

'Yet always the same Ayre, devoted ...'

'To what?'

'Life,' said Mr. Norman grandly. The Mettellii looked aghast, while somewhere in the palace a large piece of plaster (or a body) fell crashing to the floor. Philip started, but the servant who was their guide smiled reassuringly and showed them into Ayre's study, the same room in which Philip had been received before.

A table had been set for lunch. Four places, Philip noticed, wondering if the fourth was for Evan the secretary. Ayre greeted him effusively.

'So good to see you again, young man. We've missed you here in Rome. Missed you very much. Just the other day at the baths I turned to Clyde and said: "Where could that nice young American be?"'

'I was in Amalfi, part of the time,' said Philip precisely.

'I remember,' said Ayre, and an expression which could only be called furtive passed over his lizard face. 'We'll go into that in good time. But now let us dine, my dears.' Fussing and chattering, he put first Clyde then Philip on his right. And after that, the seating arrangement determined, they sat down.

'Is Mr. Morgan coming?' asked Philip, indicating the empty place across from Glenellen.

'Of course not. He's in Wales, where I hope he'll stay.'

'He *did* leave?' asked Mr. Norman, interested.

'Yes, several days ago. I must say, too, that I feel well out of it. When I think of the sacrifices I've made, I could do someone an injury.' He looked balefully at Philip, as though he were an accomplice of the villainous Morgan. Then, collecting himself, he smiled, revealing the bad teeth and nasty gums. 'You must excuse the outburst. I've been on edge lately. Very. Very on edge. But now here comes dinner.'

A white-jacketed boy brought them caviar and blinis. A feast, Philip decided; his resolve to be stern and intractable wavered. Vodka was served in small chilled carafes, and it was not until he'd finished the blinis and two glasses of vodka that he noticed Glenellen was wearing a fawn-coloured tunic without pockets or tie. He was allowed no opportunity, however, to comment, for between them Mr. Norman and Glenellen controlled the conversation, moved easily if eccentrically through history, literature, medicine and finally politics. He was forced to wait until both Glenellen and Clyde were out of breath. Then, quickly, taking advantage of this unusual hiatus, he said. 'I saw Guiscardo.'

Glenellen stared at him, his pale eyes glassy in the candlelight and his face red and shining from the vodka. 'Oh.' He looked at Mr. Norman, who looked away, worrying a pickled beet with his fork. 'Guiscardo, eh?' Glenellen cleared his throat. 'Charming, didn't you think?'

'No.'

'Trouble of some kind?'

'Yes. I wasn't able to deliver the papers.'

123

'The papers? Ah.' Glenellen looked puzzled. 'I was under the impression that you did deliver the papers.'

'Who told you that?'

'Guiscardo himself. He sent a message to me by a mutual friend, a man of the highest integrity.'

'I went to the antique-shop and Guiscardo was wearing a mask . . .'

Glenellen chuckled. 'Just like the old days, Clyde, isn't it?' Clyde agreed.

'He told me to take the papers to a certain church a few nights later. He refused to touch them.'

Glenellen's eyes opened very wide at this. He blinked furiously and a tear glittered in the corner of one eye. 'But he said that you gave them to him.'

'Are you positive?'

'Of course I'm positive. Not only do I have his word for it, but later events, unhappily, proved that he *had* received my message . . . you see, he gave it to the police.'

'The police?' Philip was frightened. 'I thought he was one of your most important people.'

'He entertained Republican sentiments in secret,' said Glenellen primly. He poured himself more vodka.

'What did the police do?'

'They sold me the papers. What else? Isn't all business done that way?'

'I'm afraid I don't know.' Philip hardly knew what to say or do. 'You . . . didn't have any trouble, did you? With the police, I mean?'

'Of course I did. You don't think I enjoy giving them money, do you? I denounced the police captain to his face, told him a thing or two, but in the end I paid. One must, after all.'

'And Guiscardo?'

'I am no longer in communication with him. I felt he'd let me down.'

'I should think so.'

He sold me a bronze which he swore he'd authenticated, an Augustan piece. Well, of course, he hadn't. I don't know how well you know him, but he is very nearly the laziest man I have ever known . . . quite slovenly in business matters. I sent him a wire saying that one of the Vatican curators had proved this piece a forgery . . . would he give me my money back? No. He sent me another bronze, a companion piece which was also fake. The man's perfidy is endless.'

'But you are still fond of him,' said Clyde sweetly.

'Of course I am. It's not his fault he is badly organized.'

'But how did he get the papers?' Philip was dogged.

'You gave them to him.'

'I did *not* give them to him.'

'Then how did he get them?' Glenellen's voice was growing irritable.

'I don't know,' said Philip, wondering if perhaps he had drunk too much vodka.

'What makes you think you *didn't* give them to him?' asked Clyde suddenly.

'First, because I didn't. I can still remember most things that have happened to me in the last month. And, second, because I broke the seal and read the message.'

'You should not have done that.' said Glenellen, unexpectedly mild. 'It would have been much better to have dropped the whole business. After all, Guiscardo did have the real message.'

'Which I could not deliver and so, having failed, I read what you had written.'

'And what was that?'

'One word,' said Philip, astonished at his own boldness. 'A Greek word, *Asebia.*'

'I don't know a word of Greek,' said Glenellen flatly.

'It would seem,' said Clyde, 'that you either delivered the message and forgot it (somewhat far-fetched but possible) or Guiscardo got it from you without your knowledge.'

'Since you say he knew the contents, then that was probably what happened. But, if it was, why did he send me off on a crazy errand to that church, at midnight, too.'

'Something of a mystic,' said Glenellen, his voice strained as he attempted, unsuccessfully, to hold back a belch.

'*Asebia* wasn't your message.'

Glenellen shook his head, his eyes bulging with indigestion, his hand on his stomach.

'It looks as though someone were playing a joke on you,' said Clyde, with his usual reasonableness. 'Perhaps Guiscardo had a servant at the hotel substitute his message for the one Ayre intended you to deliver. There are any number of pos-sibilities . . .'

'And none quite plausible,' said Philip.

'Let's forget about it, shall we?' Glenellen motioned to the boy to take the plates away, to bring in the dessert. 'I have a good reason for not wanting to remember.'

'A very good reason,' agreed Mr. Norman.

'Things are not as they were in Italy,' said Glenellen. 'Situation is fluid ... how fluid, none can say. There have been certain re-alignments which I believe you should know.'

'There has been one particular alignment which may come as a surprise to you,' added Mr. Norman uneasily. 'You see, Ayre has ...'

'Seen the light! I have abandoned the House of Savoy to its fate. Yes, I have made the plunge. It wasn't easy, believe me. I weighed the pros and I weighed the cons. I went through the entire section on Italy in the *Encyclopaedia Britannica*, and when I finished I knew that I had been wrong these many years, lulled to sleep by the decadent music of a dying order. The awakening came, however; and not a moment too soon, for I can see that had I continued much longer to wander in the morass of reactionaryism I might have ended by losing all touch with the People, who are, we will all admit, the only reason for political action, both here and abroad. On a Wednesday morning I realized with horror what I had so narrowly missed becoming. By afternoon I had acted. I cancelled all my engagements for the next two months. Letters were sent to old friends and acquaintances, giving them fair warning of the change, allowing them, if they chose, to sever their relations with me. Many did. Some few did not, among them Clyde. Others I have not heard from. Their silence I interpret as a tacit disapproval, and so I have been forced to accept, stoically I hope, an abrupt yet necessary end to involvements which, in this perilous and exacting time, did afford me some pleasure. The Pope, among others less illustrious, did not acknowledge my letter, to my great surprise, considering all that I've done for the Church. But I will not be petty. I want no one ever to say that Ayre Glenellen was petty in good times or bad. Which reminds me, Clyde, I am resigning my seat in the House of Lords.'

'Do you think that wise?' Mr. Norman seemed quite concerned.

'What is wisdom?' philosophized the peer. Seeing that there

126

was no satisfactory answer to this, he begged the question with a comment that logic was more to the point: that if one took a certain stand, then one's other deeds must of necessity be consistent with that central attitude. What then was the stand he had taken? asked Philip, confused, wondering when he might politely excuse himself.

'Ayre became a member of the Communist Party last Wednesday,' said Mr. Norman in a voice which betrayed not only melancholy but a certain pride in his friend's ability to do the unexpected.

'Sweet Jesus!' said Philip.

'It involves something higher than politics,' said Glenellen carefully. 'You see, my faith in the essential goodness of man has been reaffirmed by those members of the party with whom I have talked. In any event, you can understand now my somewhat rude lack of interest in your mission to Amalfi ... a mission which you carried out superbly, I may add. But please don't think me frivolous. My change is not only a matter of logic. It is a spiritual one as well. Lenin was the answer and he is the answer now. Death to the deviationists!' He drank a long toast to this sentiment, a toast in which neither Philip nor Mr. Norman took part.

They were just getting up from the table when a youth in a checkered shirt and corduroy trousers, with tangled black hair and the bright eyes of an animal, entered the room. With a glad cry Ayre greeted him and for a long silly moment they pounded each other here and there in an excess of manly party spirit. At last, both of them breathless, Glenellen introduced his dinner guests to Ferdinando, a Communist, a worker from Trastevere, who shook hands vigorously. As he spoke only Italian, Philip was unable to follow the intricacies of his conversation but from the expression on Glenellen's face he decided that dialectic was not the young man's forte.

'Selfless,' said Glenellen, as they sat down in front of the empty fireplace. 'Absolutely selfless.'

'Who?' asked Philip, watching the young man appropriate a handful of cigarettes from a silver box, his hand for a moment lingering on the box itself, as though assessing with his fingertips its value.

'Ferdinando. He left his wife and two children for the sake of the party. Not since the early Christian martyrs have there been

127

such men among us. I kiss the hem of his garment.' And for one embarrassing moment Philip was afraid he was going to do exactly that, but the arrival of brandy thwarted his gesture and they drank a toast instead to the current International. The young man was obviously on to a good thing. Philip decided, watching him gulp the brandy.

'I speak English,' he said, turning to Philip, prepared to charm him, suspecting that he might be a rival.

'So do I,' said Philip; he was not understood.

Glenellen then spoke to the youth in Italian and Mr. Norman turned to Philip and exclaimed: 'The subtleties of politics!'

'If it weren't for this one common denominator, I should be lost.'

Mr. Norman pretended not to understand. He warmed the bowl of his brandy glass in cupped hands, sniffed the fumes daintily as though inviting oblivion. 'Of course you don't know Ayre as well as I do. If you did you would understand better perhaps the reason for this dramatic switch. He has been preparing a long time for it, unconsciously. I don't think he himself was entirely aware of it until very recently, until last week, in fact, when a conversation with Ferdinando clarified, at one fell swoop as it were, his own position.'

'Will you also become a Communist?'

'No, I'm afraid I shall remain loyal to Savoy, but then I've never been really active in politics. My part in the movement was purely advisory. I'm a dreamer, I fear.'

Ferdinando threw his glass into the fireplace where it smashed loudly. Glenellen, delighted with this new game, did the same. Both of them then looked at Mr. Norman and Philip; Glenellen exclaimed: 'A Russian toast. Come on. Break your glasses.'

With a pained expression, Mr. Norman tossed his glass into the fireplace. It did not break. Philip said: 'I haven't finished yet.' Ferdinando got to his feet and broke Mr. Norman's glass on the hearthstone with the heel of his worn G.I. boot.

'I gather,' said Mr. Norman when more glasses had been brought, more brandy drunk, and Glenellen and his political mentor had withdrawn to the other end of the room to discuss revolution, 'that you are not sympathetic to all of this.'

'No, I'm not.'

'You must be tolerant.'

'I used to think that I must be, too. But as I grow older I find more and more things intolerable.'

'Yet in his way he's a fine person.'

'Our ways do not coincide,' said Philip with a sententiousness he'd never before equalled since his prep. school days when he had been for one whole term a polite, rather pale, but no less arrogant Rimbaud.

'Youth,' said Mr. Norman, whose habit it was to appeal to abstract nouns where more specific statements might have caused discord.

'I'd better go, I think,' said Philip, feeling somewhat drunk.

'Will you be in Rome much longer?'

'No. On to Florence, I believe. Then to the northern marches.'

'Oh to travel again, wherever one chooses, to be young!' Mr. Norman was about to slip off again. But, getting to his feet, Philip pulled him back to the mundane moment. 'I must say good night.'

The farewells were affectionate. Ferdinando hit him on the back and Glenellen wept a little.

'It has been a fine friendship. One that has meant more to me than you have perhaps realized. It must end, though, as everything must, sooner or later. Never think though that my love for Him separated us. It did not. Caesar and God, you know.'

'For him? Who? Ferdinando?'

'No ... the Spirit. Weren't you aware of it at dinner? *His* spirit. The empty place at the table.'

'Whose spirit?'

'Nikolai Lenin's,' said Lord Glenellen. 'Who else?'

In one of the tall towers a thousand candles gleamed and flickered in the soft wind, as though alive, in contrast to the fixed constellations of electric lights which circled this old tower and defined the limits of the hill-rimmed city of Florence, crossed by a winding grey river in which were reflected city light and many stars.

He stood alone in the window looking down on the city, wondering whether the pleasant scent of the warm night was from orange or from lemon, from mimosa or from the rich gardens which had been carved in terraces out of the hills of Fiesole where he was now, in a villa at a party, shortly before

129

the moonrise and the end of the green summer, the beginning of the burning autumn, bright, intense and withering. A new season. He sighed, aware of the date, but not of the fact, and he quoted to himself that line of Herrick's which has to do with rosebuds and their proper place.

'I thought I'd lost you,' said Regina, crossing the darkened library and coming out on to the balcony where Philip stood. 'Oh, it is lovely. Look, the tower! They've lit all the candles. I wonder why? It must be some saint's day or rather the day of one of the old gods. People are still faithful, you know . . . quite unchanged.'

'They gave the gods new names?'

'Names change from age to age but the gods are constant . . I think. Don't you?'

'I haven't thought of it.'

'Are you a Christian?'

This shattered him. He lived in a period where it was not polite for well-bred people to discuss their spiritual convictions or speculations and for Regina, the great materialist, to ask him suddenly whether or not he subscribed to the official religion of his culture was almost as shocking as it would have been, a generation earlier, for her to have asked him if he had ever enjoyed sexual congress.

He laughed nervously and wondered what to answer. To say he was an agnostic sounded too much like everyone else and to say that he was an atheist would place him, socially, in the same class with undergraduates who'd only just discovered to their horror that the rules of conduct they had always been taught were heavenly inspired were, after all, only a makeshift convenience, broken by everyone including their stern guardians. Yet the truth was somewhere between those two worn words. He had thought a great deal about death and he'd long ago come to the conclusion that it would be the end of that enchanting creature Philip Warren who, in the present, moved about with such grace and vitality, entertaining marvellous dreams, more marvellous than those of anyone else who had ever lived, dreams which would be set free again in the charged and busy air the day he died and ceased to move, no longer able to hold even one dream within that shell of bone where now, on the edge of Florence in the ever-lengthening eternal present, he boldly exercised this *whole* knowledge, including in itself the dream,

Regina and all the earth, the tower with its thousand candles and the sky with its endless meaningless display of stars, arranged by chance or, worse yet, not arranged at all, timeless, with neither beginning nor end; a fact which he would only partly comprehend: a structure whose origin was irrelevant and whose end was not ... since how could there be an end to that which was timeless?

Needless to say, this majestic vision had very little to do, directly at least, with Regina's question and Philip, controlling an impulse to declare, instruct, preach (he'd given up his literary ambitions, obviously), said that he was not a Christian, that he usually found himself quarrelling with their morality, while their dogma had always impressed him as being absurd to the point of grotesqueness.

'So many people feel that now,' said Regina, leaning against the railing of the balcony, the party within forgotten. 'Something will happen soon.'

'What? A new messiah?'

'I'm afraid so.'

'Has he already come, do you think? Marx? Freud? Lenin?'

'I don't think so; but I feel it in my bones and I'm never wrong about such things.'

Philip laughed. 'You could hardly have had much experience. It's been a long time since the last one, you know.'

'That isn't what I mean. I ... but it's too hard to explain. I hope the new one will respect the old gods, though.'

'You love them, don't you?'

She nodded. The moon rose from behind the hills, red as blood, like a cold sun in the east. 'They are different, you know, from the messiahs. They have nothing to do with philosophic systems. They are facts. Some are simple: the sea, the sun, the air. Some are more complex: violence, love, the mother, the father. It makes no real difference which is Queen of Heaven, Mary or Isis or Juno, as long as the idea of the mother exists, as it always will. Sometimes the mother dominates. Sometimes she does not and her son reigns. There are periods when war is regnant, or justice....'

'Or love?'

'Can you see to the end of it already?' She looked at him oddly, as though he had frightened her, but she had no reason to

131

be alarmed for he had not understood; he shook his head in bewilderment.

'I see nothing. Do you mean . . .'

'I meant only that there's a conflict between the natural gods who are, for the race at least, constant, and the messiahs who wish to rearrange the hierarchy of heaven, banishing this god, elevating that one, transforming some and murdering others, or attempting murder, for in the end it is the messiah who dies a victim of the same forces he attempted to govern. No matter how appealing or ruthless his dogma, the old gods defeat him in the end; they change their names . . . Saint This-One, pray for me, give me wealth. Saint That-One, pray for me, give me strength . . . Hail Mary, full of grace . . . as indeed she was, and is.'

He nearly saw the design, but a shadow before the moon hid the pale face beside him and the warm flower-burdened wind lulled him and he forgot in an instant what he had almost known.

'We'd better go in to the party. Your husband . . .'

'Is indifferent. But we'll go in anyway. Are you enjoying yourself?'

'Yes, I think so. It's the first really Italian party I've been to. Something of a novelty.'

'The host is very powerful in the government, behind the scenes. Rex says that when he wants anything done he goes to him rather than to the ministers.'

In the drawing-room, Philip stared a long time at this powerful man, wondering what it was that made him so different from other men; he could come to no conclusion, though. He was a man like any other: rather short, partly bald, middle-aged and, in spite of the company, bored and distracted-looking. Philip gave it up. The problem was insoluble, as he had already discovered this last week in Florence in constant attendance upon Rex Durham who had, during all that time, not made an original or profound observation on any subject. A suspicion was beginning to form in Philip's mind that a certain type of energetic mediocrity might, after all, be politically more useful in a republican society than brilliance or wit or passion. The fact that nothing Mr. Durham ever said gave him away was, no doubt, a positive virtue and although he was not capable of inspiring he did not, on the other hand, generally at least, make

132

enemies for himself or party. Pondering the nature of power and earthly dominion from one age to the next, Philip sat down in a chair between two sofas which contained a number of decorative ladies and gentlemen. Several turned to him and, shifting easily from Italian to English, included him in their discussion.

'We were discussing the Church,' said one gentleman, with a brilliant smile, glossy moustache, and sporting in his buttonhole (as the late E. Phillips Oppenheim used to say) the discreet ribbon of some knightly order. 'And we were being so anti-American,' said a thick vivacious lady.

'*You* were. Not I.'

'We were talking Church gossip.'

'What is the gossip?' asked Philip politely, pretending to listen, his eyes on Regina.

'The Roman hierarchy has come to a secret decision. I have this on the best authority. If the Russians conquer Europe they will make an agreement with Stalin that if he leaves the Church alone the Church will not oppose him. The alternative, the Romans feel, would be far more terrible.'

'Alternative? What do you mean?' asked Philip, his eyes shifting from Regina to the white teeth and gleaming black moustache.

'Flight. The removal of the Church to America and an American Pope. The Irish-American hierarchy is considered boorish by the Romans, more dangerous to the faith than an open tyrant who will fall, in time ... the Church has survived worse catastrophes than Communism. She might not, the Romans feel, survive the Irish-Americans.'

'Suppose Stalin persecuted the Church?'

'Then there would be new catacombs and more saints in heaven.'

Philip listened a little longer, drank brandy and then, getting a signal from Regina, he excused himself and joined her and Rex beneath an age-darkened painting of those sharp, shrewd features the remarkable Cosimo had, with such triumph, displayed to an earlier, more vivid age.

'Enjoying yourself, Mr. Warren?'

'Very much, sir.'

'Good boy. We'll see a lot of you when we get back home.'

Philip could never determine whether his continual omission

133

of the pronoun 'I' was the result of modesty or merely a trick to make himself seem precise, direct, a timesaver without fuss or frills.

'Regina, here, tells me you might want to take a fling at the great game. Think you'd like it?'

'Why . . . yes.' He tried to get Regina's eye but she was smiling at someone across the room. 'You're your father's son all right.' Rex chuckled deeply and Philip recalled, rather sourly, his father's contempt for politics.

'We've enjoyed seeing you these last few days. Glad to find someone Regina likes. Most people bore her to death and, of course, I'm tied up all the time.'

'I've enjoyed . . .'

'She's shrewd. Never makes a mistake. Always take her advice when it comes to people. Thinks you've got a career. So do I. You're young. Unmarried. That's good at this point. You're a lawyer; a veteran; a judge's son. Can you make a good speech?'

'I . . .'

'It's a trick. You'll pick it up. Remember to tell them only what they want to hear.' In short staccato sentences Durham outlined a political career for him. Philip watched him, fascinated, with growing respect. The man might lack inspiration and brilliance but he was a thorough craftsman: like a mechanic taking apart a car, he dismantled the ship of state in a few plain sentences and then, this done, he put it back together again, describing all the while the fundamentals of navigation, the direction and velocity of prevailing winds. When he finished, he stared at Philip with his small grey eyes, bloodshot beneath heavy brows.

'Give it a whirl?'

'I think so,' said Philip, trapped.

'Leaving tomorrow, you know.'

'Yes. Reg . . . Mrs. Durham told me.'

'Farewell party tonight as you gathered. Off to Paris first. Salt-mines. Don't look forward to it. Can't do business with the French. Talk all the time about *la Patrie,* think all the time about money. Americans just the opposite. Will you be in Paris?'

'Not right away.'

'Regina may stay over for the autumn. I'm going back to

Washington in a few weeks. Probably won't see you till the autumn.'

'Or winter, more likely.'

'That's right. Your year. Come see me in Washington, or on the river if we're there.'

'I will.'

'Good boy.' Politicians swept him away from Philip and, for the moment, he and Regina were alone together.

'You see,' she said, 'how easy it will be?'

'Why did you tell him I was interested?'

'Because you are.'

'You know I'm not and yet you insist I must be. Why?' He looked at her frowning. 'I can't see why it should concern you so.'

'But it does,' she said lightly. 'So there.'

'And what do you want from me in exchange for all this?'

'Nothing,' she said evasively, not looking at him.

'I can't believe that.'

'Is it so strange? Must every motive be selfish?'

'Yes and no. The word means nothing. I only feel . . .'

'What?'

'That you are not candid.'

'When you tell me that you want a career I will tell you what you want to know.'

'And name your price?'

'And name my price.' She laughed. 'Now I've confused you and I didn't mean to. I hate people who are mysterious, don't you?'

'I won't be able to answer you until my year is up.'

'There's no hurry. I can wait.'

'Where shall we meet?'

'Any place you like.'

Addresses were exchanged and various geographical positions charted as they compared itineraries; then the party ended. The guests went home, carrying with them all the anxieties of the age: a beleaguered church, intellectuals in search of dogmas, a barbarian horde poised upon the eastern marches, a materialistic giant beyond the western sea, neither civilized nor barbarian . . . each age has its tyrants, thought Philip, preparing for bed; and he was soothed by this knowledge as all properly educated American boys are when they come to

Europe and visit ancient rooms in which the fears of other days have been resolved by time or superseded by equivalent crises. He turned out the light and thought of what Regina had said about the old gods, and he wondered if she were right: were they constant after all? Would they reappear now that the last messiah's work had been corrupted and undone ... the son giving way to his mother and the father lost in heaven? He hoped so, knowing that when men are wise they love the natural more than dogma, more than revelation.

For an instant Philip was nearly convinced, as he hovered between waking and sleep: they were alive again, for him at least; but then he recalled the solemn humourless religion of the barbarians, both Eastern and Western, and he saw with Virgilian clarity a new, more monstrous figure appear, furiously denouncing the body and spirit, refashioning history, casting a long shadow upon the future, imposing an arbitrary orthodoxy with a fanatic vehemence which, if observed in a lesser man, would have led to exile or imprisonment, murder or therapy, certainly not to glory.

The moon set and the stars were drowning in the pale dawn when finally he slept, near-by the wind put out those of the tower's candles which had burned all night.

Part Two

*'The life of the world is only play,
And idle talk, and pageantry.'*
                    The Koran

CHAPTER SIX

At this point, the bank of the river was some twenty yards above the muddy water, a steep incline scattered with rocks and sun-withered bushes. It was late summer and the river had dwindled in the heat, withdrawing perceptibly from its winter banks, uncovering, here and there, sandbars and islands which would grow larger, support life, until the rains began again and, like so many miniature Atlantises, the islands would again vanish.

He stood on the river-bank looking down at the water gliding from south to north through the dry land. A solemn bloody sun was setting opposite him, its circle bisected already by the chalky mountains across the river. As he watched, it sank quickly, pulling the day after it, bleeding the sky of light until, when the sun was gone, the day was, too. There was no time of twilight in this season, only day and night.

He lit a cigarette; the familiar brief glow of match fire re-assured him as he turned away from the river and walked towards the colonnade beyond the row of dark palms. He wondered, as he walked, if those dead worshippers had felt the same wonder in the presence of their new buildings as he experienced among the ruins of the same temples, cluttered still with all the debris of faith and glory. He decided not, for, discounting their official preoccupation with death and the attendant details of dying, they must have been, all in all, more cheerful than not. And those few who had the leisure and the learning to speculate were, no doubt, too much preoccupied with family life, with the never-ending struggle for political preferment, to brood too much upon that last journey from the east bank to the west bank of the river.

137

He thought of his own river, cold and broad, stately in summer, gleaming with ice fragments in the winter, as unlike this muddy turgid river as possible and yet, like it, a source of life. It soothed him to walk by a river, made him feel less strange, more at home, as if he were closer to the centre of the world.

He entered the roofless temple and stood between two thick high columns, like Samson and, since there was no moon, very nearly as blind. Before him he could make out, indistinctly, various shrines, some still roofed, others shattered by weather and the wars. He stepped down on to the old pavement of the temple and, walking carefully, he proceeded to the centre of the main court where he stood, a little frightened by the dark and by the immensity of those acanthus-crowned columns, black against the blue night, which surrounded him in unbroken ranks on every side. Then, far away, he heard the sound of motor-cars, the shouts of street vendors, and, thinking of dinner, he left the temple, crossed a field and walked several blocks down a palm-edged road to the hotel where he was staying, a rambling stucco building on the edge of that town whose lights he could now see, dim and yellow along the river-bank, a town of white-washed mud with tall striped minarets and cupolas, with narrow haphazard streets, a small town oppressed, obsessed by the ruins which surrounded it, on which it perched, like a living weed in a bone-heap: the remains of palaces and temples, markets and quais, of what had been the greatest city in the world three thousand years before. Too long a time, thought Philip wearily, with a sense of having, without warning, strolled out of time altogether.

The manager of the hotel, fortunately, recalled him to the present, for, as Philip had discovered the day of his arrival, he was fascinated by America and his English, which was good, was decorated with colloquialisms either so new or so old that Philip often had trouble understanding them. Needless to say, the manager, a Mr. Koyoumdjian from Armenia, got not only his conversation but his love of America from the movies which he attended zealously, reverently, often seeing, he confessed, the same movie four or five times, learning something new each time, some detail of American life which he had not known before, some expression he could add to his ever-lengthening American line.

No sooner had Philip entered the lobby than Mr. Ko-youmdjian was upon him, his face scarlet with crisis.

'He has done it! While you were out. Just after you left.'

'Who has done what?'

'Your friend Mr. Willys ... with a gat. He tried to take his life. Such a caper!'

'What happened? You mean he really ...'

'Shot himself. Except that he missed ... just nicked the top of one ear. The sawbones came and gave him something to make him sleep.'

'But that's terrible.'

'Real excitement, though; you can bet your life. I've got the rod in my safe. Want to see it?'

'No, thanks. Is he awake now, do you think?'

'Yes, I sent one of the bozos in with some tea and toast. Though why a man who has just shot himself should be fed tea and toast I couldn't know. Maybe you'd better see him. Cheer him up.'

'I think I will.'

Philip went to his own room first and bathed. He was hot, but he never minded the heat. He always moved slowly during the day, careful not to exert himself, to keep from sweating. The nights bothered him more than the days, but, with an electric fan going, he found he could sleep quite comfortably in the great iron bed with its canopy of mosquito-netting. He dressed, putting on khaki trousers and a polo shirt. Then, ordering dinner from one of the servants, he went into Mr. Willys's room.

The would-be suicide lay inert, a mountain of flesh behind the white mosquito-netting; purple pyjamas with white piping contained those rolls of flesh which composed the wretched Briggs Willys. A bed lamp was turned on and the night table was cluttered with medicine bottles. There was a strong odour of iodine in the room.

'I hear you've had an accident,' said Philip, attempting cheeriness. 'How do you feel?'

'It was *not* an accident,' said a thin voice, emerging from the still, fat centre of the large iron bed.

'But I thought ...'

'I tried to kill myself and I failed, as I have in everything else.' A plump starfish of a hand pushed aside the netting and the bandaged head and shoulders of Mr. Willys were revealed.

139

He was not an ugly man nor was he old; he was just very fat. His features were small and rather indistinct, since one's examination of them was invariably distracted by the full shining cheeks, the ripe tier of chins, the splendid ruddy colouring which the white bandage emphasized.

'Now that's no way to talk,' said Philip sitting down in a chair near the bed.

'It may be no way to talk, but it's the way I feel. Next time I won't fail.'

'You're not going to try to shoot yourself again?'

A crafty expression rippled across the vast face and the tiny eyes disappeared altogether, until they resembled twin navels. 'No, not shoot. Poison may be my next weapon.'

'Surely you don't really want to die.'

'And why not?'

'You have so much to live for.'

'*What* have I to live for?'

There was no immediate answer to this. Looking at the matter dispassionately, Philip could see very little reason for Mr. Willys to continue living with such an outlandish body, one that not only set him apart from the rest of mankind, but one which gave him continual anxiety; for him to walk across a room was a physical effort not unlike a decathlon for someone of more ordinary proportions. But Philip was conscience-bound to be life's advocate.

'Any number of things. I don't know you well enough to be able to mention your pleasures . . .'

'Sleep,' sighed the thin voice. 'I love only sleep.'

'Food, perhaps,' hazarded Philip, tactlessly.

'Certainly not. I eat like a bird. I loathe food. A cup of consommé and a cracker is all I ever need. Just because . . .'

'I was only making a guess,' said Philip quickly; Mr. Willys fell back against his five pillows with a gentle moan of exhaustion, his eyes, as far as Philip could tell, shut.

'Still, there are so many things to do when you're alive that you can't do dead,' he continued, becoming more and more inane; it made no difference, however, for Mr. Willys was not listening. 'You can travel, for instance. You have an income, I gather. You don't have to work for a living. Think how other people envy you . . . being able to travel anywhere you like . . .'

140

'I came to Egypt to die,' said Mr. Willys suddenly. 'I was afraid I wouldn't have the courage to kill myself so I decided to come up the Nile to the hottest town with a decent hotel, and there, if I failed to kill myself I should die of the heat. I can't stand the heat. My heart is not strong. My kidneys are bad. My liver is swollen out of shape. Yet I have been here in Luxor in this hotel for two months, unable to move, unable to sleep. And now I'm unable even to shoot myself for, at the last moment, my hand shook and I only scratched my ear. Oh, it's too terrible.' Sobs convulsed the purple mountain like an earthquake. The bed creaked.

'There now,' said Philip over and over again until the crisis had passed. 'What you should do is go on a nice trip to the mountains, some place where it is cool, like Switzerland, and there, perhaps, take a cure . . .'

'Altitudes makes me dizzy, and there is no cure. None at all. It's either wait until the heat kills me or else take poison.'

'When?'

'When what?'

'When do you plan to take poison?'

'Well, I haven't picked a date yet. Soon, though, very soon. Then it will be over.'

'Have you thought what sort of poison you would take?'

'No,' said the fat man dreamily, 'I haven't. Something with a pleasant taste, however. Something quick.'

'Will you do it sober or drunk?'

'Well, I'd planned it sober, but now that you mention it, it might be easier to do if I had been drinking. Yes, that *is* a good plan. Thanks very much for the idea. I'd probably never have thought of it.'

'That's all right. I just want to make it easy for you.'

'I appreciate that, Mr. Warren.'

'Do you know much about poisons?'

'Not a thing. I did consider swallowing some iodine this evening, but I'm sure it would burn like fire.'

'No, iodine is out. What you need is something like strychnine.'

'How do you happen to know so much about these things?'

'I used to read a great many detective stories,' said Philip, quite carried away by the situation. He was alarmed, however, when Mr. Willys asked him if he would bring him some strychnine the next morning.

'I suppose you can get it without a doctor's prescription?'

'Oh, I doubt that,' said Philip. 'I'll see what I can do though.'

'That will be splendid: to be out of this mess for good! By the way, I shall want to be cremated.'

'Awful mess for the hotel, though, don't you think? I mean, your taking poison in one of their rooms.'

'Won't do them a bit of harm. The legal end of it shouldn't take more than a few hours. Besides, it will give that despicable manager something to talk about. He took my gun away, you know.'

'You could hardly blame him.'

'But I do.' A barefoot servant appeared at the door and informed Philip his dinner was ready. After promising to go first thing in the morning to buy poison, Philip said good night and went downstairs.

He had the large airy dining-room to himself. French doors opened on to a darkened garden. Flies buzzed about the electric light and fans suspended from the ceiling slowly twirled idly disturbing the hot air. A white-coated Negro, wearing a dirty fez, brought him a number of dispiriting courses of simple food, badly cooked.

The manager came by for a little chat as he was drinking the thick muddy black coffee.

'Did you see him? Was he green about the gills?'

'No, he was in the pink,' said Philip, getting into the spirit of the manager's conversation the way he had Mr. Willys's.

'Why do you think he did it?'

'He seems to be tired of life and so he tried to kick . . .'

'The bucket,' finished Mr. Koyoumdjian with a smile of one Mason meeting another in the Libyan Desert. 'I suppose it never occurred to him how disagreeable it would be for us if he killed himself.'

'It was my impression that he didn't really care, that he was more interested in his own problems.'

'Problems!' exploded Mr. Koyoumdjian. 'He has money, hasn't he?'

'A great deal, I think.'

'Then what problems does he have? He can go anywhere he

likes . . . do anything he wants. Buy any doll. . . .' The manager paused. 'He isn't impotent, is he?'

'I didn't ask; but I wouldn't be at all surprised, with that weight.'

'Weight has nothing to do with it. There's an old man about in the town here who weighs twenty stone and he's the busiest man in Lexor in regard to the frails. He has a couch specially tilted so . . .'

'I don't think that would help our Mr. Willys,' said Philip, not wanting to hear any more details.

'Perhaps not. I wonder if I should have him moved to the Mission hospital . . . it'd be their look-out, then, not mine.'

'I'd leave him alone. There isn't much he can do without a gun, and I don't suppose he has a knife . . . even if he did, it would have to be a long one to penetrate those layers of flesh.'

Mr. Koyoumdjian laughed heartily at this grim conceit. 'Perhaps you're right.'

'Are there any more guests coming this month?' The last party, a group of cotton scientists from the United States, had left that morning and there was no one in the hotel but Mr. Willys and Philip.

'Not for ten days.'

'How on earth do you make enough in summer to keep a place like this running?'

'We don't. But the owner decided not to shut up this year. We usually close in May. Of course, during the winter, our big season, we're crowded all the time.'

'Do you like having to stay here in this heat?'

Mr. Koyoumdjian shrugged. 'It's a living, Buster.'

The manager was wrong, however, for when, after an early breakfast, Philip took a stroll in the garden the next morning he discovered that another guest had arrived in the night. She was seated on an iron bench at the end of a lane of magnolias, or what Philip took to be magnolia trees: this garden was a strange one with flowers and trees he had never seen before, mysteriously set out in cabalistic designs with paths which led nowhere, a maze of heavily scented green, decorated with white and red and yellow blossoms.

'Lovely morning,' he said, approaching her.

'Yes. The only cool time of the day.'

'May I sit down?'

'Certainly.' She moved over and he sat beside her, conscious of the green world all about them; there was a hedge behind the bench and a sudden right-angled turn of the path in front of them gave the illusion of a roofless, green-walled room, oblong and carpeted with grass, while flowers still damp with night broke the solid areas of green with their bright colours. . . . For some reason he found himself thinking of a kindergarten he'd once attended, one with grass-green walls on which, in the spring, to celebrate the sickening Flora, the children had hung untidy paper flowers of their own manufacture. Looking down this natural room he almost expected to see a sand-box in one corner.

'Did you just arrive in Luxor?' he asked.

'This morning.' He liked her voice, which was cool and even, an educated American or perhaps British voice. He moved about on the bench so that he could see her more clearly. She was handsome, though not pretty in a contemporary sense, for her nose was large, like a Julian portrait bust, and her skin was white, unpainted. Yet her eyes were extraordinary, pale, grey with long dark lashes, and her hair was a fine auburn, drawn softly back from her face and gathered in a bun at the back. He suspected she was tall and, though not young, not old either . . . no grey in her undyed hair, no deep lines in her smooth face. Thirty-five, he decided, noticing that she wore no wedding ring.

'Not the best time of the year to visit Egypt,' he commented.

'I like Egypt any time of year,' she said.

'You've been here before?'

'Many, many times. In fact, my father's family used to live here a long time ago.'

'Then it must be like home.'

'Yes, like home. Have you been here long?'

The question was so politely stated, like the stylized inquiries into one's health people make on meeting one another the first time, that he very nearly didn't answer her at all: then, recalling himself, he told her he had been in Egypt for a month, that he'd been in Luxor five or six days, and that he was seeing everything there was to see in the company of an old dragoman named Said.

'I envy you, coming to it fresh like this ... even in the heat.'

'I don't mind the hot weather. The rest, of course, is wonderful. I've never felt so relaxed before. For the first time, nothing matters ... no anxiety, no memory ... nothing but the present and the past.'

'The ruins,' she said. 'That's what does it, of course. It's very hard to dream of the future when the past is all around one, reminding one that what is has been before and will be again, over and over and over. . . .'

'Proving, perhaps, that individual acts are nothing in themselves, except to the doer at the moment he acts.'

'Yet human beings love the idea of posterity.' She smiled. 'It makes us feel important. Think how confident Thutmose, the great king in these parts, must have been that his name would be immortal, a household word until the end of time; that Egypt under his descendants would remain unchanged, very much as it had been for the thousands of years that preceded his own reign. One consolation, of course, is that he doesn't know his corpse has been dug up, the wrappings removed, the bones X-rayed, the skull measured and compared with his portraits, his diseases duly noted, as though he were some prehistoric Java man instead of a successful soldier and politician. There's no long fame for mortals. None at all.'

'As Thomas Browne once said,' smiled Philip, wondering how they had got off on to this particular tack. As the reader has noticed, Philip has a tendency to drift off into abstract discussions which makes him, in many ways, the perfect protagonist for a novel since he can be counted on to get himself, at a moment's notice, into deep waters, or what are to him deep waters: the dangerous shallows of the vast sea of philosophy where many a young man's brave ship, to pursue this metaphor to its end, has run aground on the shoals of dialectic.

'Are you staying here?' asked Philip.

She nodded. 'I always stay here when I am in Luxor.'

'The manager told me he was expecting no one for a few days.'

'We're old friends, Mr. Koyoumdjian and I. He's never surprised when I appear without notice.'

'Have you some business here?' asked Philip tentatively, realizing it was none of his business and that she appeared to be

145

quite capable of reminding him that it was not. But she only smiled and said there was something she wanted to see, that she was interested in archaeology: 'Disproving, perhaps, my own theory that all is forgotten since I for one am devoted to seeing that nothing is forgotten, that every second of history is accounted for.'

'History or, rather, legend is seldom wholly forgotten,' said Philip with the careful diffidence of a man making an epigram. 'Men always are.' When this was said, as though by common assent, almost reverently, they both rose and walked silently down the green path to the hotel.

'I see you've met Miss Oliver,' said the manager, coming over to their table later that day at lunch, where Philip was toying with a number of vivid stewed fruits, all poisonous-looking and tasteless.

'Yes, we met in the garden,' said Miss Oliver, whose first name Philip had already been informed was Sophia.

'A surprise visitor,' said Mr. Koyoumdjian. 'You could have knocked me over with a feather when she walked in the hotel this morning as cool as a cucumber and asked for her old room. More investigations, eh?'

'Just one more,' she said, removing a half-drowned fly from her coffee. 'I may have to go out to the desert for a few days. I'm not sure.'

'What's the desert like?' asked Philip, hoping this would lead to an invitation; it did not. He was lectured for several minutes on life in the desert, and, by the time she finished an interesting account of the Arab method of divining the presence of water, the fly, which had been moribund, pulled itself together and flew away, heading directly, Philip noticed, for a coil of fly paper already nasty with the corpses of its fellows. He pondered the possible meaning of this omen, coming at last to the conclusion that it meant nothing at all.

'Have you seen Mr. Willys this morning?' he asked suddenly, when Miss Oliver had concluded her remarks and was thoughtfully sipping coffee, her thoughts far away, no doubt in some distant *wadi*, her eyes narrowed as though against the glare of bright sun on sand.

The manager had indeed seen Mr. Willys. 'He seems in good spirits, keeping his pecker up. I think he'll be all right now. He spoke of coming down to dinner tonight. He asked to see you, by the way. Said you had something for him.'

'Who is this?' asked Miss Oliver, the desert fading like a mirage, as Philip explained the details of Mr. Willys's obsession. She had, however, no comment to make on the situation either than a conventional word or two and a perfunctory expression of sympathy for the trouble the manager had been put to. Then she turned to Philip and, discovering that he was to go to Karnak that afternoon with his dragoman, asked if she might go along. Making a date for five o'clock, when the sun would be less violent, they parted.

Philip found Mr. Willys still in bed, but now quite nude, without even a mosquito-netting to diffuse the horror. 'Good morning,' said Philip from the door, giving the other a chance to cover himself, but Mr. Willys did not have the energy or the desire. Instead he pulled himself up so that his stomach, with its mottled pink flesh, covered his genitals, giving him the curiously sexless look of a celluloid Kewpie doll. Philip found it difficult not to stare fascinatedly at this unusual display of one of nature's bitter jokes.

'Good morning, Philip. Did you bring it?'

'Bring what?'

'The poison. You promised.'

'Ah, the poison.' Philip had no lie ready, however. 'I ... I haven't been to town yet.'

'You will remember it, though?'

'I'll see what I can do. I'll have to get a doctor's prescription, you know; and that may be difficult.'

'You're not trying to get out of this, are you?' Mr. Willys was suspicious.

'I'll do my best ... but now I have to go out. I'll see you tonight. Mr. Koyoumdjian said you were coming down to dinner.'

'I have no intention of ever leaving this room alive. I only said I'd get up to put him off the scent. I was afraid they might try to move me to the Mission hospital. But now, if you'll do as you promised, I shall be asleep by dinner-time ... for ever!' And with a gusty sigh, Mr. Willys began to turn over; the bed creaked; he groaned; the flesh sagged alarmingly and Philip fled.

'Yonder wall,' said the dragoman, in his Biblical English, 'was builded by the children of Israel before their liberation by Moses. You see, some of the bricks are made with straw; others without.'

'This tree was brought back from the land of Punt by Queen Hatshepsut's fleet,' said Miss Oliver. Philip was bombarded with information from all sides; some of it he absorbed, most of it he did not hear for he was too occupied with his own reactions. Like a man feeling his own pulse, he tried to define what he felt as he walked through the rooms and dusty gardens of three thousands years before.

When they cames to the small Temple of Pthah, they sat down in its shade, out of the terrible light of the sun which scorched the temple walls and parched the earth as it rode like a disc of solid gold in the harsh blue sky.

It is so difficult to know how to deal with well-known landscapes when one is writing a novel. There is an impulse to describe everything literally, enthusiastically, giving dimensions, dates, distances and other pertinent information; this is the guide-book approach and the dangers are numerous: for instance, should one care to describe the Sphinx, one would have to record those dimensions which are available to any owner of an encyclopaedia. Should one rely on memory there will inevitably be angry comments to the effect that the left paw is not worn away, that one haunch is higher than the other, that the bridge of the nose is still intact if one observes the face from the east, and so on. The impressionistic manner is somewhat better: to use the celebrated object as a point of departure, like Pater describing the Mona Lisa, or Henry James describing the capitol at Washington, or rather Henry James describing Henry James describing the capitol at Washington. Then there is the contemporary fashion of keeping away from celebrated objects altogether. In Paris the story, if it concerns artists, will all take place within a few blocks of the rue de Bac, or if of high life, around the Crillion and the Ritz. While in a book about Egypt most of the action will take place either in a wealthy suburb of Cairo or else in a squalid desert village with goats and lice infested children running about, eating dates and drinking stagnant water. It would be pleasant to make some sort of compromise, to be able to give a thorough instructive tour of Karnak, the Valley of the Kings, and so forth, soaring every now and then, with burnished wings, into a paradise of lyric metaphor, getting around the object, as it were, translating its aura into a few balanced melodious sentences. But, reader, you will be spared even this. The movies have already made us so familiar with foreign countries that the novel, for its own good I am sure, can no longer be usefully employed in cataloguing details of well-known landscapes, and so, except for an occasional odd glimpse of this place or that, travelogues and the monthly *Geographic* must still be our source material. It might, however, be of some relevance to quote at this point what a well-known authority on Egypt had to say in 1887 of the country in general. After first remarking on the monotony of the scenery, the authority adds: 'The monotony is relieved, however, in two ways, and by two causes. Nature herself does something to relieve it. Twice a day, in the morning and in the evening, the sky and the landscape are lit up by hues so bright and so delicate that the homely features of this prospect are at once transformed as by magic, and wear an aspect of exquisite beauty. ... The orb of night walks in brightness through a firmament of sapphire; or, if the moon is below the horizon, then the purple vault is lit up with many coloured stars. Silence profound reigns around. A phase of beauty wholly different from that of day-time smites the sense. ...' A beautiful style, alas, is not enough, while generalities are always treacherous, for as we have seen only the night before, the sun set quickly without one single bright hue in evidence. Philip, nevertheless, has found this authority a great comfort.

'The Arab women bring their babies here to bless them,' said Miss Oliver, as they stood in the close dark room, a life-sized statue of a woman with a lion's head in front of them, partly lighted by a shaft of light coming from a square opening directly overhead.

'She has great power,' intoned the dragoman, an untidy old man with a grizzled beard and wearing the national sheet-like robe, a fez on his head, sandals on his feet. He was a true Egyptian, he assured Philip when they first met, one of the last, not like those god-damned Arabs in the north. And he was not a Moslem either; proudly he had shown Philip a curious cross tattooed on his arm. 'I am a Christian. A Coptic,' he had said.

'So do all the gods, if one believes in them,' said Miss Oliver firmly.

Philip, though he liked her, found her positive assertions a little trying; she never spoke tentatively, advanced an opinion as merely an opinion and not a fact of nature. Yet, in general, he agreed with what she had to say and, in any case, he had not yet been in a position to contradict her with a superior knowledge on any subject. The dragoman, however, feeling his own position as an Egyptologist to be secure, had spent most of the morning attempting politely but tenaciously to disprove her observations and theories. She, in her turn, was far more direct; she contradicted him flatly until Philip was afraid there might be trouble but they got through the day without any unpleasantness, and it was in a friendly mood that they went back together to the hotel in a horse-drawn carriage, the top up against the evening sun.

Men sat sleepily in doorways as they drove into Luxor. Even the big-bellied, naked children sat or lay in the fly-buzzing shade of acacias, hardly moving. Only the women worked, maintaining the ancient patterns of life, preparing food, bringing water from the fountains, nursing the children and cursing the men and the flies in their deep harsh voices, cursing the fine dust which the foreigners' carriage turned up in clouds as Philip and Sophia drove through the dusty streets of the village to the highway which led to their hotel, to modern bathrooms and cool rooms.

'You failed me.'

'But I tell you the doctor refused to give me a prescription.'

'I counted on you. All day I've been happy. Happier than I've ever been before, thinking that never again would I have to open my eyes to see the morning, to look at this aching wreck and to realize that I must endure it for yet another day. . . . Oh, it's too terrible!' And he groaned piteously, the sheet which covered him rippling like a sea effect in an old-fashioned play.

'I did my best,' said Philip firmly. 'It's up to you from now on.' And, having divorced himself from Mr. Willys's project, he left the room, ignoring the pleas, the anguished entreaties from behind the mosquito-netting: 'Oh, come back! I'm sorry; I didn't mean it. You *must* help me!'

In the lobby, Mr. Koyoumdjian met him. 'We have a surprise for you!' he said, smiling, his face breaking into a number of geometric shapes none of which revealed character. 'Another lady has just arrived ... an American from New York City. You probably know her, Mrs. Fay Peabody.'

'No, I don't think I've met her. You see ...'

'New York's a big town, I know. Babylon on the Subway, that's what they call it. I'm not green. What I meant is you probably know her books. She writes detective stories ... hard-boiled. Seen some of them myself, but I have no time to read.'

'Where is Miss Oliver?'

'In the dining-room with Mrs. Peabody. They're waiting for you.'

Sophia was stately and cool in a pale blue evening dress which flattered her well-formed body and yet, recognizing dispassionately all her physical attractions, he was in no way attracted to her; she was like one of those voluptuous figures carved in ice at a winter carnival in New England. Usually he had a difficult time explaining to himself why this person or that person appealed to him but now he was amused to find himself wondering why he was not attracted to this handsome, apparently available woman. When he tried to think of her in erotic terms, he experienced the same sort of embarrassment when, as an adolescent, he had speculated on the private behaviour of his parents. He had concluded that it was the enervating heat which had done this to him, heat combined with the mood of the place and a new knowledge of the ebb and flow of all those generations whose debris, solemn and dusty, surrounded that garden which he now glimpsed, pale and shadowy, through the french windows of the dining-room.

Sophia introduced him to Mrs. Fay Peabody. The famous mystery-story writer was plump and soft, elderly, and though she had a slight speech defect (the result of ill-fitting dentures) she managed, nevertheless, to speak with very nearly as much authority as Sophia herself, though, unlike Sophia, she was limited to fewer fields: the underworld, publishing and the law.

'Well, here we all are,' she observed, after the introductions had been made and an American canned fruit cocktail was set before them. 'Probably the only Americans in upper Egypt.'

'No, there are quite a few over at the Ponsoonah Laboratories outside of town.'

'I mean, not counting professional people,' clicked Mrs. Peabody. 'Although, perhaps, I don't quite mean that either since I,

151

too, am professional, on a job.' There was a pause. Philip, aware that it was up to him to ask Mrs. Peabody who she was, did so, neatly. She told him that she was Fay Peabody and he told her that he enjoyed her books. Sophia remained silent, as though she'd been through all this before he had joined them.

'I believe in doing my research on the spot, Mr. Warren. None of this second-hand business for me. . . . Looking things up is all very well for most writers but, if I say so myself, I have quite a large body of readers who look to me for the real thing . . . and that's what I give them. When I describe the inside of Leavenworth it means that I have been inside Leavenworth, as a prisoner.'

'You must be joking,' said Sophia mildly.

'I never joke about my work, Miss Oliver. Yes, I arranged with the warden and he allowed me to reside three days in a cell, just like any other prisoner, wearing, of course, man's apparel. You perhaps remember the prison scenes in *Red, White and Blue Murder* . . . well, those are authentic scenes based upon my personal experience.' There was an awed silence after these remarks. Philip, toying with a bit of cold fried fish, wondered what to say next. He glanced at Sophia. She was no help; she asked Mrs. Peabody what she was doing in Egypt.

'I believe, Miss Oliver, that a change of place is good for all of us. Even the best. I was never one to rely on formula, although the Fay Peabody method may be considered, perhaps, to be a *kind* of formula. Yet I have been aware for some time now that there were certain limitations to the method. Not that I lack readers! No, bless them! each book sells more than its predecessor. Yet, in spite of such encouragement, one does have a duty to oneself and though I have written exclusively of crime in Philadelphia with, of course, related minor scenes elsewhere, I have never thrown down the gauntlet, you might say, and tackled a really big job elsewhere.'

'Like Agatha Christie,' said Philip innocently. The storm broke. Mrs. Christie was flayed before their eyes and her corpse, like Hector's, pulled after Mrs. Peabody's triumphal car from one end of publishers' row to the other. Sales were compared down to the last twenty-five copies sold. Mrs. Peabody had at her tongue's tip the exact sales of every mystery novel published since Conan Doyle and, while they ate the dry grey flesh of some mysterious beast, it became apparent to them that not only in quality but in sales, too, Mrs. Peabody was tops. No, she was not going to do the Christie sort of thing in Egypt. She was going to do the Fay Peabody sort of thing in Egypt and, her jaw set, she looked from one to the other of her companions, challenging them to compare her with anyone, living or dead. Philip was impressed.

'Will it have J. R. Snaffles in it?' he asked, recalling the name of her detective, an ex-prize-fighter with an aquiline profile and an appeal which reputedly drove women wild, not only in fiction but the ones in life who bought every book about Snaffles Mrs. Peabody was good enough to write for them.

'Yes, Snaffles will be in it. I can't make too large a break with my fans. I mean, if you buy a Fay Peabody mystery you expect Snaffles. Isn't that right, Miss Oliver?' Sophia nodded and the denture-clicking words of Mrs. Peabody continued, a thin trickle of saliva glistening at the corner of her mouth. 'I can only give you the barest hint of my plot ... To do more would be unfair to my other fans. Suffice it to say, Snaffles has been hired by the wealthy Great Preston of the Main Line to accompany her and her brother on a tour of Egypt to ascertain, if possible, the whereabouts of her father, who disappeared in Twenty-nine with most of his bank's available cash. (She has independent means from her mother.) Of course, he did not take the cash. . . .'

By the time coffee was brought, they knew a good deal more about the next adventure of Snaffles than any Fay Peabody fan in the world, or at least in upper Egypt.

'What a nasty taste!' exclaimed the authoress, after swallowing with difficulty one sip of the thick Turkish coffee.

'Oh, it's wonderful,' lied Philip.

'You must get used to it,' said Sophia. '*Everyone* drinks it here. Even your Mr. Snaffles will have to drink it,' she added maliciously.

Mrs. Peabody sighed. 'In that case, I'd better swallow it all, like medicine. Research! Never let anyone tell you it's easy. Take my word for it.'

It was not until they were seated on the screened-in porch overlooking the garden that Philip had his marvellous idea.

'Tell me, Mrs. Peabody, have you ever known a man who wanted to be murdered?'

'Certainly not, Mr. Warren. The whole point to mystery stories is that people do *not* want to be murdered.'

'Perhaps I should put it another way. A man wants to kill himself but he's afraid to.'

'I presume you are speaking of suicide. I do not wish to sound intolerant, Mr. Warren, but I do not approve of suicide. It is unfair to the reader. I know, of course, that you are a great admirer of Mrs. Christie. . . .' And that poor lady's body was once more dragged the length of publisher's row.

'All I meant,' said Philip, when she had stopped for breath, 'is that there's a man staying here who wants to kill himself but hasn't the nerve. He tried to shoot himself a few days ago, but missed. Now he's been begging me to get him some poison.'

'Good heavens!' exclaimed Mrs Peabody, for the first time interested in anything either Philip or Sophia had had to say all evening. Then, briskly: 'Why doesn't he buy his own lethal dose?'

'He is very fat. He can hardly get out of bed.'

'I see. You refused, of course, to do as he requested?'

'Yes, as a matter of fact I did, but I thought you might be able to help him.'

'How could *I* help him?'

'I thought perhaps you might murder him, Mrs. Peabody,' said Philip blandly.

Mrs. Peabody snorted dangerously. 'If that is your idea of a joke, Mr. Warren, then I must tell you I think it in poor taste.'

'But you said yourself that you are always authentic,' remarked Sophia, joining the game. 'How can you write about murders if you've never committed one?'

Mrs. Peabody glared at her. 'I don't think that follows at all. Besides, my novels are primarily concerned with the *detection* of the murderer, not the murder itself.'

'In any case, Mrs. Peabody, you could give him some advice on what poison to take . . . you know, some of the little tricks of the trade a layman might not know.'

'But I wouldn't dream of such a thing!' She was outraged. 'I can only hope that you're not serious, that this is some sort of private joke between you and Miss Oliver.'

'I'm afraid he means what he says,' said Sophia. I haven't seen Mr. Willys, but I've heard all about his attempts at suicide

154

not only from Mr. Warren but also from the manager who took his gun away from him.'

'What sort of weapon was it?' asked Mrs. Peabody, in a voice suddenly precise and business-like.

'A revolver,' said Philip.

'You have no idea what make? Type bore?'

'I suppose Mr. Koyoumadjian will let you look at it if you want to.'

'No. It's not important. I'm always curious, however, about weapons. In my last book I had a murder committed with a sash-weight attached to a medieval crossbow. Rather an original touch, I thought, since the murderer was able to prove he was next door at a party when the victim's skull was crushed by the weight. Fay Peabody books are noted, if I say so myself, for their unusual weapons.'

'I think you should meet Mr. Willys,' said Philip, taking advantage of the authoress's change of mood. 'I mean, it's really an interesting case.'

'But I'm quite sure that in his present state he wouldn't want to meet me. . . .

'Nonsense. In his present state he'd be thrilled to meet you.'

Philip put his head in the door to make sure that Mr. Willys was still covered by the sheet; he was. The would-be suicide was propped up in bed, modestly tented, drinking Scotch and doing a crossword puzzle. Philip introduced him to the ladies.

'I've read a lot of those books of yours,' said Mr. Willys. 'I've a great deal of time on my hands, you know, and since I've nothing better to do, I read.'

'Many great men read books,' said Mrs. Peabody gently, her ruthless material-gathering eye taking in everything: the whale-like body, the whisky, the bottles of medicine. 'As a matter of fact, my most prized possession is a letter from the late President of the United States of America, Franklin Delano Roosevelt, saying that he thought *Red, White and Blue Murder* "a swell yarn", to use his expression.' She talked on hypnotically, her eyes narrowed as though estimating a bullet's trajectory from different angles of the room, as well as places where a crossbow might be secreted, a sash-weight dropped. 'And I've heard that Mr. Churchill also enjoys an occasional tale of detection when his mind is not occupied with the multifarious activi-

155

ties of State in which his high offices involve him, not to mention his own not inconsiderable literacy activities,' she said, moving over to the night table and, as though against her will, picking up the bottles and reading their labels as she talked. She was still talking when Philip and Sophia tiptoed out of the room.

'I wonder if I should have done that,' said Philip, as they stepped out of the french windows and into the warm moonlit garden.

'I don't think much harm will be done. If what you say about Mr. Willys is true, they have a great deal in common.'

'You don't think she'll murder him?' He was half serious. Sophia laughed. 'Don't be absurd. She's an old idiot and he is a neurotic who'll never kill himself as long as he has someone to talk suicide to.' Philip had almost forgotten about people who used such words as 'neurotic' in conversation; he'd been under the impression that the ugly private language of the mental therapists was becoming unfashionable, that the cleverest people no longer talked about their psycholoanalyses; but then he remembered that Sophia would not bother to be fashionable; she would use whatever words she chose to make her point.

He often felt that he was with a foreigner when he was with her, someone who used the language intelligently but with no great facility or, rather, personal colour: no tone, no habits of speech, no peculiar phrases or repetitions. It was all so clear and direct. For the first time, he asked her where she lived.

'I live in Paris now, most of the time. But I travel a great deal.'

'Why? Any purpose?'

'I like it. No other purpose. I have "means", as Mrs. Peabody would say.'

'That monster,' Philip chuckled. They sat down on the tile edge of a small fountain. The light in Mr. Willys's second-floor room burned brightly, a warm and yellow oblong in the dark wall of the hotel.

'Were you born in Paris?'

She shook her head, but then, instead of answering, she scooped up a handful of water and let it trickle back into the fountain. Water struck water with an unmusical sound. 'Why are you in Egypt?' he asked.

156

'You ask so many questions,' she said . . . an observation, not a complaint. 'Why are *you* in Egypt?'

'To see it. I've never been here.' He explained to her about his year.

'Well, I'm here to see it, too.'

'You've been here before.'

'I like the ruins,' she confessed. 'I'm interested in archaeology and I've occasionally put a little money into expeditions.'

'Is there an expedition on now, one of yours?'

'Yes, in a way. I'm vaguely involved in the digging over at El Farhar.'

'What are they digging?'

'They seem undecided. As far as I know, it's a small temple built in the time of Seti the Second, an amiable young man who was deposed early in life, possibly because he was the son of Menephthah, the unfortunate creature who followed Moses into the Red Sea.'

'How far away is this place?'

'About sixty miles to the south. We might go over there, if you care to.'

'I'd like to very much. Is there a town near-by?'

'El Farhar is a good-sized town, with a native hotel where one can stay. The excavations are near-by . . . a group from the University of Berne are doing the work . . . thankless, of course, since the Egyptian Government confiscates nearly everything of value, but then it's a mania, like any other, a passion for know-ledge . . . much more admirable, I think, than a passion for money or for position. I actually know of people whose prin-cipal interest it is to interfere in the lives of others . . . for their own good, of course.'

Philip felt very close to her at that moment. She was the first intelligent woman he'd met who had not, at one point, revealed some sort of plot whereby through birth control, Christian Science, capitalism or enlightened deviationism the world might be saved; all opposition to the grand formula being ruthlessly abolished. Of course he did not know her well; she might perhaps have some secret dream of teaching Esperanto to every child in the world. But, for the moment, he felt in marvellous accord with her: two pure non-interventionists, seated in the jasmine-scented darkness of an Egyptian garden, each pursuing his own solitary way, paragons of human virtue and as just as

157

gods. He could not help but compare her with Regina. He even asked her if she had met Mrs. Durham.

'Regina? Of course. I've known her for years. When did you meet her?'

'A few months ago when I was in Rome.'

'Did you like her?'

This was a dangerous question obviously: Sophia, though she lacked the womanly trait of interference, was, after all, quite feminine enough to know rivalry.

'Yes, I liked her,' said Philip, deserting policy for a relative truth. 'But I think, of course, that she does answer your description: she's one of those people who want to govern other people for their own good, but I do like one thing about her: she's not simple-minded enough to have a programme. She doesn't believe in any abstract set of rules which can be applied rigorously to every situation. Power is just her particular element. She enjoys it for its own sake ... the Disraeli approach rather than the reformer's or the mystic's.'

'I don't like her,' said Sophia flatly. 'But I do agree that if one is to be interested in the world, her attitude is the least absurd; yet the result of her chicanery can be every bit as dangerous as the crusade of some fool with a four-year plan.'

Discussing the way of the world, they strolled about the garden, and Philip was sad that he experienced no desire. In any event, he was quite confident that if he did make a move she would be very surprised, as well as amused, and indifferent. He wondered if she had had lovers. The thought that she might be a Lesbian had crossed his mind, though she was not masculine ... which proved nothing, of course. Like most American men of his century he was fascinated by the whole idea of Lesbianism and his fund of information, accurate and inaccurate, was tremendous. He decided that when he knew her better he would bring the subject up to see what her reaction might be. But they spoke now of the expedition to El Farhar.

'There's another reason for going there,' she said; then she stopped suddenly, as though she'd been indiscreet.

'Another reason? What?'

'I'm not sure I should tell you yet. I'm not sure myself what it is or, rather, if the rumour I've heard is true or not true. We'll find out soon enough.'

'But why ...'

Then she said that she was tired, that the sun had been very hot that day, that perhaps they should go in.

As he passed the door to Mr. Willys's room, Philip looked in to say good night. Mrs. Peabody had drawn her chair close to the bed and was saying excitedly: 'There are four methods of making a hangman's noose. I have always favoured the traditional "double coil and slip" noose ...' Neither Mr. Willys nor Mrs. Peabody heard Philip's good night.

CHAPTER SEVEN

The car that they hired to take them to El Farhar ran out of water first, then oil, then petrol ... all of which Sophia patiently paid for, although the price for the services of the car was to have included everything. Fortunately none of the tyres blew out and they arrived at El Farhar in the late afternoon; they were taken to the only brick building, the Fuad I Hotel, and here they signed a register which was printed in French and were welcomed by a manager who addressed Sophia in Italian, a language she obviously spoke well.

Then they walked out into the glare of the day where not one sign implored them to drink Coca-Cola. There was not even a single movie-house with lurid posters predicting the thrill some old movie with bobbed-haired girls of another generation had in store for them. One battered jeep parked before the house of the local administrator provided the only contemporary note in this hot, dusty world of whitewashed mud houses and minarets with wooden balconies from which the faithful were summoned to regard the north-east and to contemplate the mercy of Allah and his dead Prophet's wisdom. The long-robed people stared at the two foreigners as they crossed the dung-littered market-place where animals and their owners milled about, kicking dust into market stalls which were sheltered from the sun by a candy-pink and white striped arcade.

'I don't think they're very friendly,' said Philip uneasily as they finally got through to the far side of the square, displacing a group of villainous-looking *fellahin.*

'No, I don't suppose they are,' said Sophia, quite composed, her sensible heels clicking on the broken cobbles of a broad sycamore-lined street.

'But why? What have the Americans done to them?'

'A great deal ... but they don't know we're Americans. All they know is that we're white and from the north, that we have money and eat pork. They don't dislike us enough to be dangerous ... yet,' she added comfortably.

The half-uncovered temple was at the end of a lane on the town's edge, not far from the dull snake-green river. To the west Philip could see the limestone mountains which separated the Nile Valley from the Libyan Desert, dead-white lunar mountains without water or vegetation. To the east, open country, dusty green where it had been irrigated and, where it had not, only dust and stone, broken here and there by clusters of slender date palms grown up about desert wells or, as Philip's authority would say, the Victorian George Rawlinson, M.A., Camden professor of Ancient History in the University of Oxford and corresponding member of the Royal Academy of Turin, in collaboration with Arthur Gillman, M.A.: 'Egypt is a land of tranquil monotony. The eye commonly travels over a waste of waters, or over a green plane unbroken by elevations. The sky is generally cloudless. No fog or mist enwraps the distance in mystery; no rainstorm sweeps across the scene; no rainbow spans the empyrean; no shadows chase each other over the landscape. There is an entire absence of picturesque scenery.' Egypt was not much like England and Mr. Rawlinson missed the grey damp days, the homely pleasures of the common cold, the soft dampness which, as Mrs. Woolf's Orlando discovered, stole over England shortly after Prinny's death, diffusing the bright sun of a more heroic age with veils of coal smoke and fog, while high spirits gave way to probity and all the poets departed, following the sun to Italy.

But Philip, a child of the sun, was perversely attracted to Mr. Rawlinson, to good form, narrow-shouldered suits, understatement and lyric poetry, not to mention grey damp days ... attracted but no more; although, now, sweating on the banks of Hapi, of the Nile, more than ever did the foggy tones of Mr.

Rawlinson come to him as a breath of cool northern air, and he could almost hear a phlegm-ridden voice intone that one bright sentence in *The Story of Ancient Egypt:* 'Silence profound reigns around.'

But there was no silence here, profound or superficial. The workmen chatted noisily as they went about their various jobs: some digging, others dusting blocks of stone with brooms.

Sophia and Philip walked slowly about the pit. The top of the temple just appeared above the surface of the ground. The excavators had dug down to the original level in front of the main colonnade. They were now engaged in completing a wide trench about the entire building. The roof of the temple had long since fallen in, but the pillared façade was unbroken and, though it lacked the familiar grace of Greek columns, it still had a fineness of its own, he thought critically, in spite of the squat proportions and the dull earth colour. Thinking of the bas-reliefs inside, hidden by earth and sand, he experienced some of the excitement which he knew archaeologists must feel when they finally enter rooms where no one for centuries has been.

Between two palms, a quonset hut had been erected, and here they found Dr. Praeger of the University of Berne, head of the expedition.

'Miss Oliver! This *is* a surprise. We thought you were in Europe. Come in. Come in.' Introductions were made and they all sat down in wicker chairs. The room was businesslike, with a clock, a filing cabinet, a water-cooler and fragments of pottery and stone carving arranged on the floor, some with little white stickers, others unclassified. Dr. Praeger was a vigorous-looking German–Swiss, red-faced, stout and earnest. He spoke English fluently but with an unusually disagreeable accent, as though he were singing the words to some atonal melody.

'We are making great progress, Miss Oliver, as you can see. In about two weeks we will be able to enter the building and see what treasures the past has saved for us,' he sang blithely, the young Lohengrin setting forth.

'Have you found the cartouche?'

'Seti the First . . . no one else so far. But we shall see what we shall see. You are interested in archaeology?'

Philip, very modestly, allowed that he was.

'Then you should be interested in certain aspects of our little temple.' He led them outside, where they stood in the shade of the quonset, looking down into the pit. 'It was erected, we now know, to the god Thoth . . .'

'As I told you,' said Miss Oliver.

'As you did, indeed. Thoth was the scribe of the gods . . . the wise man and the recorder.' And now, like a priest chanting service, Dr. Praeger told them about the temple, accepting Miss Oliver's occasional comments with a tolerant smile. 'But our greatest surprise you will never guess, Miss Oliver, not in a hundred years.' He paused, allowing the newcomers to ponder this solemn prediction.

'What is it?' asked Sophia.

'Alexander!' said Dr. Praeger. And cymbals crashed in Philip's head as he remembered Lohengrin's magnificent declaration.

'You mean . . .' Sophia looked very interested.

Dr. Praeger grinned happily and nodded, his forget-me-not blue eyes glistening with emotion. 'Alexander,' he repeated softly, gently, 'Alexander was here.'

'An inscription?'

'Better yet. A frieze . . . only a fragment, but come, look. At back of the house. We found it just outside the colonnade.'

He led them to the back of the house where a section of stone several feet square lay with a tarpaulin over it. He removed the covering and Philip saw a delicate drawing of a young man standing before a priapic god. Hieroglyphs declared, according to Dr. Praeger, that this was the divine Alexander, the sun's relative and Egypt's Pharaoh.

'Yes, it is Alexander,' said Sophia, examining the inscription without her dark glasses, running her fingers gently over the stone. 'I've often wondered why Egyptians so often showed him doing homage to the priapus.'

'A form of satire?' suggested Philip.

'Perhaps. Look how accurate they were, by the way. See, they show his slightly hunched shoulder and the small chin?'

'You mean these figures really look like the originals?'

You see? Quite against one's will the grey shadow of Professor Rawlinson falls across this discussion of Egyptian ways, making one almost agree with that contemporary English poet who once remarked that Hoboken not only has an evocative name, but that just as interesting things happen there as in more exotic locales. Nevertheless, Philip has come to Egypt, and there

162

is a good reason not only for his sightseeing among the ruins but for this uncomfortable visit to El Farhar in the middle of the summer as well. However, Alexander admittedly has nothing to do with it, and so, after an hour of trudging about in the dry dirt of the temple of Thoth, Sophia and Philip walked back to the hotel, where they were joined a few hours later by Dr. Praeger and his assistant, Dr. Peverini. They had dinner in the dining-room of the hotel.

They drank whisky during the meal, to disguise the horror of what they were eating; but the time the black sandy coffee came they were all good friends and in an excellent mood.

Dr. Peverini was a swarthy young Italian–Swiss, a Protestant, intolerant and rather prim, while Dr. Praeger, the German–Swiss, was a devout Catholic, soft and warm. Over coffee they talked of religion, to Philip's great surprise since he could not recall having often discussed anything so intangible or so abstract since he had left college: most Americans, he knew, become profoundly embarrassed in the presence of any abstraction, murmuring that, well, they thought it was probably better to do good than bad . . . dividing about equally between those who know deep in their visceras that there is a God floating about somewhere, like a stellar nebula, and those who know there isn't a God, but think religion is very nice for the other people, even though the devout have a rude awakening ahead of them, presuming one could know nothing when one is nothing, a semantical impossibility of course, but perhaps not a mystical one.

'The most interesting aspect of Mohammed's god,' chanted Dr. Praeger, 'was that he knew from the very beginning of the world who was to be saved and who was to be damned, and there was no quarrelling with God's appointment. As incredible as it may seem, the Koran, referring to the unbelievers, says, more or less: 'We have thrown veils over their hearts, lest they should understand the Koran, and into their ears a heaviness; and if thou led them to the guidance yet even then they would never be guided.'' '

'A good way of explaining the actions of one's enemies,' said Philip, recalling the same omniscience of St. Augustine's deity.

'According to Mohammed, Allah stated very precisely that if he had been so minded all men might have been saved, but that such had not been his pleasure and that he preferred to furnish hell with men as well as demons,' said Dr. Peverini.

'I wonder why?' asked Philip.

'One does not wonder in matters of faith,' said Sophia, smiling. 'One believes. One either accepts all the Messiah's revelations or none of them. Should it seem inscrutable or illogical, then one lacks faith. When one believes, all is clear.'

'Indeed it is,' exclaimed Dr. Praeger joyously, unaware of the intended mockery. 'Who are we to question the great men of our faith? Wise men have spent their lives studying the mysteries and interpreting the revelations. . . .'

'It should be remembered,' interrupted Dr. Peverini dryly, 'that Mohammedans rejected European Christianity because they thought it polytheistic. The idea of God as three persons seemed ludicrous to them and the importance of "the Mother of God" an impertinence and a sacrilege.'

'Yet all popular religions have been, on a certain level, polytheistic. Even the Moslems have Iblis, the fallen angel, the evil one, and various minor figures who do the work of heaven,' reminded Sophia. 'The people are always personalizing emotions and elements while the scholars and mystics are trying to measure and to comprehend some central power or idea from which all life comes. Even here in Egypt, with all the hundreds of gods, there was a central deity, a source of light whose name was known only to a few . . . so terrible was his name it was never pronounced. And, as always, it was the poets who discovered or rather revealed his existence. "His commencement is from the beginning; he is the god who has existed from old time; there is no god without him; no mother bore him; no father hath begotten him; he is a god-goddess created from himself; all gods came into existence when he began." '

'On a more human level, a primitive level, there will always be minor gods,' said Philip. 'The uneducated, the intellectually inadequate man will never be able to conceive of anything *not* in human terms. God must have a beard and must be jealous, irritable, vain, susceptible to flattery, stern and intolerant . . . in other words, a model earthly ruler. Catholics have gone far to propagate this nonsense, giving the people not only minor deities, but a great soaring mother as well, from whose womb God fell one day, turning the male doctrine of the Jews into a female doctrine, supplanting the classic love of virtue with a meekness which only the politicians of the Church could righteously disregard in the war on heretics.'

Dr. Praeger laughed loudly at this fierce attack on his faith, and when he answered he did so easily complacently, like a man who has the truth and can survey the errors of others with a geniality unknown to the insecure. 'I think you're a little hard on our Church,' he hummed softly. 'After all, it is no fault of the Church that the peasants have introduced some paganism into our rituals. Since we are all intelligent men without superstition, we can ignore the deviations of our less enlightened co-religionists and go to the centre of belief, to . . .'

Sophia and Philip seemed to agree that there was no continuation of personality after death, while the two doctors, if they avoided hell, as they piously hoped they would, believed in an eternity of comfort, each in a separate establishment, however: one clean and severe and filled with the austere music of fugues and oratorios; the other innocent and rich, like a mural of Fra Angelico.

'Mohammed was perhaps the most explicit biographer of heaven,' said Dr. Peverini. 'He located it as being above the seventh astronomic heaven, an enormous garden where everyone is well taken care of by handsome mamelukes and where each man will have seventy-two beautiful houris to serve his lust.'

'I wonder what the women will have?' asked Philip.

'The sense of virtue,' said Sophia. 'The happy knowledge that virtue is its own reward. Except, of course, they had no souls in those days.'

'Also, for some curious reason,' remarked Dr. Praeger, 'everyone will be allowed to drink the wine which on earth was forbidden while, as a final attraction, the prophet assures us that there will be no speeches given after the numerous banquets the blessed will attend.'

'In the meantime,' said Dr. Peverini, 'before the good reach heaven, they will have slept until Judgment Day, when, after three blasts on the trumpet by Israfel, the dead come alive again and are judged, passing over the bridge Al-sirat which spans hell, the good getting safely across, the bad and the unbelievers perishing.'

'Who defines good and bad?' asked Philip.

'No one. All that matters is whether one believes or not. The orthodox are good; the unbelievers or the Nonconformists are bad.'

'It makes it very simple,' said Philip.

'Oh, the pagans were imaginative,' said Dr. Praeger. 'And the Egyptians especially had many of the instincts which we associate with goodness. They thought the three cardinal requirements were a love of God, a love of virtue and a love of man.'

'And Yeats had a theory the soul left the body at a certain fixed angle in every case,' said Philip, wanting to make some comment.

'Who?' asked Dr. Praeger. And by the time Philip had done justice to the memory of Willian Butler Yeats, the conversation had ceased to be general and had become particular, as Sophia and the archaeologists gossiped about other expeditions, various other diggings in Europe, the possible location of the lost tombs in the Valley of the Kings. Then the doctors excused themselves and went to their rooms, leaving Sophia and Philip alone in the small empty dining-room, illuminated by a single electric bulb which emphasized its squalor, revealed the crumbs on the floor which long caravans of ants were taking away.

'I wonder,' said Philip thoughtfully, 'why we are concerned with religion when we believe nothing ourselves.'

'Speak for yourself, Philip.'

'Do you believe that the entire universe is built around human beings? that the deeds of billions of unimportant men and women are carefully recorded and judged? that on the final date the whole structure will be dismantled and prizes given out?'

'Of course not. But I believe in the *fact* of the universe that we are part of a structure which never changes, though its component parts continually change. That, of course, is the ultimate level. Closer to man, however, I believe in our desires and the elements which shape those desires, and I think that each person knows his own balance, and I resent the messiahs who try to rearrange the elements of each man's nature to conform with some particular private vision of excellence.'

'But every society does precisely that, for its own protection.'

'To a degree. But some are less absurd and less tyrannical than others, while a messiah is always a fanatic, and his single vision must be every man's vision, and all opposition must be rooted out violently. The laws of a society, on the other hand, though invariably illogical, are fortunately more complex and often more lenient, since they are the work of many men and many ages, not the product of the divine madness of one lunatic and his political party.'

'Yet they keep appearing, don't they?' Philip sighed. 'I've often thought what a pleasant place the world would be if there were no great enthusiasts. How nice to have lived in the eighteenth century where, in a certain society at least, one could consider almost any problem without having continually to make reference to a doctrine. But there's nothing to be done about it. Free inquiry is unfashionable. Faith is the order of the day: Freud, Marx, Stalin, Jesus . . . every man can now wear a complete suit of doctrinaire armour. . . .' Getting rather drunk, he continued to denounce the new dark age until he had said all that he felt, pronounced very clearly his hatred of systems and programmes, of all selfless leaders and, far worse, of those vacuous professional followers who scurry like terrified sheep from pillar to post, from Communism to Catholicism, moaning softly, ecstatically, like rutting sheep in the spring, kept always in line by a sharp-toothed dog whose brutal presence is more than compensated for by the divine, aloof yet watchful presence of some good shepherd with his crook.

'And yet,' he said, growing more calm, 'I find myself continually vacillating between anger at the stupidity of the world and a desire to do something about it, on the one hand, and, on the other, a knowledge that man is small, of no concern, that all is forgotten, that life is brief, that pain is bad and pleasure good; and so, why act at all if action makes these short years unpleasant ones? If one loathes humanity, as I do, then isn't it illogical for one ever to want reputation, to accept the detestable world's estimate of virtue and to measure oneself accordingly? To love virtue for its own sake is vain, for virtue cannot exist except in relation to something else. Virtue alone at the bottom of a well is like a work of art never executed. And I want virtue more than anything: to be just, to serve, to be admired . . . yet I find men unbearable and I feel like a stranger when I walk the streets of their cities, hardly believing I have any relation to this race or to any member of it. I have loved no one. I have admired excellence but not men, as much as the two

167

can be disassociated. For instance, I venerate the work of Dante, but I would have hated the sweating, defecating, harassed, melancholy man – would have been unable to put up with his politics, his moods, his vanity. . . .'

Sophia looked at him strangely. 'I am surprised,' she said.

Philip, drunk now, laughed and said: 'Listening to music I feel at one with every man, ready to become absorbed in the main. Who is constant? I never know from one minute to the next what I truly think of anything or anyone, and what I just described in such noisy terms is only what I occasionally feel.'

'Then you must stop being a man.'

It took him several minutes to consider this statement. After several false starts, he said: 'You mean I should die?'

'That's one way, of course. The surest.' She smiled. 'But I didn't mean that for you. I meant that you should withdraw from what repels you, turn to something that does please you. Music. Ideas. Excellence. Perhaps even the vain schoolboy hunt for "first principles" or, better yet, you like the poetry, not the poet . . . then love the idea which is real, more real than the man who made it, who invented the stories long ago, almost before there were sufficient words to describe the sun and the wind and the earth, love and anger, virtue and wisdom. That's why I have spent my life among the ruins, reading history, learning, avoiding always men and women . . . not that I'm a recluse: far from it, but I never touch them and they never touch me.'

'But why do you tell me this?' said Philip perversely, deserting his own position to attack hers. 'Why do *you* try and touch me now?'

She flushed and looked away; but when she spoke her voice was as cool and impersonal as ever: 'Since I am mortal I must entertain policy to survive. To touch you may serve that policy.' She smiled. 'That was difficult to say. I was forced either to contradict what I had just told you, what I believe, or else risk offending you.'

'You don't offend me,' murmured Philip.

'I'm glad because, as you say, I tried to touch you for reasons which may not be entirely clear to myself.' She sighed. Then, in a different voice: 'But we have an adventure ahead of us.'

'What is that?'

'Something I wish to find out, to see. A rumour I have heard, and the real reason for my coming to El Farhar.'

'A new ruin?'

'No, an old prophet.'

'What does he say?'

'The coming of the Messiah,' said Sophia. 'And I shouldn't be at all surprised if he weren't right. This is the time. I feel it . . . like a sudden silence in a room full of people.'

'That would be the end,' said Philip softly.

The next day he was ill and the hot sun made his head ache. Several times while they were wandering about the excavation, he thought that he might be sick to his stomach and, recollecting now some of the things he had said in last night's exalted alcoholic mood, he writhed inwardly, wondering how he could have been such a fool.

He kept to the shade of the quonset hut with Dr. Peverini, in the stifling but, happily, dark room while Sophia and Dr. Praeger mingled with the workmen in the trench in front of the colonnade.

'Would you like a little something to drink?' asked Dr. Peverini sympathetically.

'Just water,' said Philip in a weak voice. Unsteadily he went over to the water-cooler and helped himself. 'Everybody drinks too much in the tropics,' said the Swiss sternly. 'All the old British Colonial people used to preach heavy drinking . . . said it killed the bacteria. It may have killed a few bugs but their lives rotted in the heat and they all died young.'

'I drink very little,' protested Philip.

'You shouldn't drink at all in the heat,' Peverini continued.

'Have you found anything new today?' asked Philip, who would not have cared if they had found the Grail but wanted, rather, not to think of his pain, of the permanent damage he was sure he'd done himself.

'Nothing to compare with our Alexander. A few scarabs, but no royal cartouche yet.'

A scorpion suddenly clattered across the floor. Before Peverini could get to it the creature was gone into the blazing day. 'I hate bugs,' said Peverini.

'Oh, have you heard the rumour?'

'What rumour?'

'About the prophet here in El Farhar?'

Peverini nodded. 'There's always some nonsense like that

going on in an Arab town. I remember once, when we were digging in Syria, an old gentleman took it into his head that he was Mohammed, come to judge the world.'

'What happened to him?'

'He was crushed under his house when the townspeople pulled it down one night, while he was sleeping.'

Philip sighed. 'Perhaps he was.'

'Was what?'

'Mohammed come again.'

'In that case he would not have been killed so early in his mission. No, I'm afraid that all through this part of the world madness usually takes a messianic turn. In our country people become Napoleon or the Pope or St. Joan. Here they become the agent of Allah.'

'But this man is only a prophet.'

'So they tell me. I haven't seen him. Some of our boys have though. They're very excited, of course. Most of them believe him and they're practically counting the minutes till the day of judgment when all the infidels are sent to hell where they belong . . . hell being a place where the white men do their own digging.'

'You haven't seen him?'

Peverini shook his head. 'We've been too busy for that sort of thing. Except for our own people here, we have very little contact with the natives.'

'I think Miss Oliver and I are going to pay him a call tonight.'

'That should be interesting,' and Peverini smiled.

After dinner, accompanied by a guide and interpreter from the hotel, Philip and Sophia walked through the eccentrically twisted streets of the town. The moon had not yet risen but the stars were large and bright and in the open doorways lanterns shone, dull and yellow, flickering in the darkness; the high noise of Arab talk was in the streets as the sun-oppressed village of the day became secret and living and vital in the warm darkness when lovers met and thieves fell out, and murderers went about their bloody business, more like the slim shadows of palm trees than men by starlight and moonlight, near that shrunken summer river which was parent to them all.

Several children were playing a game of tag in the Street of

170

the Date Palm. They stopped their game and stood back in the shadows, silent, as the three strangers passed them. Then, in the Street of the Dead Camel, they paused before a tea-room where the men sat about inside, smoking water pipes, chewing hash-eesh and drinking numerous hot cups of tea. But then one looked up and saw the foreigners standing in the doorway; he scowled and turned to his companion. The foreigners moved on, walking more quickly. 'I always have a sense of danger when I walk about an Arab town at night,' said Philip in a low voice to Sophia, not wanting their grim-faced, elderly in-terpreter to hear.

'It *is* dangerous, I suppose,' she said equably, betraying no anxiety. 'But I always feel nothing will happen to me.'

'And I always feeling something will happen to me,' said Philip, realizing unhappily that the traditional attitudes of the two sexes were being reversed.

'I am more frightened in New York at night than I am here,' she said.

'I'm not. I know the danger there.'

'I know it here. But they won't bother us. They have no reason to. Besides, one is safer in a small town than a large one.'

'I have the white man's guilt,' said Philip nervously, as a man suddenly crossed the street in front of them, his robe making a rustling noise as he vanished into a dark doorway.

'Wait here,' said their guide, stopping suddenly before a building no different than any of the others in the Street of the Dead Camel. He knocked on the door. After a long wait it was opened by a small boy who stared suspiciously at them. The guide asked him a question in a low voice and the boy, im-pressed by his manner and the presence of the two white people in the street, opened the door and told them to enter.

They were left alone in a long room with an earth floor, lit by a single dim lantern. Piles of sandals were all about ... some carefully arranged in pairs on crude racks, others piled hap-hazardly at either end of the room which was filled with the unpleasant odour of imperfectly tanned leather.

'Is the prophet a cobbler?' asked Philip.

'I don't think so,' said Sophia, puzzled. 'I can't think where we are. They were not left long in doubt. The guide and the boy returned with the message that the prophet would see them, that he lived next door, and that they were in the house of his brother-in-law, Marouf the cobbler.

The boy was then paid off and they followed the guide across a slovenly courtyard where a goat was tethered, a rank, still figure in the yard. Behind the goat was a door through which they passed into a room where several silent veiled women sat playing dice. They did not look up as the strangers walked through their quarters to the next room, a bare, empty place. Here they sat cross-legged on a worn dirty rug, the only furniture in the room except for a battered lantern which spluttered and flickered, threatening to go out.

'He will join you shortly,' said the guide, sitting a few feet away from his temporary employers, as though to disassociate himself from them.

But he did not join them and, as always, Philip began to lose track of time. Had he not talked to Sophia he might have left the house with white hair, like the man who thought he'd been in a time machine for fifty years, only to discover that what had seemed fifty years was only five days.

'I hope he puts on a good show,' said Philip, with a spurious casualness.

'I do, too. I'm very curious about him. His claims, or so I've heard, are the most rational, the least suspect of them all.'

'And how many others have you visited like this?'

'A dozen. Some were Christ come again. Others were Israfel, trumpet and all. Still others were without precedent. All were quite insane ... not that insanity ever gave a mystic pause. But their madness was of such an obvious kind that they all lacked plausibility, even for the illiterate, for the most superstitious.'

'Do you seriously believe a man can predict the future?'

'No. That would be granting too great an importance to the human race we should like to despise. ... No, but I think there's a significance in the *fact* of a prophecy. One often knows intuitively when one is in personal danger ... or one often knows that there is something seriously wrong with the body even when there's no pain, when a doctor has found no trace of disease, has not located the cancer whose presence the body instinctively knows. Well, I have a theory it is the same with prophecy. Some men feel more sensitively than others that some great event is pending. Usually the less educated, more simple man is better able to divine what the world wants than the educated man who relies too much upon logic, upon an empirical method, missing the often quite simple need of the race which creates the Messiah or the leader as . . .'

'Tolstoy would say,' said Philip smiling, amused by the nonsense, willing to be impressed; it was like having a horoscope cast. He didn't believe but, for several moments at least, he was usually able to suspend scepticism, he recalled a remark Santayana had recently made to a friend of his in Rome: 'I have never been a mystic but I can imagine what it must be like.'

'Tolstoy or not,' said Sophia severely, 'every great event has been preceded by omens and prophecy and I believe that if one studies the portents the general shape of the immediate future becomes clear. If, all of a sudden, enough men are suddenly inspired with messianic visions then, very likely, there is one standing in the wings, ready to make his entrance at the proper time, a creation not of God's but of the old need of the race.'

Before Philip could dispute this, the prophet entered the room. He was a small wiry little man dressed in desert rather than town fashion, his head bare and his beard wild and tangled. His dark grey-streaked hair was long and uncombed. His face was more Arabic than Egyptian, with a large beak of a nose and black eyes; the skin was dark and wrinkled and the only modern touch to his Biblical austerity was a pair of steel-rimmed spectacles through which the bright black eyes, somewhat magnified, stared at the visitors.

His name was Abu Bekr.

'The prophet greets you,' said the guide, equalling the gravity of their host, who made a salaam and then seated himself before them on the rug, in the centre, Philip noticed with some interest, of a cabalistic design on the carpet. At first he was not sure if this was intentional or not but, when the prophet carefully pulled his robe within the circle, Philip was quite prepared for the carpet to ascend gently with all of them on it and float out the door to the land of Oz.

'We would like to hear the exact prophecy Abu Bekr has made,' said Sophia firmly to the interpreter, who repeated this sentence with various ceremonial flourishes to the old man who mumbled a brief reply.

'Abu Bekr would like to know *which* prophecy you want to hear.'

'Do you think he wants money?' asked Sophia of the interpreter.

'Certainly not. He is a holy man, inspired by Allah.'

'I wasn't sure. Ask him what prophecies he has made.'

The holy man's answer was a little longer than the preceding response. 'He wants to know why you've come to see him and what you want to hear.'

'We want to hear the truth and we have come to him to know the future. We have been told that he has had a revelation, that a new teacher is born.'

The prophet answered at length, his voice growing louder, more excited as he talked, gesturing with his hands, moulding the air as though creating out of nothing the figure of a divine child. When he finished, the interpreter began his translation, haltingly, confusedly.

'The world is an evil place today, more evil than ever before. The men kill each other with machines and the women go without veils and act like men in the streets and bazaars, while both men and women have deserted the faith and the angel of Allah stands at the gate of heaven looking down upon the earth, ready to blow the trumpet which will put out the sun and shake the stars out of the night and level the mountains, the cities in a sea of flame. But the angel's moment has not come for a new token of Allah's mercy has appeared in a land to the west, a village by the sea. He will grow up a holy man and he will teach the word of Allah to all the world. The people shall hold him in reverence and call him Saviour for he will teach them not to fear death.' The interpreter stopped and looked expectantly at Sophia.

'Why will they not fear death?' she asked, looking directly at Abu Bekr, ignoring the interpreter. 'What will he teach the people that will make them unafraid?'

The older man's answer to this was mumbled and he stared at the design in the rug while he talked, one hand wound in his beard. 'Abu Bekr says he does not know, that he is not the Saviour but only a man to whom part of the future has been revealed. He adds, from the Koran, that a true believer need not fear hell.'

'When was the Saviour born?'

The answer was prompt: 'Two months and nine days ago when the moon rose he was born and, the same night, an angel came to Abu Bekr in a dream and told him what had happened so that he might prepare himself and the men of his tribe for the cleansing.'

'Will he be a king or a warrior or a priest?' asked Sophia.

'He will be a man,' said Abu Bekr, rising; the audience was over.

All the way back to the hotel Sophia and Philip quarrelled; the interpreter was silent as he led the way down the Street of the Dead Camel to the town's centre and their hotel.

'You don't really believe such nonsense,' said Philip, obscurely angry at what they had heard.

'Of course I do.'

'But how can you? He's just an ignorant old man living in a godforsaken village on the Nile. He obviously knows the Old Testament and he's made up his mind that it might lessen the monotony of daily life if he were to become John the Baptist and attract as much attention as possible, which he seems to have done.'

'He knows the Koran, too,' said Sophia mildly. 'The first speech he made us was a paraphrase of Mohammed.'

'I'm still not impressed. I think it amusing and all that, like palmistry, but I refuse to take any of it seriously.'

'But he gave us an opportunity to check what he had said. He told us the exact day of the birth.'

'But didn't mention the place.'

'We can find out easily enough. I don't think he knew himself where the place was.'

'How can you find out?'

'There aren't too many sections of the world where the new moon rose in a country to the west, on the sea, on a day that we know.'

'A line of longitude is several thousand miles long. I'm sure that a town on that line will be easy to find. Yet even if you should discover that the old man meant Tacoma, Washington, it will probably be thirty years or more before the mission becomes known.'

'It's something to look forward to in our old age,' said Sophia, laughing softly in the dark.

'Why do you care so much?' asked Philip suddenly. 'Even if every word the old man said were true, what difference would it make?'

'A great deal to everyone.'

'There's nothing you can do to affect it, is there?'

'No. Of course not.'

'What would you do, if you *could* do something?'

'I would kill the child at birth,' said Sophia. 'But, of course, like Herod, I should fail. These things happen. No one can stop them from happening. We can only endure.'

CHAPTER EIGHT

'Welcome home, young man,' said Mr. Willys cheerily. 'How were the ruins? Hot work, isn't it? Archaeology, I mean.'

He was sitting up in bed, his thin grey hair combed, the head bandage removed and the torn ear nearly healed. He wore a Chinese dressing-gown of white silk with a blue dragon picked out in it.

'Very hot, and I'm glad to be back: the food was terrible. How have *you* been?'

'On top of the world.' Mr. Willys beamed. 'I can never thank you enough for introducing me to Mrs. Peabody. I never imagined any woman could be so wonderful. She knows everything, literally everything . . . in her field, that is. It's been a real education, I can tell you.'

'Is she getting on with her book?'

'Oh, she's not *writing* here. She's just doing field-work. Collecting data, that's all. She will later dictate the entire work in five days into a tape recorder.'

'Prodigious,' said Philip, sitting down beside the bed in such a way that the afternoon sun was not in his eyes. 'Then you're taking a more cheerful view of things, I suppose.'

'I certainly am,' said Mr. Willys. 'I feel better than I have in years.'

'You've stopped all of that nonsense about wanting to kill yourself?'

'Well . . . yes and no.' Mr. Willys suddenly looked as crafty as his open pudding face would allow. 'If you mean have I given up hope of being able to kill myself, I will say yes, I have. I just don't have the courage to do it.'

'Well, that's good news. You probably won't be staying here much longer.'

'No. Not much longer.' He smiled craftily.

'I'm afraid I don't understand you.'

'Can I trust you?' Mr. Willys narrowed his tiny eyes until they disappeared.

'Of course you can.' Philip was curious.

'You'll not try to interfere in any way ... if I tell you?'

'I promise.'

'I know I shouldn't tell you, but I can't help it. I *must* talk to someone, and you're the logical person since, without knowing it, of course, you brought the whole wonderful thing about.'

'What wonderful thing?'

'Fay Peabody.'

'Well? *Is* she a wonderful thing?' Philip had a vision of Mr. Willys and Mrs. Peabody being married in a Hollywood chapel full of lilies of the valley ... providing, of course, Mr. Peabody had presented no legal difficulty, if there was still a Mr. Peabody to present difficulties. But his guess was wrong.

'You can take it from me, young man, that she's a mighty bright little lady, with her heart in the right place. She's consented to do it.'

'To marry you?' Philip did not want immediately to give up his dream.

'No, to administer the poison. We've had a number of long talks and she's consented to do for me what no other person of my acquaintance would do and what, as you know, I couldn't do for myself. As a matter of fact, she's quite thrilled by the whole thing.'

'You had no trouble in persuading her?'

'A great deal ... especially at first. She had all sorts of scruples, but when she saw how serious I was and how much I needed help she took pity on me. She has a heart as big as all outdoors.'

'And she isn't afraid?'

'At first, she was. But since then she has steeled herself to the task ... especially when I reminded her who she was: the greatest murder mystery writer in America. You know what President Roosevelt said about her book, *Red, White and Blue Murder*.'

'He said it was a swell yarn.'

'That's right. I never cared much for him, by the way. Did you?'

'I hate all politicians this year,' said Philip. 'But how is she going to do . . . what you want her to do?'

'I don't know.' He sighed. 'Isn't it wonderful? I don't know how or when . . . only why . . . the motive, as Mrs. Peabody would say.'

'You must be scared to death,' said Philip tactlessly, carried away by the novelty of the situation.

'I've never enjoyed life more . . . if that doesn't sound inconsistent. To know that any day now it will be over for good. . . . Well, it's far better than I bargained for, believe me. There was a spell last week when I thought I was going to go on for ever like this, without relief.'

'Is it to be a perfect crime or will it resemble suicide?'

'She hasn't told me and I haven't asked. I don't want to pester her. I mean, what if she should suddenly refuse? No, sir, I'm not asking any questions. I wouldn't interfere for a million! I figure that little lady has done pretty well in this field, the writing end of it, anyway, and I don't want to put my oar in.'

Philip wondered whether or not Mr. Willys was quite sane. Perhaps the heat and the fat and the near-suicide had made him subject to hallucinations, made his dream of death seem nearly realized. Presuming that not a word of what he had said was true, Philip decided to humour him.

'I should think Mrs. Peabody would be nervous, even if *you* aren't. After all, you want to die. But she, I suppose, wants to live, and she is, you know, risking her very valuable life to satisfy a whim of yours.'

'I should hardly call my wish to die a whim, and although I may not have been very much in my life I think I should tell you that, as a citizen, there was a time when I was very highly regarded in Philadelphia: I was a director of the Quaker Greeting Card Company, before the depression.'

'I didn't imply your death was a matter of no importance. I only meant that it would be a real tragedy if Mrs. Peabody were to be caught.'

'Fay Peabody caught? Never! Even though this is her first

178

attempt at this sort of thing, she is a complete master of both method and theory. I wouldn't worry about her.'

'But I do,' said Philip. 'For all her competence, she is still only a theoretician.'

'Well, have no fear, Mr. Warren. *I* have none.'

'I hope she pulls it off.'

'I'm sure she will.'

'When do you think . . . it will happen?'

'Some time during the next week, I suppose. I haven't given it much thought.'

'Poison?'

'I believe so. The only stipulation I made was that it should happen so quickly I couldn't be aware of it until it was all over.'

'Sounds like poison then.'

'I should think so. To help her, I've taken to ordering enormous meals . . . all my favourite dishes: not that I have much appetite, but I was something of a gourmet in my younger days, so I've got that manager working his tail off. Tonight he's promised a *sauce béarnaise* made with his own hands. He's an amateur chef, he tells me. . . . Who knows *what* may be in that sauce?'

'Who knows, indeed?' said Philip, rising. 'I hope everything works out for you.'

'Thank you very much. You realize, of course, that what I've told you is in the strictest confidence. You won't repeat a word of it, will you? Not even to Mrs. Peabody?'

'Of course not.'

He did not see Sophia that evening until they joined Mrs Peabody for dinner; he had wanted to discuss the whole matter with her, to try and determine what, if Mr. Willys *had* told him the truth, should be done. Although he knew of course that he himself would probably do nothing since it was no concern of his what Mrs. Peabody and Mr. Willys chose to do with the earthly residence of Mr. Willys's soul.

Sophia was in a good mood. She had spent the day across the river near the Valley of the Kings and she had bought a contemporary cartoon of Ikhnaton which one of the natives had found the week before in the wreckage of an incompleted tomb. She showed them the fragment of plaster on which a cruelly sophisticated artist had, in a few strokes, sketched the long head and heavy-lidded eyes, the full mouth and sharp chin of the great monotheist, gratuitously adding whiskers, revealing Pharaoh as he looked when he had not shaved for a week.

'What a fool he must have seemed to his contemporaries,' said Sophia, putting the sketch back into her purse.

'What a fool he was,' said Philip. 'From a practical point of view. He was given a first-rate country to govern and he wrecked it, all for the love of God.'

'What did you say his name was?' asked Mrs. Peabody, liverish in a gown of fever-red with garnets at her throat.

'Ikhnaton,' said Sophia. 'He ruled over three thousand years ago.'

'Such a long time!' mused Mrs. Peabody, toying with her fork. 'You say he was a Christian?'

'No, Mrs. Peabody. He tried to replace the old religion with a form of sun worship which various authorities have ever since the nineteenth century at least, found singularly prophetic and attractive; actually, he was a mystic and he did the usual amount of harm those people do. His theology was soon forgotten, but the damage survived him, as it always does.'

'"And the good is oft interred with their bones,"' quoted Mrs. Peabody, under the impression she was reciting a sacred text from the Bible. 'How sad it all is! I am sure he must have been very fine. The face you showed us was sensitive; I can tell; I know a thing or two about faces. When I was doing field-work for *The Dark Pullman Car Murder.* . . .' As she told them about her research, Philip examined her narrowly for any sign of anxiety or guilt, but she seemed much as ever and he decided that Mr. Willys had indeed gone mad with the heat. In fact, the authoress was uncommonly animated tonight and dressed with more than usual care; she had even given her hair a fresh rinse, and it was now a lifeless, frizzled maroon by artificial light. When she had finished discussing faces, Philip asked her how her work was coming.

'Very well, all things considered: I don't care too much for the heat, you know . . . so I've taken to wearing an old picture hat with a heavy muslin veil . . . stuffy, but at least it protects me from the harsh rays of the sun.'

'You've done a good deal of work, though?'

'Ah, Mr. Warren, that is something I can never tell until the moment I start to dictate. Then, if I have done my task well, the book takes form splendidly and another Fay Peabody work is born. But, if I have a false start, I know that I have failed of my goal, that I have done insufficient spade-work, and so, willy-nilly, I am driven back into the field. At the moment my guess is that my rate of progress has been average. I spent the morning with the manager studying the train schedules. That sort of thing is important, very important. How many a work of imagination has failed because of faulty verisimilitude!'

'How many indeed,' echoed Philip and Sophia, in excellent humour.

'Get the facts, I tell young people who are contemplating a career in the field of detection writing. That, and plenty of elbow grease, spell success.'

There was very little to say after this until the dessert, an elaborate Arab affair of crushed nuts and thin pastry, was put before them; then, just as Fay Peabody, eyes glistening, had brought a large forkful half-way to her thin lips, Philip asked her how Mr. Willys had been. She was obviously caught between delaying her answer for several awkward, perhaps even suspicious, moments while she chewed the longed-for confection, and disappointing her salivary glands by delaying the anticipated treat to answer him. She exercised her will. She put the fork down, swallowed hard and, the dessert still untasted, said: 'Poor Mr. Willys. I fear he is morbidly inclined.'

'He has very little to live for,' said Sophia.

'Is not life itself enough, a precious gift?' Mrs. Peabody chewed contentedly now, her dentures making odd little clicking noises.

'I should have thought that you, of all people, Mrs. Peabody, might have sympathized with Mr. Willys's attitude,' said Philip, watching her face. She was admirably controlled, however.

'Come, come, Mr. Warren. Merely because I have devoted my life to the problems of detection does not mean that I have, along the way, jettisoned that moral code which I learned long years ago at my mother's knee in Cleveland. Quite the contrary. My fieldwork has dramatically demonstrated to me that crime is bad.'

Philip waited a moment before he answered, not sure whether she had completed her statement or not; she had.

'I have never looked at it that way,' he said humbly. 'But I'm sure you're right. Still, a suicide is not precisely a crime.'

'It is considered a major crime by both State and Church, far worse, morally, than murder. As a device in novels of detection, it is only to be deplored. It is not fair to the reader. Fortunately, most authors do not use it as a device, recognizing that it is not Fair Play.'

'But I should say that Mr. Willys could only hope for death to come quickly of its own accord or else to pray that someone will murder him.'

The effect of this statement convinced Philip that Mr. Willys had been rational after all, that Mrs. Peabody was indeed contemplating murder. The startled expression that had fluttered across her soft, ordinary face was succeeded by a debonair smile, the sort movie heroines wear when they want to dispel the suspicions of another character, yet wish to remind the audience that, at the same time, they are involved in some noisome plot and that their smiles and gentle words are quite as false as their pearls. Fussing with her bodice, as if fingering those same (invisible) pearls, Mrs. Peabody declared herself guilty when she said: 'I shouldn't imagine he was in very good health ... with all that weight.'

'He might have apoplexy any day,' said Philip, wondering what he should do next, whether to interfere or not.

'He has a bad heart, I believe,' said Mrs. Peabody, finishing her dessert.

'Perhaps nature will take care of him soon and solve his problems once and for all.'

'I pity him,' said Fay Peabody as they left the table. She then excused herself, murmuring that an authoress's work was never done. Sophia and Philip wandered out into the garden where they discussed his discovery.

'Now the problem is what to do.'

'But why do anything?' Sophia sounded surprised. They stopped walking and stood in the middle of the path; palm trees hid the hotel.

'I think she should be stopped.'

'Why? For one thing it's no business of yours and, for another, she's doing a good deed. If I were tempted to do a good deed, which I am not usually, I might have taken on the assignment myself.'

'I'm afraid I must seem conventional to you,' said Philip, more from a sense of duty than from any real conviction.

Sophia laughed. 'It's also the funniest thing I've ever heard! I could have sworn that woman wouldn't have been able to kill a fly.'

'That's the main thing that bothers me. Suppose she is caught?'

'Who will catch her? The authorities here aren't going to bother about the death of a fat man whom no one knows, a semi-invalid.'

'Your attitude seems rather cold-blooded.'

'Then let's go and tell the police.'

'We can't do that either,' said Philip, confused, in an agony of spurious conscientiousness.

'Let's wait and see,' said Sophia. 'Perhaps she won't go through with it . . . She may give up, you know.'

But Fay Peabody did not give up. She did not lose her nerve. And, even when the situation looked darkest, she was able to draw strength from the knowledge that she was, after all, the incomparable Fay Peabody, peerless in the world of detection writing, a woman whose field-work was a legend throughout the civilized world.

The first attempt on the life of Mr. Willys was made at breakfast the next day. Philip first heard of it when, somewhat late, he came downstairs to find Mr. Koyoumdjian despondent, in what our grandparents called 'a blue funk'.

'That guy Willys ought to be in an institution like a hospital.'

'What's the matter? Has something happened?' Philip's hands grew cold, as though he himself were the murderer.

'He got sick to his stomach after breakfast. The local sawbones is upstairs giving him the word. I told him I wanted Willys moved to the hospital, but the doc said no dice. He stays here. Next thing he'll probably die on me.'

Philip thought this very likely, but he did not say so. 'Where is Miss Oliver?'

'Up early and gone across the river for the day.'

'And Mrs. Peabody?'

'She's out in the garden. Says she wants to do some flower arrangements for the dining-room. The gardener will be fit to be tied, but the customer is always right, like they say.'

Mrs. Peabody, wearing a straw picture hat, gave a start when

183

Philip, coming up behind her as she was leaning over some purple blossoms with a pair of garden shears, said: 'Good morning.'

'You startled me!' she said, dropping the shears. Philip got them for her; then, as though suddenly exhausted, she sat down heavily on a near-by bench. 'The heat,' she sighed.

'Mr. Willys is sick this morning.'

'I should really look in on him. I plan to take him some of these gorgeous blooms after I do the downstairs arrangements; I hate untidy bouquets.'

'Mrs. Peabody, do you think it wise? Do you really feel you should risk your own life just to oblige Mr. Willys?'

Mrs. Peabody, now very pale indeed, dropped the shears again; this time neither made a move to pick them up. 'What do you mean?' she asked, in a voice so tiny that had he not been sitting beside her, he might have thought a bee had flown by, or a cicada had whirred somewhere in the green foliage.

'I'll be frank with you, Mrs. Peabody: Mr. Willys once made very nearly the same proposition to me that he made to you . . . only I refused to be a party to it. You, on the other hand, were taken in. I don't know why, and I don't really care. Whether it was out of curiosity or out of a real desire to help him, makes little difference. The facts are the same in either case: you agreed to murder him.' Philip paused.

'Mr. Willys told you this . . . fantastic story?' She got a grip on herself again: the panic of the moment was now succeeded by nonchalance; she even picked up the shears and put them back into the half-filled flower-basket.

Philip nodded; then, pressing his last bit of advantage, he declared: 'And I also know that you poisoned him this morning at breakfast, but that something went wrong.'

Mrs. Peabody rose with great dignity and said: 'Follow me.' She led him to the far end of the garden where, in the shade of a gnarled eucalyptus tree, she said: 'Since we are now completely alone and there are no witnesses I will be candid, although I vowed my lips would remain sealed until the day I died, but since the plot is already getting tangled and you are, whether you like it or not, involved quite deeply, I will confess to you that I took on this perilous job and that I mean to see it through, come hell or high water! My motives were, and are, of the highest. My method has, to my own amazement, been faulty. I erred. I blundered. I took a hypodermic needle early this morning and filled it with a colourless, tasteless poison of local origin which I inserted into the soft-boiled eggs he had ordered for breakfast. The chemist had informed me, prior to my purchase, that the dose was not only lethal, but that it would kill a host of rats. It failed, however, to kill Mr. Willys. From my room I could hear the doctor talking to him, and I gather he was only midly nauseated.'

'Which is probably just as well for you, Mrs. Peabody.'

'Let me tell you, Mr. Warren, that should you attempt to go to the police you would only be laughed at since, obviously, I would deny having confessed to you while Mr. Willys would never testify against me.'

'I have no intention of going to the police. I was just reminding you of the risk involved, should you try again.'

'I will take that risk, Mr. Warren. Rome was not built in a day, you know. I am not discouraged. I shall strike again.'

'I don't see how you have the nerve,' said Philip wonderingly; but then one look into the bright little eyes of Fay Peabody convinced him that she was a fanatic, an artist. She would not be stopped by anyone until her demon was satisfied, until Mr. Willys was dead.

'It proves,' she said, in an ordinary voice, 'that one can't rely on foreign products. If I'd had more time, I'm sure I would have been able to try the poison out on some creature to see if it were efficacious, but, as you can see, I was forced to rely on the word of a native chemist and all my plans "gang aft a-gley", as Bobbie Burns would say . . . like a false start on my dictaphone . . . yet when I fail to get the beginning right, I go back into the field with renewed vigour and I have never, never failed to bring home the bacon,' she said slowly, fixing Philip's eyes with her own serious ones, loose flap of the muslin veil now shadowing her left cheek and eye, giving her a curiously slovenly air.

'Well, I won't interfere, Mrs. Peabody . . . beyond saying that I think that what you're doing is dangerous and that the morality of the thing is confused, to say the least.'

'I will do my duty as I see it and, though I appreciate your concern, I can . . .' Suddenly she stopped talking and for a moment Philip was afraid she was going to faint. Quite pale, she made for the bench and, with one last spurt of strength, she got to it and crumpled, her hand to her heart and her eyes wild with fear.

'What in God's name is the matter?' asked Philip, startled, positive that she was having a heart attack.

'The hypodermic,' she whispered, growing paler by the instant. 'I left it in the pantry.'

'Good Lord!' Then: 'You must get it back immediately. Perhaps they haven't found it yet.'

'It's been there several hours. How *could* I? How could I have blundered so? The plan was perfect. Oh!' She moaned into the muslin veil which now completely covered her face.

'There's no use in your losing your nerve now, Mrs. Peabody.

'Go to the pantry and see if the needle is there. After all, Mr. Willys isn't dead yet.'

'That's right.' This thought comforted her and she emerged for a moment from behind the veil. 'We must hide the evidence.'

'*You* must hide the evidence, not I. I'm not going to be one of your – what do you call them? – accomplices . . .'

'After the fact; only there's legally no fact at all. Come to the pantry.'

The hypodermic was where she had left it and, since there were no servants in sight, she hid the weapon in the flower-basket; then with something of her old assurance, she went into the lobby accompanied by Philip.

'Ah, flowers,' exclaimed Mr. Koyoumdjian brightly. 'I hope you'll take some up to Mr. Willys. Cheer him up. He's been asking for you.'

'Poor dear man! Has the doctor gone?'

'He just now left. He's getting to know Mr. Willys very well . . . it was him who patched him up after he tried to take a powder.' Philip was pleased to find that the manager could make an occasional mistake in his well-loved vernacular.

'What did he say was wrong with our Mr. Willys?'

'Nothing much . . . just stomach trouble. He picked up a bug in Cairo, I wouldn't be surprised.'

'I have just the medicine for him,' said Mrs. Peabody, marching off, her flower-basket swinging jauntily on her arm.

The second attempt on the life of Mr. Willys was made during the night when his bed collapsed, the iron cross-piece

186

which held up the mosquito-netting missing his head by several inches. Philip, when he heard the noise, thought to himself: 'That's done it'; then he went back to sleep, refusing to be even a witness to Mrs. Peabody's plot.

In the morning, on his way to breakfast, he looked in to see what damage had been done. The room was the same as ever, however, and Mr. Willys was sitting up in bed, gravely sipping water through a straw.

'What was all the racket last night?'

'The bed,' said Mr. Willys. 'It collapsed. Gave me quite a shock. My heart's pounding so that I can barely breathe.'

'Mrs. Peabody?'

'Mrs. Peabody.'

'She's failed twice.'

'I know,' said Mr. Willys gloomily. 'It's getting on my nerves. I had no wish to be hurt, you know. I can't bear pain. The thought makes me quite ill . . . and the suspense! I tell you I don't know when or where she'll strike next.'

'Make her stop.'

'Oh, I couldn't do that. She's gone to such trouble. It would hardly be fair.'

'I don't see that fairness has anything to do with a situation like this.'

'Perhaps not. Actually I still want her to pull it off . . . if only she weren't so damned sloppy. First of all, I knew those eggs were poisoned. She left enormous holes in the shells and they tasted god-awful, but I ate them, anyway, and got sick. Then, last night, the bed caved in. How she managed that, I'll never know. I suppose she loosened the ton piece while I was taking a bath. I must say she's ingenious. What a mind that little lady has – like a steel trap!'

'One which won't close, though. If you weren't a willing victim, she would be in jail now.'

'Well, we must remember that it's all quite new to her: there's a lot of difference between writing about something and actually doing it.'

'I could do a better job than she's done,' said Philip scornfully.

'You wouldn't take it on, would you? I'd be very grateful . . . I could make it worth your while. You can name your price, within reason, of course.'

'No, I'm afraid you're stuck with Mrs. Peabody. It's a little like the medical profession . . . you engaged her and until *she* consents to call in specialists it would be most unethical for you to get someone to replace her.'

'This is *not* a joke.'

'I realize that it isn't, but there's nothing I can do about it except tell the police you want Mrs. Peabody to kill you and that she's trying to, without much success. No, I'm afraid you will just have to trust to luck and the "Fay Peabody Method".'

'You're not very encouraging.'

'Now, why don't you be sensible and tell her to stick to her writing while you go to Switzerland and lose weight.'

'I can't. . . . Glands.'

'Then take shots.'

'They don't work on me. No, my mind is made up. Yet I don't wonder what she'll do next.'

'Probably drown you in your bath.'

Mr. Willys shuddered. 'I hate the idea of drowning: strangling to death, that's all it is. Well, I'll keep the bathroom door locked. She won't be able to get in . . . it bolts on the inside. Besides, we have an agreement to the effect that the business must be done in an instant.'

'She's a desperate woman, though; remember that. She's failed twice. Rather than fail a third time, she's quite capable of losing her head and setting fire to you.'

'Oh, she wouldn't do that.' He was alarmed, and Philip hoped that the fear of pain might yet force him to change his mind. 'I'm sure the next time she'll be able to do it, easily, without any fuss.'

'I think you're optimistic,' said Philip darkly, and he left the room and went downstairs to join Sophia and Mrs. Peabody, who were already at breakfast.

'Did you hear the noise last night?' asked Sophia, cool in green, unlike Mrs. Peabody, who looked more dowdy than ever, tired as well, her eyelids red and granulated from fatigue. Her hands shook as she drank the bitter black coffee.

'Mr. Willys told me his bed collapsed on him in the middle of the night.'

'Poor Mr. Willys,' said Sophia maliciously. 'So many things seem to happen to him.'

'He's very unlucky, poor man,' said Philip, watching the murderess *manquée* out of the corner of his eye: she appeared not to be listening.

'One could almost believe in a malignant destiny. How could one man have so many things happen to him?'

'Foul play?' suggested Philip.

'It's possible. But who would want to hurt poor, harmless Mr. Willys?'

'Mr. Willys himself.'

'Possibly. But no one else. The whole thing is so strange.' Then, having made Mrs. Peabody suffer for her projected sin, they changed the subject and spoke of the trip they were to make that day to some tombs near the Valley of the Kings and, to their great surprise, Mrs. Peabody asked if she might accompany them that afternoon because: 'I've never done those tombs . . . the ones where the nobles were buried.' And so, since there was no polite way to refuse her, she was allowed to join the expedition.

Ater leaving the hotel, they went down the steps to the river where a rowboat and their dragoman were waiting. A number of naked boys stared curiously at the women who refused, pink-faced, to stare back. Then, crossing the slow, warm river, they passed a sand island where donkeys were being raced to the delight of a large group of men. How the donkeys had got there and why they were racing one another Philip could never learn, for the dragoman, though he spoke English fluently, invariably expressed himself in such cryptic phrases that Philip preferred not to ask him questions. He was necessary as an interpreter, but that was all for, among the ruins, Sophia took over; even the dragoman had finally come to recognize her authority.

Mrs. Peabody was silent all the way across the Nile. When they got into their horse-drawn carriage on the other side, she said she disliked horses, but except for that single observation she made no further comment or objection as they drove off in the heat, across the dusty countryside which stretched, dark green and grey and white, to the all-white hills with their tree-less cliffs and level summits where, hidden away, was the valley in which the great kings were buried, deep in the soft limestone. But they did not drive to that valley; instead, they drove along the road to the two Colossi of Amenhotep III, serene and immense, looking across the river to the sun and to the living city. Thebes-Living and Thebes-Dead were the names by which the east and the west banks were known to the natives. And this was indeed a dead city, thought Philip, looking about the ruins, the funeral temples, the small sun-baked villages built on the foot-hills so that the Nile, when it flooded, would not wash them away . . . a place all desolate and strange, a bleak land inhabited by a listless people, victim of that same sun which the child of the Colossus Amenhotep had wanted all the world to worship, the glowing origin and the scourge of life. As they drove past one of the villages, a warren of adobe huts on a be-tunnelled rise of white porous rock, a figure, tall and spare in flapping robes, stood in the hot wind looking at them, silhouetted against the glowing sky; then, with an abrupt gesture, he unfurled a piece of cloth which snapped and rippled in the wind like a banner, like a signal to the ghosts that strangers were approaching their tombs.

'What can he be doing?' asked Philip.

'Beating a rug,' said Fay Peabody; it was her first remark since they had got into the carriage, and both Sophia and Philip looked at her with greater respect than they would ordinarily have done had she been conversing as usual. The rug theory prevaled. Mrs. Peabody had, with one sure phrase, created her own atmosphere, and Egypt flattened out, receded, became a back-drop, and this was only fieldwork, after all.

At the base of the largest foot-hill, their carriage stopped in the shade of a withered acacia and the explorers got out. Before them, as though carved by the tributaries of a long dead river, were a series of small ravines cut a dozen feet into the soft rock and all connecting, like the design of a delta fashioned in the stone, a web containing the tombs of the very rich, those nobles who had once adorned the vanished capital across the river.

The day passed pleasantly. They visited many of the tombs, small cheerful little rooms cut in stone with bright wall paintings and tiny chapels. The colours were new and fresh, preserved by the dry heat; and they read in pictures about the lives of the dead and looked at representations of their country houses, children, friends, and all the activities of three thousand years before.

Mrs. Peabody took many notes. She spoke very little, but what she did say was to the point. They were, Philip decided, seeing the true Fay Peabody, the tireless workman, the master craftswoman giving her fans the best that was in her.

Once when Sophia and the dragoman were quarrelling over a figure of Osiris, Philip got Mrs. Peabody off in one corner of the tomb of the Second Chief Accountant of the Royal Household and asked her in a low voice why the last attempt on the life of Mr. Willys had failed.

'A miscalculation. I miscalculated the position of the cross-piece,' she said bitterly, implying she would rather not have made this admission.

'But it was clearly in the centre of the bed. I don't see how you could have expected it to drop anywhere except in the middle of the mattress or on his stomach.'

'It was weighted,' she said, looking at him with undisguised malevolence. 'It was so arranged that when he turned over the entire thing would drop, from a considerable height, on to his head. Had it done so, he would no longer be with us. I had not counted, however, on his head being on the very edge of the bed. The odds were ten to one it would be close to the centre where the weight did fall, missing him.'

'I think it's getting on his nerves, these false attempts of yours.'

'Getting on *his* nerves!' She glared at him. 'Do you think it a picnic for me? Do you? Do you imagine I enjoy making a fool of myself before all the world? . . . or at least before you and Mr. Willys. You seem to forget that I embarked on this project for completely selfless reasons. I have twice failed of my object . . . I admit that. But I hardly feel that others should criticize me for not being able to do easily what they would never dare attempt to do in the first place. I want it clearly understood, by both you and Mr. Willys, that I will brook no criticism of my methods, *and* if I do not have the fullest co-operation and confidence of Mr. Willys at least, I may be forced to withdraw altogether. Do you understand?'

'Perfectly.'

'You will repeat this to Mr. Willys?'

'I will.'

'What time is it, by the way?'

'Four o'clock.'

'Ah! Then you will probably be spared the onerous task of repeating what I have said, for, unless some unforeseen contingency has again arisen, Mr. Willys is dead.'

Here, among the tombs, the announcement lost much of its inherent awfulness.

'But how . . .'

She would not answer his question, though. Instead, she un-pinned her veil, shutting out the world with muslin.

Mr. Koyoumdjian was in a rage. 'I'm going to have him moved today. I won't have him here another minute. The servants are thinking somebody has got the evil eye and they won't go near him. He's jinxed.'

'You mean Mr. Willys?' asked Philip.

'I certainly do.'

'Has . . . something happened to him?' asked Fay Peabody, one hand on the corner of the desk as though to steady herself.

'Asthma!' Mr. Koyoumdjian moaned. 'He nearly choked to death. The doctor's with him. I'm going to get him out of this hotel if it's the last thing I do.'

Sophia looked at Philip and smiled. Mrs. Peabody, without a word, went to her room.

'What do you think she could have done to him?' murmured Philip, as he and Sophia followed Mrs. Peabody up the stairs.

'I haven't any idea. Do you think she tried again?'

'Oh yes. She told me so this afternoon. She intimated that he would be dead when we got back.'

'Poor woman. She must be desperate. I hope she doesn't lose her head and blow up the entire hotel.'

Mrs. Peabody did not lose her head, however, Instead she came down to dinner even more carefully dressed than usual, her garnets complemented by a double strand of pearls which were dingy enough, small enough, to be real. She was obviously aware that both Philip and Sophia knew her scheme and she carried the dinner off as well as possible under the circumstances, discussing fluently and instructively the large world of detective writers and readers among whom she was still a figure of the greatest magnitude, a thought which obviously sustained her now in her hour of defeat.

During dinner, the manager entered with the latest bulletin: 'He's going in the morning. The doctor says he shouldn't be moved, but when I told him I couldn't have any more of this monkey business in my hotel he said they'd send a car over tomorrow and take him to the hospital. I've never seen anything like it. My staff is just about ready to leave. They say a demon is loose in the hotel.'

'Is he feeling better?' asked Mrs. Peabody, with an air of gentle concern.

'I think so. He stopped choking ... looks weak, though. Doesn't want to leave, of course, but I had the doctor tell him he would have to go in the morning.'

'He's certainly an unlucky creature,' said Sophia.

'I sure wish he'd be unlucky somewhere else,' said the manager.

In the lobby, after dinner, Philip had another chance to talk with Mrs. Peabody. She tried to avoid him, but he was too quick for her. 'What went wrong?' he asked.

'I would rather not discuss it.'

'You won't try again, will you?'

'It's no business of yours,' she snapped. 'But to satisfy your curiosity, no, I *won't* try again. Now, if you'll excuse me . . .'

'Do tell me what you did this last time.'

'I placed a certain deadly, air-polluting poison in the pistils of a large number of flowers which I then set about his room so that, in a few hours, the atmosphere would be completely malignant. I had not, however, taken into account the fact that Mr. Willys had an allergy to all flowers and that he nearly choked to death before they could be removed.'

'Frankly, Mrs. Peabody, I'm astonished you failed. I can't imagine anything simpler than killing someone who wants to die in a country where there probably would never be an investigation.'

'I should like to see *you* try it.'

'People do it every day. How can you explain it? Thousands of murders go undetected every year ... people get away with it all the time. I can't understand why you, with every advantage, can't do as well.'

'Perhaps because *I* am not a criminal,' said Mrs. Peabody; and she went upstairs.

'How did she do it this time?' asked Sophia, when the other was gone.

'Poisoned flowers . . . to contaminate the air.'

'She's much too subtle. What went wrong?' Philip told her and she laughed. 'If only her fans could see her now.'

That night, before going to bed, Philip visited Mr. Willys. He looked the same as ever, but his thin voice was more weak than usual and talking seemed to tire him.

'It's all over with me,' he said. 'She won't try again.'

'Just as well. I was always against the idea.'

'I can't imagine her quitting now, though; after wrecking my nerves and health she refuses to finish the job . . . it isn't fair. It just isn't fair.'

'I'm sure you'll be well in no time.'

'I expect to be an invalid for the next twenty years. I can hardly move as it is. The strain of getting out of bed and going to the bathroom gives me such palpitations that I can hardly bear it. Oh, it's so terrible,' and he moaned plaintively, his eyes tight shut, as though to blot the world out for ever.

'It nearly worked last time,' said Philip illogically, hoping that this would please him, this reference to the plan which had failed; it did not.

'The fool . . . the incompetent fool!' Mr. Willys turned on his former idol with a ferocity made all the more frightening because his voice was so weak, so incapable of bearing the passion of a denunciation. 'Any half-wit Arab could have done better, if he thought there might be a plug nickel in it for him; but the brilliant Fay Peabody, given every chance in the world, flops. She could have asked me about the flowers. But no, she waited until I'd gone to the bathroom, then she put them all around the room like a funeral parlour. It was half an hour before I could get enough breath to shout for help.'

'Do you think that anyone suspected the flowers were poisoned?'

'How? They were thrown out right away, while I was strangling. I suppose if she had put a few more in the room, nature might have done the trick.'

'Did she have any excuse to make?'

'She attacked me for having an allergy. Said it was the most ridiculous thing she'd ever heard of, that if she'd put it in a story nobody'd believe it.'

'I hope you told her off.'

'Don't worry! I said that if she'd ever . . .' He began to wheeze alarmingly, shaking the bed, fat rippling dangerously as he gagged, tried to get his breath. When finally he did, he was pale and exhausted, too sick to acknowledge Philip's sympathy.

The next morning, refusing the litter which the doctor had

194

sent over, Mr. Willys dressed himself and slowly descended the stairs, supported on each side by a fragile native boy. It was the first time that Philip had seen Mr. Willys on his feet, and he was surprised to find that he was a short man, broader than he was tall, with ludicrously small hands and feet. He wore a crumpled white suit and a loud tie decorated with reindeer, a souvenir no doubt from his greeting card days. He was very pale and breathing hard when, against the doctor's advice and the manager's wish, he insisted on joining the others at breakfast.

'Good morning,' he puffed, as a place was laid for him.

'It's nice to see you up,' said Sophia politely.

'I'm vertical, if that's what you mean. I am hardly *up*. I can hardly breathe in this weather . . . a large breakfast seems in order though.' And he had them bring him sausages, eggs and potatoes, as well as toast and coffee. 'A real American breakfast,' he said, eating as quickly as he could, his white face glistening with sweat.

'Do you think you should eat so much in this heat?' asked Philip, somewhat sickened by the other's unnatural appetite.

'I need a hearty breakfast,' mumbled Mr. Willys.

'I believe that toast and coffee is all *anybody* needs,' said Fay Peabody. 'Except, of course, working men who must labour with their hands.'

Mr. Willys snorted but made no answer as he speared a fried potato.

Philip looked out the french windows at the green gardens flickering in the heat. For several moments the only sound at the table was the wet noise of Mr. Willys chewing and swallowing food.

Sophia mercifully broke the silence: 'Where do you intend to go next?'

'Switzerland, if I can survive the altitude. Start taking glands and things. See if maybe they can do something. Doubt it, though.'

This speech was dragged out to an inordinate length by long stops for breath and nourishment. Philip could not take his eyes off him as much as he would rather have looked anywhere else than at that grey shapeless face with the loose lips which quivered as Mr. Willys gasped and talked and chewed, all at once. Philip almost wished, if only on aesthetic grounds, that Mrs. Peabody had succeeded.

'Will you be in Europe long?' asked Sophia, who, of them all, was the only one not officially in on the conspiracy which had failed.

'Can't tell. May go back to Philly. Though it's hot there, too. Waiter, bring me some more toast. One place pretty much like another to me, except some are hot and some are cool. Want a cool place now.' Then he did things to a soft-poached egg which Philip never wanted to see done again.

'Did you get to see much of Egypt?' Sophia was intent on being polite.

'Saw the Sphinx my first day in Cairo. Then had a heatstroke, and I've been laid up ever since. First there; now here.'

'I'm sure you'd have enjoyed Karnak.'

'Don't think so. I did want to see the Sphinx, but outside of that I'm not so keen on sightseeing. It's hard on a man my size.'

'Why did you want to see the Sphinx?' asked Sophia.

'Always heard about it.'

'Did you like it?'

'Not much. Face all gone.'

'At least you're able to get a bit of reading done,' said Philip helpfully ... only a few minutes to go.

'Don't read too much; my eyes can't take it. I like detective stories, though;' he put down his fork, swallowed noisily and stared at Mrs. Peabody, who had the grace not to stare back.

'I'm sure Mrs. Peabody is pleased to hear that,' said Sophia. 'I've never read a detective story, I'm afraid ... a terrible confession to make in front of you,' she said, turning to the authoress.

'Not at all. I am aware that the vineyard in which I have for so long toiled produces nothing more than a good table wine. At least so the connoisseurs in these matters seem to think; but it is good enough for me and for a great many other people as well, both at home and abroad.'

Mr. Willys looked at her with loathing, but he said nothing while the others talked about Mrs. Peabody's vineyard.

The manager came in just as Mr. Willys was debating whether to have more coffee. 'The car's waiting for you outside, sir. I've also got the bill for you and some other things out in the lobby if you'll be so kind as to take care of them for me.'

'Let us go then,' said Mr. Willys, pushing back from the

table, the two frail native boys moved forward, got him to his feet and escorted him out of the dining-room and into the lobby. Mrs. Peabody, with a bleak little smile, excused herself and left the room for the morning-fresh garden.

'Well, that's the end of that,' said Philip.

'She seems rather crushed by it all.'

'And he doesn't, which is suspicious. He seems almost cheerful.'

'A great deal of attention sometimes has a good effect on people who are often alone. I don't suppose Mr. Willys has ever been the centre of attention before in his life, except as a minor curiosity in public places.'

'All that food!' Philip shuddered.

'He could hardly walk.'

'Let's go and see him off,' said Philip, and they went into the lobby where Mr. Willys stood unsupported in the doorway, his baggage all around him, and Mr. Koyoumdjian, beaming with relief, was wishing him a quick recovery.

'Ah, there you are,' said Mr. Willys as they approached. 'This is it, I'm off at last.'

'Have a good trip,' said Philip, shaking the cold damp hand. 'Are you going to stay at the hospital for very long or are you going down to Cairo?'

'Cairo. I'll be at the hospital overnight for a check-up; then I'm leaving this goddamn country for good.'

'I was going to say if you were at the hospital for any length of time, we would come visit you.'

'Very kind of you, I must say. You've been wonderful about the whole thing . . . very kind. But now I must be off. Good-bye, Miss Oliver; it's been a pleasure.' Then, unaccompanied, he walked into the sunlight where he collapsed, a few feet from the motor-car which was to have taken him to the hospital. His last recorded words were: 'Get a doctor.'

The sudden death of Mr. Willys shocked them all, even though they had for so long and so nervously awaited his murder at the hands of Fay Peabody. To Philip it seemed, somehow, grossly unfair while to the manager it was the end: he did not believe anyone could be as jinxed as he was, or as the hotel was. Several servants resigned on the spot while the remaining ones gave him a vote of no confidence but did not press for any immediate action, either on his part of theirs. The body was removed the moment the doctor announced that the anguished, flesh-burned soul of Mr. Willys had departed this vale of tears. Philip told the doctor that the deceased had wanted to be cremated and his ashes cast into the Nile. This last touch was Philip's own. The doctor thought they might have trouble finding a large enough oven for this purpose but that there was a possibility the brick kiln on the edge of town could be hired to do the job. Fortunately Mr. Willys had had sufficient cash in his pocket to make a fine cremation possible ... the other details such as the disposition of personal effects and the writing to the next of kin was assigned to Mr. Koyoumdjian.

That night at dinner the two ladies wore black and Philip wore a blue serge suit.

'What did the doctor say he died of?' asked Sophia, after a long, lugubrious silence.

'A heart attack,' said Philip, in a low reverent voice. 'Excitement, the heat, and all that food he ate finished him off.'

'What were his last words?' asked Mrs. Peabody softly, her hands folded before her on the table, as though in prayer.

'He asked for a doctor,' said Philip; a sudden suspicion crossed his mind.

'It doesn't sound as if he was very *sincere*,' said Mrs. Peabody, unaware of the suspicion in which she was held by Philip. 'All that talk about wanting to die and then, when he does get his wish, he is frightened ... a lack of moral fibre, I should say.'

'You ... you weren't responsible?' asked Philip, forgetting that Sophia was not supposed to know about the attempt on Mr. Willys's life.

'No, I wasn't,' said Mrs. Peabody. 'I debated whether or not to give it one last whirl. His rudeness to me at breakfast, however, restrained my essentially kind impulse and I allowed him to depart for what I hoped might have been a long life of physical distress and melancholia. Fortunately, for him, nature intervened.'

The next day the manager brought Philip a shoe box which contained all that was mortal of Mr. Willys. 'You go throw them in the Nile,' said Mr. Koyoumdjian, 'and do it quick because if the boys find out that even that guy's ashes are in the hotel, they'll leave me flat.'

Philip said that he would conduct the last rites immediately and so, accompanied by Sophia, he walked to the bank of the Nile and climbed down the rocky embankment to the water's edge. Sailboats glided across the water. A dozen men were bathing near-by, indifferent to Sophia's presence, their lean hard bodies gleaming like polished metal in the sunlight, as unlike his memory of Mr. Willys as it was possible to be, thought Philip, opening the box which contained some grey black lumps of bone and ash.

'Who would have thought he could have been compressed to this?' he said in an unconscious paraphrase.

'Give me the box,' said Sophia, and she took it from the bemused Philip and emptied its contents into the green water. 'You see how easy it is?' she asked, throwing the box away.

'How easy what is?'

'Dying.'

'No, I don't.'

CHAPTER NINE

He pressed his eyelids and saw two black suns, two eclipses in the red darkness. His head ached from the glare and heat of the day which, fortunately, was very nearly over. He opened his eyes again and looked across the desert at the near-by pyramids: large buff-coloured objects as meaningless as a child's toys upset in a sand-box. The sky was lovely, though: a pale luminous pink, cloudless and now, as the red disc slipped over the desert's edge, sunless as well, leaving the sky still full of light. To his left was Cairo and to his right the desert. The green Nile Valley ended abruptly at his feet. One foot touched the grass; the other the brown desert: the line between was unnaturally precise, as though drawn by a giant. He turned and looked at the city, coral pink and white, deprived by the Nile, edged by dusty green which was, in its turn, circled by the wide flat desert at whose edge he now stood, a few yards from Mena House where he had been entertained that day with lunch and a swim in the hotel's new pool. Thinking of his host, wondering if he should go back into the lobby and look for him, Philip strode slowly up the steep road which led to the pyramids. He was nearly at the top, when he heard someone call his name. He stopped until, out of breath, his host and new friend Charles de Cluny joined him.

'I had things to do. The manager wanted to know about a party some friends of mine were giving. How I hate this hill! It's so steep. I'm quite out of breath. The sky. Isn't it a fine colour? This is the time of day when I find myself really loving Egypt. Rose. Wonderful rose colour, the sky, and cool out here in the open without the sun. Here we are.'

They were now at the top of the sand hill near the base of the great pyramid. Below them in the roseate distance was Cairo while across the desert, indistinct by twilight, were the other pyramids, like so many broken metronomes.

'Magnificent sight. I never tire of it. I'm always staggered when I recall the age of these buildings. Think what they must have seen. Think!'

Philip thought and then de Cluny, shifting from contemplation of the past to the scandal of the present, pointed to the only house in the desert, a small cube of a building with great windows and a soldier standing guard in front of it.

'His,' he whispered. And from his tone Philip knew that he meant Farouk, the King, a plump young Albanian, a ribald successor to those austere Pharaohs who had reigned before him over the same green valley.

'He brings his women here,' his guide whispered as they moved towards the great pyramid. 'Including the dress models, the ones from Paris.'

'Is it true . . .'

'About the cigarettes?'

'Yes.'

And he repeated to Philip the current bit of scandal: a couturier had come to Cairo with a number of models and his latest collection to be shown to the royal ladies. The king, so the story went, attended the viewing and amused himself by flipping cigarette butts, presumably lighted, at the models in the hope of landing a butt in the décolletée. Cairo was amused. The ladies and the couturier were not. They had promptly gone back to Paris, leaving behind one of their number, a moonglow blonde.

'A gloomy-looking place,' said Philip, as they passed the sentry. 'No trees, no garden . . . just sand.'

'But the view! Think of it! Having the pyramids in front of you on a starlit night, with a beautiful woman beside you . . . how evocative: to recall in the midst of an orgy that one owns the pyramids out there and all the desert around, to know that one is king. What a lovely prospect for a young man! No wonder it's gone to his head.'

'Do you think he enjoys it?' said Philip who often, in self-defence, liked to take the popular American view that the rich and powerful were hopelessly miserable with no whims left to be granted, no use at all for their wealth and even less for their power which was, of course, invariably attended by guilt and shame. The old woman who dies in a tenement house with fifty thousand dollars sewed in her mattress or the Texas millionaire who lives on cornflakes and weak tea are recurrent American folk types . . . but even Philip had to agree that the King of Egypt probably never suffered from much more than an occasional hangover or a moment's anguish at the lithe figure he had sacrificed to a robust appetite.

Philip's companion explained all these things to him as they approached the great pyramid at whose base guides and ragamuffins were gathered in cheerful discussion groups, assemblies which quickly adjourned at the approach of the foreigners. In a moment Philip and his companion were the centre of the annoying, chattering Cairo crowd; everyone had something to sell . . . in this case, a tour of the pyramids, a visit to the Sphinx, post cards, a ride on a camel, a debauch with one enterprising twelve-year-old boy who made it clear with gestures that he would give either or both, together or separately, a good time. Philip's first impulse was to ignore the crowd, to walk as though they were not there. But, as he soon discovered, this was not possible. They made too much noise; they pulled at his sleeves, got under his feet, His companion dismissed a number of them with a few significant words in Egyptian; the rest continued to mill about, however, as Philip, ready to throw stones, walked to the base of that pyramid which is ascribed to Cheops. Up close, it was like a geometrical mountain or rock pile. One of the boys scurried up it, out of sight, like Jack on the beanstalk. He returned, a moment later, breathless. Philip's companion gave him a coin and the child indignantly asked for more. The foreigners fled, shaking off all their pursuers except the boy.

They stopped, breathless, on the edge of a valley where, handsomely silhouetted against the sky, was, yes, the inevitable attraction, the Sphinx. To Philip it looked smaller and less tidy than he had expected; to our authority, Professor Rawlinson, it is 'among the marvels of Egypt, second to none. The mysterious being with the head of a man and the body of a lion is not at all uncommon in Egyptian architectural adornment, but the one placed before the Second Pyramid (The Pyramid of Shafra) and supposed to be contemporaneous with it, astonishes the observer by its gigantic proportions. It is known to the Arabs as *Abul-hôl*, the father of terror.'

And Philip, ignoring the whining boy, stared into the mild, faintly smiling face and saw nothing at all, only an ancient monument; and yet, though what he saw was not in itself impressive, the associations of thousands of years affected him as strongly as it had at Luxor and he experienced once again that grave serenity, that secret knowledge of the endless flow of life, of generation and regeneration, never-ending, never-constant, the endless structure which contained all time and matter, the waking dream behind his own blue eyes, eyes which could hold it all.

Then the sky turned grey and silver specks appeared overhead; the ruddy-faced Sphinx turned the colour of slate and Philip muttered that frightening name. Abul-hôl, to himself as he and de Cluny walked back to Mena House, the boy, like a dog, snapping at their heels all the way.

Later he sat in the dark rose-smelling garden of the hotel and drank whisky with Charles de Cluny, his friend of several days now, a traveller like himself, but a knowing traveller, one who had been here often before. He was French and he had lived nearly everywhere, Philip gathered: in Central America, in Europe, in New Orleans; now, for this month at least, he was in Cairo. He had never been up the Nile and he had no wish to go, although he did have a certain real love of history, as well as a

glib and authoritative fund of stories with which he amused
Philip, telling him about the Pharaohs, anecdotes based not on
fact, Philip was positive, but on a thorough knowledge of Sue-
tonius, from whom he made free and imaginative adaptations.
But Philip was more interested when he spoke of the contemporary world which he knew well, of exiled royalties and
rich tourists, of the voluptuaries whose deeds always awed and
excited him, no matter how tawdry he knew they must be in
actual fact.

'When does she arrive, this friend of yours?' asked Charles
suddenly.

'Miss Oliver? Next week, I think. She's in the desert now, I
have no idea where, but I suppose she'll be here when she said
she would.'

'She sounds like a very intelligent woman,' said Charles, dis-
approvingly.

'Very,' said Philip. 'She's good company. That's all.'

'Ah, Then you're *not* in love?'

'Good Lord, no! She's the last woman in the world I'd be
interested in.'

'Do you think *she* knows that?'

'I doubt if she's ever given it a thought,' said Philip, who
sometimes wondered whether she had or not; his vanity often
insisted that she *did* love him . . . a real fire beneath the cold
surface. His reason, however, thought it unlikely.

'Is she wealthy?'

'I expect so.'

'I wonder if she might want to buy some jewels. I have an
impoverished cousin – as a matter of fact, I have dozens of
impoverished cousins – but the one I have in mind has some
exquisite pigeon's-blood rubies which she'd sell for nothing. Do
find out if Miss Oliver's interested. It would be such a help if
she were. My cousin, by chance, happens to be right here in
Cairo.'

'I'll ask her,' said Philip, wondering how de Cluny himself
earned a living.

'I should appreciate that.'

After a long silence, de Cluny asked Philip if he knew Zoe
Helotius.

'Only slightly. Is she here?'

'Just for the week . . . out of season, too. But then there's to be a great party, and wherever there's a great affair, Zoe's on hand. Amusing woman. When did you know her?'

Philip told him. A number of names were then exchanged. They had several acquaintances in common which they had not, until that moment, bothered to discuss. They had met as strangers and neither had made too much effort to fix the other's place in the world since the identities of both were so clearly apparent: a young American of apparent leisure and a French adventurer with a taste, but not a flair, for philosophy and a flair, but no taste, for a fashionable life on an income which seemed uncertain.

'If you care to,' said de Cluny, when Philip's attitude and position had become more clearly defined after the naming of the names, 'I might get you invited. It might interest you. A real Cairo affair to celebrate the wedding of . . .' And here he named both the host and the bridegroom, two Egyptian men so highly placed that they could have touched the throne itself if they had been so minded. 'Only it will be a Western party . . . although we won't see the bride, of course. Both gentlemen are enlightened, more or less, but not that much. Other women will be there, however . . . in spite of the Prophet.'

'Sounds interesting,' said Philip, going through the polite ritual of 'but' until he was sure that he was really invited; then he accepted.

There was too much of everything at the reception: too many people, too many flowers, too much food and champagne, and more jewels than Philip had ever seen before. The non-orthodox Egyptian women were especially gaudy in lace and damask with huge yellow diamonds, square emeralds and rubies like gouts of blood; their glossy black hair coiled and contorted by Paris hairdressers, dusted with gold or bright with diamond moons and stars. Philip had never before seen such a display, as he walked from one large, airy room to the next, through Moorish arches each guarded by servants in livery while others, in white Western-style jackets, served wine.

De Cluny was an excellent guide. He saw to it that they never remained too long with the very dull or missed meeting the occasional odd or interesting citizens of Cairo who stood, usually, at the centre of large groups, receiving homage, constructing epigrams or diatribes or platitudes or whatever their speciality happened to be, their genius joyfully applauded by the distinguished and decorative audience which moved from one point of interest to the next, like tourists in a museum.

The host, a large imposing man in a morning coat, welcomed them gravely in French, declaring that his house was theirs. That was the last they saw of him.

'And there,' said de Cluny, in a low voice, as they crossed the largest of the rooms, 'is a Russian spy, under the chandelier . . . calls herself Princess.'

The spy was a small pretty woman in her forties with dark hair and wearing an Indian sari. She smiled engagingly at de Cluny. 'How are you?' she said in French, as he kissed her hand. 'And how are *you*? I've seen you in Shepheard's, haven't I?'

Philip said that she had.

'Oh, let's find some chairs. Everyone stands. It just makes me wilt, standing in the heat.' She went over to one corner where three gilt chairs were placed against the wall. Two of them were empty; the third was occupied by a small Egyptian. The spy gave a dazzling smile. 'Princess would like to sit down,' she said.

The small Egyptian looked puzzled.

'I said, *Princess* would like to sit down,' repeated the spy, more sternly; with a frightened expression, the little man got to his feet and fled.

'That's better, isn't it?' They sat down. 'They have such bad manners, Egyptians.'

'Are you from India?' asked Philip naïvely, not realizing that in Cairo no one asked the spies direct questions for fear of seeming not only gauche but, worst of all, indelicate and prying.

'My mother is Indian,' she said, repeating the same dazzling smile that so confused the former occupant of the chair; then she began a long involved story about the peregrinations of her family and herself, a melange of nationalities and resounding titles.

'But I am talking only of myself,' she exclaimed, when both de Cluny and Philip were afraid she might never talk of anything else again all evening, holding them close to her with her brilliant smile, with her tiny gesturing hands which, every now and then, touched Philip's sleeve as she named yet another

205

country in which she had lived. 'But I am talking only to myself. Tell me about you.'

'I'm an American,' said Philip. 'There isn't much more to tell.'

'Come now. Princess doesn't believe that. I'm sure you must be a wonderful business-man building oil-wells and making dollars all over the world.' For a moment he was afraid that this might be a preface to an attack on capitalism, but she meant it literally.

'No, I'm a tourist, just out of school,' he said; her interest waned perceptibly.

'How wonderful for you to come to see our old countries. To breathe the same air that Cleopatra did! Oh, history is my passion! How I should love to have lived in those times and gone to the sources of the Nile in a pleasure barge. Princess would like some champagne.'

It took him a moment to separate the request from the rhapsody; by the time he did, de Cluny had already clapped his hands and a boy came with champagne for them.

'Aren't you drinking, Charles?' she asked, noticing that de Cluny refused the wine.

'I'm a good Moslem today.'

'Now you're making fun of me. Princess is a *real* Moslem, but she believes the Prophet would not mind too much since he has promised us all the wine that we can drink in Heaven.'

'Only the men were promised that,' said de Cluny with a smile.

'You *are* old-fashioned. Tell me, though, how are your cousins? I was at a dinner not long ago with one of them, but I forget her name.'

'There are so many.'

'How wonderful it must be to have distinguished relatives all over the world.'

'And all struggling to survive,' said de Cluny.

'The old ways change,' said the Princess gravely, putting down her glass; then, making the usual farewells, she walked off.

'I don't believe she's a Russian spy,' said Philip, as they moved towards another large room where an orchestra was playing waltzes.

'I'm sure she's not either,' said de Cluny agreeably, 'but she's just like the ones they used to have here during the war. *That* was a time ... believe me! Everyone was a spy and ... Oh, look, there *he* is.'

They stopped in the doorway of the ballroom where a dozen couples were dancing to the music of an orchestra which was hidden behind a group of potted palms. The parquet floor had been newly waxed and, from time to time, the dancers slipped and stumbled, amusing spectators who stood chatting around the room, all eyes for the most part discreetly centred on a short, burly figure in a tuxedo who was, de Cluny murmured to Philip in a low voice, the King of Egypt. Philip immediately recognized the curiously stiff figure and immobile face, half hidden now by dark glasses which made him look, more than ever, like an interesting experiment in taxidermy. The blonde with whom he was dancing was a head taller than he and very beautiful.

'He's incognito,' said de Cluny. 'In other words, no one is allowed to fuss over him. But, on the other hand, no one can approach him without his consent ... a happy arrangement. But here are the guards.' Philip looked and saw that in each corner of the room stood a man in a business, suit, hand in pocket, revolver barrel pointed.

'What a nuisance,' commented Philip; then they came to the last of the rooms, a small Chinese one, with carved teakwood furniture and crimson silk banners on the walls. Here a group of sedate Westerners were gathered, talking politics. De Cluny knew them all and he introduced Philip, saying the names rapidly and precisely; then, since there was no place farther to go, their journey ended, they sat down and de Cluny promptly talked politics with the severest and greyest of the men, and, listening to his friend, Philip could not help but feel that he was perhaps too fluent, too affable, to ready to see the other person's point of view and to argue it with even greater eloquence than the other person was himself capable of, at the expense of his own apparent convictions ... presuming he had any.

Zoe Helotius entered the room like some predatory bird of prey with white leather face and sharp nose, her blood-red lips in an ikon's smile, as she attacked, surrounded by equerries, advisers, friends and enemies who spread out like an army, flanking the room, picking off this person and that person, rounding up the residents until a series of concentric circles had been arranged, the lesser figures close to the periphery, important ones at the small centre where Zoe herself stood, talking quickly casting febrile glances around the room to see if she were missing anything. She was not. She was the centre of attraction; the main event.

'Ah, Charles, my dear, It's been a long time.'

'Five years, madame.'

'Too long a time. And how is X? and Y? I love them so. I never see them any more. You must come and pay me a call while I'm here ... in the afternoon at five. I'm staying with Z.' A shudder of delight went through the circles, like waves from a stone cast in water, the circles ever widening until at last they spent themselves against the insensate silk-hung walls.

'Mr. Warren? Have we met? In Capri? Ah, Regina's friend. I remember now. You were attached to the Embassy at Rome. I love your Ambassador. Tell him I look forward to that dinner in Venice ... he'll know what I mean. Is Regina here in Cairo? But of course not. I saw her in Paris a week ago ... so much more like a queen than any of the queens one knows, if you follow me. Do you know her, Charles? Yes? No? Ah, you would love her. She has such style and *he*, well, one defers to the most powerful man in the world, which he is nowadays. But,' and she lowered her voice and opened her eyes very wide, her onyx irises circled now by white, 'I hear *he* is going to divorce *her*.' Philip was by now sufficiently used to the varying degrees of emphasis with which people in Cairo mentioned otherwise unidentified pronouns to establish correctly the intended reference: *he* was Farouk; *she* was the lovely but seldom seen Persian he had married.

'I hope not,' said Charles, neutrally.

'It is what *they* say. But here is Anna Morris. Where have you been hiding? This is Charles de Cluny, Mr. Warren.'

Charles kissed the lady's hand; Philip bowed to the newcomer, a dark-haired girl, Philip's age, with large hazel eyes and, he quickly saw, a husband who joined them a moment later, a burly, rough-voiced man with a limp. An industrialist, Philip gathered. In steel.

'Some party,' said Mr. Morris, in a tone which could easily have been hostile. 'Never seen so much jewellery in my life. Pay off the whole Egyptian debt with one roomful of it.'

'You have no love of beauty,' said Mrs. Helotius, who had

and who told them all about it while Philip talked to Anna, learning that she was originally European of mixed nationality and that she was now married to the industrialist with whom she was touring Europe and North Africa for her pleasure as well for his business: he had come to Egypt to sell steel. Philip was charmed by her, by her voice, which was low and melodic, faintly accented and appealing, like no other voice he had ever heard. He was fascinated, prudent, diffident, too, not sure of himself, over-awed by the virile, bull-necked husband in whose broad shadow she now stood unmistakably interested in Philip and yet obviously attached to her husband, moving always closer to him as they talked, moving away from Philip as though she wanted, somehow, to include or seem to include her husband while in no way sacrificing this moment's privacy with the young American who attracted her.

'It is too much,' she said, in answer to a remark of Philip's about the reception. 'Too heavy. I prefer lightness, I think.'

'The *Petit Trianon*?'

'Oh, I'm sure I would have loved that. Have you been there?'

He shook his head. 'I've never been in France. Next month I'll be there, in Paris.'

'I lived there a long time . . .'

'Is it . . .'

'It is.' She smiled. 'You'll never want to leave.'

'I'm sure of that.'

'But when you do leave you'll not be the same.'

He laughed. 'Now, that's an exaggeration. I've known hundreds of people who've gone there, been enchanted, and returned the same as ever.'

'But not you. I can tell.' She looked at him gravely while he looked not at her serious, shining eyes, but at her mouth instead, wondering at its Botticelli shape, like a bird gliding, the upper lip childishly pursed.

'I can believe anything,' he said. 'This is my year of belief, I think. Until recently I doubted everything and trusted no one. Now the wilder, the more improbable the story I am told, the more eager I am to believe it. Tell me there are serpents in the sea and I will believe you; the next time I travel by ship I will see one a mile long, attended by mermaids with seaweed in their hair.'

'There *are* serpents in the sea,' she said, smiling, one hand touching the odd-shaped bit of crystal she wore about her neck on a silver chain.

'Then I shall surely see one.'

'Mermaids, too?'

'A platoon of them, all wearing naval officers' caps.' She laughed and then, aware that her husband was saying farewell to Mrs. Helotius, she turned to Philip and gave him her hand. 'Perhaps I'll see you when you come to Paris. Where will you stay?'

'I've no idea. Where do *you* stay?'

'We,' and the pronoun was suddenly forbidding, 'always stay at the Ida, rue d'Olympie ... a quiet place. We'll be there for several months, I think – this autumn. Or at least I will stop there while Vane is travelling about.' The 'I' was a promise; and so they parted.

Mrs. Helotius, the room exhausted, each person drained of information, catalogued and filed, looked about; then she raised one arm slowly as though to adjust her hair; but this was no spontaneous gesture, Philip saw: it was a military signal, like a cavalry officer's command to charge and, led by Lady Julia, mad in green-watered silk, her cohorts, assembled about her and the invaders withdrew, in a flood of sound.

'Did you ever hear the story about Zoe Helotius and Bernard Shaw ...' began Charles.

'Many times,' said Philip sternly. 'I have vowed never to hear it again.'

'In that case I shall respect your wishes. There are too many stories about her, anyway. Shall we move on?'

Not until they had regained the ballroom, now crowded with dancers (the royal one gone) did Charles mention Anna Morris.

'I could see you liked her,' he said.

'Why? Did I stare? Turn red with excitement?'

'You did indeed ... I don't blame you. She's an attractive woman.'

'Got a bad character, hasn't she?'

'Of course not, as far as I know. Why do you say that?'

'I don't know. Isn't that what one always says about beauties?' asked Philip, wishing the orchestra would play no more Strauss waltzes, hoping Charles would have more to say; he did.

'You mean is she faithful to her husband? In that case, I can tell you, to your great delight, that she has been unfaithful on occasion; but she has good taste.'

'In lovers?'

'In everything. Not that I know her especially well, but I have followed her career with some interest these last few years. She has quite a vogue in Paris, you know. Less of one in America, I should expect . . . too delicate for them. . . . That doesn't offend you?'

'Nothing offends me,' said Philip happily; but he spoke too soon: the Russian spy, her somewhat crumpled gossamer sari floating behind her, approached them, smiling stonily, like the Gorgon conforting two doomed mortals. 'Princess has been looking for you,' she said.

Philip was not surprised to find that Sophia and Charles had everything in common except mutual sympathy, and so, after one grim dinner together, he kept them apart, devoting most of his time to Sophia, who had arrived early in the week from her journey into the desert where she had inspected a newly discovered city of the Twelfth Dynasty and interviewed yet another holy man who had gloomily predicted the end of the world next spring, in the first week of Ramadan.

They kept mostly to Shepheard's, for Philip, once he had seen the great museum and a few of the mosques, had no real desire to explore Cairo, not liking the heat or the filth or the men and boys who followed them everywhere they went, begging and selling, their voices alternating between intimate whines and shrill cries of anger. He usually pushed past them, striking out at the brown hands which tugged at his coat: he hated being touched by anyone, especially these people, strangers who acted as though, by touching him, shaking him, money might fall to the ground like fruit from a tree. None ever did, for he was adamant; yet, even so, such stern behaviour was a strain, and so he found it pleasanter to stay in the hotel, to wander about the garden and, when he did go out, to leap quickly into a taxi, before the mob was upon him.

One afternoon he had tea with Sophia in the garden at the back of Shepheard's and he asked her what had become of Abu Bekr at El Farhar and his prophecy.

'I never saw him again,' she said, her grey eyes lovely, almost compensating for the thin mouth and square jaw. The wind rustled the branches of the treee overhead scattering lozenges of sunlight across the white table-cloth. A Negro servant wearing a fez, tight jacket and bloomers, leaned against the wall of the hotel, lazily trying to catch flies with one hand. An English family sitting at a table with a striped awning were the only other people in the garden. They looked very red and hot, untidy in white crumpled linen.

'I suppose he will stay there all his life, making prophecies as long as people will listen.'

'They will always listen. Whether they believe or not is another question.'

'Do you?'

'I'm not sure. In general, yes. Something is about to happen. Where and when and how ... not to mention *what,* are all a puzzle. I look for keys.'

'The keys are at Rome,' said Philip obscurely, not knowing himself what he meant.

'Rusty keys,' said Sophia, pouring herself more tea. Philip put a whole scone in his mouth and chewed thoughtfully. Still leaning against the wall, the servant caught a fly; smiling happily, he dried his palm on his bloomer leg.

Then Philip told her that he would leave for Paris in a week's time ... by plane, he added, assembling details as he spoke, pleased with the suddenness of his own decision.

'Oh, I'm sorry. I had hoped you would stay here another month. I thought you might be interested in some Ptolemaic things they've come across near Alexandria.' If she was in any way distressed or put out, she did not show it; she talked of ruins in Alexandria until the fact of his going had been absorbed by both and accepted as immutable, a day of sure departure at last selected, a time of change.

'You'll be coming to Paris, too?' asked Philip politely, yet not hypocritically, for he did like her.

'I'm not sure. My plans are seldom definite. How long do you think you'll be there?'

'A few months. Perhaps most of the winter ... I'm not sure. I shan't know until I've tried it, I suppose.'

'If you're there several months, we shall see one another again.' And the sentence came out cold and formal, obviously against her will, for she smiled and tried, unsuccessfully, to be, for a moment, warm and spontaneous. Her failure both surprised and embarrassed him. He covered it quickly, volubly, agreeing that they would see one another, pouring himself tea and inquiring quickly, irrelevantly about Mrs. Peabody.

'Mrs. Peabody? Ah, I'd almost forgotten about that nightmare. She's gone back to America, I think. I saw very little of her after you left. She avoided me, too, for that matter. I think she was suddenly rather horrified at what she'd very nearly done. Last I saw of her she was going down the Nile to Alexandria on a freight ship ... the regular passenger ships have been discontinued since the war, but, undaunted, she found a place for herself aboard a terrible little freighter, and, if she managed to survive that phase of her field-work, she's probably at this very minute sitting, dictaphone in hand, composing *The Karnak Corpse*.'

'That is *not* the title.'

'Indeed it is. She told me so herself the day she left. Suggested I look for it when it was published next spring.' They laughed. A bird chattered in the branches of a tree near-by while another, like a scarlet shuttlecock, swooped in an arc from the sky to the flowers.

'Poor Mr. Willys,' said Philip, thinking back on those weeks at Luxor as though three years instead of three weeks had passed since they had stood on the edge of the Nile and scattered the ashes.

'Poor? He got his wish, didn't he? That's more than most of us get.'

'What a terrible wish, though. What a terrible life!'

'I agree that the life was a piece of misfortune, a bad trick of chance, but the wish was something else again.'

'I can see how at times one might want to die, to escape all the trouble and bother, but I'm afraid that I think both the wish and the fact are terrible.'

'But logical ... the wish, at least. If living is no longer a pleasure, if the body or the world gives one pain, then why prolong the pain? Why not select your moment of departure in the same way you, for instance, decided to leave Egypt for France, where you know you will not suffer from the heat or the flies or from beggars in the streets.'

'It's not the same,' said Philip, remembering guiltily his irrational decision. 'After all, there is usually hope of some kind.

If there were really none, then I could see how one might, in great pain, choose to die. But not under any other circumstances.'

'Then why shouldn't you choose your own moment to die? To make the only defiant gesture man is capable of: the real triumph of the spirit over the flesh. No, I see it as a splendid deed . . . the logical conclusion to a life which, for one reason or another, ceases to give pleasure.'

'But the animal dies hard. The animal doesn't want to die, ever. Even Mr. Willys didn't have the courage to shoot himself, and if any man had a good reason for suicide, he had.'

'Of course, that's the point. The animal. You're quite right. It doesn't *want* to die. Yet the whole essence of civilization is the spirit's dominion over the flesh: of course that dominion is only temporary, but the deal remains and the ideal is ultimately best served through the sacrifice of the animal to the spirit . . .'

'Which dies, too.'

'It ceased to exist in its present form, yes.'

'You haven't become a Hindu, have you? Or a Platonist? The soul going into the bodies of other species . . .'

'Not at all. I mean that the structure of the universe contains us all. We're always a part of it, in one form or another. Do you think a man can be seen from another planet? No, but the earth where the man is can be seen. Or can the earth be seen from another galaxy? No, but the galaxy which contains the earth can be seen, and, should there be even vaster divisions, so will the part of fire and gas and void which holds all our stars and planets, ideas and men, be seen, and so it will continue to exist, timeless, changing yet always in essence the same and, though your body decomposes, it is always a part of total life, of the whole.'

'And the spirit? in this case me, the I of Philip Warren. What of it? of him? of me? Does it die?'

'It changes. What is a temperament or a spirit or an identity but a particular combination of abstractions and sensations which are, at least as far as human life goes, eternal? The idea of virtue which you have is a variation on *the* idea of virtue which, as Aristotle would say, exists perfectly . . . your fear of pain, your love of pleasure . . . those are all constant. You are nothing but a combination of senses and ideas which exist perfectly, as far as our race goes, and, though your momentary arrangement is lost when you die, neither the ideas nor the senses are affected: they exist perfectly, relatively at least, just as matter exists eternally.'

'Yet there's not much consolation in regarding oneself as an arrangement of flowers which in time withers and dies and is thrown out, becoming earth and new flowers in due course, roses and lilies and so on which, as types, exist for ever, as you say, or apparently for ever . . . but though I accept your image, I think it only part true. I think the arrangement has more than ornamental value. I *must* think that it has, since I am it and love it as myself . . . or that part of conscious life which, accidentally I agree, I am, regarding myself at this instant regarding myself in all time, like mirrors in a tailor shop reflecting the same figure over and over again . . . but now I've lost the thread completely,' he laughed. 'Presuming I had it.'

'Nearly,' said Sophia. 'I don't quarrel with your putting a value on the combination of atoms or tissues or of essences which compose you. It would be very odd for a mortal not to. You have nothing, after all. But you do not value everything equally if only because nothing *is* equal to any consciousness. If you had to lose your sight or your left arm you would have the left arm cut off first. And, being civilized, as we employ that somewhat loose adjective, you would, I think, ideally at least, prefer your arbitrary will to the confused demands of the flesh. There are times when the body would like the rest, but you make it work, or when it wants to make love and you refuse to indulge it, your controls guiding, more or less well, the animal . . . guided in turn by the flesh which controls the work of the spirit; you will, I am sure, prefer the spirit to the flesh if you should be forced to make that final choice.'

'Perhaps . . . I don't know.'

'Of course, you would. And should the body give you physical pain or mental (social to be precise), then I think it the most logical thing in the world to end the pain, to dominate the animal for good, to scatter the no longer satisfactory arrangement across the earth, like those dead roses and lilies you mentioned.'

'I don't want to die,' said Philip, recalling vividly the horror of certain death-dreams he had had from time to time all his life; even when he was a child, he'd often awakened alone and desperate in the impersonal night, trying to visualize what

215

nothing must be like, what it would be like to be no longer himself, to have no parents, no house, no world and no life. The dream had changed very little over the years; the terror and the despair remained as he realized that one day he would die, that he would *not* be. He shivered in the warm flower-scented wind and he touched the table, the cups, as though to prove to himself that he was still alive, that the present was all.

'Why should you want to, now? But one day you may want to die . . . then remember what I said.'

'I'm more interested in how to live than how to die,' said Philip, feeling silly at the heroic ring of this statement: how often had he found some really recondite, brilliant insight or moment of vision become, when reduced to words, a dusty bromide falling of its own accord into the worn phrases of ancient platitudes: all men are brothers, for instance, a sentiment without which no religion had ever got moving . . . qualified, of course, by policy: all men who believe as I do are my brothers.

'There is only one way to live,' said Sophia, pushing a strand of hair out of her eyes. 'To do as you want, making of course the obvious allowances for the rules your neighbours in place and time have established. To live in the present is the best, of course. So many people live for some event which may never happen, jettisoning the present for the sake of a grand future. Sometimes I think that the beast in the jungle should replace the eagle as our national totem.'

'And live according to the body,' said Philip, wondering if he should accept de Cluny's invitation to visit a bordello that evening.

'That is part of it. But one comes closer to the way through contemplation. I feel a greater affinity to those men who built the temples of Luxor than I do to living men. The idea of the dead is pure and unconfused by the senses; we cannot see or hear or touch them . . . the irrelevant flesh has been swept away and only the idea of Thutmose or Amenhotep, Socrates or Plato, endures. I am selfish, of course, and I know what pleases me. I am dedicated to the idea and not to the man, but since you are obviously closer, through affinity and choice, to the man, you will be able, I think, to understand this better if you stood off at a distance with only the idea confronting you.'

'Spend my life among the ruins? I haven't the vocation, I'm afraid; as much as it may fascinate me.'

'Then spend it with the shadows of men. Their books or attitudes which are so much purer than they themselves, the uncorrupted vision.'

'I could do that altogether too easily. I've done that most of my life. I hate involvement in other people's lives. My serene disposition is a result of a childhood vow that I would keep my distance from all the trouble in the world ... let no one touch me.'

'And yet the farther you seem to withdraw from the world of the living, the closer you come to life itself,' she said urgently. 'You see it dispassionately and, as they say, you see it whole. You see not a man but the idea of a man. The idea which holds him and, at least, you will see and know yourself to such an extent that you could, if you chose, destroy the flesh at will.'

'Ignorance and superstition may not be so bad,' said Philip smiling, chilled by the shadow of his own death which had fallen across the day like an eclipse at noon. 'What you say has a certain appeal. I could all too easily spend my life in a library reading and dreaming, coming closer to what you call the idea of man. I may even do that one day. I don't know. I'm more tempted by that sort of life that I am by one of busy fraudulency. But I can never imagine with any pleasure committing suicide under the vain impression that I was dominating the body once and for all ... spitefully. I have no grudge against the senses. They've given me little pain. I have no guilt.'

'You are still young,' said Sophia, sitting back, rather like a lawyer who has just finished an inconclusive yet important cross-examination of a principal witness – a lawyer who has not yet appealed to the jury.

Philip looked at his watch. 'I'm afraid I'd better go in and shave. I'm going out for dinner.'

'Oh, I'd forgotten. With Charles?'

Philip nodded. 'I believe we're going to the French theatre afterwards.'

'Give him my regards,' she said, too wise to state her disapproval of the volatile Frenchman.

'I shall,' said Philip; and he did, just as he and Charles entered the narrow, dim alley which led to the brothel of the Three Sisters of Fatima from Beirut.

Part Three

'And I wish that all times were April and May, and every month renew all fruits again, and every day fleur-de-lis and gillyflower and violets and roses wherever one goes, and woods in leaf and meadows green, and every lover should have his lass, and they to love each other with a sure heart and true, and to everyone his pleasure and a gay heart.'

An anonymous student,
Thirteenth Century, Paris

CHAPTER TEN

'It usually happens at twelve,' said Glenellen. 'Seldom later than twelve-thirty. Well worth seeing, you know. People come from all around, but very few of us get this close. Takes a lot of managing, believe me.'

'I certainly do,' said Philip, remembering the four locked doors and the villainous *concierge* at the gate.

'You see the great thing is: what shall it be?'

'Does it vary?'

'Continually, from day to day. One never knows what to expect.'

'What will it be today?'

'How should I know? That's one of the reasons I came. In any event, it's one of the seven wonders of Paris, if not of the world.'

'And the other six?'

'I was speaking rhetorically. I don't think you properly appreciate the situation.'

'I was only joking. I'm sorry.'

'Americans always joke,' said Glenellen, sulking. Philip sighed and looked about the room. It was a cube, large and shabby with a dusty gold throne at one end and a number of scallop-shell Venetian chairs, on two of which the visitors sat while the chamberlain, a small dour gentleman wearing the rusty striped trousers and morning coat of a minor French civil servant, complete with worn white cuffs and pearl-grey spats, sat on a frayed wart-like, salmon-coloured pouf; he lacked only the furled umbrella for which, absently, Philip searched with his eyes, deciding that it must be on the other side of the towering bookcase which stood between two of the room's four windows. A door covered with green baize and studded with rusty nails led into the Presence, the shrine.

'Is there anyone else coming?' asked Philip, oppressed by the room's silence, by the lonely far-away sound of the traffic in the street below, muffled by heavy plush curtains which shut out light and air until the cool morning seemed like a lowering twilight . . . he almost expected to hear thunder and the noise of warm rain against the window-panes.

'How should I know?' Glenellen was petulant. 'With considerable effort I have arranged this audience and you sit and make jokes.'

'I'm sorry,' repeated Philip, tired of Glenellen, wishing that he had not accepted the invitation.

The chamberlain on the pouf answered him, however, in French. 'We never know how many will attend the levée . . . seldom less than five, though. Occasionally as many as a hundred, in times of national crisis especially.'

'I see,' said Philip.

'It is also an expensive thing to arrange,' muttered Glenellen. 'One could dine at Maxim's for the cost.'

'If you'll let me, I'll gladly. . . .'

'But you're my guest,' said Glenellen, recovering his usual equanimity. 'I wouldn't hear of such a thing.'

There was a tinkling at the door and the chamberlain rose, stiffly, and walked over to it. Then, after first straightening his coat, he slowly opened it to admit a beautiful young woman with short hair, wearing a shirt, neck-tie, tweed skirt and a pair of sensible shoes; under one arm she carried a swagger stick. 'On the scene yet?' she inquired in a blurred English voice. 'No? Not yet? I'll wait then.' She went over to the bookcase, ignoring Philip, who had risen at her entrance, and Glenellen who had not,

'She comes here every day,' said the chamberlain in a low, proud voice. 'She . . .' but the tinkling of the bell sent him back to the door: this time a slim blond boy, unmistakably American, with a crew-cut and saddle shoes entered, accompanied by an older man with steel-grey hair brushed carefully back from a smooth baby-fat face ... the sort of man who had his nails manicured daily, thought Philip intolerantly, not moving as the newcomers were led by the chamberlain to chairs only a few feet away. The old man looked first at Philip with an expression which he had long since learned to interpret and not to resent; then, seeing Glenellen, he waved one of his well-tended paws and exclaimed: 'Ayre! Why aren't you in Capri?'

'Edmond! My God!' retorted Glenellen, as though stunned; he rallied: 'Haven't seen you since ...'

'The Baths of Nero ... small world.' He looked uneasily at the girl in tweed, as though unsure whether it was safe to speak out; obviously encouraged by the severe lines of her tailored back, he said: 'But I hardly expected to find you here. You don't come regularly, do you?'

'No, this is the first time.'

'Many, many friends of ours come here religiously, all the time. They find it soothing, and I must say I have to admit that I do, too. I mean one shouldn't be ashamed of one's pleasures. ... And is this the charming Mr. Morgan I've heard so much about?'

'No,' said Glenellen, 'it isn't.'

'But do introduce us. I like to know *all* the young Americans in Paris. My name is Edmond Twill,' he said, warmly shaking hands with Philip, both leaning far out of their chairs, neither getting up. 'And this is Jim, an American, too,' said Mr. Twill. The handsome youth with the crew-cut nodded distantly at Philip, not speaking. 'As a matter of fact, we're all Americans here today except Ayre ... quite unusual, too, because as a rule Americans seldom come here ... I can't think why, can you?' he asked Philip, with a smile which revealed very even white false teeth, as clean and neat and expensive as his pearl cuff-links, as well cared for as the round pink finger-nails which tapped out restless messages on the arms of his chair.

'I wouldn't know,' said Philip. 'I've never been here before.'

'I'm sure you'll come again and again, though, the way many of us do. Would you like a cigarette?'

'Cigarettes are forbidden at this time,' said the chamberlain, who was now sitting cross-legged on the pouf.

'I must have lost my head,' giggled Mr. Twill. 'I wonder why

220

I haven't seen you around town, Philip. I thought I knew nearly everyone.'

'I don't know,' said Philip, who knew perfectly well why they had not seen one another before. 'I've been here since the first of August.'

'A whole month! Well, we must do something about that. You and Ayre must come and have dinner with me one evening this week. Will Tuesday be all right . . . at seven?'

Philip shook his head, amused. 'No, I'm afraid I'm tied up that night.'

'Mr. Warren has his *own* world,' said Glenellen, in a warning voice which Mr. Twill, recklessly, chose not to understand.

'But how *special*! So few people have their own world any more. I had one but I gave it away . . . traded it in for the great one. But then we're none of us twenty, are we, Ayre?'

'Speak for yourself, Edmond,' said Glenellen irritably, making various decisive gestures as though he could, with a wave of his hand, dismiss Mr. Twill for ever. But Mr. Twill was not that easily discouraged. He renewed the siege. 'In any event, you and Ayre must stop by my house one day this week for a drink. You'll love the place . . . only a few blocks from here. Used to be the hôtel of the Duc de Lyon et Grénoble. I have a floor in it . . . really fine set of rooms.

'That would be very nice,' said Philip non-committally.

'Do see he comes, Ayre . . . like a good fellow.'

Glenellen glanced at him, not answering. The ringing of the door-bell put a temporary stop to Mr. Twill's offensive. This time nine thin young men of various heights, with a number of exotic arrangements of face hair decorating their sallow countenances, entered; the chamberlain ordered them to stand out of the way, against the wall opposite the bookcase where the girl in tweeds still stood, reading the titles of the books to herself like a rosary, her mouth half open.

'*Messieurs, mesdames*,' said the chamberlain, climbing on top of the pouf, both hands raised to silence the room. 'The moment approaches. Those of you who have never before been presented should take cognizance of the following ceremony. At the moment of Entrance, all must rise to their feet and bow very low until The Seating, after which you, too, may sit down, in absolute silence, however, until The First Statement of the Day. Is that understood by everyone? Are there any questions?

Good.' He jumped to the floor and paused for a moment, as though straining to hear some celestial melody. No one spoke. Then, from behind the Baize Door, came the unmistakable sound of an alarm clock going off, followed by the tolling of a dinner-bell. Slowly the door opened and, preceded by the chamberlain, who backed into the room, a tall figure, with head erect, moved as though sleep-walking across the room to the throne. Philip, who was standing like the others, his head bowed, caught a glimpse of the man, a tall, pale creature with dark red hair, shoulder-length; and wearing a white undecorated gown which touched the floor. When he was seated, the worshippers sat down and waited silently for the First Statement.

The figure on the throne looked straight ahead, the unseeing eyes glassy. Philip wondered if he were drugged. Then, suddenly, remarkably, the eyes became focused, the pupils dilated and in a high toneless voice the man said: 'Augusta.' There was a round of applause.

'Oh, I'm so glad!' exclaimed Mr. Twill. 'I like her best, don't you, Ayre? But I forgot, this is your first time. Believe me, though, when I say it's a real treat you're getting. You just happened to hit it right. You'll adore her as much as we do.'

Throughout the room there was a murmur of approbation following the applause. Everyone seemed pleased and there was a curious atmosphere of good fellowship to which Philip responded with some wonder, not understanding yet what it was these people were experiencing as they moved excitedly around the throne, making remarks about (but not to) the now smiling figure. The chamberlain disappeared into the sanctum behind the Baize Door; he returned a moment later with a large box which was placed on the floor to the left of the throne ... a chair which looked to Philip like a discarded theatrical property, the gold paint mostly gone and the red tassels torn.

'Now comes The Robing,' said Mr. Twill delightedly. 'The best part. I always lose my head during The Robing, don't I, Jim?' But Jim, too, was part of the vast conspiracy to snub Edmond Twill, for he made no answer, only sat passively in his chair watching the others as they opened the large box and reverently removed a number of articles of women's apparel.

'What happens now?' asked Philip.

'Augusta is to be dressed,' answered Mr. Twill, eyes glistening. '*We* do that. It's part of the ritual.'

'Who's Augusta?' asked Philip.

'She sitting on the throne, silly.'

'Oh,' said Philip, his masculine pride suddenly pricked at being called 'silly' by Mr. Twill. He let it go, however. The ritual was now under way. The habitués were crowding about Augusta, each carrying some part of the ceremonial costume. Mr. Twill had seized upon the hat, a toque somewhat similar to that affected by the stately dowager queen of England. The young woman in tweed held a large frivolous-looking brassière, ready to snap it in place at the proper moment ... which soon came, for, at a signal from the chamberlain, Augusta stood up, only to vanish in a sea of clothes and chattering courtiers. All participated in this rite except Glenellen, Philip and the silent American boy.

It was soon over, to the sorrow of the worshippers who were now dangerously excited, shouting to one another in French and English, touching reverently the figure which they had robed with such speed and accuracy: Augusta now stood magnificent, if slightly rumpled, in a floor-length tea-gown of apple green, a feather boa about her shoulders and numerous coral and amber beads attached to her person like decorations on a Christmas tree and with much the same logic and cheerful effect. Over one eye, at a jaunty angle, was the toque, Mr. Twill's triumph.

'The Robing is completed,' announced the chamberlain, and the devotees withdrew slowly, admiringly, their eyes upon Augusta, who stood for a long moment staring at the floor; then she sat down.

'Now wasn't that wonderful?' exclaimed Mr. Twill, joining the non-participants.

'Very fine,' said Glenellen sincerely, his pale eyes interested. Could this be a new hobby? wondered Philip.

'Did you see me manage the *chapeau*? I do it the best, the chamberlain says, and he should know. I mean after all people do it every day yet on the occasions when I do it I add a little something, a nuance, or so he thinks.'

'What does Augusta think?' asked Philip.

'Who can tell? I believe she appreciates it. One can tell a lot from the way she holds her head. When it is thrust slightly forwards, you had better watch out ... she's on the warpath.

When it's to one side, she is nervous ... when the chin is held high, however, that means all is well ... like now. She's always in a good mood when I officiate at The Robing.'

'That's a great honour,' said Glenellen. 'You should be proud.'

'I am indeed. You must take part in the next one, Ayre. Tell the chamberlain you want to. He can fix it.'

'How much?'

'Don't pay more than a thousand francs, That's all *I* ever paid. Some people, Americans mostly, pay as high as ten or fifteen thousand, which is outrageous.'

'Does the money go to Augusta?' Philip was curious about the details.

'Who knows? It certainly goes into the establishment; then of course there are the missions.'

'What missions?'

'Oh ... missions,' said Mr. Twill vaguely.

'Is he booked up, do you think, for the next Robing?' asked Glenellen. 'I would like to attend, you know.'

'Oh, nothing could be easier, if you're properly sponsored and I would be very, very happy to sponsor you, Ayre. You know that.'

'That's awfully kind,' said Glenellen warmly, his former frosty manner quite thawed by the other's generosity as well as by the vision of Augusta seated on her throne, head back, eyes blissfully closed. Absorbing the devotion of the worshippers like a lizard in the noonday sun.

'I suggest you come Friday. It is always Augusta without fail.'

'When is it *not* Augusta?' asked Philip.

'Well, yesterday it was not Augusta. And it probably won't be tomorrow.'

'What was it yesterday?'

'Augustus,' said Mr. Twill. 'That's the whole point of the Hour of Meditation and the First Statement which precedes The Robing. During the hour, the First Statement is decided upon behind the Green Door. No one knows what agony of spirit wracks that frail body during the lonely hour of decision. But always the choice is made; the facts are faced and the First Statement is delivered, calmly and unequivocally, no matter how difficult, how painful the decision behind the Green Door has been. Such courage!'

'Very real courage,' murmured Glenellen, admiringly, 'real character.'

'Such mysticism, too!'

'Obviously. One can see that.'

'The only functioning hermaphrodite in Paris, France,' said the young man named Jim in a low Southern voice which, though the message was heard by no one except his immediate companions, sent a ripple of unanticipated sound through the room; hostile glances were turned upon them and even Augusta was seen to move uneasily, as though aware of a disturbing and unharmonious presence.

'Now, now, Jim,' said Mr. Twill, anxiously, smiling, looking about the room feverishly, exonerating himself, neutralizing with apologetic smiles the effect that that low voice had had on the Post-Robing Assembly. 'You must not say such things here, not in the presence of Her. You are entitled to your opinion like everyone else, but you must have the courtesy, not only to Augusta but to me, to refrain from outbursts like that.'

Jim only grinned, pleased with himself. Philip rather liked him for this unexpected honesty. He wondered idly what he was doing here with Mr. Twill. The obvious explanation seemed unlikely but then Philip never knew. His attention was distracted by Mr. Twill who was discussing the lineage of Augusta. 'You mustn't think that the influence Augusta has and the reverence so many intelligent and unsuperstitious people do her is entirely the result of the unusual condition to which Jim just now alluded. No, indeed! Augusta is directly descended from the goddess Venus and those volumes in that bookshelf prove it . . . and not on the male side (which is never accurate, due to the frailness of women) but through the female line so that there can be no doubt of her legitimacy.'

'How do you know this?' asked Philip, squinting, trying to read the titles on the spines of the books.

'We know it because her genealogy has been traced back to Julius Caesar who, in turn, traced his own ancestry to Venus. Look, she even has the Julian nose.'

And so she had, Philip saw, trying unsuccessfully to recall the details of those busts he had seen which were reputed to be of Caesar.

'Then she is Italian,' said Philip.

'No, she is Augusta,' said Mr. Twill, bowing slightly in the direction of the throne. 'But now comes the Naming of the Names.' And, to Philip's horror, the names of every eldest daughter of the house of Julius in the one hundred generations since that great man's murder were pronounced, slowly and distinctly by the chamberlain, to the obvious pleasure of the worshippers who grew more and more excited as the chamberlain passed from the Middle Ages into the sixteenth century until, by the time the nineteenth century was reached, they were singing and cheering so loudly that they almost drowned out the final name which the chamberlain, in a religious ecstasy, shouted so that all might hear: 'Augusta!'

'Wonderful, wonderful!' said Glenellen, mistily, his eyes tearful with excitement. 'Wonderful! Absolutely wonderful.'

'It is our best moment,' said Mr. Twill simply, wiping his own eyes with the back of a shaking hand. Philip and Jim looked at one another dry-eyed; then Philip looked quickly away as though he was in danger of being detected in a conspiracy.

After the last cheers had died away, Augusta rose and, attended by a profound silence, left the room, the Green Door closing noiselessly behind her. The levée was over and the chamberlain went to the door through which the visitors had originally entered and opening it with a flourish, he bade them all farewell.

In the street, Philip and Glenellen left Mr. Twill and his companion in a flurry of plans; dates and places were still being discussed when a taxi carried off Mr. Twill and the silent Jim.

'What did you think?' asked Glenellen, as they left the rue des Saints-Pères and crossed the tree-lined Boulevard St. Germain.

'Very unusual,' said Philip, not wanting to dampen the other's enthusiasm. 'I liked The Robing very much.'

'Oh, it was magnificent! Really so! I must look into the possibilities of bringing all this to the attention of the world.'

'I suppose their missions do that, don't they?'

'I am speaking on a grand scale. Do you realize that this could catch on? Like wildfire! Something everyone has been waiting for: workers, intellectuals, everyone.'

'I thought you were a Catholic.'

'That has nothing to do with it. The two don't conflict, as I see it. One will complement the other splendidly. I shall wire the Vatican tomorrow.'

'And the Party?'

'What Party?'

'The Communist Party. You were a member when I saw you last spring in Rome.'

'Ah, the Party ... but that was Italy. This is France. Can't you tell the difference? The air is different. None of us is the same: even *you* are changed, in Paris.'

'How am I changed?'

'Well, for one thing you had dark hair in Rome. You are now a blond; that is the principal physical change.'

'I had blond hair in Rome, too,' said Philip sharply.

'Oh, come now, you don't expect me to believe that, do you? Besides, you look very nice with blond hair ... no reason to be ashamed. Many boys dye their hair these days.'

Philip made no comment and in silence they walked down the rue du Bac to the river. In front of the white gleaming Pont Neuf they parted as casually as they had met the day before in the street. Glenellen hoped that they would see a great deal of one another; then he disappeared into the Metro while Philip crossed the bridge, enjoying the warm sun and blue sky, the design of the green gardens on the other side of the river.

One pleasant, aimless day followed another. The summer grew dry and dusty and the leaves darkened on the trees. Here and there, in the Tuileries gardens, an occasional vivid red leaf suggested autumn: the southerly flight of birds, the return of the tourists to the west, a cold time when Paris would become French again, the trees bare-branched and the winter skies as grey as the nineteenth-century façades of the buildings which lined those wide avenues the last Napoleon had carved out of the confusion of narrow medieval streets, avenues still green and gentle with the waning summer.

Neither Anna nor Regina was in Paris. He had inquired after both of them but no one knew when Regina would return. Anna, however, would arrive in six weeks, or so the desk-clerk at the Ida Hotel had assured him that first day in Paris when he had moved in a happy dream through a silver afternoon, so different from the harsh hot country he had left behind early that morning.

He had been fortunate in finding a hotel for himself, a dark congenial place in the rue de l'Université, a block from the rue du Bac. Here he spent his time reading, when he was not sight-seeing or meeting old friends from America who had come over to drink a great deal of cheap wine and to see night clubs where the girls took off all their clothes, so exciting the American boys that Philip almost believed the remark of a French brothel keeper who had once told him, quite seriously, that all Americans were *voyeurs*, except for the aviators who liked to be beaten.

But these old friends of his were in the minority that year for the city had been conquered by his homosexual countrymen, and he watched with wonder as the scandal grew, as mask after mask fell from familiar and ordinary faces to reveal the unexpected, the Grecian visage. Business men from Kansas City, good Rotarians all, embraced bored young sailors on the streets at night or paid high prices for slim Algerian boys at those bordellos which catered to such pleasures. College boys, young veterans, the ones Philip had always known in school or in the Navy, athletes and aesthetes both, ran amok among the bars and urinals in search of one another, the nice girls back home forgotten, as they loved or tried to love one another in this airy summer city.

Like most of his generation, Philip was, of course, tolerant of everything. It was an age in which, as a reaction to the horrors of the various European pogroms and experiments with genocide, his countrymen had been driven, somewhat hysterically, into the opposite direction, until the intolerance of intolerance had become so remarkably virulent that one Jew or one Negro or one Italian not admitted to certain residential districts in America caused more disturbance in the newspapers than the gas chambers at Belsen. Fortunately those people who must always have someone to hate could, if they chose not to be tolerant of intolerance, attack one another on grounds of sexual behaviour. But this last cherished area for intolerance was suddenly declared out of bounds by a celebrated statistical report which revealed that one third of the nation's men had, at one time or another, committed a homosexual act. This survey promptly lessened everyone's guilt and, if only by weight of the numbers given, it made the idea of pederasty much less remote, no longer exclusively associated with managers of flower shops or with a fearful fumbling in the back row of a darkened movie house. Those sturdy youths who had been ashamed of their secret practice now took much pleasure, at least in Paris, in openly doing what they pleased and, with all the enthusiasm of zealots, they proselyted furiously.

It amused Philip to think that his own puritan nation of Baptists and Methodists and good sound Americanism should, in its moment of empire, become so gaudily Roman, so truly imperial in one generation. Yet he disliked feeling out of things. The groups that gathered on the landing of his hotel would stop their intense conversations when he walked by and he was aware, or thought he was aware, of a real contempt in their eyes for a countryman who, because of some basic duplicity or sexual inadequacy, refused to play the game. Nor did he enjoy being treated like a pretty young girl who could be rolled into bed at a moment's notice by a properly aggressive man. The tragic novel of the age, he decided irritably, would not be about the anguish of the sensitive neurotic youth who wanted to make ladies' hats but about the confusion of the undistinguished, womanizing youth who came to the big city to make his fortune, only to find that everywhere he turned men desired him and that the ill will his refusal to surrender his virtue created was so great that he was forced either to adapt himself to a life of pederasty or to go back home, not returning to the big city until age had so lessened his physical attractions that he was rendered safe from abuse.

He had, however, two allies who felt the same as he did: apostates, for they had been lovers for seven years, first in high school, then in the Army, then in college and finally here in Paris, in a room next to his own. They were both twenty-five, robust, and charmingly simple. The following June, when they graduated from college, they were to be married to two girls they had known for a long time in their home town, Spartanburg, South Carolina, and their future was to be as simple and as well-directed as their past, living next door to one another, working in the same business. They would even, they confided to Philip name their children for one another.

'What will the wives think of all this?' asked Philip, putting his feet up on the bed. He was in their room, a small one with two big beds, an old bureau and a bidet hidden by a torn curtain. The window was tall, however, and the room was cool and full of light. Clothes were scattered everywhere: as well as tennis rackets, bathing-trunks, even a pair of boxing gloves for they were obsessed with their bodies, eating carefully, drinking very little, keeping their bellies flat with exercise. He could hear them every morning, doing push-ups, puffing and straining, He had never heard them make love, however, even though the walls were thin ... not that he had wanted to, quite the opposite, yet the idea had a real fascination for him, a morbid appeal, like the time when once, at a resort, he had slept in the room next to his parents and had heard everything until he could stand it no longer, until he had covered his head with a pillow. Unlike the other occupants of the hotel, these young men were quiet and well-behaved. Regularly, often in Philip's company, they picked up girls and brought them back to the hotel, increasing rather than diminishing their love for one another on these occasions when, side by side on the same bed, they possessed the women, to use a good Victorian verb, an applicable one, thought Philip, since their devotion and respect for each other was essentially nineteenth century: neither would have dreamed of humiliating the other, unlike most American combinations, orthodox or not. He was continually beguiled by the Southern courtliness with which they treated one another.

'I don't suppose they'll think anything about it at all,' said the taller one, a fair-haired, dark-eyed boy named Stephen. 'I mean, they've known we've always been friends. They'd think it was unnatural if we stopped seeing one another after we got married.'

'Besides, the girls get along,' said Bill, a stocky young man with a boxer's figure and dark curly hair which grew low on his forehead. 'I guess it would be impossible if they didn't like each other.'

'You seem to have worked it all out very carefully,' said Philip, not concealing his admiration for a long-range plan which had, so far at least, worked out.

'We figured the whole thing out in high school,' said Stephen with gentle pride, scooping all the dirty clothes up and tossing them in a corner.

'How do you plan to get away? I mean ... see each other?'

'We'll be living in the same block and everybody knows we like to go hunting in the season, on week-ends, when the weather is good. And the girls, they would never go hunting. We'll have a lot of week-ends together. Oh, there'll be plenty of time for everything.'

'Well, you've done a good job,' said Philip, sighing, thinking of his own loveless, aimless life which, though it usually pleased him, was obscurely incomplete: he could hear the beast in the jungle so clearly that he felt he knew what it would be like when, finally, at the end of a long difficult chase, he found it. But he envied these lovers for having stumbled across it at an age when he had not even suspected that the jungle contained another living creature beside himself.

'I think so, too,' said Bill, leaning back on the bed, stretching his legs till they cracked, his head against Stephen's thigh.

Philip was both envious and depressed . . . the trail had never before seemed so dark to him, or the quarry so elusive. He hated them for one ungrateful instant.

The evening was warm and windless when they arrived at the Café Flore and took their places at a table outside, close to the street where the curious and the fantastic stared at one another solemnly. Young men with beards wearing blue jeans and open red-checked shirts contrived to look more like Iowa than Murger, while the young women, their hair long and tangled, also wore open shirts and blue jeans, as dirty as the boys and quite as happy, as they too pursued the grand grim business of expressing themselves, imitating the French of that quarter who, with no effort at all, managed to be far dirtier, far more dishevelled . . . in every way fine models for these children of the new world who had temporarily forsaken ice-cream, Coca-Cola and the linoleum-floored new high schools of the West.

The sight saddened, rather than amused Philip, who truly disliked this display of conventionality on the part of his simpler contemporaries as they attempted so hungrily to absorb the nineteenth-century romantic manner in a world which, for better or worse, was changed in every way. The rebel with combed hair and clean shirt could pull down the temple far faster than all these sad dirty boys from Iowa in concerted action could. He thought of the yards of virgin canvas these children had smeared in their dusty rooms, the thousands of poems composed entirely of commas or of nouns only, the endless novels of anguished misunderstood youth drugged with self-pity among the myriad stars, so far from earth that in the vast resounding emptiness of sky no other person could ever

231

intrude upon the endless pain and delight of that self-absorption, the bitter-sweet pleasures of the onanist ... the very young, lost to man, if not for ever, for at least that one season of youth when, humourless and blind, they moved through the streets of an old city, indifferent to others, licensed in their stumbling way by a perfunctory offering to the unknown majesty of art, all other faces blurred yet no stranger's face so remote as the one which peered at them from mirrors and the glass of dark windows, the faces they showed the world diffidently or defiantly, it made no difference which until, should they be in luck, the true identity was revealed at last in a work, or, best of all, twice reflected in the eyes of another.

The two Southerners were amused, pointing out the various freaks to one another, without malice or condescension, examining with wonder the superficial variety of which man is capable. Every now and then a murmur went through the crowded café as a celebrity of some sort passed by or the rumour of a celebrity who might have passed by and, immediately, all eyes turned in the same direction and two camps, one friendly, one hostile, discussed the poor creature freely, to his face if he was unwise enough to linger here.

'Did you ever try writing anything?' asked Stephen turning to Philip.

'Not seriously,' said Philip, recalling Cyril Connolly's protest that he never again wanted to read a novel where, referring to a character who was an artist, another character asked: 'How's his stuff?'

'I'm surprised,' said Stephen. 'You always struck me like you might be a writer or something.'

'Just my pedantic manner,' said Philip who had himself often been struck with the superficial resemblance he, on occasion, bore to those who fashioned the one bright book of life.

He was about to give them his considered views on contemporary literature in America and its marked resemblance to the hat business, when a slim familiar figure walked past their table, paused, and then came back. It was the boy who had been with Edmond Twill at Augusta's levée. He was very handsome, thought Philip, looking at the golden hair and dark blue eyes. He was dressed like a conservative schoolboy in dark grey trousers and a sports coat. 'You're Philip, aren't you? I met you last week ... at that place.'

'I remember,' said Philip. 'Stephen, Bill, this is Jim.' It was like the Navy, he thought, the old anonymous days of first names. The three Southern boys gravely shook hands. 'Want a drink?' asked Philip.

Jim shook his head. 'I've got to go,' he said, in his low expressionless voice. 'You want to meet me here tomorrow at six?'

'Why ... all right,' said Philip, suddenly, surprised not only at the invitation but at his own prompt acceptance.

'I'll see you then ... at six. Good-bye.' He nodded to the others and walked away.

Bill chuckled. 'Looks like you got yourself a buddy.'

'Do you a world of good,' said Stephen.

'I'm sure it will,' smiled Philip, who saw no reason to protest.

Under a violet summer sky, they met at six. A storm threatened and the leaves of the trees along the boulevard fluttered white and green in the sudden wind. The air smelled of sun and stone but there was a wet sharp edge to the hot wind which came from the north-west where the night and the thunder waited. An awning had been unfurled over the outdoor tables; here a few quiet tourists sat, waiting for Sartre.

'Let's get out of here,' said Jim. 'It's going to rain.'

Philip, surrendering himself to the other's care, followed him across the square to the church of St. Germain de Prés behind which was a narrow street, damp and shadowy, where above a restaurant Jim lived. 'We can have a drink there,' he said. 'Then if it rains, we can eat downstairs.'

Philip said that sounded all right to him although he wondered, a little uneasily, what was expected of him.

'This is the dump,' Jim said, opening a door, revealing two high-ceilinged rooms furnished haphazardly. A large carved bed of dark wood with four posters but no canopy stood in the centre of the second room whose windows looked out on a grey court, littered with broken tile and discarded furniture. Unframed drawings by Tchelichew and Picasso were propped on the grey marble mantelpiece, a relic of the house's one-time splendour. To Philip's surprise, the drawings were originals and one of them, the head of a lean Picasso boy, was familiar to him and, presumably, of great value. There were no books anywhere except for a beautifully bound set of Balzac scattered

233

carelessly on a plain kitchen table, as though placed there on arrival and never touched again.

'I've even got a bathroom,' said Jim, as the storm broke over Paris with a sudden roar. 'Oh . . . there she goes.' They went to the window and looked out at the grey diagonals of rain which splattered in the street below; the gutters became rivers while the rain made sudden coronets of water in the puddled streets; men and women ran for cover with newspapers and umbrellas unfurled. The day was over and evening, dark and secret in the rain, moved across the wet city, following close upon the lighting of the street lamps.

'I like the rain,' said Philip, aware that someone always said that.

'I don't,' said Jim. 'But then I don't give it much mind.'

'That's a Southern expression,' smiled Philip, as they turned away from the window and went back into the dark room. Philip stumbled against a chair, Jim turned on a single lamp.

'I am Southern,' he said. 'Sit down and I'll get you some wine. Or do you want Pernod? I got both.'

'I'll have Pernod. Where did you come from originally?' Philip found himself for some reason fearing silence, not wanting to be alone in the room with Jim with only the sound of rain against the windows; he was ill at ease, without words.

'From Virginia.' He brought two wine-glasses out of a cupboard and carefully filled them both. 'Here you go.' The apéritif slopped on to Philip's hand. 'I'm sorry,' said Jim. 'Need a handkerchief?'

'That's all right. I've got one.' He wiped the stickiness off his fingers, slowly, deliberately, wanting to prolong the operation, to delay the moment of revelation which he was sure, resided in the baroque clock on the mantelpiece . . . when the long and short hands came to a predestined conjunction he would be forced to handle, with tact and severity, his companion's suggestion. A moment later, Philip saw he had made a mistake: the clock was broken; both were spared. Relieved, he said: 'I like Virgina, what I've seen of it . . . around Warrenton I come from New York.'

'I figured you were a Northerner.'

'Have you been in Paris long?'

'Three years.'

'A long time.'

'A real long time. But I like it here.'

'You don't want to go back?'

'No, I can't go back, even if I wanted to.'

'Oh . . . I'm sorry.'

'Nothing to be sorry about. I got into trouble. Lot of people get into trouble. So I left. I've had a good time.'

Philip was puzzled by the other's bleakness. He was curious about the trouble but his own years in the Navy had taught him not to inquire too closely into the lives of others . . . partly from fear of embarrassing them, partly because they might embarrass him with too complete an account of their lives. Mystery was often best.

'Are you working now? In Paris?' This was tactless, Philip knew, but he persisted.

Jim smiled at him, a slow engaging smile and, with the first show of warmth either had displayed that evening, he said: 'I don't work. You know that.'

'Oh.' Philip was stopped. Not knowing what to answer, he grinned foolishly and drank his Pernod in two long fiery swallows.

'I just drift along. It's easier.'

'Do you . . . like Twill?' asked Philip.

'No, I don't like any of them.'

'They like you.'

'Yes . . . funny, isn't it? I've often wondered why.'

'You're good-looking.' This was not the sort of remark Philip liked to make to another man, but having accepted the other's line, he was bound to it.

Jim made a face. 'They can get a better-looking piece of flesh with a bigger thing for a dollar in any street in this town.'

'Maybe they're attracted by your hostility.'

'I've thought of that. But then I'm always very quiet when I'm around them . . . a real good boy who doesn't say much.'

'And you get money?' Philip sounded to himself like a college boy talking to his first prostitute, asking her how she could possibly have become so degraded.

'I get everything.' He waved his hand briefly at the apartment, the drawings, the set of Balzac. 'One old guy settled a hundred a month on me for life.'

'For his life, or yours?'

Jim laughed. 'For mine. Get property . . . that's the thing. So many kids, when they start in, just go around chiselling drinks until they get fat and dull and nobody wants them any more. But I get cash if I can . . . or jewellery or pictures: I've learned a lot about painting these last few years. I once spotted a phony Degas some old guy tried to get me to take.'

'You make the deal in advance?'

'I'm not that crude. I get things without asking. That's what I mean when I say I don't know what it is that they see. I've often thought that if I knew what it was, I'd really be able to cash in.'

'I suspect,' said Philip, 'that the fact you don't know may be your charm. Self-consciousness often produces great art, but I doubt if many find it a lovable trait, in others. The secret to wide popularity is a kind of mysterious negativity . . . something that can't be imitated. Not that I mean you're actually negative, or mysterious (though you may, for all I know, be both), but you give that appearance.'

'How did you figure that out?'

Philip, half-way through his spurious character analysis, suddenly realized the implication of his blunder. He had started talking nervously, affected by the rain and the dark, by the Pernod gulped too quickly on an empty stomach and, carried away by his own solemn attempt at analysis, he had managed to create a false impression on several levels at once . . . a considerable trick, he thought wryly, undoing the damage, reorganizing what he had said.

'I was putting it more in terms of the president of a high school class,' he said glibly. 'When I was in school the handsomest and quietest boy in class was always elected president. No one envied him, no one feared him; he was admired because of the strength of character his pleasing silence obviously hid. Boys who boasted were always thought liars; it never occurs to simple people that a loud, conceited person may be more competent than a modest quiet one.' They were now a long way from the centre and Philip examined the idea of popularity until, sick of it himself, he stopped suddenly in the middle of a sentence and stared at the Picasso sketch, the monotonous noise of the rain succeeding the equally monotonous sound of his own voice in the room.

'We'd better have another drink,' said Jim, filling their glasses.

Half-way through the second glass of Pernod, Philip's unease vanished and he talked about himself, freely, and Jim seemed nearly as interested as he himself was. Yet the pleasures of egotism were brought to a rude halt when Jim suddenly asked him if he liked boys.

'No,' said Philip, freezing, aware that a misstep would distress them both. 'I never have.'

'Not even once, in school?'

'Not even then. I have all the earmarks of a pederast. I suppose . . . or so a friend of mine at Harvard used to say; but I've never done anything about it.'

'Would you like to?'

'No, I don't think so. I'm too old to change my habits . . . and they tell me it's mostly habit.'

'You wouldn't like to try?' The invitation was abrupt.

'No, I wouldn't. I'm sorry.'

Jim sighed, but not sadly. 'You might have liked it.'

'I wouldn't know what to do.'

'You wouldn't have to do anything.'

'I'm not that passive. I could never enjoy lying still while somebody else thrashed around.'

'But you'd give me pleasure,' said Jim, smiling, some of his early abruptness gone; he was almost gentle.

'That's the worst of it,' said Philip, a new idea occurring to him . . . one which might be very significant. 'I don't want to give anyone pleasure, especially a man.'

'You want to give a woman pleasure.'

'Yes . . . no. Consciously I do, for the usual selfish reasons; unconsciously, I want to take care of myself and go home.'

'Even when you're in love?'

'I've never been in love.'

'I'm one up on you.'

'Did you like it?'

'That's a stupid question.' Jim's voice was unexpectedly sharp. He apologized quickly. 'I'm sorry. I didn't mean that.'

'Forget it,' said Philip, his curiosity aroused. But then, remembering his new idea, he worried it a bit. 'I think maybe that's the difference between men and women, between men and certain kinds of pederasts; the man's instinct is to take his pleasure, the woman's to give it, to receive the man.'

'That could explain the old guys in the latrines, looking for

237

sailors. They get a charge out of that.'

'Of course I know women who wanted men the same way men ordinarily want women, but there don't seem to be too many of them ... yet who knows? Perhaps the difference in attitudes is only a social one. . . .'

'I don't think you know very much about it,' said Jim, nicely.

'Am I wrong?'

'Damned if I know. I haven't got any theory. All I know is that it's one thing to love somebody and another thing to have sex with somebody you don't know or don't care about, the way I do all the time.'

'Women, I know, often get their greatest pleasure out of the man's excitement. They ignore him. He's just so much sweating, heavy bone and flesh on top of them but when they realize that it is their own lovely, desirable body which has made an animal out of him, they are quite carried away by this vision of their own desirability and they reciprocate, loving themselves being loved in his arms.' This very nearly said it, thought Philip, not wanting to see any cracks in the dike of his reasoning, pleased with the area he had rescued, if only for a moment from the floor of a confused sea.

'You make it sound like acrobatics,' said Jim mildly.

'Isn't it? It's usually that in ... well, in the other world.'

'I don't think so. I suppose I've been mauled as much as anybody can be but, in spite of all that, I think it's possible to care about one person and to forget the acrobatics and think just of him and not the two bodies. But I suppose I hold that romantic notion because I'm just a whore and know how little sex has to do with loving. I've got a theory that the more you do it, the more likely you are to love somebody when the time comes.'

'When is that?'

'Only once for me, so far . . . maybe again. I hope so.'

'Never for me, so far. But then, how can one tell? What's love for me may just be an ordinary experience to another person . . . or a leap into the abyss for still another.'

'I've ... It's stopped raining,' said Jim, who apparently disliked theorizing as much as Philip enjoyed it. 'Shall we go across the street and have dinner? It's better than the place downstairs.'

'I'd like to. I didn't have lunch today.'

'They got wonderful snails across the street.'

'I don't like snails.'

'Have you ever tried any?'

'No.'

'Well, how do you know?' They both laughed and Philip realized the crisis had passed. He was relieved. He was also surprised how callow and inexperienced he felt beside this youth whose life had been, or so he would have supposed, so much less than his own, so differently balanced.

He thought of Henry Miller's rhetorical title, 'The Wisdom of the Heart', and, while he ate snails with Jim in the dingy restaurant, he wondered what, if anything, the phrase might mean: intuition? Possibly. And what was that? Accuracy in emotional matters achieved by chance, quickly, illogically, without recourse to any deliberation. That was intuition, he thought, not liking the snails. But what then was accuracy? Emotion was not a logic and one person's definition of a state of being or of a situation which involved himself and a lover, say, might not be remotely like his partner's ... the wisdom of one man's heart could very easily seem like a shocking ignorance to another's. Without ultimates it was impossible to define anything except in immediate, in relative terms. Perhaps, he thought suddenly, the heart's wisdom was the knowledge that two people in a certain relationship *together* possessed, for that moment at least, in that one place, a special joint knowledge of mysteries which, separately, was denied them. He looked curiously at the snail-eating Jim, and wondered if he *knew*, if he had really *been*. . . .

After dinner, somewhat against Philip's will, they went back to Jim's apartment. 'Just for a moment,' he said, as they climbed the damp-smelling stairs. 'I have to practise my vice.'

When they got to the front room, Jim turned on a lamp, an orange and black Japanese lantern; then he placed what looked to Philip like a Bunsen burner from a chemistry class in the middle of the table. A blue flame blossomed at the end of a lighted match.

'Have to be careful,' said Jim, lighting the burner. 'I don't want to set the place on fire.' From a cabinet he took out a yard-long wooden pipe, brightly decorated with Moorish designs, and a thin metal spoon in which he placed a single dark pellet. 'This is the tricky part ... the cooking. Have to have a

239

steady hand.' Holding the spoon in one hand over the flame, he prodded the melting pill with the end of a safety-pin. A strong odour like incense, like medicine, filled the room. 'Now,' said Jim, 'here it goes.' The hot viscous remains of the pellet were poured into the chimney of the pipe and quickly, all in one integrated movement, Jim turned off the blue flame, put down the spoon and raised the pipe to his lips and inhaled so deeply and so long that his face grew red and his eyes stared. Then, slowly, he exhaled a pale cloud of smoke. 'Oh, that's good stuff,' he said happily, smiling at Philip. 'That's better than anything I know. Better than loving.' He took several more lungsful of the smoke before he offered the pipe to Philip, who declined on the unusual but accurate grounds that, since he did not smoke tobacco, he wouldn't know how to inhale.

'Well, it won't work if you can't inhale,' agreed Jim. 'Anyway, you ate the snails. That's enough for one night.'

'How do you feel?' asked Philip curiously.

'Like I'm dreaming . . . a little like a dream of flying.'

'Better than love?'

'Wouldn't you rather fly than make love?'

'Any day.'

'This way I feel like I'm doing both.'

'Shall I go?'

'Oh no . . . not yet. Stay with me until I'm asleep. It won't be long.' He walked over to the carved bed and carefully, like a figure in a motion picture at half speed, he lay down, the pipe still clutched in his hand. 'Sit over here,' he said, pointing to the edge of the bed. Philip did, both of their faces in shadow now, the dull orange lantern far away in the other room, like daylight at a tunnel's end. 'Would you take my shoes off? I don't like to move when I get this far.'

Philip untied the scuffed, schoolboy's shoes and put them neatly side by side on the floor, scrupulously, neurotically careful not to touch the other's body, to avoid receiving the sensual shock warm flesh against warm flesh invariably had, no matter what one's habit was. 'Now I feel better,' said Jim softly. 'I can't think of anything unpleasant when I'm like this. Can't think about you.'

'About me?'

'About the ones like you I've known . . . but it all seems fine

240

now I'm flying.' He inhaled again and again. The sweet heavy odour was making Philip sick; he wanted to go.

'I don't eat the dregs,' said Jim suddenly. 'Some people do, but not for me. It's the worst of all. When you start to do that, you can't ever walk again, never touch the ground until they bury you in it. . . .' His voice grew softer and softer as he talked, now of flight, now of a river and one green day long ago in June. For a time Philip sat beside him in the shadowy room and listened to him talk. But then, when he was sure that the other was no longer conscious of him, he got quickly to his feet and, blowing out the paper lantern, he left the apartment.

In the street, he paused. A thin grey rain was falling now and he was grateful for its coolness and for the fresh night air which he breathed in great gulps until he could no longer taste or smell the smoke on which, far away, Jim drifted, momentarily beyond the gravity which would, Philip knew, pull him back one day to the hard inevitable earth beneath that pale cloud which now maintained him, for one eternity at least, safe and dreaming above the land. The rain was cold in Philip's face, as he hurried down the rue de l'Université to his hotel.

'We were picked up,' said Stephen, when Philip got back to the hotel.

'That's right,' Bill chuckled. 'Friend of yours, too. He said to send you his love.'

'Who was that?'

'An old queen named Edmond Twill. We didn't know you were handling the carriage trade.' They laughed mockingly.

'I met him once,' began Philip, feeling suddenly guilty.

'At a religious ceremony,' said Stephen. 'He told us all about it.'

'I wish he'd told *me* all about it. I'm still confused.'

'Perhaps he will tomorrow. There's a party and we're invited . . . you, too.'

'What kind of a party?'

'Can't you guess?' said Bill.

'We're going,' said Stephen. 'For the hell of it.'

'He said he wanted some men for a change . . . I thought that was real flattering.'

'Are you sure he wants me to come?' asked Philip.

'Sure,' said Stephen. 'He wants you special. He told me so. He also said that you were being kept by Lord Somebody-or-other, but that you had stolen his car and sold it.'

Philip whistled. 'That's a wild one.'

'You didn't sell it, did you?' asked Bill.

'Never knew he had a car. I've only seen him once since I've been in Paris. I wonder who started that story.'

'According to Mr. Twill, everybody knows it. He said the only reason you weren't in jail was because you had too much on him, on Lord What's-his-name.'

'That's quite a story,' said Philip, more amused than angry.

'Anyway,' continued Bill, obviously enjoying himself, 'he's going to have the old guy at the party just to see what will happen . . . only I'm not supposed to tell you that he'll be there. Mr. Twill wants a scene.'

'I told him you weren't one of the boys,' said Stephen, 'But he wouldn't believe me.'

'They never do,' said Bill.

Mr. Twill occupied a floor of one wing of the former Hotel of the Duc de Lyon et Grénoble, a Marshal of Napoleon, who had grandly renovated the one-time town house of a ci-devant aristocrat whose head had fallen nobly into the basket during the Terror, to the cheers of the blood-minded women of Paris, one of whom had stolen it, according to legend, and rolled it all the way to the aristocrat's house where she had then, in a fit of poetic justice, heaved it through a window, frightening the clerks in the government bureau which occupied the house at that time. A generation later, the Duc de Lyon et Grénoble, having robbed the quarter-master corps of a great many golden napoleons, restored the house to a point considerably beyond its original splendour. Traces of the Marshal's private vision of elegance were everywhere in the suite Mr. Twill now ornamented; although two Watteau fans and a heavenly stole occupied the place of honour over the mantelpiece where once the portrait of the Emperor had hung, beneath two sabres crossed by the baton of a Marshal of France.

Money was as much in evidence now as it had been during the years the Duc had lived in these high-ceilinged rooms with their white and gold walls, marble floors, resplendent (if dusty) chandeliers which were suspended like inverted frozen fountains from ceilings where cherubs and Napoleonic deities consorted archly with one another against a cerulean sky.

Mr. Twill received them in the first of two drawing-rooms. He looked much as ever, thought Philip, in spite of the feathered hat he wore and the white flowing gown which sparkled with brilliants.

'Do you like it?' he asked, giving Philip his hand. I have the most wonderful little man who can copy anything. I don't suppose you recognize it, do you? It's from a Winterhalter portrait of the Empress Elizabeth. She was my ideal, you know.' He turned to Stephen and Bill, who were staring at him with frightened eyes. 'My two Southern lambs! How sweet of you to come. I've always said Southern boys are the loveliest. Don't you think so, Phil? But what have I said? You're not Southern!'

'South of Albany,' said Philip, pleased with his own *sang-froid*. He thought of a message a British secretary of Legation in Asia was supposed to have sent the Foreign Office: 'A rebel army sawed H.M.'s Minister in half and committed other diplomatic improprieties.' Philip had just witnessed the division of the Minister; he was now prepared for anything. But anything proved only to be several middle-aged gentlemen in evening gowns and twenty or thirty young men in Brooks Brothers suits. They were gathered, for the most part, in the second drawing-room, seated on Louis Quinze gilt chairs and fauteuils. On one wall a tapestry depicted Sebastian receiving, with certain smugness, the arrows of his fate. Two Japanese boys in white jackets served champagne and brandy.

It was superficially like almost any party, thought Philip, yet in essence it was radically different ... unfocused, even if one were to disregard the presence of the monsters in their lovely gowns. In the other world, when men without women were together in the same room, an entirely different atmosphere was evoked: one that was louder, more fraternal, dull but easy, not like this decorous group of watchful creatures whose eyes never for a second ceased to shift from person to person, judging, calculating, comparing. Cats and dogs, thought Philip grimly, following Stephen and Bill into the room aware of the excited interest which burst over them like waves over the bow of a ship leaving its calm harbour for high seas.

Stephen and Bill were immediately separated by three young Frenchmen with narrow shoulders and pink healthy faces who

moved between the lovers with all the cunning of a star bas-
ketball team in a classic manoeuvre. Philip, in his turn, was
borne to the still centre of the party by a nervous, hair-chested
Frenchman in a low-cut crimson gown, slashed with gold, a
large cameo about his neck.

'*Joli gosse, n'est-ce pas?*' he commented to two older conventionally dressed men who sat side by side on the largest
couch in the room, a number of young men arranged around
them, some speaking English, others French, their sibilants
cracking like whips across the room, no matter which language
they spoke. Philip was introduced to everyone and he smiled
amiably, taking his place on the couch between the two older
men, one of whom was, to his delight, Clyde Norman.

'My dear Philip. It's been an age.'

'Half a year.'

'Ah, the year ... the precious year. I see you haven't forgotten, have you? *Toujours fidèle.*'

'To whatever it is.'

'But don't you know?'

'Three hundred sixty odd days ... no more.'

'You still haven't decided?'

'No. I'm afraid you were right. It's not so easy. Nothing short
of a major revelation will do it now. If anything, I'm more confused than I was. Too much experience is worse than too little.'

'It wasn't experience you lacked, only conviction ... and conviction takes a lifetime to come by.'

'I hope not. I don't want to go on for ever like this.'

'Why not? Aren't you enjoying yourself? You're young and
pretty ... why live in the future?'

'Why live at all is the question I ask myself,' said Philip,
wanting to change the subject which, fortunately, a Japanese
bearing champagne interrupted; when he withdrew, Philip was
able to ask Mr. Norman where he had summered.

'Torquay, of all places ... the British Riviera. I stayed with a
sister I'd forgotten all about. Now I'm on my way back to
Rome.'

'Is Glenellen here?'

'Not yet. He told me he'd seen you. He's got a new interest,
you know. Augustus, or whatever his name is.'

'I know,' said Philip. 'By the way, I understand I've been
accused of stealing his car.'

'First I ever heard of it,' said Mr. Norman. 'But now, tell me all about Egypt.'

Philip told him, his eyes as watchful as all the others, sizing up each newcomer, commiserating with Stephen and Bill who, having been taken captive separately, were being devoured alive by the bright-eyed little Frenchmen.

'What, by the way, are you doing here?' asked Mr. Norman, after he had swallowed his third glass of champagne and could dare to be less delicate than usual. 'You haven't by any chance ...' But three glasses of champagne were not sufficient to give him the courage to finish that sentence; so he merely gestured weakly with one hand and frowned.

'Oh no,' said Philip. 'I'm just a tourist.'

'I thought so. But, with Americans, it's often hard to tell ... with the young especially.'

'I met Mr. Twill at Augusta's levée, a place Glenellen took me to,' said Philip carefully. 'Then I ended up here.'

'In the secret shrine of the lodge, as it were.'

'Where are the articles of worship?'

'There's only one ... the sacred totem which each man carries with him and to which our *laus perennis* is addressed.'

'There are, of course, deviationists,' said Philip.

'Worse ... schism! Since the very beginning there have been interventionists.'

'Better to give than to receive?'

'This philosophy precisely. But there is a movement afoot, not organized of course, to bring the two groups closer; for one to complement the other.'

'Don't they do that now?'

'Often in individual practice, but, since the initial heresy, various interdicts have been hurled back and forth and the gap has widened terribly in certain countries. I must say, however, that we look to America for the third way which both of the traditional Western parties could accept ...'

'And the third way?'

'All Americans know it,' said Mr. Norman roguishly. 'It is the practice of the young nation ... no matter what your interests, whether you belong or not, you know instinctively *the way*. That is a rule. I've known many Americans and all accepted, even if they did not *live*, the third way.'

'I knew something fine and spiritual would one day come out

of America,' said Philip, who was fast losing track of the conversation. 'I never thought it would be that.'

'Neither did any of us. One's first reaction to the idea of America is: look at all that money! those vigorous pioneers! uncouth fathers of thousands of children! But when they came over here during the last war, ah! we were surprised. Since the last century of course we have been used to the American exquisites, the careful New Englanders, the opulent New Yorkers who collected our paintings with the same energy that their daughters collected our titled men. They were too gentlemanly, too civilized to be endured, especially the bachelors who accompanied their mothers obediently from spa to spa, entranced by each new dowager, revelling in our old world of manners which might have expired sooner than it did had it not been for the heady and unexpected applause of our Western cousins. But the war ... that was something else. Those lovely golden youths without guilt, like an Athenian army come to save an outlying province from the Persians. It was not until I'd come to know those youths that I realized what the frontier had been like. We'd forgotten in Europe what a world without women could be like. We grew up in rebellion against an old society, the organized world of our mothers, the elaborate conventions which contained, with remarkable success, the native exuberance of the young. We turned away from what we knew, not loving the other but rather hating what we had known. Then, suddenly, the children of that last frontier descended on us and showed us what it was, traditionally to love one another: not out of hate or inadequacy, but spontaneously like the Moslems, like those Asiatics whom we call inscrutable. It was a refreshing experience, believe me. The third way. ... Such a relief after the accretion of attitudes and fetishes which have so long burdened both our camps that our activities have become as formalized and as ritualistic as a ballet. *Le vice anglais*, that sort of thing was unknown to those frontiersmen who lived without women and who loved one another, men who needed men in every sense.'

'We're several generations removed from the frontier,' said Philip gently, thinking of the nervous pederasts on the beaches of Southern California, descendants of the forty-niners, their dyed hair carefully arranged as they searched continually for those lusty youths who would tolerate them for a price, who often in a neurotic frenzy beat them to their great delight: oh, pioneers! 'We have our rebels, too,' said Philip, 'but our world is almost as rigidly stratified as yours. The frontier is gone, its myth ignobly preserved by Wild West movies.

'Where the hero never kisses the girl.'

'Where the hero kisses the horse's ass,' said Philip. 'And, speaking of horses, there is Glenellen.'

The peer, wearing a plum-coloured smoking-jacket and a gold chain about his neck, the sort wine stewards in the better restaurants affect, approached the couch where Philip and Mr. Norman were seated, the bleeding Sebastian behind them and the youths in a semi-circle before them. 'There you are. I'm exhausted, absolutely shattered.' And he sat down heavily. 'Such a day . . . there were a hundred this morning.'

'Where? A hundred what?' asked Mr. Norman.

'A hundred in attendance on Augusta at The Robing . . . you've never seen such a madhouse! Then I spent all the afternoon at the new mission. We now have an abbot and eleven monks there. I am following the medieval church in my reorganization of the various missions. Such a task! Absolutely Augean! Doubt if I shall survive it.'

'Where will it end, Ayre?' asked Mr. Norman, no longer an ally.

'In a world conversion . . . I demand nothing less. I've been entrusted by Augusta with The Chain.' He fingered the chain about his neck which, Philip saw, was indeed a wine steward's badge of office for the small cup which was pendant to it bore the legend 'Ritz Hotel', in a handsome engraved script.

'A very great responsibility,' said Mr. Norman.

'It makes one, somehow . . . humble, to feel the weight of such a responsibility on one's shoulders. I sometimes feel myself hardly equal to the task.'

'About the car,' said Philip, interrupting.

'What car?'

'I don't know. I heard some crazy story that I'd been accused of stealing your car.'

'I don't think I accused you.'

'But you're not sure?'

'Not entirely. I vaguely recall having drawn up a list of suspects for the *Sûreté*. Your name might possibly have been on that list.'

'Even though I didn't know you had a car? that I had seen you only once, briefly, since I'd been in Paris.'

'One can never tell.'

'I would appreciate it if you told Mr. Twill that I didn't steal it ... told him right now.'

'My dear fellow, you're taking much too pedantic an attitude about this. Besides, the police discovered I'd left it myself on a side street; *they* didn't make a scene ... took it very well, as a matter of fact.'

'You should exonerate Mr. Warren,' said Clyde. 'It is only fair.'

'Later,' said Glenellen. 'By the way, Clyde, I've arranged for you to attend the Friday levée. It's always the best.'

'I'll be there. Any special costume?'

'We like a morning coat, but, alas, so few people have them nowadays. Only the English Lesbians dress properly ... vigorous crew: backbone of our missions, both here and abroad.'

'Abroad?' Mr. Norman's eyebrows arched. 'Has it spread so far?'

'Indeed it has. Nicaragua, Germany and Norway all boast Missions, while we have Conveyors of the Word in England, Italy, Spain and Switzerland.'

'Not in America?'

'Potentially our largest plum. I am leaving for New York September first, a trip which may change the history of the world ... you realize that, Clyde?'

'It is possible. So many things are continually changing the history of the world that your journey could very easily be one of them.'

Mr. Twill swept over and they made room for him on the couch, between Philip and Glenellen. 'Ayre, my darling, where did you get that ghastly thing about your neck?'

'If you'd been at the services for the last month, you would have known that it was presented to me by Augusta herself when I was made Guardian of the Green Door.'

'But I had no idea! Do forgive me! That was nearly blasphemous, wasn't it?'

'Very nearly. Why haven't you been in attendance?'

'The crush,' said Mr. Twill, adjusting his white elbow-length gloves. 'There are too many people there nowadays ... too many of the wrong sort. But, although I may not be there in person, my heart is with Augusta.'

'You are a back-slider.'

'Oh, Ayre, don't be cruel! I tried, God knows I tried to get there, but I have so many appointments ... and I don't get up till noon nowadays, anyway.'

'There is a story that you are ashamed to go back because of the time you dropped the toque.'

'You are merciless, Ayre,' said Mr. Twill, genuinely if briefly wretched.

'It is only for Augusta,' said Glenellen gently. 'We must do everything for *her*. We must not let *her* down.'

'I'll be there tomorrow. I'll move all my appointments up an hour so that I can attend. You are absolutely right: I've been selfish, headstrong, and I *was* upset when someone knocked the toque out of my hand. I confess now that I swore I would never go back ... I was in such a pet. But you're right, this is no time to be small.'

'You have made us very happy, Edmond, very happy indeed.'

'Will I ... be able to handle the toque?'

'You will indeed. And should it be Augustus instead of Augusta, I think I might be able to get you assigned the Privilege of the Braces.'

'Ayre!' Too moved to say any more, Mr. Twill managed a high whinny of pleasure.

'By the way,' said Philip, 'I didn't steal Lord Glenellen's car.'

Mr. Twill looked puzzled. 'But isn't this the one, Ayre, who was at the levée?'

'The same one ... but it seems that I lost the car. No one took it after all; my suspicions were groundless.'

'Oh, what a pity! I so hoped he had. I like a bold reckless boy!' He squeezed Philip's thigh ... once out of sheer exuberance; a second time to corroborate the favourable impression of the first squeeze. Philip moved away. 'Such a solid boy, isn't he? I love that combination ... blond hair and violet eyes.'

'He looked better in Rome,' said Glenellen critically. 'He had dark hair then.'

Philip sighed but said nothing.

'Well, I'm glad he changed it.' And he cast a sidelong flirtatious glance at Philip, his eyes small and bloodshot behind artificial beaded lashes.

Then, as though a stage manager had given a command, everyone changed his position: group dissolved, reassembled in new combinations, presenting all sorts of possibilities. Large quantities of brandy and champagne were consumed and the lights had been so dimmed that Sebastian had quite faded away, only the golden arrows still visible against the wall. In the next room the gramophone played the songs from the latest of Mr. Cole Porter's musical comedies, and the doors to two bedrooms were already locked.

For one brief moment Philip found himself with Stephen and Bill, both bewildered and far less amused than he. 'Don't take it so seriously,' he said. 'It's not so vicious, after all.'

'I don't think it's very funny,' said Bill, his face flushed and his dark curls sweaty from the room's heat and the brandy he had drunk.

'He's a big hit,' said Stephen, the less outraged of the two. 'That joker in the red dress has been goosing him all night. Just now he offered to take him on a Mediterranean cruise; then when Bill told him we were buddies, he said he would give us each a hundred dollars if we'd let him watch some time.'

'Easy money,' said Philip, enjoying himself.

Bill snorted and then, seeing the fat figure of the red-gowned man moving towards him, he walked quickly to the next room, Stephen close behind him.

'You're not so bad, either,' said Red Dress drunkenly, pausing in front of Philip, his breath hot and unpleasant with wine and garlic. 'You want to take a little trip with me? Moonlight ... Mediterranean. We could have a swell time, you and me. We could ...' But Philip was gone before Red Dress had finished telling him what they might do together.

He crossed the room and stood for a moment between the ghost of Sebastian and the couch where Glenellen still sat; surrounded now by a group of young belles. Voices were growing louder and there were now over fifty people in the two dimly lit rooms. Amorousness in dark corners warned Philip that it was time to go.

'Excuse me,' said a dignified grey-haired man, a Frenchman

who spoke excellent English and looked exactly like Philip's idea of a Quai d'Orsay man, with the rank of minister at least. 'You're American, aren't you?'

'This is my first trip to Paris.'

'This is a part of the grand tour now, isn't it?' He indicated the room with a scornful gesture of his long white hand.

'A very interesting part.'

'For a young man, yes, but not for me. I've seen too much, I suppose. I'm bored with this sort of thing . . . so obvious, so feverish, so pointless.'

'But worth seeing once.'

The Frenchman raised his dignified brows. 'This is not your *métier*?'

Philip shook his head. 'I'm here under false pretences . . . incognito, a spy.'

'But how charming! You dabble, of course?'

'No. I don't dabble.'

'But surely you plan to one day, don't you? You're not fighting that hard against it.'

'I'm not fighting it at all,' said Philip blandly. 'I'm a grown man, perfectly contented.'

'How rare! How refreshing! But then my instinct is always infallible in these matters. Placed in a room with twenty men who all look alike, who all share the same tastes except one, I will, unerringly, go to *that* one, to the incorruptible . . . my fate, alas.'

'Isn't that rather sad for you?'

'Fortunately I live in Europe where a gentleman can buy very nearly anything he wants, including the incorruptible.'

'That's fortunate.'

'Indeed, yes, but tell me, have you found a comfortable hotel?'

Philip told him where he was staying.

'How very nice, so Bohemian. You people should live that way, for a time at least, even though the facilities are not always the best. Do you have a bath? That's lucky. So many of those places have no hot water. In which case I should have offered you my own place for bathing. . . .' He laughed and added: 'Quite legitimate, as you people say, I never force myself on people. What about the laundry situation, though? That's always so difficult this time of year.'

251

Philip, a little bored, said that he had had no trouble in getting his laundry done.

'I see. If you cared to, however, you could give it to my woman to do ... she's quite marvellous, no starch ... the way Americans like their shirts.'

'Thank you very much, but ...' Philip declined his offer, looking round the room in search of Mr. Twill; he was ready to leave.

'Tell me,' asked his companion, 'do you wear what the Americans call "jockey shorts"?'

Philip looked at him startled. 'Why on earth do you want to know?'

'But do you?' The other was insistent.

'I do.'

'Are you wearing a pair now?'

'Yes, but why ...'

'I will give you ten thousand francs for them.'

Philip fled. In the black marble foyer he found Jim, who was just arriving.

'What the hell are you doing here?' asked Jim, surprised.

'I'm beginning to wonder myself. I was just getting out while I could.'

'Good idea.' The boy's face was very pale and his eyes were half shut. 'Can't stand the light,' he murmured.

'Are you flying?' asked Philip gently.

'And how! I'm real gone. I'm never going to touch the ground again. Why, I can't even see you from where I am.' He smiled at Philip, opening wide his silver eyes and Philip saw the tears.

CHAPTER ELEVEN

She looked exactly the way he had remembered her that day in Cairo when Zoe Helotius introduced them in the room with the silken banners on the wall. She was sitting with Charles de

Cluny at a table opposite the door. Philip looked at his watch: twelve-thirty at the Ritz. He was on time. With a smile, he went over to her table, suddenly self-conscious, aware that he needed a hair-cut, that his shoes were not shined.

'I'm so happy we found each other,' she said warmly as he greeted her and Charles, and sat down.

'So am I,' said Philip. 'It's nice to see you, too, Charles. How long've you been here?'

'Just a few days.'

'Oh, do you know each other?' asked Anna.

'We're old friends,' said de Cluny. 'In Cairo.'

She nodded. 'Now I remember . . . at the party. This is an unexpected meeting, isn't it?'

'It certainly is,' said Philip. 'I checked with your hotel every week until they finally told me you were here.' This was indiscreet, he thought, aware suddenly of de Cluny's knowing glance; but he carried it off. 'They must have got tired of me.'

'On the contrary, I was told that a gentleman with a very nice American voice had inquired for me and the manager was extremely solicitous, hoping, I am sure, that he would be allowed to assist in an intrigue. He couldn't have been more disappointed when I told him what a great friend Mr. Warren is of my husband's. We saw each other quite often in Cairo,' she said, turning to de Cluny; Philip admired her for the clear and sensible way she arranged the facts, confirming all de Cluny's suspicions.

'Are you in the steel business now?' asked Charles maliciously, his cigarette-holder pointed at Philip like a conductor's baton.

'I'm *very* interested in steel,' said Philip, suggesting by his tone innumerable secret committee meetings where wars were decided upon and governments broken, all for the love of steel.

'Mr. Morris is a giant among men,' said de Cluny, placing the cigarette-holder between his teeth, smoke for an instant hiding his narrow face.

'He'll be in Paris soon,' she said, as the waiter brought the cocktails.

'I hope you will all do me the honour of dining at my house.'

The invitation was accepted with a friendly vagueness.

'Will you have lunch with us today, Charles?' she asked.

'If only I could! But I have to be with Hélène de Lyon et Grénoble. She's deaf and blind, but she has an uncanny gift for divining whether one is talking to her or not. I don't know how she does it, but, when one is not at her house, she knows it, and, though most of her faculties are gone, she is not yet mute. What a tongue! So, if you'll excuse me, dear lady, and you, Philip, I shall make my way to the Faubourg ... regretfully. Don't forget about our dinner, though, when Mr. Morris has returned. Philip, I'll call you tomorrow.'

More graceful words and then, with several bows and flourishes of the cigarette-holder, he was gone.

'I like Charles,' she said, not looking at Philip, as though she were suddenly shy at finding herself alone with him. 'He's been acting the part of the courtier so long he has finally become one. The role has swallowed up the man.'

'The courtier with no court?'

'That's his charm: he makes each of us the centre of the world ... he has a hundred *roi-soleils* and, though they realize how absurd he is, they love him for his attentiveness, for his good manners. And where would we be without the snobs, without the people who value tradition?'

'Where would we be?' repeated Philip. 'Well, I'm afraid we'd be exactly where we are now since all the old traditions are gone and new ones are still aborning.'

'It's a pity, I suppose,' said Anna, watching the bar-tender shake a cocktail so hard that the eye was confused and his hands and the silver shaker became a single blue in space, reflected by many mirrors. 'But perhaps there is an advantage to living in a time of great change ... though every time is one of change. ...' They looked at each other for the first time, and he saw his own face twice reflected in her hazel eyes.

'I called your hotel,' she said, suddenly personal, her voice changing as she discarded the eternal manner which became her not at all.

'Today?'

'Yesterday when I arrived. But you were out and I didn't leave a message. I wasn't sure you'd remember me.'

'You knew I'd remember.'

'Perhaps. I have a good memory, too. I remember your telling me that you would get your mail through the Embassy. I called them and they gave me your address.'

'Would you have called today if I hadn't telephoned you?'

She nodded. 'Yes ... what an immodest admission, though!'

'I'm glad,' he said, and then, to bridge the awkward moment, this time of shy and difficult declaration, he ordered two more cocktails. 'I drink too much in Paris,' he said. 'I don't know why. I go for months at a time without taking anything; then, all at once, I find that I want to be amiable and relaxed and sentimental like other people ... like some other people at least.'

'I'm sure it's good for you,' she said, hardly touching her own glass. 'I don't need it, I'm afraid. Nature made me sentimental from the very start. I think that if I drank I should be maudlin.'

'Or perhaps the opposite ... very hard and aloof.'

'Never ... even though there are times when I should like to give that impression.'

'But not with me, I hope.'

'No, not with you.'

They lunched in a small restaurant around the corner from the Crillon, a place with Chinese red walls, lacquered and gleaming and decorated with banks of roses and ferns not yet wilted, still fresh with morning.

'I see why you chose it,' said Philip. 'The Chinese room ... with all the banners.'

'The same mood, without Zoe.' She laughed.

The day went easily, carefully. Each deferred to the other and their conversations alternated between a delicate formality and a lover-like intimacy: the usual prelude to an affair. But Philip for once could not determine the nature of the fugue yet to come.

He was often able to see at the very beginning the end of an affair, with a painful clarity which had, in recent years especially, done much to diminish the intensity of his own emotions. Too fine an understanding was far worse, he knew, than the confusion with which most young men blundered into love affairs. He'd always known, for instance, not only how far he would commit himself with Regina, but also at what point his withdrawal would, imperceptibly, commence, and, though this prescience was saddening, it gave him a sense of security, of power which made the affairs, at least while they lasted, singularly agreeable, lacking in the usual dissensions, the blind misunderstandings; then, too, as he grew older, he had become more kind; he prided himself now on having become an adept at the art of separation, the gradual retreat which left neither anguish nor rage behind. But, being a child or the grandchild of the Romantic Movement, living in a culture still dominated on a vulgar level by the high romantic poets of the nineteenth century, he longed instinctively for the flames, for the one attachment: 'my last and only love', the love which increased from moment to moment until the lovers strangled for lack of air among those peaks which touch the edge of heaven, close to the consuming sun in whose fire, united at last, they perish to the accompaniment of French horns and frenzied woodwinds, the voice of Isolde, strong and pure, lingering in the vast golden dome of heaven where angels, out of sympathy, deluge the earth below with their pity. And in the back of his mind each time he began the intricate ritual he hoped that his own knowledge would be proven false by the unexpected conquest of that suspected but never before attained dimension in which he could indulge not only his secret passion for romance, for immolation, but also achieve that instant which each man awaits as though it were his due, inevitable, the moment of recognition that there is someone else in the world with whom the mortal's loneliness can be shared and finally overcome, the last of the fluttering moths from Pandora's box, caught and speared.

But I am a realist, said Philip to himself, disliking this self-estimate, aware that it was true: he was not a romanticist or a visionary.

Yet for Philip, for the realist (what a disagreeable word: it has become so associated with unpleasant, humourless pragmatists that it is very nearly as unfashionable as 'cynic', which has almost gone out of the language, or 'sophisticated', which has become synonymous with 'superficial'). Yet for the realist who recognizes the more obvious limitations of both flesh and spirit, the hope of a great romantic experience is tempered always with the grim knowledge that nothing is constant, and that even though a certain height might, temporarily, be attained, descent from it is inevitable and painful, unless one chooses to perish at the grand moment, a gesture which did not attract Philip, although the rich, dark tragedy at Mayerling had fascinated not only him but others of his generation, as directionless as he, all of them like compass needles gone awry, awaiting the pull of some magnet to set their courses for them, true north no longer the centre it had once been. But Mayerling or not, he had no wish to die. He would, he knew, go as far as his temperament would permit into a separate world with one other person, but since it would not be his only world, since he was possessed by other demons, the pure expression he dreamed of seemed unlikely, although, as he talked to Anna, he thought it would be difficult ever to become bored with her and that was more than he could ever have said of any other woman he had known, at this point at least in the ceremony of union. As he talked he recalled the loveliest of the *Minnesänger's* songs: *'Unter den Linden, An der Heide, da unser sweier bette. . . .'* A bed for us on the heather would be very fine, he thought, and, as it always had before, his desire drowned his love and he could only think of an act, the excitement, the mysteries revealed, a new conquest and, as he succumbed to the familiar itch, Anna ceased to be, her face and character were veiled, only the body was real and immediate. But she countered him, to his surprise, for just when the moment seemed very nearly achieved, the way clearly indicated, she withdrew, leaving him staring angrily into his half-empty coffee-cup.

'I have to do some errands on the rue du Rivoli; and then I promised to meet some people at Rumpelmayer's. I ran into them yesterday and they made me promise.'

'Tonight. . . .'

'A silly dinner. But tomorrow why don't we get Charles to give us dinner at his house. He has a lovely one, or rather some rooms in one, opposite the Isle de la Cité.'

'I've always thought there was a happy symbolism in the choice of St. Germain's name for our left bank boulevard. He was a remarkable man, a Bishop of Paris at the end of the sixth century and, having that rarest of maladies, ancient or modern, a Christian conscience, he went about Europe raising funds for the liberation of slaves. By the time he died, he had very nearly shattered that barbarous practice in Europe. Now the young people come from all over the world to live here on his boulevard, to lose their superstitions, to become emancipated. It is very touching.' But nothing de Cluny said ever sounded as though he quite meant it, thought Philip critically: Charles had cultivated the ironic manner to such an extent that his most casual words were redolent with self-mockery and double-meaning. Yet he talked well enough, Philip conceded to himself, happy with the dinner they had just eaten, with the view from an open balconied window of Notre Dame against the stars, with Anna who wore Chinese red like a Chinese bride, the curious fragment of crystal about her neck.

The evening had been perfect and they now sat in a book-lined study, neither shabby nor elegant, made unique by the view from two tall windows. Philip and Anna had talked little, pleased with the moment, not wanting to upset the delicate balance with irrelevant words. De Cluny, aware of this happy situation, seized the opportunity to speak of himself and, while his guests looked at one another, he talked of his recent sojourn in Central America.

'An incredibly lifeless place, all things considered ... and in my dozen years there I did consider nearly everything, including suicide. Not that my job wasn't interesting ... I was adviser to the President, Alvarez Asturias. You may have heard of him.'

Philip and Anna murmured in unison that they had not.

'He was a dictator, one of the better ones. But he was deposed and I followed him into exile. Had he remained in private life all might have been well. We were very snug in New Orleans but he attempted a revolution in which I took part, a ghastly affair and disastrous for everyone concerned, except me: it galvanized me into a feverish literary activity. I had lain fallow for so many bitter moons that I thought it unlikely I should ever bloom again. But I did. We escaped by helicopter ... an exciting time, I might add, with Government troops firing on us. Fortunately we got as far as Guatemala where we fell, for some reason no one has ever been able to determine, in the middle of Lake Attitlan ... on a clear day, mind you. I have a theory that the pilot was drunk but we shall never know for he was knocked unconscious when we crashed, and sank like a stone. The rest of us were rescued by a fishing-boat and I went back to France as soon as I could, where, fortunately, I had certain properties saved from the deluge.'

The moment had come when the dinner must be paid for. Philip and Anna looked at one another ... it was agreed silently that she request the reading. She did, graciously, with an air of real sincerity.

'I know what an ordeal it is to be read to, especially in French, but of course you, dear lady, *are* French and Mr. Warren speaks it beautifully.' And he shuffled papers on his desk, assembled a staggering number of manuscript pages which he then read to them in a loud ringing voice, the cadence as regular and as monotonous as the alexandrines at the Comédie Française, without benefit of scenery or of entr'actes or of talent.

Gently, Philip dropped off to sleep. He was awakened with a start, aware that a question had been asked, that the others were looking at him intently, awaiting an answer.

'Fine.' He croaked; then, clearing his throat, he sat up and said, with as much resonance as his light voice would permit: 'Very fine.'

'You don't feel that the scene in the park is a trifle grandiloquent?'

'On the contrary, I thought it remarkably muted, considering its theme,' added Philip confidently, blundering into a trap.

'But what do you really feel *is* the theme? I mean the underlying motif at that point? I have kept it oblique, I think, awaiting the proper moment to develop it more fully; yet it *is* there, all the way through the scene, like an echo to what is said ... a faint counterpoint to the obvious theme.'

'Ah,' said Philip, looking at Anna helplessly. She only laughed at him, silently, with her hazel eyes.

'The echo I think is the broken statue,' hinted de Cluny eagerly.

'A sense of loss, I should say,' said Philip, gambling everything with a flourish. A longing for what will never be.'

'You have it! I *knew* it was apparent but I was afraid it might be lost. You have no idea how relieved I am! Shall I get you more brandy? Yes?' He left the room to find another bottle.

'Where shall we go?' asked Philip, suddenly, when their host was gone.

'Wherever you like, Philip. To the Ida?'

'No, that wouldn't be wise.'

'To your hotel?'

'It's so . . . dark. I don't want that, do you?'

She smiled. 'No, we must have light.'

'Then we leave Paris. Go somewhere else.'

'When?'

'Now . . . tonight.'

'But where?'

'To the sea. What about Deauville?'

'But . . .'

'Saint Malo? That's better, isn't it? We could stay there.'

'But how . . .'

'You have a car, haven't you? We'll take that. Please. If we leave right now we'll be there before noon.'

'Before noon,' she repeated, taken aback; then she laughed. 'Do you really want to take such a chance? You hardly know me.'

'I'll take it, if you will.'

'Oh, I will, of course.' Her lack of hesitancy surprised and pleased him.

'But your husband?'

'He won't be in Paris until the end of the month.'

'We'll have two weeks alone.'

'You are very brave Philip.'

'Shall we go?'

She nodded.

'Tonight?'

'Whenever you like. It will be a lovely night for driving.'

'Where's the car?'

'At the hotel . . . parked in front. I have the keys with me.'

'Let's not take anything with us. We'll go just as we are.'

'I would like that,' she said, surprising him for the last time.

'This brandy,' said de Cluny, 'has been in my family for fifty years. Look! Cobwebs!' He put the bottle down on the table and wiped his hands with his handkerchief. 'One's voice needs a little . . . lubrication after a long reading, I find. The audience, of course, deserves a stimulant.'

'A sedative,' said Philip gallantly, exuberant, more pleased than he had ever been before. 'After all you keyed us up.'

'Now you exaggerate,' said de Cluny, his face darkening slightly with pleasure; he poured the brandy.

'You read so well,' said Anna. 'Like an actor . . . your face is very like Jouvet's.'

'Do you think so? Ah, that *is* a compliment indeed! André Gide was most sympathetic the other day when I paid a call on him at the rue Vaneau. Most sympathetic.'

'Did you read for him?' asked Philip.

'Alas, no. He didn't have the time. He's very old, you know, but he told me he had every confidence that I should maintain my old level ... he was most encouraging. Such a vigorous man for his age, too. Physically, like a hard, barrel-chested peasant ... not always kind either: when I made some reference to Claudel he said: who? Imagine! But then I suspect he dislikes discussing his contemporaries or near-contemporaries. He talked for the most part about a delightful manuscript of pornography, handsomely and primitively illuminated, the work, I swear to you, of a retired Anglican bishop living in Italy. He had sent it to the master with a *dédicace* and, as the master said, it was fine but a trifle too literary in tone.'

'He sounds very agreeable,' said Philip.

'A fine manner. And isn't that, on a human level at least, the most important of virtues? Genius exists only in the work, not in the man, or I should say one can only approach it in the work ... where the man is disembodied, as it were, made pure. Naturalness, of course, is supposed to be one of the most engaging of American virtues, but is it really what one wants? is it truly civilized? A country of first names! Only the Negroes have manners I found. They are most scrupulous in calling one another Mr. and Mrs. The white people, especially the ones in business, at their first meeting with a stranger call him by his Christian name, even if he is old enough to be their father.'

'But they have their own manners, I think,' said Philip, unsurely. 'If one is informal in a certain way, consistently, the informality becomes the convention, with its own rules, its own definition of good form.'

Then Philip made a great scene over the hour. What time did de Cluny's watch say? and the orante clock on the mantel? the broken Dresden clock in the bedroom? his own often inaccurate watch? Was it really so late? and the evening, was it really gone? Then, the symposium on time concluded to everyone's satisfaction. Philip and Anna said good night.

The false grey-pink Paris dawn had already begun to glow when they drove across the city through dark and silent streets; neither spoke until they were in the open country, the towns of

Eastern Touraine before them and, beyond Touraine, the fields and orchards of Normandy and the northern sea.

'I'm glad I wasn't wearing an evening dress,' said Anna, as the day illuminated the dark sky with gold, with rose; then a ghostly yellow sun appeared over the green and misty land and the sky shone blue with morning.

'A few more hours,' said Philip.

'Do you want me to drive?'

'No, I don't want to stop for a minute, until we're there.'

'Neither do I.'

'No breakfast?'

'Nothing . . . until we're there.'

Three miles east of Saint Malo they stopped and got out of the car. In the distance, partly hidden by the sea mist, they could make out the pyramidal shape of the ancient castle, set far out in the sea. Half a mile away was a stone cottage with a thatched roof, the only building in sight. The land undulated, soft and green, white-dotted with rocks and grazing sheep. The clover-scented air was still and warm as they stood by the side of the car, looking out upon the dark blue sea which broke on a dun-coloured, rock-strewn beach at the meadow's edge. Then, without a word, they walked across the coarse turf to the beach and, finding a stretch of sand that was sheltered from the road by tall trees, they paused among the grey, smooth rocks, relics of an age of glaciers and still not speaking, the hot sun in their faces, they undressed. It was noon.

He took her in the cool sea, their lips tasting of salt, blue above and all around them except for the green land they had left behind. Gulls circled slowly overhead. Salt water stopped his watch, holding the sun for ever in the centre of the sky; high noon, as they moved to a sea-like rhythm in one another's arms until, at last, the tide drove them back to shore again and the sun fell in the west.

Between two guardian rocks, they lay on the sand, side by side, their bodies touching, creatures belonging neither to the sea nor to the land from which each had come to this beach between earth and water, the air above them and, far below, their own element fire, swathed in sea and air, earth, stone and metal, a smothered sun at the centre of the world.

He sat up on one elbow and looked at her as she lay, white and perfect, upon the sand. He touched her carefully, as though she might melt like the snow princess in the legend. But she was mortal. She sighed and opened her eyes, her dark hair cushioned by seaweeds and shells, crystals of salt glittering like a powder of fine snow on her white skin, dried by the warm air.

'I was asleep,' she said. 'Were you?'

'I think so. Look, the sun has set.'

'The day can't end.' She shut her eyes again, her arms crossed upon her breast. He plucked the shells and seaweed from her long hair and, when she opened her eyes again, he half-expected to see the pearls that were her eyes. ' "Full fathom five," ' he whispered to himself.

She looked at him a long time, her hand gently stroking his arms and his chest as she gradually followed the line of blond hair to the now limp and child-like origin of life; then they made love again, closer to earth than to sea, once more whole: a double-star, a third sun suspended between the other two, the one below and the fiery one which now lingered in the western corner of the sky.

They lay together, joined, until the sun set and the pale grey sky was pierced by a single star, a gleaming point of silver in the nascent evening. 'Ah, there it is,' she said. They separated and got to their feet, unsteadily, like invalids or like children who had just learned to walk. 'Have you made a wish?' she asked.

'I have,' he said, his arm about her waist.

'Have you made the wish?'

'There is only one.'

'Only one,' she murmured, and they dressed at last on the dark beach while, among the trees which bordered the meadow, fireflies gleamed like a swarm of old stars falling.

The room was large with small shuttered windows and rough beams showing; a four-postered bed, square and massive, was set in the centre of the tile floor. Brass gleamed in the fireplace and the room smelled of smoke and linen, wood and roses.

'It is our best room,' said the old man, grumbling and snorting like every French character actor Philip had ever seen. 'Feathers.' He punched the thick mattress. 'The *vase de nuit.*' He indicated a blue and white chamber-pot beside the bed. 'Only candles. We have no electricity here.' He paused, challengingly, prepared to attack the new age, but they had already surrendered and the room in the stone house, a half-mile from their beach, became home, all meals cooked by the patron's wife.

Since he was always with Anna, Philip had little time to contemplate his own emotions, like a physician taking his own pulse. Yet he was sharply aware that at the centre of those easy days there was a pain equal to the delight of loving . . . the dark side of the love, the parallel emotion without which nothing could be measured or identified: no day without night, no life without death, no love without this cold pain, this separateness. For, at the last, he was a creature of his world, time-haunted and future-loving, obsessed with hours and minutes, terrified by days and years and the loss of youth, the end of the good present in which he now moved, like a man who dreams and knows that he is dreaming in a world all his own, where he reigns a god but, unlike a god, is conscious of the world outside his dream, its noises intruding fitfully, unbidden, until at last, half-blind and angry, he awakens, the dream scattered in a hundred fragments by the ruthless light, the significant design for ever gone, only the anguish and the sense of loss lingering to mock the day.

But his watch was broken, rusted by sea water, and neither spoke of the hour for many days.

He sat cross-legged on a rock and watched her walk out of the sea wringing water from her dark hair, her body gleaming white in the sun. Birds chattered in the orchards. Grey gulls circled over the sea. The sun burned gold and hot in the sky.

'How brown you are!' she exclaimed joining him on the sand between their two tall guardian rocks, Gog and Magog she had called them.

'And you're still white,' he said, touching her cold wet thigh.

'I never tan. I can't think why. I should like to look like one of those bronze amazons with golden hair. I admire them so.'

'I don't,' said Philip, stretching his legs, the short hairs sun-bleached and glistening on his brown arms and legs, only the lower belly and thighs still white, the line of a bathing suit still marked on his skin. 'It's like going to bed with a man, to go to bed with one of them.'

'Did you ever?'

'Go to bed with one of them? Oh yes. In my college days all the girls were six feet tall and liked to engage the boys in various competitive feats of strength. Fortunately that was before the days of jiu-jitsu, so all but the slighter boys got their way ... the weak ones were either thrown back into the sea or else raped by their conquerors. One young man named Mac-Dougall was forced to surrender his virginity to a giantess from Smith College ... three times in one terrible hour in his room while his two room-mates, roaring with delight, watched through the keyhole. ... they had locked the door so he couldn't escape.'

Anna laughed, wonderingly: 'It sounds like the end of the world,' she said, lying back on the rock, her hair like a dark rain-cloud against the sand.

One eminent man of letters (whom many think the first among us) once wrote in a novel that when his hero made love to his heroine the earth moved and celestial firecrackers went off in the void where presumably his audience, a benign eternity, applauded rapturously each mighty thrust. A lesser more superficial man of letters (equally celebrated but less well-regarded at the moment) chided his peer, saying that nothing of that sort ever happened when a man and woman made love ... at best they had a good time. To which the great man responded: '*You* could never understand,' retiring like any good priest into mysteries which cannot be defined in familiar terms: either one *knows* or one does not.

In Philip's case it would be untrue to say that the course of his life was altered by that moment with Anna: it was not ... at least as far as one can determine which events do affect character and to what degree. He got out of bed the morning after their first night together as he had got out of bed the day before and as he would get out of bed ten years later. He was the same man in the usual sense of sameness: he did not go out into the street and preach the Word; he made no attempt to proselyte; he gave up nothing he had liked before (including promiscuity), nor was he inspired to become a marvellous artist because, as it has been earlier demonstrated, he had no particular talent and, contrary to a certain opinion, vision alone is not enough in the arts ... although it may serve one handsomely in life. But in one important sense he was changed. Where before he had believed, he now knew and that, as any mystic will attest, is the difference between night and day. And, for the rest of a long life, he would glimpse the fire again and again, always reflected, however, in a woman's eyes ... never the way it had been that first night when, briefly, his flesh and bone, memory and will had been consumed and he became a part of all that is.

When the Duc de Lyon et Grénoble died, twenty years ago, his vivacious widow, who was then only sixty, moved into a small but stately house on the Faubourg St. Germain, selling her husband's hotel to a speculator who made several apartments of it, in one of which, as we have already noted, Mr. Edmond Twill now resides steeped in his own rich atmosphere of drugs and debauched street boys, no trace of the stern Duc or his still handsome Duchess remaining in that old building ... even the cobwebs in the cellar have been changed for the Duchesse is very mean, as everyone knows, and she is supposed to have taken the family spiders and mice with her when she moved into the smaller establishment where she has re-created an imperial atmosphere which is the despair of all the Bonapartists, none of whom, not even the Murats, has been able to equal in grandeur or in authenticity.

Needless to say, the better Royalists have very little to do with her and she, in her turn, has nothing to do with any member of the Republican government, excepting always those old friends who have blundered into high office: for those unfortunates, she gives small teas in her boudoir, not allowing them, however, to attend her carefully chosen receptions or those formal dinners where she entertains the relics of the Empire and the older members of that world of high fashion which used always to amuse her before she became deaf and blind. She is, according to Charles de Cluny who insists he knows, a hundred and seven years old. No matter what her age, it is a fact that she was on intimate terms with the Empress Eugénie and dined with her once a week until that lady's death. The Duchesse has had no close woman friends since, although her friendships with men are still much talked of; she is known to have been the cause of a number of duels, suicides, divorce cases, as well as the life-long love of one lyric poet's short-termed existence. She is now living with her one-time coachman, a portly silver-haired gentlemen who is seldom in evidence although early callers report that he brings her breakfast to her each morning on a tray, with a bouquet of fresh violets across the morning paper.

Philip and Anna were led by de Cluny to the centre of a grey and silver drawing-room where, directly beneath a chandelier, the Duchesse stood, a straight small figure with bright red hair held in place by a fillet of green velvet and wearing a long somewhat wrinkled dress also of green velvet, in the style of the 1880s, modified somewhat during the early years of the twentieth century to set off a figure which had once been handsomely proportioned but now had grown thick at one end of the torso and grotesquely frail at the other, where the narrow shoulders were hung with discoloured pearls as filmy and as dark as the eyes which darted this way and that, not seeing, the world shut out by whiteness ... having attained certain Alpine peaks, thought Philip poetically as he studied those dim eyes, she had been blinded by the glare of light on glaciers.

'Charles!' Her voice was surprisingly full for one so old; loud too from deafness. 'Did you bring me the young people? Ah, yes, here are their hands. She is a lovely blonde with white skin and he is a fat American boy. I can always tell by hands. Such a comfort to have some communication with the living since, obviously, I have none with the dead ... although many of my friends think they can talk to the dead, I don't: all nonsense. Besides, why should one want to talk to an absolute stranger with whom one has nothing in common? "I am Yvette, a midinette, and I died in Seventy-four. ..." ' She mocked in a high voice, still holding the hands of the lovers in her own, her touch as smooth and as dry as old silk.

'Fortunately, everyone I used to know is dead, including the ones who attended séances. They certainly realize *now* what nonsense it was all. Well, go on ... there are young people here, I think. Bore one another.' And with a shadow of what must have been a brilliant smile, she let go their hands abruptly and they found themselves in a room full of strangers, of whom none were young. They sat in a brocade love-seat next to a spinet where a tired-looking man played Mozart with a faded grace, the thin, elegant sounds lost in the party's chatter.

Above the mantel was a portrait of the Duchesse as she had looked when Bismarck entered Paris. On the spinet, on every table, were miniatures and photographs of an earlier time, a lock of Napoleon's hair, dark brown and lustreless in a heavy case of gold and crystal, a silver rattle which had belonged to the King of Rome, Murat's spurs and the baton of the first Duc, all preserved under glass with yellowed cards identifying them for those casual visitors who had strayed, like Philip, into this drawing-room with no real knowledge of what it meant, of what it had been in other more vigorous days, when ladies sewed golden bees on to handkerchiefs for French boys who were to die, most of them, far from home.

Then Anna was finally taken away by an old acquaintance and he was left alone by the spinet with de Cluny, who smiled and bowed continually at figures across the room, talking to Philip at the same time.

'Love of unfamiliar, outworn ways is a weakness, I suppose,' he said genially, bowing very low at a poorly assembled mass of lace which passed close by, exuding a musty odour like a closed room suddenly opened. Philip half expected the ambulatory lace to be attended by reverent outriding moths.

'It's natural,' said Philip.

'On the contrary, most unnatural. Have you noticed the hatred with which lower-class people (and much of the middle class, too) regard the past? One sees it at a cinema where they laugh derisively at the costumes of another time and on those occasions when confronted, in school or in the theatre, with some classic literary work, they respond with confusion and anger, mocking the language not only of the past but, worse still, of all art, since they are as afraid of the new as they are of the old. No wonder one loaths the mob.'

'But why loathe people who don't share your taste? It seems bigoted to say the least.'

'Taste is another thing. No, I don't really mind if the working classes mock Corneille, but I do mind when they attempt, as they periodically do, to destroy all art, to reduce the great to their own level. That is the terrible anti-human constant in all our affairs, and that is why I, for one, do loathe the mob. The people who deposed Aristides and poisoned Socrates. ...' He kissed a dingy alabaster hand which emerged for one brief moment from yards of faded yellow silk.

'But what can one do?' asked Philip, as the yellow silk crumpled into a near-by fauteuil.

'Nothing at all ... but curse and occasionally pray that what is bad will not, in one's own lifetime at least, grow worse, as it often does. Of course, a love of the past like mine is a madness equal in intensity and, perhaps in absurdity, to your country's love of the future. In either case it means the same thing: romanticism, love of an idea, an essence which may exist as a universal in the mind but which has never existed in fact in this world, past, present or future. The romantic disregards evidence; he feels. Rousseau when asked why he believed there was a God went into a rapture, saying that when he beheld the dawn and the glory of the sun, he *knew* there was a deity, a Creator. That is all very well, but what Rousseau *knows* is not much of an argument to support the existence of a deity ... the true romantic feels that each man must come to his own conclusion through his emotions, rather than through his reason ... he is never to consider cause and effect while natural evidence is to be resolutely disregarded, especially if it contradicts the judgment of *la sensibilité*. Romanticism, carried to its logical extreme, would be chaos; carried to a possible extreme, it was Hitler. He could not logically prove that the Jews were bad. Since he controlled the state, that was enough for the Germans: they knew too, and they killed off the Jews. Irrational cause; logical effect.'

'I've always had a frivolous theory,' said Philip, 'that the reason so many Europeans hate the Jews is not because they crucified Christ, but because they produced him in the first place.'

'A romantic conceit. More original than most,' said de Cluny, greeting a squadron in black which glittered with jet and paste. 'But in spite of everything, I am, in practice, a romantic like the rest of my generation, since the only immediate alternative is science, and you know what ill-educated boors scientists are.'

'I think we are all balanced somewhere between the extremes,' said Philip, wondering about himself. 'I am attracted to the past, but I have no serious nostalgia for what might have been and, as for the future ... I expect nothing: some of it will be good and some bad. There will be periods of relative prosperity and other periods of war and unpleasantness. The future is only the present until one dies; then, in personal terms at least, time stops and all human affairs are finished.'

'Now that *is* romantic.'

'In conception. But in practice, I'm a good Epicurean devoted to free inquiry and the avoidance of pain.'

'Perhaps. Odd, isn't it, how each age has its panacea ... its banner, as it were. In the Middle Ages it was Faith, in the eighteenth century it was Reason ... later, it was Progress. ...'

'And what, I wonder, is it now?'

De Cluny smiled. 'I know.'

'What?'

'I don't dare say.'

'That's hardly courageous.'

'Love!' said de Cluny, bringing one long finger down on the keyboard of the now deserted spinet. An eighteenth-century E-flat tinkled faintly, like a derisive echo in the air.

'That has never been the ideal of more than a few,' said Philip sternly.

'I'm not speaking of amity or charity or the brotherhood of man. I am speaking of sexual love. Think for a moment: man is no longer the centre of the universe as he once was, or thought he was, which is much the same thing. His displacement began, in modern times with Copernicus and ended with Darwin. The idea of a personal god who watches over man with a worried eye, giving out marks for deportment and arranging celestial bliss or eternal discomfort for the good and the bad, is dying in the West. While a belief in the universals of Aristotle has been succeeded by a conception of relativity ... morality is relative and variable, change is constant and the Protagorean conception that man is the measure of all things is, in practice, if not in orthodox belief, quite general. Where, then, is man? The universe in his own image has been succeeded by a universe in its own image *containing* him, and he is now beginning to perceive what two thousand years of Western culture tried to hide: that his race is not the central adornment of the universe and that its control over nature is as precarious and as limited as its control over itself; man is important only to himself. The fiction of a partisan deity has become so transparant that even the most uneducated are able to see through it, to see the infinite impersonal void beyond this world, this single particle in an indifferent galaxy ... child of earth and of starry heaven indeed! I doubt if even the most eccentric, the most persuasive mystic will ever again be able to personalize the void, to subordinate it to this one race as our fortunate ancestors did. Man has nothing except himself; so, without hope of heaven after death or of Utopia on earth, he is left nothing but games like art and power, the satisfaction of various hungers and, of all the games and of all the hungers, the most exalted, the most god-like is the sexual act, since in human terms at least, it is the most important of all our deeds: continuation of life, while, as sensation, there is nothing to compare with it, in the vigour of one's youth at least. And of all the old gods of the West, Venus alone is pregnant. Two can face the void with less terror than one. The moment of orgasm fills the dark with light, or seems to, which is enough, I think. Everywhere in the West, one sees this sudden preoccupation with sex, in our literature, in art, in science ... there's even a new philosophy of sex with men like Lawrence and Freud attempting to define it, either mystically or empirically, in spite of the opposition of an older generation which still hopes for a heaven in life or a heaven in death. One knows now that love is the last illusion, the only magic, and unlike other pleasures ... the exercise of power, mysticism, the creation of works of art ... it is physically possible for nearly everyone while, in a spiritual sense (or whatever word one wishes to use to characterize so tenuous a state of being), it is a challenge to the few, a proof of virtue, a temporary defeat of the impersonal reality, black magic in an age of science.'

'That only leaves death to be accounted for,' said Philip thoughtfully.

'Death accounts for us, not we for it,' said de Cluny, as the room was split in two by Zoe Helotius.

Philip moved close to the room's centre where Zoe paid court to the Duchesse and the party paid court to Zoe.

'Darling Hélène, I'm late. I came as soon as I could, but was in the house of X, and you know how difficult it is to get away from them.' The reference to X was sufficiently lofty to impress even the oldest of the Bonapartists.

'I can't hear a word you're saying, Zoe,' complained the Duchesse, which was obviously not true since Mrs. Helotius' voice could have penetrated walls of lead.

'Darling, can you hear me now?' The voice reduced the room to silence.

'Just barely. You must learn to speak without mumbling. When I was a girl, we were taught elocution by La Meynard of the Comédie Française. "Speak up," she used to say. "Speak up!" '

'My childhood was less privileged!' bellowed Zoe, and then, ignoring the old lady's occasional remarks about her diction,

271

she gossiped and Philip, among these relics of the first Napoleon, thought of Madame de Staël and her loud progress through these same drawing-rooms a century ago, in search not only of lions, but of ideas.

'She is lovely,' said Charles admiringly.

'You think so? I think she's terrible.'

'I meant Anna.'

'Oh. I thought you meant Mrs. Helotius. Yes, she is.'

'Did you enjoy your trip to the sea?'

'How did you know?'

'I know everything.'

'Yes, very much.'

'I knew in Cairo this would happen.'

'So did I. Do you think she did?'

'Certainly. What do you intend to do now?'

'I don't know. I haven't thought. Go on, I suppose.'

'He'll be coming back.'

'We haven't discussed the future.'

'Sensible. I hope you'll know what to do when the time comes, however.'

'When what time comes?'

'The moment of choice. There's always one in every relationship.'

'I don't like generalities. You know, as well as I do, there are no rules to these things.'

'True, but I know better than you the nature of the choice *you* must make ... if only because I am older and once selected, long ago, impetuously, my own way.'

'Which was not the right way?'

'Right, wrong, it makes no difference; we die in any event. No, I should say one chooses what one must, of course, but I believe there is an instant of free will, a moment when one can assume direction. The trick is to recognize that moment.'

'I'm not sure I follow you.'

'Don't follow me! That's precisely it. There's your answer.'

'There will be war, Hélène!' shouted Zoe.

'More what, my dear?'

'I have it on the best authority ... within ninety days. Then the end. Pouf! No more Europe. Nothing. Where will *you* go?'

'Know what?'

272

'I shall die with the world I have loved. I will not desert. Never! I shall be at Antibes, waiting. I shall wear all my jewels and, when *they* come, I shall receive them on the lawn. They will drive their tanks through the boxwood and over the roses, the pink ones named for me, and I shall be drinking champagne with the Duke of Windsor on the terrace when they shoot us down!'

'I haven't been to Antibes in twenty years ... it was a new resort in those days. I went there with Paul Avril. You remember him? He dedicated his *Titania* to me. They do it now at the Comédie I hear, but I no longer attend the theatre. Crowds confuse me, except here in my own house.'

'No, none of us will survive this war ... and who will want to? Who?'

'New? What, my dear, is new? You are naïve, but it's your charm, Zoe. Never let them take it away from you.'

'Call me Cassandra! I see what I see.'

'But I love the sea as much as you and perhaps, if these treatments I am taking work, I may be able to visit you at Antibes.'

'I should love that, Hélène.'

'They're giving me the glands of sheep. Imagine! To be a sheep, after all these years.'

'Ninety days, Hélène; that's all we have. Ninety days. One really doubts if there is Someone above.'

'Love? But, my dear Zoe, *who* loves you? And how nice for you. Tell me, I must know.'

'You see,' said Charles, turning to Philip, pausing in their journey across the room, beneath a portrait of Josephine.

'Yes, I think so.'

Through black lace and black broadcloth, he saw Anna at the far end of the room, waiting for him.

CHAPTER TWELVE

'It is twelfth night: the moment of revelation ... the hour of truth!' Glenellen paused, arms outstretched, glowering at the crowded room. The worshippers stood or sat in a dense circle about him, leaving hardly any space around the empty throne in front of which he now stood. Two young women, hearty in tweed, guarded the Green Door.

There was a sigh of anticipation, a murmur of excitement at this pronouncement. One young man near the bookcase fainted from tension while, in other parts of the room, there were several audible moans of religious fervour, including one resounding 'Hallelujah!' from an American night-club singer, a New York Italian girl who had attempted, with complete success, to pass herself off as a Negress, thus insuring a considerable following among the credulous French.

Then Glenellen, red-faced and tense, stepped to the Green Door and stood, head bowed, in front of it, waiting. The silence was broken at last by the ringing of an alarm clock; then the dinner-bell tolled and the Green Door slowly opened, revealing Augusta, completely nude, a tall pale figure with primary and secondary sexual characteristics of unusual variety. With a serene smile the beloved figure moved through the cheering worshippers to the empty throne. But then, before the first Statement of the Day could be made, a dozen gendarmes shouting: 'Exhibition! Exhibition!' broke into the room.

The noise was deafening. Most of the young women jumped out of the window (the shrine was on the second floor of an eighteenth-century building) while several of the young men fainted and were severely trampled by the panicky worshippers and the no less hysterical gendarmes who rushed this way and that, shouting Republican sentiments, invoking *Legalité* as they tried unsuccessfully to arrest the fleeing Augustans, all of whom, within several minutes, had got out of the door, excepting those vigorous young women who had sprained their ankles on the hard pavement below and the young men who had

274

fainted and lay now like corpses after a battle, while the gendarmes hammered on the Green Baize Door behind which Glenellen and Mr. Norman together protected the cowering Augusta as she lay on an iron cot, shuddering convulsively, the various articles of worship covered with a torn linen sheet.

'Go away!' shouted Glenellen. 'This is sacrilege! This is a private institution! I shall go immediately to the British Ambassador if you persist! Do you hear me?'

The gendarmes continued to batter at the door, demanding the arrest of Augusta, professing shock at the obscenity of the exhibition they had witnessed.

'You had better let them in, Ayre,' said Mr. Norman quietly.

'Never!' shrieked Glenellen, moving an old wardrobe against the door. 'Desecration!' he roared at the gendarmes on the other side, but they were too busy with their hammering to hear the solemn curse which, presently, he thundered at them, leaning against the wardrobe, one hand clutching his chain of office.

Mr. Norman sat down on a three-legged stool, the only furniture in the room besides the cot and the wardrobe. Calmly he lit a cigar and then, exhaling, a model Englishman in a confused moment, he looked about the small airless room curiously, at the shrine which until now none but Augusta had seen. Dust was everywhere and the single window with its dirty panes of glass had obviously not been opened for many years, while on the floor, on the bed, on the window-sills lay old candy wrappers and tag ends of food, fragments of stale cake and biscuits, while several ominous floor-level holes in the wall suggested that Augusta shared her feats in much the same way that the saint from Assisi had shared his.

'That should hold them,' said Glenellen, his curse completed, his last thunderbolt launched at the gendarmes who had found some sort of battering-ram and were now, at regular intervals, hitting the door, splintering it methodically as flakes of plaster fell from ceiling and walls upon the motionless figure of Augusta, like a corpse beneath her sheet, and upon the two Englishmen who conversed quietly, pausing only when the regular noise of the battering-ram crashed through the shrine.

'What shall we do when the door finally goes?' asked Mr. Norman.

'Fight them with our bare hands,' said Glenellen grimly.

'Come now, Ayre. Neither of us could handle an angry child, much less the pride of the gendarmerie.'

'A token resistance, then ... we shall not surrender easily.'

'I suppose they'll book us on some charge or another.'

'Martyrdom!' exclaimed Glenellen, his face transfigured for an instant as he considered grace.

'Should the movement triumph we will of course be included among its first martyrs, but should it not prevail we shall have wasted our time in unnecessary humiliation.'

Glenellen looked at his companion sadly. 'You too, Clyde?' he whispered.

'I was speaking realistically, my dear old friend. You know that. I shall never desert you ... although I have at times disagreed with your methods in the conduct of the Missions ... especially when you deposed dear Edmond from his post as Bursar, even though I begged you not to.'

'You should never have taken his side.'

'At a time like this ... a climacteric, as it were ... I should not think it advisable to be too finicky.'

'Let me tell you, Clyde, since you wish to discuss the squalid affair of Edmond's fraudulency, that you yourself have been, on more than one occasion, accused of selling audiences with Augusta and, worse still, of receiving a retainer from a certain Brazilian for the Privilege of the Braces.'

'*I* sell audiences! It is fortunate indeed that you are my old friend, or I might forget myself.'

'That it is you dear Clyde, who are the offender, justifies or, rather, ameliorates the deed and precludes penalty.'

'Penalty!' A large section of plaster, shaped like a map of France, fell to the floor at Glenellen's feet. Augusta whimpered and turned her face to the wall.

'Remember Savoy!' said Glenellen furiously. 'The House of Savoy! Remember? Did we desert Umberto, the first gentleman of our adopted country, our rightful lord, for this? That we end by selling audiences to the Incomparable, dirtying our fingers for the sake of ready cash, exploiting our co-religionists ... Oh, I should rather have remained a Communist and cursed the bourgeoisie than such an Augustan!'

'Don't turn on me, Ayre. I won't have it. I won't! You forget, I am a believer too, more devout than you. . . .'

276

'Stop it, Clyde! You know you're not. You have no vocation.'

'I have.'

'And *I* say you haven't.'

'I shall lose my temper with you, Ayre, if you don't watch your tongue.'

The mirror on the wardrobe came loose and smashed on the floor. There was a shout of triumph from the gendarmes on the other side; they renewed their battering.

'You bore me, Clyde.'

'Is it possible?'

'Listen to me, Clyde. Don't interrupt and stop glowering at me like an idiot.'

'Great heavens! . . . has it come to this?' Mr. Norman was genuinely anguished.

'Yes, my dear, all this . . . and more. Fret all you like because from now on I shall be quite serene, undisturbed by these outbursts. . . . I find you ludicrous, Clyde. Do you hear? Absolutely ludicrous.'

'Then it is over. . . .'

'You say you are more devout than I . . . such insolence. Prove it. Tell me one vision you have had which might substantiate your pretensions.'

'Now you wrong me, Ayre; I'm sorry. I said I was *as* devout as you . . . I didn't say more, did I?'

'I don't care if you did.'

'When we served Umberto you would not have spoken to me like this. You know it. You no longer care for me, Ayre. Augusta has drained you of all humanity.'

'I do not like your faults.'

'If you were a friend you would overlook them.'

'If I were sufficiently insincere, I suppose I could pretend not to see the Eiffel Tower.'

'I am tired,' sighed Mr. Norman, with the gesture of one rehearsing for a crucifixion. 'I hope the gendarmes come soon and take us to the station. I can't bear your carping, your hatred . . . this morbid concern with my imagined faults. I'm too weak, too exhausted to bear all this.'

'Oh, Clyde! Clyde.' Glenellen turned to the window as the top panel of the door splintered above the wardrobe.

'I can't bear your contempt, Ayre ... your indifference.'

'I'm not indifferent, Clyde. I was ill-tempered when I said that.'

Mr. Norman rose from his three-legged stool, tears in his eyes. 'I am happy you said that. Give me your hand.'

'Gladly.' They shook hands gravely, too moved to speak, as the wardrobe toppled over and landed with a crash at their feet. Through the shattered upper panels of the door they could see the gleaming vandalous faces of the gendarmes, outlined by ribbons and shreds of torn green baize.

'To the barricade!' shouted Glenellen, throwing the stool through the gap in the door. But the shrine was occupied by the blue-uniformed men at whose loud centre Glenellen still struggled, while the recumbent Augusta shrieked like a tropical bird, and Mr. Norman, wringing his hands, was led away.

First of all, the immortal dwellers in Olympus made a Golden Race of moral men. These lived in the days of Cronos, when he was king of heaven. They lived like gods, with hearts free from care and from painful toil and trouble. And miserable old age came not upon them; but, ever the same in strength of hand and foot, they feasted in delight apart from all evils; and they died, as it were, overcome with sleep. All good things they had; the earth of herself bore them the harvest of the corn she gives in plenty without stint, and they with good will lived at peace upon their lands with good things in abundance. Now, after that this race was hidden in the earth, by the will of great Zeus they are become good Spirits, above the ground, guardians of mortal men; they keep watch over the right and over unkindly deeds. Clothed in mist and darkness they go to and fro through all the earth.

Then the next thereafter the dwellers in Olympus made a far worse race of Silver, not like to the Golden either in body or mind. For a hundred years the child was nurtured beside his good mother, playing, a foolish infant, in his home. But when at last they came to the full measure of manhood, they lived but for a little while, and suffered by their folly; for they could not keep their hands from violent outrage one upon another, nor would they do service to the Immortals or make sacrifice upon the holy alters of the blessed gods after the lawful manner of men in every land. Then Zeus in his anger put them away, because they paid not due honours to the blessed gods who dwell in Olympus.

And Father Zeus made a third race of mortal men, a race of Bronze, in no wise equal to the Silver ... and they were strong and terrible, and delighted in deeds of dolorous war and in insolence. Their weapons and their dwellings were of bronze, and with bronze they wrought: dark iron was not yet. These, slain by their own hands, went to the cold dank house of Hades, nameless. Terrible though they were, black death took them, and they left the bright light of the sun.

Now after that this race also was hidden in the earth, Zeus made yet a fourth race upon the bountiful earth, a divine race, better and more righteous, of Hero men, that are called demi-gods, the race that was aforetime upon the boundless earth. They were destroyed by evil war and dread battle, some before Thebes of the Seven Gates in the land of Cadmus, contending for the flocks of Oedipus, and some were brought in ships across the great gulf of the sea to the land of Troy, for fair-haired Helen's sake. There in the end the cloud of death enfolded them.

Oh that I lived not in after days among the fifth race of men, but either had died before or been born later! For now indeed is the race of Iron. They shall rest not by day from labour and trouble, nor from the spoiler in the night season; and the gods shall give them grievous cares. The father shall not be like to his children, nor the children to their father; the guest shall not be true to the host that shelters him, nor friend to friend, nor brother true to brother as in the old days; parents shall grow quickly old and be despised, and shall reproach their children with bitter words. Wretches that know not the visitation of heaven! He that keeps his oath or is just or is good shall not find favour; but they shall honour rather the doer of wrong and violence. Right shall be in might or hand, and the spirit of truth shall be no more. The rogue shall do hurt to the better man with crooked words backed by a false oath. There shall be among miserable men a spirit of striving, a spirit ugly-voiced, rejoicing in evil, with hateful eyes.

Hesiod: *Words and Days.*

Regina returned to Paris on a bitter and lugubrious February day when all alliances seemed purposeless, all motives suspect and the immediate prospect of a war was not only possible but, in the general apocalyptic mood which prevailed, desirable: a fitting climax to the greyness, at last proof of Lucifer's victory so many millennia before in that not so dubious battle on the plains of heaven.

They met in her rooms at the Ida, to Philip's amusement, aware as he was that in the corresponding suite on the floor above Anna Morris occasionally received him, though as a rule they met at his hotel, now nearly empty, the visitors from the West gone back to school, to jobs, to mother and to real life.

As they talked, he could hear the far-away sound of the wind as it assaulted the mansard roof of the hotel.

'Did you get my letter?' she asked.

'No, did you write?'

'Twice . . . to American Express.'

'I never go there. I told you . . .'

'I forgot. I said nothing in particular. Like a good politician, I never commit myself on paper!'

'How is your husband?'

'Very well . . .' She laughed. I was almost going to say "thank you"! I wonder why we are so formal?'

'Well, we've been separated by quite a few months . . . nearly a year of them.'

'The year is almost over, Philip.'

'Time to go home.'

'To what?'

'I wish I knew. To whatever I was before, I suppose.'

'You feel unchanged?'

'I'm afraid so.'

'You've had no revelation after all?'

'No, and now that the year is gone I see how foolish it was of me to have ever thought I could so arbitrarily resolve all doubts and make a final choice, just like that.'

'That's one discovery, at least.'

'Perhaps, but not much of one. I find it demoralizing to realize that there is no such thing as future time, only a long present . . . that all acts are essentially meaningless, except of course to one's self. . . .'

'Professional idealists often make that discovery when they go into politics. They think of themselves as rigid Jeffersonians or disciples of Locke or good Christians; then, when they come to power, they discover that every day they are confronted with crises which they only partly comprehend, situations in which the morality, according to any ethic, is so confused that by the time they have determined where, as devout Jeffersonians, they should stand, the State would be in considerable trouble. Philosophers and intellectuals have never been very successful in public life ... a fact which they have always found distressing.'

Philip refused to accept this lead. 'I think it unlikely I will be ever able to accept a dogma of any sort. Yet it would be nice,' he added wistfully, 'to have some attitude, to be able to pretend at least to myself that I am consistent.'

'You want a great deal.'

'I know. If I could only accept some simple standard ... like money, for instance, or the State. If I could only make myself believe that what made money for me was good and that what did not was bad, I would be so happy ... like most of the people I know back home.'

'Are they happy?'

'Often ... at least they never doubt; they have no sense of futility as long as they are making, or even losing, money. Or if only I believed service to the nation was virtuous, that the whole was more important than any of its parts, I would feel at least I had something I could surrender my time and attention to. I realize now the supreme desirability of a true martyrdom, the ultimate attraction of Christianity, say, and even of Communism ... to give one's life to an attitude, a dogma: what could be more satisfying? The knowledge one was a total success. . . . "Not to desire to be called a saint but to be one," as Benedict said.'

'Do you need success that much?'

'I don't think so. But there's always an urge to dominate the countryside, to be envied and praised ... only an urge.'

'But your one weakness, your one connection with the world. . . .'

'Weakness?'

'Of course. You've made yourself so separate from the world that separateness becomes in itself a kind of perfect good, an attitude. To be affected, then, by the opinion of others is to be inconsistent.'

'I'm not that separate,' said Philip, and he thought of Anna as he spoke. 'As long as one exists more or less this side of the mad, one must cope with the world. Yet I do feel none of it matters ... how can it? when the world ends the day one dies, when even the greatest work done is forgotten.'

' "The Prince of this world is not for me"?'

'And there is no other.'

'Prince?'

'World.' He sighed. 'None of the choices now available is very tempting. I have no wish to be a Catholic or even a Christian. Eastern philosophy, though morally charming, is hardly something a non-mystic like me would find attractive. Communism is obviously impractical while Socialism is much too functional and, though inevitable, not a happy prospect: the world as a nursery. Then again I doubt if I shall ever make the pleasing of my senses a central activity nor do I want to instruct or to please or to govern or to believe while, if from time to time, I should want to act, to become engaged, it is only because I am energetic and in good health and at times capable of identifying with others.'

'That is enough,' said Regina.

'Is it? I wonder. Yet I have no feeling of uselessness. I am seldom bored. Both people and situations interest me; I have little guilt.'

The dialogue proceeded, as it always did between them: from the general to the particular, from the sensibility to the reason and back again. Philip, unknowing, went farther in it than he ever had before. If he had gained little in this precious year, he had lost a great deal. What had been only a vague awareness of the long present had at last become a conviction and he was no longer alarmed by this knowledge since it was, finally, the point from which the temporary arrangement of matter that was himself surveyed the material world, without guilt or shame, afraid of death but resolutely concerned with life, preferring harmony to vision.

Outside snow began to fall. The sky turned black before the sun had set, and the river stopped. Frozen birds fell in the icy streets and shattered like porcelain figurines on the pavements. A number of people died of exposure that evening, as they always did when the winter was hard, while one of the energetic philosophers of the day published a novel, produced a play and composed a dozen pamphlets suggesting that although there was no God, no governing spirit, one should still act and, in the act, forget that all was meaningless: constructing not a philosophic system, as the philosopher had hoped, but reporting merely what the majority of the more thoughtful people of the day felt, paradoxically, offering himself as a figure to be believed in and, to an extent, as paradoxically, some did believe, rendering black February less a burden.

At what point, wondered Philip, with that part of his awareness which was always disengaged, even during the dialogue, did a post-war period become pre-war? At the half-way point? Or would it all seem like the Hundred Years War to future historians?

'I shall be here for a few months,' said Regina, as the dialogue came to its usual indecisive end.

'Until the first of May?' asked Philip, smiling.

Then, carefully, soberly, they duplicated their former passion and both found it wanting, though Philip as always was attracted to her, against the advice of his reason, and she in turn, though loving, seemed concerned with something else, something unspoken and as yet undeclared.

The moment ended when a window-pane broke and the room was filled with an ice-cold wind on which, like the white petals of frozen flowers, snowflakes whirled for one brilliant moment; then the wind upset the lamp and the room went dark as the light bulb smashed and the lovers fled.

He who wins fresh glory in his tender youth, soars high in hope. Achievement worthy of a man lends wings to uplift his thought above low cares for wealth.

In a little while the delight of man waxes to its height; and in a little while it falls to the ground, shaken by adverse fate.

Creatures of a day, what is a man? what is he not? Man is the dream of a shadow.

Only, when a gleam of sunshine comes as a gift from heaven, a light rests upon men and life is smooth.

Pindar: *Pythian.*

Fay Peabody was stately in a long gown of russet, her garnets and pearls in evidence and her usually pale face pink, not only with excitement but with the unaccustomed application of cosmetics to a complexion which had once been called peaches and cream and which had, consequently, not often been painted; since, as she would have said, had she been guilty of vanity, there is no point in gilding the lily.

The French Academy of Detection Writers, several hundred ladies and gentlemen in full fig, rose to their feet as she walked out on the platform, her note-book under one arm, escorted by the officials of the Academy who arranged themselves about her with the decorous impassivity of a number of potted plants in a hotel lobby.

When the last bit of applause had died away the president spoke: '*Messieurs et mesdames de l'Académie. Nous sommes assemblés ici pour faire les hommages a Madame Pébodie, l'incomparable. Elle a gagné le grand prix de notre métier: le Poignard Doré pour le Mérite. Elle nous a donné le genie et aussi l'inspiration pour continuer dans un métier qui demande tout l'esprit d'un artiste sans réputation serieuse. Madame Pébodie, au nom de l'Académie de la Détection Française je vous donne le poignard Doré et j'espère que vous acceptèrez en même temps l'admiration, l'adoration de vos confrères français pour qui votre example est toujours une inspiration … pour nous et pour tout le monde.*'

There was prolonged applause at the end of this speech and, although Mrs. Peabody was not French, the confidence in her shown by the Academy was quite real and, considering her foreignness, all the more impressive.

She received their applause with a gentle smile and then, putting down the gold dagger which the president had given her, she opened her black note-book and read in a ringing voice her response: '*Chers amis français, chers confrères, chers auteurs de la Détection Fiction, je vous remercie d'un coeur plein. Votre confiance ce soir sera toujours un des jours rouges de ma vie. La vie d'un artiste, comme vous la connaissez, est dure, mais pour moi, dans ce moment, votre confiance est vraiment merveilleuse … elle me donnera le courage pour écrire, pour continuer le travail que j'ai commencé il y a trente ans en Cleveland quand j'étais jeune fille et quand j'ai eu beaucoup de rêves qui sont morts enfin, malheureusement. Mais maintenant, toujours, à cause de votre amitié, je trouve le chemin moins difficile. Ce soir je veux parler un peu d'un sujet qui est près de mon coeur: la suicide dans les romans de detection.*

*Plusieurs d'auteurs anglais ont essayés, sans succès, à faire
un roman avec un suicide. . . .'*

We are all dullards in divinity: We know nothing.
                                Anaxandrides: *Canephorus.*

He found his way with some difficulty down the dark hall to
his own room where, in the circle of red and blue light from a
single paper lantern, his bed was illuminated, like an altar
awaiting sacrifice, in this case his own body, pale and lean as,
quite naked yet not shivering, not noticing the cold, he did what
he had been forbidden to do: he took the long wooden pipe out
of its hiding place in the medieval chest and, with steady hand,
lit the blue flame of the burner. There was only one pellet left,
he remembered ... almost the only thing he could remember,
he thought, suddenly happy at the familiar odour, redolent of
past pleasures, the smoke rising in a pale slender spiral from the
blue flame to the far-away ceiling, dark and menacing, where
the ghosts and villains and all the unbeloved outrages awaited
the extinguishing of the blue flame ... when he would float
away from its comforting light to them, to the shadows above,
to the nightmare world of the ceiling across which he must
journey, occasionally floating, sometimes running, other times
struggling to move even a hand, a finger, as the dreary shadows
held him tight above the room, embraced his body with a loving
greed, draining it of will and memory, even of pleasure, so that
when he was released he fell like the discarded husk of a locust
from the dark ceiling to the bed below, and what was left of
him could hear the dry crackling of the rest, like brown paper
rustling in a Virginia kitchen: it was June again and like a
faded, cracked movie, sometimes too fast, sometimes too slow,
he saw himself speak to this person, speak to that person, saw
lips move in question and response ... a silent movie, for the
dialogue did not matter since he knew the order of the mass
already; and though he might try feebly to exert his will and
change the course of ancient events he could never intrude upon
that flickering cinematic world which viciously unreeled, over
and over again, leading him each time to the same delight and
to the same despair as it had done since that first day when there
were indeed voices and the trees were green, not grey and white,
and he'd been out on location and had accompanied that slim

285

hard figure with its helmet of short wiry curls down to the edge of a river, the camera of memory taking it all in, mercilessly, blackmailing him for life with that one image to which, at last, he came, dry tears in burning eyes, as he saw the bodies touch by firelight and then, with a sense of loss, he moved on in time through a world of faceless men, until the act of violence turned everything about, till he saw with terror that each of the faceless men had now assumed identity, the egg-smooth whiteness of their featureless faces covered with masks: some were vultures, others sheep, others eagles; some were lions, and several apes, while one of them with the monstrous face of a toad nuzzled him until he felt a scream rise like a tide from his groin to his throat, only to die on his lips when he saw himself, as he always did, with terror and eternal astonishment, reflected in the gelatinous globule of the toad's eye, and his own face was as smooth, as white as the shell of an egg: the worst was over then. The film ran backwards at great speed and he blinked his closed eyes, growing dizzy in the flickering light.

'Do you think he'll remember he asked us to come by?' asked Stephen.

'I don't know. He seemed all right to me.' They knocked at the door again. He heard them knocking but he could not speak or move. The good part was next, he remembered.

Stephen opened the door and, followed by Bill, entered the bedroom. The flame still flickered in the rusty burner and by its blue light Jim's body looked as if it had been rolled from some deep sea's bottom to a reef; Stephen almost expected to find seaweed in his hair and the mark of shells upon his skin.

'Is he dead?' whispered Bill.

Dead, dead, dead: what an ugly word it was, thought Jim, contented in his paralysis. Yes, he wanted to say, I am dead. Then, among the soft clouds of his other dreaming, he wondered: am I dead? is this what it is after all? an old movie winding forwards and backwards for ever. . . . 'I am not dead!' he shouted; but he had no voice. The now caressing clouds held him in their arms and stopped his voice: no sound in a vacuum.

'I don't think so,' said Stephen, and he put his hand on Jim's breast and felt through warm skin the slow thud of the heart. 'No, he's on the stuff again.'

'Didn't the doctor say it would kill him?'

'Sooner or later.'

Not dead, he thought, delightedly. That was a relief, and he viewed the clouds about him spitefully, contemptuously. They were his still; he was not theirs. Lovely Stephen, pretty Stephen, come lie with me.

'I'd better cover him up,' said Stephen. 'He'll freeze to death.'

'He looks all right,' said Bill, as they pulled the blanket over him.

'You'd think he would look worse, considering what he's done to himself,' said Stephen, turning off the blue flame, changing the character of the room, banishing much of the horror as warm red lantern-light replaced blue.

He remembered, as they talked, that he had asked them to come and see him that evening but, somehow, time had got a little muddled and he now had a distinct recollection of having seen them earlier, that the evening in question had come and gone some weeks (months?) ago and that they had had a pleasant time and the conversation, not to say the circumstances, had been very different from this. He tried to offer them a drink but he was facing in the opposite direction, he discovered sadly, and it would never do to attempt communication with his back to them and with all those shadows between. He was grateful, however, for the red light as opposed to the blue: it made all the difference in the world. He felt now as though he was at the warm secret centre of an odourless velvet-leaved rose through whose petals sunlight came, ruddy, diffused, penetrating his blindness like an intimation, a prescience of light to a new-formed eyeless embryo still safe at home.

'Doesn't look like the sanatorium did him much good,' said Stephen.

'Poor kid,' said Bill. 'He was like a ghost this afternoon.'

'No memory. You remember he couldn't think of our names? And he talked so slow, as though he'd forgotten how to talk.'

No memory! At the heart of the rose he chuckled silently, stirred even, like an uneasy foetus anticipating birth. Was it not enough that he *knew*? Was it necessary for him to *remember* as well?

'I don't think those shock treatments do any damn good. You remember. . . .'

287

'That guy in the Army, in the hospital? Shocked his mind clear out of him . . . poor bastard.'

'Do you think he'll die?'

'Who, Jim? I don't know.'

'The doctors all say that if you keep on after a certain point you never get off the stuff, you just dissolve.'

The red stuff of the rose melted about him and he was alone in the dark again, the voices of the two Southern boys, gentle and soft, far below him, as he floated upon a dark tide which transported him quickly away from the viscous carmine puddle where the rose had been. His arms and legs were without sensation; he wondered if they were still attached, or was it only a memory? an odd fantasy that in some other existence he'd been a creature with two legs, two arms. Where was he going? he wondered lazily, as layer after layer of darkness opened to receive him.

'Seems funny for a boy like him to have ended up like this,' said Bill, looking at one of the Balzac volumes on the table: '*Louis Lambert.*' He read the title aloud, automatically.

'I know,' said Stephen, considering the melodramatic fate which had so logically, if not tragically, befallen Jim. 'Well, we'd better leave him a note to say we're going back to the States.'

'If he'll remember our names when he sees it.'

'If he can read.' Stephen wrote the note carefully, explaining that they had come, as invited, but that since they had found him asleep they had gone away without disturbing him. And so this was good-bye, they were going back home to school. 'If you should ever be in Spartanburg, S.C.,' he wrote in big firm letters, 'Look us up any time. Yours truly, Steve and Bill. . . .' Followed by their addresses.

'I don't guess there's anything more,' said Bill, looking down at the face of the dreamer. 'Looks like a baby, doesn't he?'

'Well, he's not much older than us.'

'But he's taken it every way, one time or another.'

He was not aware when they left. He had long since ceased even to hear their voices. He was interested now in trying to recall who and what he was and why, disembodied, he should be caught in all this darkness, with no physical sensation except that of motion . . . forward, outwards, away from the tiny red light below.

288

Then he understood what was happening and he was terrified, preferring any pain, any unpleasurable sensation or anguish, to dissolution, to the enfolding darkness. He tried to speak, to move, to turn back, not wanting to die. He stared fixedly at the red point in space until, slowly it drew him back to it, grew larger and larger until the leaves of the rose held him once more safe inside. He had a moment of peace, of satisfaction, before the old movie began to unwind once more; and it was June again and his father and mother moved jerkily as the faded strip of memory displayed its images, the light behind as full and as constant as the images themselves were cracked and dim with use.

Each of us when separated, having one side only, like a flat fish, is but the indenture of a man, and he is always looking for his other half. Men who are a section of that double nature which was once called Androgynous are lovers of women; adulterers are generally of this breed, and also adulterous women who lust after men; the women who are a section of the woman do not care for men, but have female attachments; the female companions are of this sort. But they who are a section of the male follow the male, and while they are young, being slices of the original man, they hang about men and embrace them, and they are themselves the best of boys and youths, because they have the most manly nature. Some indeed assert that they are shameless, but this is not true; for they do not act thus from any want of shame, but because they are valiant and manly, and have a manly countenance, and they embrace that which is like them. And these when they grow up become our statesmen, and these only, which is a great proof of the truth of what I am saying. When they reach manhood they are lovers of youths, and are not naturally inclined to marry or beget children . . . if at all, they do so only in obedience to the law; but they are satisfied if they may be allowed to live with one another unwedded; and such a nature is prone to love and ready to return love, always embracing that which is akin to them. And when one of them meets with his other half, the actual half of himself, whether he be a lover of youth or a lover of another sort, the pair are lost in an amazement of love and friendship and intimacy, and will not be out of the other's sight, as I may say, even for a moment: these are the people who pass their whole

*lives together; yet they could not explain what they desire of
one another. For the intense yearning which each of them has
towards the other does not appear to be the desire of lovers'
intercourse, but of something else which the soul of either evi-
dently desires and cannot tell, and of which he has only a dark
and doubtful presentiment.*

*In Elis and Boeotia, and in countries having no gifts of elo-
quence, they are very straightforward; the law is simply in
favour of these connections, and no one whether young or old,
has anything to say to their discredit; the reason being, as I
suppose, that they are men of few words in those parts, and
therefore the lovers do not like the trouble of pleading their
suit. In Ionia and other places, and generally in countries which
are subject to the barbarians, the custom is held to be dis-
honourable; loves of youths share the evil repute in which philosophy and gymnastics are held, because they are inimical to
tyranny; the interests of rulers require that their subjects should
be poor in spirit and that there should be no strong bond of
friendship or society among them, which love, above all other
motives, is likely to inspire, as our Athenian tyrants learned by
experience; for the love of Aristogeiton and the constancy of
Harmodius had a strength which undid their power.*

Plato: *Symposium.*

'It is doubtful,' said de Cluny, 'that there is an original idea
left in the world. But that, of course, is of no consequence since
only children believe in new ideas: rather one wants to have the
old ideas rearranged in a relevant pattern ... and no one has
done that properly, in our time at least.'

'Perhaps not for you,' said Philip, 'nor for me. But you would
be surprised how attractive certain banal arrangements are to
some quite intelligent people.'

'I'm never surprised by anyone's enthusiasm ... except occasionally my own. Of course, philosophers are often to blame
since most of them, out of a profound native incompetence,
write badly. Those who write easily are considered suspect and
superficial because an obscure statement is thought, quite in-
correctly to contain an obscure thought. A simple statement
like: It is good not to cause pain to others, is thought simple
because it is clearly stated, existing as an idea without apology.
Poorly educated people are always attracted by the elliptical

statement, the cloudy phrase, the gnarled ugly prose of the bad (and occasionally the good) philosophers. Between Bergson and Marx, say, the uncouth would, emotionally at least, be drawn to Marx for his style and his arrogance ... A master is really what they need and, conveniently, he announces that he is one, in a ghastly prose style.'

Philip frowned, thinking of Marx. 'I wonder if anyone has ever traced the history of the notion that the State, the body politic, is superior to the individual, because that idea is, certainly, both in practice and theory, one of the few constant themes in the world.'

'The romantics you profess not to admire were against it. They recognized in their illogical, emotional way that now that the machine, the newest image of Lucifer in our guilty lives, has given anti-humanists an ultimate weapon with which to reduce all Nonconformists to the same grey, easily controlled level, there would be no controlling the conception of the State as all-good, as divine.'

'I don't think romanticism is the right weapon, however. I don't think the mystical, the visceral approach to reality is as effective a way of combating the horror as reason, as logic, as knowledge, as wit, as a fundamental conception that what serves the nature of one man without infringing on the safety and well-being of another man is good, and that what denies a man's non-aggressive nature is bad. I always thought the romantic movement hysterical in its anger. How much more valuable was Voltaire or Swift, those unfashionable, vigorous souls who fought every attempt of any institution or dogma to reduce human beings to some artificial pattern, to force everyone to conform to some sinister ideal of correct behaviour.'

'You should like a Frenchman attacking America.'

'Or an American attacking French politics. I don't think it makes any difference what one's nationality is, or what one's party label, because the real war is on and we are forced to choose sides: to join the conformists or to join the humanitarians (those labels are inaccurate, but you know what I mean). I think I have chosen my own position. I hate the proselytizers; yet I realize that for the rest of our lives, and perhaps civilization, they will dominate. ...'

'A civilization which may be nearly at its end. ...'

'I shouldn't be surprised. What good can you expect of a

291

world where all governments and most institutions seriously believe that human personality and individual capacity can be analysed and measured empirically?'

'You reason like a romantic.'

'Or a true rationalist. In any case, I feel like Peacock when he roared against the first of the competitive examinations for clerkships at India House where he worked. My own country has a reverence for statistics which borders on idiocy. We give intelligence quotient examinations to all children in school to discover how intelligent they are, and also to soldiers to decide whether they are intelligent enough to become officers or not ... tests which are a part of every child's, and of every soldier's, life history, holding him, officially at least, to one level as long as he lives in the Army or, worse, in school, where a child may fatalistically accept the verdict of a test that he is stupid and let it go at that. Those particular examinations were given the military, during wartime at least, on the same day a man entered the service, his system full of artificially induced tetanus and typhus germs. But, of course, no account is taken of the human factor: that a man who has had sufficient sleep and who is physically and emotionally at ease might be better able to take an intelligence test than one who is tired and nervous.'

'You sound as if you hadn't done too well in that particular test,' chuckled de Cluny.

'I did well enough, but when I saw various accountants and clerks get genius ratings while easily the most intelligent man in my training camp, a poet, was found to be intellectually subnormal, I realized that such tests, like most university examinations, can never measure either information or imagination, two elements of greater importance, even to an Army officer, than tweezer dexterity.'

'You must admit that only Americans would have faith in such tests.'

'They were invented by Germans, I think.'

'Naturally ... the Germans are worse, I admit.'

'Then, having measured one's intelligence, they test mechanical skill. Now, the latest fad at the colleges, even in such venerable places as Harvard and Yale, is to have students photographed from three angles nude.'

'Sounds like a pederast's dream of paradise.'

'It often is. The photographs are not requested: rather, they

292

are taken automatically at the first physical examination and if anyone complains he is shunted off to a psychiatrist.'

'That I cannot believe.'

'I'm afraid it's true, though. It even happened to a friend of mine who objected not only to being photographed but also to answering the psychiatrist's questions. When asked why he took this perverse un-American stand, he replied that he considered it an invasion of privacy. He might as well have said he was a Pelagian heretic: he was not understood. Such behaviour was unheard of and the psychiatrist sent the president of the college a report to the effect that he did not think my friend happy and that, all in all, it would be best for him to submit to six months' analysis as a condition of his matriculation.'

'I find this very difficult to believe.'

'You would be called a reactionary at Yale, however, if you objected to their health services ... you would probably be thought neurotic. In any case, my friend went to another college. I've often thought, though, what it would have been like if they had had photography in Byron's day and if, by some queer chance, Oxford had insisted on recording the bodies of its undergraduates. You know as well as I do that every psychiatric text-book today would carry photographs of Byron at seventeen, seriously overweight, the club-foot in evidence, perhaps an especially enlarged inset of it, as well as his genital measurements and general physical type.'

'Byron would never have consented.'

'I'm as tough as Byron was, I think, and I let it be done at seventeen, when I was herded through a physical examination.'

'What reason do they give?'

'Posture.'

'You're joking.'

'No, that's the official designation. Actually, these studies are made for a naïvely earnest psychologist in New York who has decided that there is a great deal of relation between behaviour and physiology ... which, to a point, there no doubt is. But in spite of numerous breakdowns and graphs, he has come up with no generalities more startling than the familiar one that heavy people tend to be more cheery than thin people because their blood pressure is higher. Nevertheless, it is touching to observe with what whole-hearted enthusiasm institutions have gone out of their way to help him in this work, with or without the consent of those who are to be photographed and analysed.'

'All those statistics,' de Cluny sighed. 'It is quite obvious where it is all leading: complete domination of human beings by a central authority which will weigh and measure them, analyse their capacities, assign them work, feed them, breed them intelligently and raise their children. ... What a feeling of satisfaction the controllers will have that they are doing a tidy job, that nothing that matters is being wasted.'

'No longer any questions of right or wrong, certainly, when everything is related to the State and a man who does not serve the State, who does not conform, is done away with; or, very likely, in the great days coming, if he is a good physical specimen, a lobotomy will be performed and then, quite docile, he will be used for work and breeding, just as though he had not, for one moment, indulged himself by opposing the public good with his own wicked, private will.'

'I find the presence of the psychiatrist in your universities more ominous than the taking of photographs. After all, nudity may one day be a popular custom. But I cannot see how any institution to which one freely comes could make any of its members, despite their protests, available to psychiatric examination.'

'Perhaps the naked mind may one day be a popular custom. ...'

'Say no more!' exclaimed de Cluny. 'We must try to recall that all our anger is, in the form of eternity, meaningless. The capacity of our race to adjust itself to any and every indignity and mortification is perhaps its most distinguishing characteristic. One can train people to believe anything, to accept anything. Look at the Catholics with their schools ... all that incredible mishmash of superstition and silliness, the tag end of every mystical religion from Orphic Rites to the Book of the Dead can be found somewhere in that collection of Judaic myths so many Europeans have elected to believe is the work of the Deity.'

'Perhaps my reaction to the State's total control is reactionary,' said Philip thoughtfully. 'There's no doubt that it *is* coming, and the new rulers will certainly rewrite the texts, depicting people like you and me as old-fashioned monsters who attempted to retard progress.'

'But then, as certainly, State control will give way to something else. Nothing is constant.'

'Give way to what, I wonder?'

'Chaos.'

'War?'

'Yes, and soon I hope.'

'But you can't want that.'

'Oh, can't I?' De Cluny was grim. 'I value human life to such an extent that I would be willing to see half the world slaughtered rather than witness the complete enslavement of the living.'

'I couldn't go that far. I've seen too many men who looked like butcher meat.'

'And I've seen three wars and I've no pity for the dead ... only the ones who have to live either in the bleak prison your country is constructing for us in the West or the one *they* are making for us in the East. A new war is the only answer ... the ruin of the cities, the shattering of the machines, the new beginning.'

Philip shuddered. 'I wouldn't want that,' he said.

'Why not?'

'I don't want to die.' The central motif, the dark theme to which all life was counterpoint.

'You must, sooner or later.'

'I don't want them to die, either,' said Philip.

'How didst thou dare to come down to the house of Hades, the dwelling of the senseless dead, the phantoms of men outworn?'

And I answered and said to him: 'O Achilles, son of Peleus, greatest of the Achaeans, I came to seek counsel of Teiresias, how I might return home to rugged Ithaca; for I have not yet come nigh to the Achaean land, nor set foot in my own country, but it goes hard with me continually. But thou, Achilles, art the most blessed of men that have been or shall be hereafter; for afore time, in thy life, we Argives honoured thee like the gods, and now thou art a great prince here among the dead. Therefore grieve not that thou art dead, Achilles.'

And he answered me and said: 'Seek not to console me for death, glorious Odysseus. I would rather be on earth as the

295

*hired servant of another, in the house of a landless man with
little to live upon, than be king over all the dead.'*

Homer: *Odyssey.*

'We *must* have her, Zoe.'

'But, Julia, she won't fit.'

'You'll have to *make* her fit. You have been at her house
twice this year and she's not been to yours *once.*'

'But she can't see . . . she can't hear.'

'She knows, however, that she *is* where she is.'

'Would the Murats come if I had her?'

'The Duchesse always attracts the Bonapartists, you know
that.'

'All right, darling, put her name down.' Lady Julia Keen
wrote Lyon et Grénoble in her tiny but vigorous hand while her
employer, Zoe Helotius, occasionally patted the quart of dry
mud which made her face look like a mummy in danger of
unravelling. The bed where she lay was shaped like a ship, with
an enormous gold Eros for a prow. The remains of Zoe's breakfast (Holland Rusk and weak tea) decorated the night table.

'Now, what about the Windsors?'

'Well, what about them, Julia?'

'Will they be in Paris in time for the party, and will they
come?'

'They will not be here in time,' said Zoe evenly, like a chief of
government who has just lost an important minister in a cabinet
crisis.

'I . . . I'm terribly sorry, Zoe.'

'That's all right, Julia. These things must be faced squarely. It
never does to cry over spilled figs.' (In moments of crisis she
tended unconsciously to relate all things to the source of her
wealth, the rock on which her fortress stood.)

'It seems like only yesterday. . . .'

'Never look back, Julia. It doesn't pay. Go on, go on: that's
my motto. If one were to stop each time fate dealt one an
unkind blow one would remain stationary. We will invite. . . .'

'*Him?*'

'Yes, Julia.' For a moment the mummy seemed almost to
smile with triumph.

'What a thrill! And her?'

'She will come too.'

296

'But how ... I mean, well, when?'

'A week ago. It was all arranged. I was saving it as a little surprise for you.'

'And what a surprise! The biggest, absolutely the biggest of all.'

'I know.' The earlier dereliction was forgotten.

'I could not be more thrilled,' said Lady Julia, writing two names under Lyon et Grénoble.

'Back to work,' said Zoe, holding her arms up like a mantis praying, so that the veins in the backs of her capable hands would grow smooth.

'Regina Durham?'

'By all means,' said Zoe. 'Is the husband here?'

'Not until May.'

'Too bad. The politicians one wants always come if Rex Durham is about.'

'Now, darling, what shall we do about the young man?'

'What young man?'

'Mrs. Durham's.'

'Oh, I remember. He's with the Embassy.'

'No. He doesn't work. He was in Capri. ...'

'I know, Julia. I *do* remember things, you know. There are times when you treat me like an utter fool.'

'Zoe!'

'Yes, by all means have him.'

'But there is a complication.'

'I should have known, Julia, from your tone, that you were planning a complication for me. What is it this time?'

'Anna Morris.'

'What about her?'

'And Philip Warren.'

'Who is he?'

'I thought you said you remembered.'

'You mean Regina's friend?'

'I do indeed.'

'And he is Anna Morris's lover now?'

'He is indeed ... and she is coming to the party too.'

'Now that's very interesting,' said Zoe, waving her arms like a man signalling a ship with flags, exercising the wrinkled wattles of flesh which hung from her sturdy bones, attesting to that age which her face, thanks to certain miracles of quasi-medical science, did not reveal at all. 'You think there might be a scene, Julia.'

'I doubt it.'

'Then we are safe if we have all three.'

'I should think so. I felt you should know, however,'

'But, of course. Now that you mention it, I have heard talk. I must say, he's done well for himself. Is he a gigolo?'

'I don't believe so. He has money.'

'I wonder what his charm is?'

'He's quite good-looking, and young.'

'That combination is easily come by if one has money, if one is Regina Durham.'

'And then I've heard . . .' And Lady Julia lowered her voice, although they were alone and, flushing slightly, she whispered something into Zoe's ear. The only word an eavesdropper might have overheard was 'butterfly'. The ladies laughed heartily or, rather, Lady Julia did, for because of the mud Zoe could only snort, blowing a cloud of fine dust the length of the bed. Then the telephone, which was hidden in Madame de Maintenon's chamber-pot, rang. Lady Julia answered it. Her eyes grew round with delight and her voice became warm and personal; then she put her hand over the mouthpiece and hissed: 'It's *her*, Zoe . . . the Duchess!'

'My God!' Zoe sat up abruptly and the mud cracked and crumbled about her ravaged shoulders as she seized the telephone.

Hiero the tyrant asked Simonides to explain the nature of the deity. The poet asked a day for reflection. When the question was repeated on the morrow, he asked for two days. Thus he kept on doubling the number of days, till Hiero, in surprise asked the reason. 'The longer I think about it,' he answered, 'the more obscure the question seems to me.'

Cicero: *On the Nature of the Gods.*

For three days during mid-April there were violent storms. But when at last the sun shone winter was gone and Philip began to contemplate departure as he read the various letters from home which suggested, mildly, yet with an underlying urgency, that he return to the valley where his life was to be.

'What did you do all winter?' asked Sophia curiously, as they drank coffee on the rue de Rivoli, a glimpse of new green in the Tuileries Gardens across the street, its fence of gold-tipped spears bright in the sun.

'I wonder that myself,' he said. 'When you ask me like that, abruptly, I can't think of a thing. I have an image of myself reading English novels in the bathtub.'

'That's something,' she smiled.

'I have some recollection of having kept a diary.'

'Now that's very interesting. ... Why only a recollection, though?'

'Because I've kept a journal off and on all my life, but I continually lose them, and I've never written in one more than three days consecutively.'

'What did you write in this one?'

'What would I have written, is more likely. Because the more I think of it the less sure I am that I *did* keep a journal during the winter ... but if I had I would probably have done what I've always done: commented on whatever I happened to be reading, what conversations I had overheard, what profundities occurred to me while crossing the Place de la Concorde, dodging motor-cars, late to an appointment. I've often been late recently, to almost everywhere.'

'Sounds as if you were at least having a social success.'

'I suppose I intended it to sound like that; acually I've seen very few people ... mostly Americans, at that.'

'Like Mrs. Durham?'

'How did you know?'

'I've been here a few days,' said Sophia, with as much malice as her ordinarily serene detachment would allow.

'I've seen a little of her ... these last few weeks.'

'Poor Regina,' said Sophia.

'Why poor?'

'Her husband is such an oaf.'

'At least he leaves her alone.'

'Perhaps,' said Sophia mysteriously.

But Philip refused to challenge her and they spoke no more of Regina, which did not displease Sophia, who was now eager to discuss the character of Anna Morris.

'I like her very much,' said Philip, wondering what had so abruptly caused the usually impersonal Sophia to confront the character of other women with that same intensity which she ordinarily reserved exclusively for facts, for generalities, for the contemplation of those syllogisms which gave her such pleasure.

'I have known her such a long time,' said Sophia, 'such a very long time that I suppose I am too close to her to know what I think.'

'Yet,' said Philip to himself.

'Yet,' said Sophia, unconscious for once of the effect she was having, 'I can't help but feel that she has been somewhat dishonest emotionally.'

'Dishonest?'

'I think that's the word. It's not that one objects to her having affairs. Most women in her position do these days. Rather it's her prodigality. I mean, each time she goes to bed with a man it can't be as earth-shaking, as unique an experience as she maintains it is. Oh, there've been so many! Each time you would think that at last she had found the half for which she had been searching all her life; then, a month later, there's someone else.'

'You make her sound more frivolous than she is.'

'Deluded. No human being could survive that intensity which she claims she experiences each time.'

'She is serious,' said Philip.

'I'm quite sure she is ... resolutely so. I question only her sincerity ... or her reason.'

'Not everyone is alike. Perhaps she's exactly the way she seems. Some people are.'

'I remember she loved a general once, a young man, and she followed him about everywhere ... it was a great scandal.'

'How did it end?'

'The way it always does.'

'And how is that?'

'He lost interest. The man always does. Men aren't constructed for such intensity, simulated or not. Poor Anna ... she is always deserted in the end.'

'Which proves her sincerity.'

'Or bad judgment.' Then, having said what she had wanted to say, realizing instinctively that she had perhaps gone too far, she spoke of other things, amiably, recalled mutual acquaintances, asked even about Charles de Cluny, as though they had, at one time, all three, been the best of friends.

He told her that he planned to go back in the spring.

'Will you be sorry to leave?' she asked.

'No. I don't think so.'

'But you *have* enjoyed it?'

'Oh, very much ... even if I can't remember what I've done.'

'You'll remember later.'

'I often do.'

'That's right. A bad habit though: not to appreciate the moment except in recollection.'

'I'm not so sure.'

'But I am, for me at least. Do you look forward to going back home?'

'I think so. I don't really know. I have a terrible feeling that nothing matters, that it will make very little difference whether I spend the rest of my life in Egypt poking about in the dirt or whether I have a political career in New York.'

'It seems very different to me.'

'Not when I think of death ... not when I think there is no reason to be alive ... but I *am* alive, of course, and don't want to die.'

'Afraid of hell?'

'No.'

'Of pain?'

'Not very.'

'Of what?'

'Of *nothing*. Isn't that enough to fear?'

'One could learn to prefer it,' she said. He laughed at her until he saw that she was serious; he tried then, out of politeness, to present an argument that would support her curious, nonsensical announcement, discussing gravely with her the inadequacies of the alien garment of the flesh which they both wore with such distinction, each aware, in such different fashions though, of that day when awareness would be lost in the whole reality: the flesh gone and the breath properly contained in the larger breathing of the world.

Her told her about the International Typewriter Company which maintained an enormous factory near his home town of Hudson. The paternalism of this institution (so low has the father fallen in American life that his social function, when recognized at all, is identified with tyranny) has assumed significant proportions. Total security is offered in exchange for total resignation to the order. Wages are high. Company-owned houses, all alike, are sold to workers on easy terms. No union is allowed even to contribute to the delicious harmony which prevails between pater and his children, and, when a child wishes to remain home a day to endure or to feign an illness, a registered nurse is sent him post-haste, by broomstick, by magic carpet, to make sure that he is really ill and not playing hooky, as the children of even the very best, the most indulgent fathers will do on occasion. In every lavatory of the new glass-and-chrome factory, in every hall, in every office, there is a placard which enjoins each boy and girl to REMEMBER, signed J. Branson, Etting, their father, himself the eldest son of the grandfather of them all: the noiseless International Type-writer. 'Now, more than ever,' quoted Philip to himself, as he discussed the penultimate phase of that eccentric yet occasionally colourful civilization into which he had been born, so near the end ... yet so near the beginning, he suddenly thought, with some surprise, of still another, of something else again, as yet unknown: I am the *alpha* and the *omega*, the first and the last, the beginning and the end. But which? Or did it matter?

Sophia thought not.

For when is death in us, when is it not? As Heracleitus says: 'It is the same thing in us that is alive and dead, awake and asleep, young and old. For the former shift and become the latter, and the latter shift back again and become the former.'

For as out of the same clay one can mould shapes of animals and obliterate them and mould them again and so on un-ceasingly, so nature from the same matter formerly produced our ancestors, and then obliterated them and generated our parents, and then ourselves, and then others and yet others, round and round. The river of birth flows continually and will never stop, and so does that opposite stream of destruction which the poets call Acheron and Cocytus. So the same first cause that showed us the light of the sun, brings also the twilight of Hades. Perhaps we may see a similitude of this in the air around us, which makes ultimately night and day, bringing on life and death, sleep and waking.

Plutarch: *Consolation to Apollonius.*

302

The hour of the equinox was celebrated in such a way that what Philip had suspected might be true was proven true, that repetition for the first time in his life became confirmation rather than the familiar boredom which he had inevitably experienced with everyone and everything, more soon than late. Could it be that this body was in some way different from all the others he had known? that this head which he now held cupped in one hand was really so strange: a round glove of bone wreathed in dark hair and containing a mystery which he did not know, would never know ... thus, through ignorance, was he held by an attraction far more intense than the usual centre, the dark groin where the other mystery resided, the one he had always known, the centre from which he had at last successfully strayed to the true centre, to that unseen mystical altar before which only kings are anointed, adjured and crowned.

'Nor am I jealous,' said Anna suddenly.

'Jealous?' They had been silent for some minutes as their racing hearts quieted in unison and the breathing grew more easy, less quick and harsh. 'I don't know what you mean.'

'Oh, but you do.' She sat up on one elbow, the pale light of early spring across their bodies, across the grey-cold, winter-old city and its gardens and the fields far, far beyond the gates of St. Denis. Would there be lilacs soon? he wondered, touching her breast carefully, like an unobserved boy in a museum caressing the stone fantasy, the dream lover of some Greek two thousand years dead, the marble evocation of his pain, serene and unbemused among strangers in a distant city, fondled by a boy.

'You mean about Regina?' he asked, falling back upon the crumpled pillows, his arms crossed upon his chest like a Crusader on his bier.

'About Regina. You knew her first.'

'But not as well.'

'She's doing everything she can, you know.'

'Everything?'

'To win you.'

'But why?'

'Don't you know yet?'

'I'm afraid not. I've often thought about it, of course ... why should she be so interested in me?'

'Because she loves you.'

'Now you're making fun of me. I'm not that vain. Women

303

like that never fall in love, or if they do they would love a completely different sort of man . . . a Rex Durham.'

'And me? What sort of man would I love?'

'I wonder.'

'You?'

'Yes, I think so. For a while.'

She looked away and when she answered she spoke to the pale daffodil light on the wall. 'I never end it,' she said softly. 'I am always there when the other leaves . . . when you go back next month, to your real life. . . .'

'This is it, right now.'

'You've made me talk of the future,' she laughed. 'What a bad influence you are! I don't believe in the future. There's no such thing.'

'But there is.'

'There is change in the present and, when you leave, the present will change for us both.'

'I could stay.'

'No, you couldn't.'

'I suppose not.'

'But I am vain enough to like hearing you say it.'

'Why can't I see you in America?'

'Because . . . oh, so many reasons. Perhaps you won't want to. Perhaps *I* won't want to. And then, I won't be coming back for some time.'

Philip sighed and wondered what to say, wondered what he should feel . . . it would be nice, he thought, to be able to have definite responses to everything, to know always not only what one should feel, but, more important, what one did feel.

'On the other hand,' said Anna sharply, suddenly out of character, 'you will be seeing a great deal of Regina when you go home.'

'I suppose so,' said Philip, almost resenting this display of less than god-like emotion. He had created her, after all, he suddenly realized with some wonder. The body he held in his arms, the perfect response to all his needs on every level, had not existed except in his own imagining. She was not real, and he knew it now. The perfect love had been himself, loving himself; the arms of a stranger whom he had never known had held him while his own reflection had come between their two bodies, like a silver mirror or like an old curse: you will never know another, never walk through the reflecting glass to the true world, to the one outside. Who was she? he wondered, suddenly frightened at having revealed so much to a stranger: was she a spy? a blackmailer? Some sort of saint? or, worse yet, a patient fool who mocked him from behind the smooth implacable glass which separated them. Where am I? He touched the iron bedstead . . . was it iron? Who am I?

'Philip.'

'Yes.'

'What do you want?'

'What do I want? Knowledge.'

'Of what?'

'Of everything, of someone else, of you.'

'But you know me.'

'Never. You are I.'

She smiled. 'Haven't you always known that?'

'No, no, no.'

'Isn't that what you wanted?'

'To know myself?'

'To know yourself and through yourself to know me?'

'Or the other way round.'

'Is it the same.'

'But it shouldn't be.' Not even the iron of the bed was real. 'I want something more than myself.'

'There's nothing more, Philip. There's only you.'

'No one else?'

'Only when the dream becomes so intense that you forget yourself. . . .'

'Like St. Malo?'

'Like that . . . and, then, I am dreaming, too, at the same time. You are I . . . I made it all.'

'But not the same thing.'

'Never the same.'

'That could be unbearable.'

'It could, but it won't be for you, as long as you imagine me.'

'Or Regina?'

The iron was cold and smooth beneath his hand; it chilled his fingers at the same time the warmth of his flesh made the iron less cold. Then the room grew warm with light, and through the window he saw the sun.

305

The Cyprian Queen, my children, is not only the Cyprian; there are many other names she bears. She is Death; she is imperishable force; she is raving madness; she is untempered longing; she is lamentation. Nothing that works or is quiet, nothing that drives to violence, but as she wills. Her impress sinks into the mould of all things whose life is in their breath. Who must not yield to this goddess? She enters into every fish that swims; she is in every four-footed breed upon the land; among the birds everywhere is the beating of her wings; in beasts, in mortal men, and in the gods above. No god with whom she wrestles, but is thrice thrown.

If it be lawful to say it ... and lawful it is to speak the truth ... in the breast of Zeus she reigns, a tyrant that needs no armed guard. There is no design of mortal or of god that is not cut short by love.

Sophocles: *Fragment.*

CHAPTER THIRTEEN

During April the letters began. At first they were wistful; by the end of May, however, they had grown urgent and he knew that the time had come for him to choose, to return, if he could, to the summer valley and the grey river of home.

Zoe Helotius, who had no secrets (other than the central one concerning her obscure birth), had, nevertheless, one peculiarity which none of her intimates suspected, not even Lady Julia; like most people with a private fancy, a secret life, she was enormously cunning and resourceful and consequently no one was aware that she talked to herself. Most people on occasion will think aloud, but Zoe differed from the majority in that she was quite aware that she was talking to herself and, since she was essentially a conventional woman, she was ashamed of her habit; even so, whenever she was alone she would address herself, in baby talk, as 'Tiny Tot', an adorably, sly-boots of a child who was often naughty but always forgiven and indulged. On those busy days when social engagements followed one another too closely, Zoe would grow nervous and irritable, like an addict deprived of drugs, craving desperately the company of Tiny Tot to whom she could confide her latest plan or some bit of gossip, with whom she could share her brilliant triumphs and her glum defeats. When she could bear this separation no longer, she would abruptly leave even the most celebrated of her guests and hurry to the nearest bathroom, where, seated on a commode or on the edge of the bathtub, she would commune with Tiny Tot, apologizing abjectly for not having come sooner, for having neglected her darling duck, her fig, her *choux fleur*, her only love.

Needless to say, the party for the birthday of the British King (which is celebrated in June) occupied Zoe's every moment for several weeks, enraging the spoiled Tiny Tot, who exacted, on the rare occasions when she and Zoe now met, elaborate apologies for her creator's dereliction. On the afternoon of the party, Zoe suddenly broke off a spirited debate with her caterers and hurried to the ladies' retiring-room of the *Bain de Ligny*. Here, alone at last, in front of a Venetian mirror, she crooned to her love, her fig.

'I've been a brute ... I know, I know ... a beast ... you must forgive ... that's a darling, a true lamb ... I couldn't endure it another minute ... five days away from you, I know. Can you ever forgive me? Please ... please' And she was forgiven at last, as she always was. Then, briskly, she discussed the arrangements for the fête.

'It will be better than the Eiffel Tower ... I feel it, I do, Tiny Tot ... you'll be so proud; just wait and see, my darling. It will be Mummy's best, her very best. It took courage not to rent the Tower this year, but nothing lost is nothing gained as they say. It will be an evening like no other! I have done the whole boat like a Byzantine pavilion, like a Venetian palace ... and there'll be gondolas in the pool and banks of flowers; then, at midnight ... yes, you've guessed it, darling, your favourites: fireworks! and a portrait of *him* in rockets as the orchestra plays "God Save the King". There'll never be another party like this in our time ... my masterpiece: and everyone is coming. Yes, darling, yes, yes! Yes! and she will come, too ... yes, yes, and even her!

Imagine! A triumph ... everyone! And when it's over what stories I shall have to tell my darling Tiny Tot, my own dear. ...' And at this point Zoe Helotius' voice became low and guttural as she murmured endearments in her native tongue, a language which she'd not spoken in thirty years, except in private to Tiny Tot.

Lady Julia put her head in the door of the ladies' room, which had been decorated to resemble an Ottoman harem. 'Zoe, the conductor wants to go over the music with you ... and also the costumes for the musicians ... they never arrived.'

'One minute more, Julia, and I'll be done.' She pretended to examine an eyebrow as Lady Julia withdrew: the only person in the world who had even the slightest intimation of Tiny Tot's existence. Zoe was aware of her secretary's suspicions and she often trembled at the effect an exposure might have on her darling, who was now listening raptly as she completed the list of those who were to come that evening, the important dozen guests ... the less important five hundred who were to be scenery, props, supernumeraries.

'Oh, and there may be trouble ... yes, a marvellous scene, perhaps. Regina Durham – I've told you about her, haven't I? – is coming and her ex-young man who is now Anna Morris's young man, but Anna's husband will be here, too. I hope I shall have time to watch them. Julia will know, in any case, and when she tells me I'll tell you *all*, word for word, my darling, the moment I know. I've already made up my mind that at twelve-thirty, after the fireworks, I will sneak in here for a quick, comfy chat ... I know how restless you get when there's a party. Now be a lamb while I talk to the musicians, and remember that you are my own love, no matter what anybody says.'

The *Bain de Ligny* is an enormous barge on the Seine, moored to a quai on the left bank. Inside the barge is a swimming-pool of filtered river water with a narrow sun deck on four sides, two storeys of cubicles, a restaurant and a bar. During the summer the *Bain de Ligny* is very popular with city-bound Parisians and tourists who swim there by the hundreds during the day; at night it is deserted ... but not this night, for Zoe had transformed it into a new Venice, a new Byzantium, a new Babylon with glowing lanterns everywhere and burning torches held by half-nude Algerian boys while garlands of flowers festooned *papier-mâché* arches supported by delicate fluted columns of gold-encrusted plaster. In the pool (illuminated from beneath by jade-green lights) gondolas plied languidly back and forth, to the music of a symphony orchestra whose members were dressed, for some curious reason, in early dynastic Egyptian costumes.

At sundown the guests began to arrive. The costumes were exotic though not always Venetian as the invitation had suggested. The moon was full at the black sky's centre and a warm wind made the torches gutter dramatically, a flickering light upon bright jewels and festive eyes.

Philip arrived alone, in Venetian costume, wearing a mask like the other guests. His identity, however, was quickly checked by two non-Venetian thugs who examined his invitation carefully. Then he was allowed to present himself to Lady Julia who stood just inside the gate, by the pool; she greeted him warmly. 'How marvellous you look, Mr. Warren! I'm sure you must've been an Italian in another life.'

'You never can tell,' said Philip, inadequately, but Lady Julia, a column of scarlet satin, was gone ... a pillar of fire by night, thought Philip, moving towards de Cluny who stood near the bar, talking to a massive lady.

'Charles!'

'How did you recognize me? I thought I was invisible.' The heavy lady giggled and retired. The orchestra began the 'Nutcracker Suite'.

'A sixth sense,' said Philip, glancing at the other's spidery legs which black tights did not flatter.

'Lovely party.'

'Very.'

'Lady Julia just told me that she sent to the south of France for a thousand glow-worms but they arrived dead. . . .'

'It might have been too much.'

'Perhaps ... the last impiety: "When the flower of pride has blossomed, death is the fruit that ripens, and all the harvest reaped is tears" ... as the Greeks would say.'

'A grim message for such an occasion.' Then Philip saw Regina; she was seated alone in a gondola which was moving towards them; by torchlight her black gown glowed with tiny pearls and on her head diamonds flashed messages of light in some exotic code.

'Who is that?' asked de Cluny, impressed.

'A friend of mine,' said Philip, excusing himself. Proudly he helped her from the gondola.

'I saw you,' she said. 'From the other side.' Beneath her black mask, she smiled.

'Well met by moonlight,' said Philip; and they sat down on a white iron-wrought bench beneath an arch of pink camellias and new ivy.

'What a job she's done,' said Philip conventionally.

'I wonder if the orchestra intends to play *all* the "Nutcracker Suite"?'

Two unidentified couples paid brief court to Regina. Then, alone again, Regina said: 'I've seen so little of you these past few weeks. Have you been busy?'

'Oh yes,' he lied. 'I've been seeing all the sights of the city ... places I hadn't bothered to visit before.'

'Are you leaving, Philip?'

He nodded. 'Next week.'

'Then the year is finally over.'

'It seems like only a month ago that I came to Rome, not a year.'

'Are you ready now?'

'For what?'

'Our plan ... I can go back when you do. Rex is expecting me next week.'

Philip did not answer.

'It will be so easy, believe me ... and it will happen soon ... if only because I haven't the time Rex and I had when *we* started, years ago.'

'Tell me why you want all this.'

'Because I lost Rex,' she said the truth at last. 'Lost or shed him ... it's hard to say which. Now he lives one life and I lead another, an aimless one. He has no use for me any more: his career is made.'

For the first time Regina had touched him; he took her hand awkwardly and held it, not knowing what to say.

'You wonder perhaps why I don't have a career of my own ... I sometimes wonder that, too. It would make it so easy if I did, if I could be self-sufficient; but I can't. I can only act through the man ... I live only through him.' She smiled. 'Don't mistake me, Philip, it's not love I want. . . .' And she lost him for good.

'I was the wrong choice,' he said gently. 'We want different things. I want a private life, not your public one.' And he let go her hand.

'She did this, didn't she?'

'Who?'

'Anna.'

'I don't think so.'

'She did . . . she did,' said Regina, as though her own anger gave her pain, as though she had, like some furious scorpion, turned on herself. 'Would you give up the world for someone like her?'

'No,' said Philip coldly. 'I wouldn't. I'm not giving up any world, except yours . . . one which I never had, in any case. She had nothing to do with it.' But did she? He could not be sure.

'Don't listen to her, Philip. You'll find she's wrong . . . believe me you will. I know. I've seen all this before.'

'You don't understand, Regina. You take so much for granted.'

'You'd better go to her then. I understand she's here to-night.'

'I suppose I should.' He got to his feet.

She caught at his sleeve. 'I didn't mean that, Philip. Please stay!' But he pulled away from her and stepped out of the camellia-decorated alcove on to the deck. Torchlight made her diamonds burn like a fire of ice. 'Philip!' But he was gone, separated from her by a band of chattering ladies in harlequin masks.

'A triumph, Zoe! A triumph!' exclaimed Lady Julia.

'I know,' said Zoe, gentle with pride.

'They all came.'

'Are you surprised?'

'No . . . yet I had hardly dared to dream. . . .'

'Even our wildest dreams become, on rare occasions, reality, said Zoe, who was saving this particular line for Tiny Tot, but saw no harm in rehearsing it now with Julia.

'I know . . . I know. Oh, darling, who are those two young

311

men over there? sitting next to the bar ... the ones who are wearing old clothes?'

'They are Americans, Julie. Anna brought them. They are writers.'

'Oh ... how odd they look.'

'We live in a changing world, Julia.' On this philosophic note, the ladies parted.

The Duchesse de Lyon et Grénoble rode in a gondola, back-and forth across the pool; she was dressed in the wedding-gown of the first Duchesse of her name, an intricate tent of yellowed satin and Brussels lace. Tonight she was enjoying herself immensely, humming toneless arias from forgotten operas, not always sure precisely where she was, but pleased at being in motion, on water, with a gondolier to whom she occasionally gave irrelevant commands that he ignored as he poled their frail bark across the chartreuse pool which reflected, like fire in an opal, the light of torches, the gleam of rainbow lanterns.

Standing at one end of the dance floor, watching the couples waltz, de Cluny observed that he seldom minded those tyrants who treated their subjects as though they were animals since, after all, men *are* animals, but he did object to those new tyrants who treated their subjects like machines, which they were not: the one sin against the Holy Ghost. Philip agreed; then, catching sight of a Tintoretto girl, he deserted de Cluny and danced three waltzes, until the disagreeable scene with Regina had been forgotten, until the girl was claimed by a bearded Moor.

Philip wandered up to the second storey, to a long balcony overlooking the pool, one which had been transformed into an avenue of laurel and adorned with Renaissance interpretations of classic deities, white upon the green which skilfully hid dressing-room doors. At the end of the avenue a figure in grey, a woman, stopped him and said: 'Good evening, Philip.'

It took him a moment to guess who she was, for the light was green and dim and, too, he had not expected to find Sophia here.

'I couldn't resist it,' she said, as though apologizing.

'Nor I,' said Philip. 'How have you been?'

Slowly they walked the length of the avenue and then, as

slowly, they walked back to the spot where they had met. 'Do you look forward to leaving?' she asked.

'Very much … I was getting to the point where I could absorb nothing new here. And then I'm a little home-sick, too. There is a lot to be said for living in a country where the people speak your language.'

'I suppose there is.' Sophia paused before a broken Hermes. 'What shall you do back home?'

'Practise law … in the town where I was born.'

'A quiet life?'

'Who can tell? Perhaps. I don't think of the future any more. Everything is finally here, in the present.'

'I believe that, to. Will you go into politics, do you think?'

'I may,' said Philip, surprising himself a little. 'I think I might like it … but who can tell?'

'Who can tell?' sang an American night-club singer, engaged for this one song: 'Who can tell that I'm in hell and not so well and not so swell for the wonder of you and me, the blunder of you and me, the wonder of you you you.'

'Do you know?' she asked suddenly.

'I think so.'

'Is it clear at last?'

'Very nearly.'

'And you? Are you certain?'

'Yes, I know it now.'

'In terms of what?'

'Of people. …'

'Regina!'

'Not Regina. I never took her seriously.'

'But you take the world seriously.'

'There is nothing else.'

'The idea, each time. …'

'That, too, but in proportion.'

'Earth smothers fire.'

'Fire comes from earth.'

'Don't!' she said abruptly. 'Don't listen to Regina. The other is more important.'

'I know what I need. No one loses what he needs.'

'But men do.'

'And your way is wrong, too …. for me, if not for you. I

313

can't tell. No one ever really knows about anyone else . . . and that's the point.'

'What point?'

'Discovery of someone else . . . recognition . . . all that.'

'But you just said no one ever knows another. . . .'

'No one does . . . but each should try: and, finally, there is illusion which is so much better than knowledge, as any lover will tell you.'

'I don't understand.'

'I do, but I can't explain. But suppose . . . suppose that I was born on an island without people: I should be an animal then, without a language, without words, without reason . . . an animal with a certain instinct for survival, and nothing more. So, in a real sense, I would never exist until I had been identified, until I saw myself as my own kind saw me. But if others should come to the island and give me words and attitudes, I should know who I was, not in ultimate terms of course, but in terms of them, the only terms there are. Then, for better or worse, I should exist, created by them; and I would know that some would be attracted to me for my face or my manner and others would be hostile for the same reasons. Of course at the deep centre I should always be the island animal, volatile, instinctive, nameless. but I should have a new, more important life in terms of others . . . and, finally, at some point, if I'm in luck, I would find another like myself, a stranger for whom I would exist in a new and terrible way . . . the way she will exist for me and then, for moments at a time, we shall identify with one another, the true coupling of those island beasts. . . . Do you see? Do you see what I mean? Do you see why I can never go back to the island?'

'You came from the world.'

'No, I am an islander, and I know where the island is even now . . . on dark days I see it clearly, inviting me to return, to lose the myriad faces and all hope of another, to live alone, like Prospero with his dreaming. I am tempted; but I shall not go there now.'

'Is the woman Anna?'

'Yes . . . no.'

'What sort of answer is that?'

'I'm not sure what I mean. She was the first I knew. . . ,'

'You are a fool!'

'Through her I knew what it could be like ... isn't that enough?'

'It is all the same.'

'Except where before there was one there are now two; a difference.'

'She'll never leave her husband.'

'Why should she? I may never see her again after tonight.'

'I don't understand.'

'You? – not understand?'

'You tell me she had done a miracle, that you are finally touched, no longer tempted by withdrawal ... and then you leave her, too.'

'Strange, isn't it?' said Philip joyously. 'She understands.'

'She always does.'

'Why do you sound so bitter?'

'Only sad. . . .'

'Look! The fireworks!' Philip hurried to the end of the avenue of laurel and stood on the upper deck looking down at the pool where, from a raft, fireworks were being set off. The lanterns had been put out and it was dark, except for the light of occasional torches and the fountains of fire on the raft, the exploding constellations in the sky.

In her gondola, the Duchesse heard the noise of fireworks near-by, caught a gleam of light through her grey-filmed eyes, and she asked querulously: 'What is it, boatman? Don't mumble. What's happening?' But the gondolier, a Paris tough in an embroidered vest, knowing that she was blind and dead, did not answer, his eyes on the spectacle.

Alone for a moment, Zoe whispered: 'Look at them, my darling ... look! better than last year, better than the Eiffel Tower. And the rose, see? The rose all in rockets ... for you, for my own darling Tiny Tot who loves roses and beauty ... all for you, *mignonne*. Soon I'll leave all these people and we'll talk ... and what news I have for you! You'll never guess. But here comes Julia.'

When Philip turned to speak to Sophia he found her gone. The avenue of laurel was deserted; one of the marble figures, which had been insecurely fixed to the wall, had fallen face

315

forward upon the deck, wreathed all in withered laurel, like funeral flowers. He moved down another balcony, one which was light and airy and hung with fern and roses. Here couples made love by the light of rockets. Suddenly, the King's portrait appeared in the sky and the orchestra played his anthem. For a moment there was silence. Then a gondola caught fire, to the delight of everyone, and by its ruddy glow Philip continued his progress down the balcony, watching lovers hide among the fern and rose.

She was waiting for him at the end of the balcony, in a grotto of shell and starfish, of seaweed and mother-of-pearl. She was unmarked, in white, with a summer flower in her gleaming hair. As he looked at her by firelight, saw her smile, the silver mirror dissolved before his eyes, dispelling its ungrieved ghosts like smoke upon the night, and beyond her in the dark, a promise at the present's farthest edge, a dreaming figure stirred and opened her golden eyes.

Edgewater: 21 August, 1950 – Key West – Barrytown.
New York, 21 June, 1951.

Scendi propizia
  Col tuo splendore,
O bella Venere,
  Madre d'Amore;
Madre d'Amore,
  Che sola sei
Piacer degli uomini,
  E degli dei.
                    Metastasio

Other Panthers For Your Enjoyment

Man and Woman

☐ Gore Vidal   **MYRA BRECKINRIDGE**
                                                40p

The elegantly outrageous novel that demolishes lots of American sexual myths. Vidal's piercing invention is at its most dazzling in this story of Hollywood sex-changes.

☐ Martin Seymour-Smith   **FALLEN WOMEN**   **40p**
The strumpet in literature – from the Old Testament right up to today's highly professional porn. The author does it with insight, sympathy and wit, and his conclusions are controversial – or, as the *New Statesman* puts it, 'Provocative'.

☐ Trans. Charles Plumb   **THE SATIRES OF**
                                        JUVENAL   **42p**
The vices – and what vices! – of Imperial Rome by one who was there. A translation for the 1970's – direct, witty, lewd.

☐ Jean Genet   **QUERELLE OF BREST 60p**
The criminal-homosexual world so sensuously evoked by Genet is a taboo subject in suburbia. Elsewhere, Genet is 'Matchless . . . any comment at once becomes presumptuous' – Terry Southern

☐ Jean Genet   **OUR LADY OF THE**
                                        FLOWERS   **40p**
The great sensual novel about the criminal-homosexual world with which Genet overturned middle class values.

☐ John Rechy   **CITY OF NIGHT**   **40p**
Rechy's city of dreadful night is any downtown American city after dark, when lonely homosexuals begin their frantic prowl in search of companionship.

Fictional Diversions

☐ **Violette Leduc** **LA BATARDE** **60p**
In this famous autobiographical novel a great writer lays bare the
secrets of her checkered life and her loves – largely for other
women.

☐ **Violette Leduc** **RAVAGES** **50p**
'Violette Leduc has a wonderful feeling for all kinds of sensual
happiness' – *Daily Mail*. A novel with all the candour and
poignancy of LA BATARDE.

☐ **Angus Stewart** **SANDEL** **30p**
The well-reviewed novel of a young man's relationship with a boy.
'A controlled and beautifully written love story, at once
passionate and pure' – *New Statesman*

☐ **Henri Barbusse** **HELL** **30p**
Life in a Parisian girl's bedsitter viewed through a hole in the wall by
her next door neighbour, an impoverished and struggling young
student. Cold, French realism working at its coldest. By the famous
author of *Under Fire*.

☐ **Maureen Duffy** **WOUNDS** **30p**
A man and a woman making love: tenderly they explore each
other's body and mind. No taboos, no shame. Flesh is there to be
caressed, thoughts to be exchanged. But – outside this sensual, very
private world the world is harsh. This story of pain and pleasure
has an honesty rare in contemporary fiction. *Here*, says the author,
is, where life inflicts its wounds.

☐ **Kingsley Amis** **I WANT IT NOW** **35p**
A poor little rich girl, Simona, and a TV interviewer, Ronnie,
meet, merge, and strive for the things that *they* want tout de
suite. In a word, that knowing, sardonic Amis is at it again in
another bestselling high comedy. 'Wickedly entertaining' –
Sunday Times

Obtainable from all booksellers and newsagents. If you have
any difficulty please send purchase price plus 7p postage per
book to Panther Cash Sales, P.O. Box 11, Falmouth, Cornwall.

I enclose a cheque/postal order for titles ticked above plus 7p
a book to cover postage and packing.

Name ————————————————————————

Address ———————————————————————

————————————————————————————